"Fast-paced, compassionate, and hilarious, this debut from Sarah Reida grips from the first page and keeps the reader invested with every new chapter and every new character. A sharply written dissection of secrets, wealth and murder in the suburbs, its cast of compelling characters give the story its heart."
—AMY TECTOR, AUTHOR OF THE *DOMINION ARCHIVES MYSTERIES*

"*Neighborhood Watch* is the best kind of crime novel: fun, fast-paced, and full of characters who have something to hide. You'll want to pour yourself a drink, settle in somewhere comfortable, and spend some time with the delightfully deceptive residents of Oleander Court. A wickedly entertaining read that takes readers back to *Desperate Housewives* in its prime."
—JILL ORR, AUTHOR OF THE *RILEY ELLISON MYSTERY SERIES*

"Sarah Reida is a fresh and invigorating voice in the thriller universe. Her debut novel, *Neighborhood Watch*, zings with mayhem and mischief. Prepare to be dazzled!"
—SUSAN WALTER, BEST-SELLING AUTHOR OF *GOOD AS DEAD* AND *LIE BY THE POOL*

"A page-turning caricature of suburbia, *Neighborhood Watch* is Agatha Christie meets *Desperate Housewives*."
—SARAH LANGAN, AUTHOR OF *GOOD NEIGHBORS* AND *A BETTER WORLD*

"Reida captures the dark intensity and subversive hilarity of suburbia with a relatable cast of characters and a page-turning mystery. *Neighborhood Watch* will have readers looking around in their own neighborhoods and wondering what secrets are hidden behind the pristine picket fences."
—MAUREEN KILMER, AUTHOR OF *SUBURBAN HELL* AND *HEX EDUCATION*

NEIGHBORHOOD WATCH

ALSO BY SARAH REIDA

All Sales Final
Monsterville: A Lissa Black Production

NEIGHBORHOOD

WATCH

A NOVEL

SARAH REIDA

KEYLIGHT
BOOKS
AN IMPRINT
OF TURNER
PUBLISHING

KEYLIGHT BOOKS
AN IMPRINT OF TURNER PUBLISHING COMPANY
Nashville, Tennessee
www.turnerpublishing.com

Neighborhood Watch

Cover and book design by William Ruoto

Library of Congress Cataloging-in-Publication Data
Names: Reida, Sarah S., author.
Title: Neighborhood watch : a novel / Sarah Reida.
Description: Nashville, Tennessee : Keylight Books, an imprint of Turner
  Publishing Company, [2024]
Identifiers: LCCN 2022050091 (print) | LCCN 2022050092 (ebook) | ISBN
  9781684429639 (hardcover) | ISBN 9781684429646 (paperback) | ISBN
  9781684429653 (epub)
Subjects: LCGFT: Thrillers (Fiction). | Novels.
Classification: LCC PS3618.E549 N45 2024 (print) | LCC PS3618.E549
  (ebook) | DDC 813/.6—dc23/eng/20230130
LC record available at https://lccn.loc.gov/2022050091
LC ebook record available at https://lccn.loc.gov/2022050092

Printed in the United States of America

for them

NOW

ADELAIDE

Adelaide notices her Lyft driver's expression as he turns into her subdivision. A waterfall trickling down layers of granite into the koi pond below welcomes the residents, while an iron NO SOLICITORS sign deters the riffraff. The whole first glimpse of Oleander Court is hoity-toity.

And wasteful. Don't people know fish are for deep-frying and sticking in ketchup, not for decoration? That's exactly what Adelaide's mama said the first time she came to visit, looking around her daughter's new neighborhood like she'd landed on Mars. Adelaide couldn't stand to tell her that Pam, the head of the HOA for Oleander Court, had bragged about the koi costing five hundred bucks a pop.

Adelaide fixes her gaze out the window, observing the Christmas decorations that popped up while she was in L.A. Soft twinkle lights illuminate the glossy hedges of many homes, and massive wreaths ornament the doors. A life-sized sleigh, complete with eight reindeer and the jolly man himself, perches on one slanted roof. Not blow-up, of course. That would look cheap.

When the car slides to a stop at the end of the cul-de-sac, Adelaide tilts her head up at her home. The whole thing is white brick and has always reminded her of a wedding cake—the kind you don't want to slice into because it's too fancy to eat. "Blow out the candles," she'd said to William the first time she'd seen it, referring to the pillars that hold up the second floor balcony.

Even though she and William will be married for two years as of this Tuesday, Adelaide still has trouble believing she lives here. It's a far cry from her mama's trailer park in Bedford, Arkansas, and not just because the homes aren't on cinderblocks. Oleander Court in Alpharetta, Georgia, is the kind of neighborhood where you can forget the keys in your car overnight. In Bedford, the mistake would mean a donation to the less fortunate.

Adelaide uses the last of her phone's battery to tap an exorbitant tip into her Lyft app, knowing William won't care and her driver certainly will. Then she extends the handle of her luggage. The wheels bang against the stone steps as she drags it to the enormous oak door that complements the sandstone porch.

William has left her a note in the kitchen: *Home by 8:30. Look in the bathroom for a present. Can't wait to see you.*

Adelaide sighs. She'd prefer William over a present. But William's a surgeon at Wellstar North Hospital, and them body parts ain't gonna cut themselves off. After helping herself to a bottled water in the refrigerator, she heads upstairs, her hand lightly trailing the polished wooden banister. Today was Magda's day to clean, and everything shines.

When Adelaide reaches the bathroom, she smiles. On the vanity, between the his-and-hers sinks, her favorite pajamas are laid out, folded clumsily to reflect a man's handiwork. A shimmery blue bag bearing INDULGE in loopy script rests next to them, and Adelaide crosses her miles of ceramic tile floor to find a small box inside.

She knows what this is. Just the other day, Adelaide and William had popped into the shop at the Avalon, the swanky shopping complex nearby. Indulge specialized in "high-end luxury bath items" and therefore thought it had the right to charge sixteen dollars for a bath bomb. Adelaide had refused to give them a red cent on principle.

Nestled in the box are four bath bombs. Adelaide lifts out a pale pink one shaped like a rosebud. It touches her heart to think of William spending his lunch break in Indulge, sniffing on different options to figure out which one she'd like best.

Adelaide strips down and turns the taps in the bathtub, watching the water gush onto the immaculate porcelain. She plugs the drain and sniffs the round object in her hand, which indeed smells like a rose. When she gently tosses it into the tub, the water froths pink until the bath bomb breaks apart, releasing dried rose petals that rise to the surface.

Adelaide exhales as she lowers her slender frame into the hot water. She wills herself to clear her head and enjoy this. Today had been rough. Adelaide still smarts when she remembers the casting director's words: "Too mature a look." That's Hollywood-speak for "Too old for the part."

Why drag her bony butt all the way from Georgia to audition to be a high school sophomore, then? They knew she was twenty-eight and what she looked like. They had her CV.

Adelaide slides down until the water is up to her chin. The fragrant water fizzes, and she can feel the tightness in her upper back melt away. Maybe that sixteen-dollar price tag wasn't greedy, after all.

The heat and comfort have almost lulled Adelaide to sleep when an alarm chirps to signal the opening of an outside door. "Adelaide!" William bellows from the bottom of the stairs. "I'm ordering Thai!"

An evening in with William sounds perfect. Lord, she loves him. Also, he'd saved her the humiliation of having to move back to Bedford. Other than a short stint on a streaming series that got canceled after its first season, L.A. hadn't exactly been working out for Adelaide. Adelaide hollers back her approval of their dinner choice and slips lower into the water, closing her eyes again.

Only a few moments pass before Adelaide's tranquility is again interrupted, this time by the screaming of police sirens. She dips a washcloth into the water, folding it in half and draping it across her eyes. Pressing the edges of the fabric against her ears, she waits for the sound to pass.

It doesn't. It grows louder and louder, and then blue and red lights flash over the cloud-like bubbles.

Adelaide maneuvers to the middle of the tub, poking her fingers through the wooden slats of the Venetian blinds to see the cul-de-sac below. Three police cars have pulled in front of the McMansion next to hers.

She doesn't recognize the woman sobbing in the front yard. She's blond, with slim legs extending from a black parka. She paces, weaving off and on the walkway leading to the street. One of two police officers present puts his hand on her back, but she shakes him off, burying her face in her hands.

There's a gentle knock on the door, and William eases it open. "Ah, you're spying too," he says, raking his hand through his dark hair. His white shirt is open at the collar, his trousers rumpled. He still smells like the hospital, Adelaide knows. The scent of antiseptic always clings to him after work. "What do you think's going on?"

"I don't know," Adelaide says, her eyes returning to her neighbor's lawn. "Nothin' good."

Adelaide is not surprised at the sight below. Hailing from Bedford, she's waited for the other shoe to drop ever since her prince whisked her away to this lovely neighborhood.

A Bedford girl knows there's no such thing as a fairy tale.

THEN

LAURA

The weekend before Labor Day, Laura surveys the lower floor of her home, a shiver of anticipation running through her. It looks gorgeous. She'd spent the entire morning cleaning, sending her husband Pete and their children to Costco for enough food and beverages for the neighborhood ladies of Oleander Court. When the family had regrouped at home, they'd cranked up some music and gotten to work—arranging plastic cutlery and dishes, laying out dips and chips, and heating up frozen pierogies and spanakopita.

"Okay, people!" Laura says, swiping at a stray strand of brown hair. "Finishing touches!"

"I'll do the flowers," Nicole offers, and Laura beams at her. Now twelve, Nicole's suddenly become more helpful, while Ben at eight acts majorly inconvenienced by the smallest chore.

Which reminds her.

"Where's Ben?" Laura asks as she arranges frozen taquitos on a cookie sheet.

"He said he had to go to the bathroom," Nicole says as she emerges from the pantry with two chunky vases. "Like, twenty minutes ago."

"Ben!" Laura yells. "I need you!" She runs a sponge across the stovetop, which is already shining. Everything needs to be perfect. Laura has idly day-dreamed about having a party like this for years—one where she had the space to entertain guests without everyone knocking elbows. Where the food wasn't cheap pizza. Pete has spent almost a thousand dollars at Costco. He's even bought a wheel of shrimp, the kind with cocktail sauce in the middle.

Her youngest slinks into view, slouched in the unmistakable posture of a child protesting manual labor. "What?"

"You know what. Wash your hands and put the vegetables on this tray."

"I just washed my hands."

"Well, wash them again."

The doorbell chimes. "Oh, man," Pete says as he uncorks a bottle of wine. "Someone's here already?"

"Just Faith," Laura says as she goes to open the door. The Evite said three o'clock, which means they shouldn't expect their first guest until a quarter after. Faith is coming sooner, to help. But when Laura pulls open the door, an elderly woman stands on the porch, her face tilted in the warm September air.

"Hello!" the woman says, her eyes as bright and alert as a robin's. She leans her heavy frame on a cane, and Laura's surprised that she made it up the sidewalk by herself. "I know I'm early. I thought it would make up for not having read the book."

Technically, Laura's party is a book club party. She'd reasoned that it would provide a fallback topic of discussion.

"Oh, that's fine," Laura replies, eyeing the casserole dish teetering in the woman's free hand. "Both things. Glad to meet you, and probably no one's read the book. I'm Laura," she adds as she rescues the dish from its precarious hold.

"I'm Helen," the woman says as she shuffles inside with the aid of her cane. Her shrewd eyes take in everything—the family photos arranged on the walls, Pete's office to the right, the hardwood floors. "Love the house. Already looks like it's lived in."

Laura's still trying to figure out if she's been served a backhanded compliment when the woman wanders farther, into the kitchen. "Hello there," she tells Laura's family. "I'm Helen. Helen Beecham." The name rings a bell, but Laura can't place it.

"Nice to meet you, Helen Beecham," Pete says as he turns a cork-screw in another bottle of wine. "You know, there's an artist named Helen Beecham, too."

Ah, there it is. Pete had dragged her to an art exhibit in the Smith-sonian because two of the woman's paintings were on loan. "Salvador

Dali-esque," Laura had deemed them, not knowing anything about art but wanting something to say.

"That's me!" The woman sounds delighted.

Pete pauses mid-twist. "Seriously? Don't toy with me."

"I suppose I don't have any actual proof. Could I draw a picture on a napkin for you?"

"Oh, wow." Pete puts the bottle down. "If you're the real Helen Beecham, you can draw on my butt for all I care."

Laura reddens. She loves Pete's sense of humor, but he has no filter. And Helen is ancient. Laura doubts she appreciates crude humor.

But Helen laughs. "It's an unpredictable canvas, I'm afraid."

"Oh, yes. Lots of bumps and ridges."

"Da-*ad*," Nicole says, embarrassed. She's literally hiding behind a spray of yellow roses. "Don't talk about your butt to a stranger."

"I'm not a stranger; I'm a neighbor," Helen says as the doorbell rings again. This time, it *is* Faith, dressed up in a light blue summer dress.

"You look nice," Laura says, smoothing her own dress. She'd debated between it and another for almost fifteen minutes. Finally, she'd decided on dark blue. Simple, classic.

"Cocktail attire, right?" Faith asks, raising her eyebrows as she steps into the house. The clutter that usually characterizes the foyer is gone, the mess having been forced into the hall closet.

"Our first guest is one of Pete's favorite artists," Laura tells Faith as she closes the door behind her. "What are the odds?"

"Like, zero?" Faith offers as she hangs her satchel on the hook at the door. "Sorry I'm late."

"You're not. She was early," Laura says in a whisper.

As far as Laura's concerned, Faith never has to apologize for anything. She's been a dream, far exceeding the Nobles' expectations for an entrepreneurial nineteen-year-old advertising her childcare services online, which was how they'd found her. Laura would open her pantry to find that Faith had organized it, or notice that the clean laundry dumped on a bed had been folded neatly and put away. Having Faith around was like having a very helpful elf.

The doorbell rings again, and again and again. Soon, the lower level of Laura's home is filled with people, half of whom she hasn't met. Strangers now, but friends soon. Hopefully.

Laura pauses by her bar, also known as the kitchen table, to pour herself a glass of malbec. As she does, an Asian woman around her age glides toward her. Laura's about to introduce herself when Pam Muenster appears from nowhere. The other woman changes course so abruptly, her glossy hair swishes shampoo commercial style.

Laura smiles politely at Pam, whom she'd met right after moving into Oleander Court over the summer. When Pam had come by to deposit a basket filled with gifts from local Alpharetta businesses—a box of loose-leaf jasmine mint tea, a wheel of Brie, a bottle of Champagne, several shakers of spices, a bottle of olive oil—she'd announced herself like the presenter at a fancy garden party: "Pam Muenster, HOA president!" Then she'd asked Laura so many rapid-fire questions that Laura had felt like she was being quizzed: "Why did you all move to Alpharetta?" "From where?" "Do you have kids?" "Ages?" Pam was surprisingly aggressive for such a tiny person, like a bloodthirsty Chihuahua.

"Laura." Pam greets her warmly, almost proprietarily. "Thank you for hosting us."

"It's my pleasure," Laura replies, taking a sip of malbec.

Pam is eyeing the drink selection. "Goodness," she says. "So much Kirkland wine, isn't there?" Kirkland is the Costco store brand.

"It's our favorite—priced right, and the same ratings of the fancier brands." Whatever those ratings mean. Laura and Pete have never had palates for wine. Even with their recent influx of cash, their selection is still tied to price tag. Why spend more if it all tastes the same?

Pam's pert nose wrinkles ever so slightly. "Absolutely," she says, reaching over a row of bottles for a non-Kirkland sauvignon blanc.

Was Pam making a point? Should Laura and Pete have avoided Kirkland? Maybe it seems cheap. And the hors d'oeuvres—was it too late to hide the bags under the other trash in the bin? Laura had thought Pete had done a wonderful job choosing appetizers, that they were good enough. But maybe a party like this should be catered.

"You know," Pam says. "I forgot to ask. What, exactly, do you both do?"

"We're in tech," Laura offers, lifting her hand as an African-American woman approaches. She's striking—tall and statuesque. "Hey," the woman greets them. "I thought this was a book club. We gonna talk literature, or what?"

Pam shrugs. "I haven't, in other book clubs," she says, her tone suddenly cool.

The other woman snorts. "There's a surprise. Always *people* to talk about instead." She cups her hand around her mouth and whispers loudly to Laura, "This one walks her Yorkie so she can stare into windows. Keep your clothes on."

"That's not funny," Pam says stiffly.

"What's the matter?" the woman asks, shaking her dark curly hair. "I'm merely offering a helpful tip. You know, being neighborly. And, speaking of neighborly, Adelaide got your HOA citation letter. She says thank you for the interest in her lawn, and for you *not* to go fuck yourself."

Maybe it's intended as a joke, but it doesn't land like one. After a half-beat, Laura laughs nervously.

"Oh, Ray," Pam says. "Can't you *ever* behave yourself? Beverly!" She waves, but Laura can't tell the recipient. There might not be one. "I'll circle back with you," Pam tells Laura as she sidles away, ignoring Ray, who shrugs at Laura.

"My bad," she says.

"So . . . you're best friends with that one?'" Laura asks.

"The best." Ray points a finger toward the living room. "Next topic. Your husband's a cutie. And it's nice of him to stick around. Most husbands would've fled the scene."

The kids have. They're in their rooms, probably buried in electronics. But Pete's sharing the couch with Helen and looks thrilled to be there. Every time he's caught Laura's eye, he's pointed to Helen and mouthed, *Helen Beecham!* Laura hasn't seen someone so excited since Nicole was into unicorns.

"He's being a groupie," Laura tells Ray, leaning forward. "Did you know she's *famous*?"

"We have our share here. An actress, too."

"An actress?"

"Yeah, Adelaide was in some teenage zombie show. She's one of my favorite people."

Ah. Adelaide of the HOA letter. "Are you famous, too?"

"Nah, I'm a kept woman. My wife's a lawyer. My job's keeping the house and the babies. Our dogs. What do you do?"

"My husband and I have a company that does IT solutions for health-care. We just got acquired." The whole story has been featured in several magazines. "The Cinderellas of Tech," *Scientific Community* had dubbed her and Pete. Before, they'd scraped by for years, with Pete as the mad scientist and Laura pushing the paper and doing the marketing of their home-based firm.

"By whom?"

"MacIntyre Corporation." It was the patents they wanted, securing the rights to three of Pete's inventions. When the patents went through, Pete and Laura had leveraged a buyout that included the purchase of themselves. Now they're the employees of the Atlanta division of MacIntyre that uses their former intellectual property.

Pete and Laura don't need to be employees of anywhere. There were enough zeroes in the deal. But after a lifetime of working, the concept of idleness is inconceivable.

"Self-made woman," Ray says approvingly. "I like it." Her gaze shifts away. "Oh, geez. Bookends of evil. Good luck."

Before Laura can decipher Ray's meaning, a blond woman breaks from the crowd to greet her. "I'm Beverly," she announces, clasping Laura's free hand in her cold, dry ones. "I live in the house with the stone lion out front. Thank you so much for throwing a party. And after having *just moved*." She clucks her tongue.

Up close, Beverly looks older than Laura had expected her to be from farther away, with deep lines etched around her eyes and mouth. *Objects may be older than they appear*, she thinks. Given their ability to afford cosmetic surgery, the adage may apply to many of Laura's new neighbors. "Was that Ray Willis you were talking to?" the woman asks, guileless cornflower blue eyes staring into Laura's. "Stay clear of that one."

There's something almost reptilian about the way she blinks, the way she cocks her head. "You know," she offers when Laura doesn't say anything. "She's a . . . lesbian."

"I gathered," Laura says, taking another sip of wine. She gets Ray's *bookends* comment now. Pam and Beverly. Cute.

"Not that there's anything wrong with that. Of course, *I* don't think so."

"Right." Laura glances at the crowd, noticing the woman again, the one with the shampoo commercial hair. Doesn't she live across the street, in the house with the white wicker porch furniture? Laura had hoped to talk to her because she has a daughter around Nicole's age.

Beverly turns to see who Laura's looking at. "Soon-Li Jung," she tells her. "Barely speaks English. Chinese," she adds. "I don't understand that. Coming to this country and not making an effort to learn the language." She sighs, as if Soon-Li's language barrier represents a huge personal inconvenience to her own existence.

Pete appears, saving her. "Nice party, honey," he greets her, looping his arm around her waist. "Good turnout."

Laura gestures to Beverly with her wine glass. "This is Beverly. She lives in the house with the stone lion."

Pete snaps his fingers. "Right! Next to the one with the greenhouse. That thing is awesome. Who does that belong to?"

Beverly's eyes narrow. "That would be Ray Willis."

There's a story there, Laura notes, but Pete is tapping her shoulder. "Hey. Don't forget Faith," he reminds her softly.

They'd talked about this. Faith is scrounging for money for college during her gap year, and Pete and Laura had wanted to use the party as an opportunity to help her out. "We were there once," Pete had noted yesterday, in bed. "Let's do what we can for the kid."

"Right! Excuse me, Beverly." Laura extricates Faith from the kitchen, where she's arranging pierogies on a cookie sheet. "Faith, I need you." She grabs her wrist, careful to avoid the silver bracelet Faith always wears, the one with silver charms so tiny it looks like a circle of barbed wire from a distance. Laura steers her to the living room and taps on her wine glass.

"Hey, everyone! Thanks for coming. I'm glad we finally got to do this." She puts her hand on Faith's shoulder. "And I'm sure I'm embarrassing her, but I'm going to do this anyway. This is Faith. And she's amazing. If you need anything—kid care, organizing, help—Faith's your girl. Shoot me an email and I'll have her reach out."

After the room returns to its low babble, Laura surveys the party. Almost everyone who had RSVP'd has shown up. There's enough food, and everyone appears to be enjoying themselves despite the abundance of the Kirkland brand. Hopefully Laura was unnecessarily fretting about that.

She smiles to herself as she raises her wine to her lips, thinking of her family's cramped apartment in Arlington, the two-story walk-up. She and Pete have earned this. They've worked so hard, and here they are.

Movin' on, movin' up.

FAITH

aura didn't have to do that—dangle her in front of all those snobby women and tell them how great she is. Faith doesn't care what they think of her, thank you very much. And she doesn't want to work for them, either. She saw how they were at the party. Like, hello. How hard is it to say *thank you*, ever? And they were guests. Aren't you supposed to be nicest when you're a guest? They'd probably be awful in their own houses—sitting at their marble kitchen counters reading *Vogue* and sipping pink cocktails while Faith scrubbed at their feet like Cinderella. Offering her tap water even though their refrigerators were filled with bottles of mineral water infused with unicorn tears.

Then Faith gets the first text from Laura: *Lady from party wants you to dog sit. Serious $$! Interested?*

This piques Faith's interest. What's "serious $$?" And dog sitting can't be so bad, especially since the owners will be gone. She'll only have to see them to take instructions and then payment, ha ha. So she texts Laura back: *Sure. Give them my number.*

She also knows Laura's intentions are good. She knows all about Laura's and Pete's company from reading about them on the Internet. Wow. They're like Apple on a smaller scale, if Apple had been run by a dorky (sorry), nice middle-aged couple with kids. Maybe now that they have crap-loads of money, they're trying to pay it forward a little. Laura gives Faith way too much to watch her kids—and Faith likes doing it, anyway. Nicole is super cool, and Ben cracks Faith up. He's like an eight-year-old Pete.

The lady who needs dog sitting is that woman, Ray. Faith had liked her. At the party, she'd offered to help out in the kitchen. In a real way, not the *can I do something?* question where the eyes drift from yours and they're already walking away as they ask it. Ray and her wife have three chocolate labs that have tons of energy, so Faith walks them twice a day and even takes them to the dog park on Saturday. The house is fancy, like every house on the block, but it's not the kind of place where you feel like you can't touch anything. The same way Laura's and Pete's house is. They have tons of DVDs and a movie room, which Faith takes advantage of since Ray had told her to "make herself at home" and left instructions for turning on the stereo equipment.

While Faith is staying at Ray's house, Laura pings her: *Two more emails! Can I give them your number?*

Faith is quicker to respond this time: *Sure.* That same weekend, she mows the grass for Conner, a guy whose wife, Tracey, had gone to the book club meeting.

Conner is hot for an old dude. He has to be at least forty-five, but he doesn't have a beer gut or back fat or anything. Faith knows because he does yoga on the front porch while she runs the lawn mower over his front lawn. The back yard is built out with an in-ground pool and hot tub, so there's almost nothing to mow there. Just a little around their ginormous playground, which is wooden and filled with cool nooks and crannies to hide in. After Faith's done, he Venmos her a hundred dollars even though it only took her an hour.

Faith also cleans for Pam, who is the worst. Pam spends the entire time complaining about so many people that Faith can't keep their names straight. Her dog pisses on the floor twice while she's there, and Pam looks at her until she offers to clean it up. Pam pays her even more than Conner did, but it's probably because she has no clue how much she should pay and not her being nice.

By the end of the weekend, Faith itches to get back home. It's not because she misses her own bed, but because of the neighborhood. There's something weird about it, like no one—except maybe the Nobles and the Willises—is real. How does no one do their own yardwork or housework? Do they think it's *beneath* them? If that's how they feel, should Faith feel insulted that they're asking her to do it instead?

They're all so wasteful, too. Pam told her to throw away anything in the fridge that was even a day expired. Faith had filled a trash bag—cage-free eggs, sliced mangoes, Greek yogurt—and, when Pam wasn't looking, stowed it in her own car. As she slammed her trunk closed, she'd looked up to see a beautiful end table sitting out on the curb. Probably an antique, probably worth a fortune. But someone has tossed it without a thought.

That had ended up in Faith's car, too.

Real people don't act this way. They trim their own hedges and clip coupons and only go on vacations they've saved up for. They don't let beautiful furniture end up in a landfill.

The people in Oleander Court are freaks, living in a setting that reminds Faith of a horror movie—one where something awful unfolds because everything's way too perfect, and there's no such thing as a utopia. Like the people who live there need to be taught that.

Faith has the feeling something's about to happen. Something bad. She can't put her finger on it, but she knows it's coming, the same way she wakes up sometimes and knows it's going to rain. Something so perfect can only hold for so long until it falls apart.

Especially when it's rotten at the core.

"**I**'m going to kill that bitch!" Ray screams. "What kind of a sick, vindictive, closed-minded piece of—" she sputters, examining the neat sheaf of papers that had arrived in a manila envelope.

Or rather, had *been served* in a manila envelope. Over the weekend, as she and Juliet had been enjoying their anniversary weekend at the Four Seasons in downtown Atlanta, a process server had appeared on behalf of Beverly Grant. Faith had accepted the documents he'd extended, apparently not even realizing what was happening. Ray hadn't seen them until this morning, when, after feeding the dogs, she'd gone to peruse the minimal stack of mail Faith had left for the couple on the kitchen counter.

"This is so completely unnecessary," Ray continues as Juliet snatches the papers and scans them. Ray can practically see her lawyer's mind clicking away, considering the couple's different options against the evil troll who lives next door.

"It is," Juliet agrees, running a hand through her short brown hair. It's only seven thirty, yet she's already fully suited up, ready for the drive into Atlanta. "I don't get why."

"Really?" Ray stares at her. "*Really?*"

Hades's toenails click on the linoleum as he goes to his master, abandoning the remnants of breakfast that still occupy Apollo and Zeus. Of the three Labs, he's most in tune with Ray's moods, most concerned with comforting her. Ray's fingers twine around his short brown fur as she scratches between his ears. "It's okay, boy," she mutters.

"I like to believe she's not that closed-minded," Juliet says. "This can't all be because of our orientation."

"Why not? Have you *seen* the way she looks at us?" Ray releases Hades to rest her hands over the back of a kitchen chair, squeezing. "Juliet. What if it isn't that? What if she *knows*?"

"She doesn't know," Juliet says automatically, flipping a page. "Don't think about it."

"But she could."

"No, she couldn't. There's no trace."

"We can't be sure."

Juliet pries Ray's right hand off the chair, clenches it in her tinier ones. "Sweetheart. Don't worry. We've covered your tracks. And besides—who cares?"

"Yeah, yeah, yeah," Ray grumbles. "Tell that to the angry mob." The doorbell rings, and Apollo emits a short bark. "Maybe it's the bitch," she says hopefully. "I can kill her if she's on my property, right?"

"Very funny," Juliet says, moving aside the yellow curtain. "It's some woman and her dog."

Holding her dogs back, Ray opens the door to find Laura, who is struggling with a very excited brown terrier mix. "Whoa," Ray murmurs to her fur babies, keeping the door cracked so they can't rush out. "Who's this?"

"Costco," Laura says, pushing her hair out of her eyes.

"Now, that's consumer dedication," Ray observes, and Laura smiles.

"I got him at the shelter over the weekend. Interested in a walk?"

"Sure," Ray says. "Let me grab the leashes." She opens the door wider. "Stay," she commands the dogs, and they do.

Juliet appears from the kitchen, having traded the court papers for a toaster waffle, which she nibbles from a paper towel. "Hey, I'm Juliet. You're the one who had the party, right? Sorry I missed it." Juliet had been working. She's always working.

"No worries. Want to join us for a walk?"

Juliet shakes her head. "I have to get out the door."

"Oh, right. You're an attorney. They probably expect you to actually be in the office."

That was one of the only benefits of the coronavirus. Suddenly, most businesses realized their employees could be trusted to work from home in the comfort of sweatpants. But not Juliet's firm.

Juliet makes a face. "Yes, they do." She taps Ray on the back as Ray slips on her sneakers, leashes and poop bags in hand. "Have fun."

Once outside, Laura's new dog immediately heads for Ray's hyacinths. "No! No! Bad dog!" Laura strains against the leash. It's the wrong kind for a large, exuberant puppy—not a harness, which would make him much easier to control. Ray tells her so, but kindly.

"I know that. Now. He slipped out of his collar earlier and ran for it. I nearly had a heart attack."

"Haven't you ever had a dog before?"

Laura shakes her head. "My dad's allergic, and Pete and I never had the space for one before."

"Where are we walking?" Ray asks. "Neighborhood loop?" Oleander Court is shaped like a lopsided T, with Magnolia Lane off the main road and Jasmine Lane intersecting halfway. Years ago, it was only Jasmine Lane—a curving, lazy street with a handful of houses nestled in the woods.

"That would be great." Laura grins, and Ray grins back. There's something about this woman that endears her to Ray. She's eager and well-meaning, the way Ray's little sister was. Still is, probably. Ray wishes she knew.

Costco pulls Laura again, and she yelps as she yanks at the leash. "Maybe I should have gotten a smaller dog," she muses as she wraps the leash around her wrist. Ray's dogs are bigger than Laura's, and she has three of them, yet she's having an easier time.

"I'll give you the name of my trainer," Ray says. "She's brilliant. Mine were a mess before her regime." Ray breathes out, willing her heartbeat to slow. She needs to manage her temper. Deal with her issues constructively, like her therapist says she should. "And also," she says, "I'll give you the scoop on the neighborhood." She waves at Conner next door, who is energetically engaged in pushups on his front lawn. "That's Conner," she tells Laura. "Hedge fund manager, big fan of himself. Wife is Tracey. Super nice. Super great with the kids."

Super unobservant, she wants to add. Poor Tracey. She deserves someone better than Conner. Every time Ray sees her, she's with the kids, looking lonely and exhausted and a little bit older than the day before. Meanwhile, Conner's probably out banging someone he met at a happy hour.

"The huge house in the center of the cul-de-sac is Adelaide's. The actress," Ray adds.

Ray wishes Adelaide was in town. Adelaide's always up for an afternoon bottle of wine, feet on the table as the two flip through trash television options. Her accent becoming less Southern and more redneck with each sip.

One wouldn't think someone like Adelaide would be friends with someone like Ray, but both know what it's like to carry a past. That's better friendship glue than a shared love of Whole Foods.

"Zombie parts must be really lucrative. Pun intended."

"Her husband William is a surgeon. He's lived here for years." Ray stops herself from further elaborating on William. William's always given her the creeps. And who moves a new wife into the house you'd shared with your dead one?

She points to a house with toys scattered all over the lawn. "The Atkinsons. Nice people, but they keep to themselves. Busy. Always one school event or another."

"How old are the kids?"

"I dunno. School age?" Ray ignores the twist in her gut when she thinks about school-aged kids. She and Juliet have researched their options for years, but they've never pulled the trigger. And now they're both on the wrong side of forty. Sighing, she points to a gorgeous Spanish-style home with a tiled walkway two houses down. *"Pam* lives there. And Buster. He's probably shit in your yard about a hundred times already."

"How nice."

"Yeah, dog shit under a certain size is exempt from HOA guidelines. I'm sure it's in the bylaws somewhere." Ray imagines Pam penning it in, stamping the document with a seal to make it official. One that looks like something Voldemort would use.

"The Jungs are across from you on the corner. You have to meet Soon-Li. She cracks me up." At Laura's quizzical look, Ray grins mysteriously. "You'll see."

"Here's the Denton family. Nice people. Warm, kind of goofy. And then the Holidays. Bambi's a treat. Basically, the cartoon, crappy version of Adelaide. And you know what they say—the original's always better."

Though, if one were concerned with accuracy, Bambi had been there first. With most of her original parts.

"There's your husband's new girlfriend." They're at Helen's house. "The HOA's always getting on her about that lawn." It's obvious where Helen's property line ends, as the grass is a full three inches shorter on both adjoining sides. Tripp Schulman, the worthless politician, is backing his car out of the driveway next door. Ray's fairly certain he's powered by batteries instead of the four food groups.

"Is the house next to ours vacant?" Laura asks Ray. "I haven't seen anyone yet."

"Yes and no. The Colemans retired to Florida a while ago, but they didn't sell the house so their daughter can use it. Jade. She's twenty-eight, I think? She's a 'professional social media influencer.'" Ray makes exaggerated air quotes.

"What does a professional social media influencer do?"

"Beats me. I'm old school." Ray doesn't think much of Jade's job, but she's always liked her, her parents. Originally from Colombia, Anita Coleman is warm and bubbly, and had more than a few times walked excess food down the street in an attempt to fatten up Juliet.

"Hmm."

"How are you liking the neighborhood?" Ray asks Laura to fill the gap in conversation. Does Laura think she's shit-talking? The last thing Ray wants is to be put in the same category as *Pam*.

"It's nice." Laura yelps as the dog yanks her again. "But it's hard getting used to a house so big."

"Hire a cleaner. That's what most people here do."

"You don't?"

Ray shakes her head. "Nah, I can't justify it. Not with my current . . . sabbatical."

"I thought you were a 'kept woman'?" Ray isn't surprised Laura remembered her quip.

"Somewhat. I was an attorney, too. I'm taking a break." Ray leaves it at that. It's not the whole truth, but it's also not an inaccurate way of putting it. Which makes it a lawyer way of putting it. Maybe she's still got it.

As they near Ray's house, Beverly is meandering down her walk. Ray slows, hoping Beverly will be gone by the time they pass, but no such luck. She's blocking the sidewalk, using a sponge to scrub at invisible dirt on the stone lion at the end of the walkway. It's almost like she's waiting for them.

"Coming through!" Laura warns cheerfully, and Beverly gifts her with a broad smile while ignoring Ray completely.

"Oh, *hello, dear*," she says, the sponge paused mid-air, spotting the sidewalk with water droplets. "And who is this beautiful guy? I don't believe I've seen him before!"

"Costco." Laura leans to scratch his head, then notices Beverly's No Dogs on the Grass sign. "Oh! I'm sorry." The dog is about two inches over on the lawn. She tugs at the leash but he sits down, scratching at his ears with his back leg while displaying an impressive erection. Laura purses her lips, clearly embarrassed.

Beverly waves her hand like a queen pardoning a subject. "Don't worry about the sign. It's only a precaution."

"A precaution against what?"

Ray can't stay without punching Beverly in the face. Or taking the sign and shoving it up somewhere dark and dusty. "Come on, boys," she says, clicking her tongue and continuing down the sidewalk.

Laura trots to catch up. "What was that about?" she asks when she reaches her.

"Sorry. I hate her," Ray says shortly, focusing on her breathing. She'll do yoga in the back yard when she gets back. That, or open the bottle of malbec on the kitchen counter. Maybe she'll drink *while* doing yoga.

"What did she do?" Laura asks, and Ray appreciates the phrasing. Laura doesn't assume she's so petty she'd hate Beverly just for being Beverly. There'd have to be a reason.

Suddenly, though, Ray doesn't want to talk about it. She talks about it all the time, and Beverly isn't worth that. She shrugs. "I can't get into it right now. But I will say this—I sure do wish I didn't have to see her every damn day. I can't be responsible for what I might eventually do to that woman."

HELEN

She's tried to stop, she really has. But lately Helen finds herself watching the hands on her wall clock—the old-fashioned kind, no checking iPhones for her—and waiting for four o'clock. Four o'clock is an acceptable time for her first Moscow Mule. To squeeze the lime, to pour a generous portion of vodka in a square crystal glass. Hand shaking in either simple anticipation or genuine need, Helen doesn't know and doesn't care to know. She'll be seventy-nine next year, and she'll do what she damn well pleases.

Helen needs to retire to Boca Raton. She's already purchased a lovely little condo along the water, in one of those assisted living places with varying levels of support based on stages of decrepitude. The closing was three months ago, but Helen can't bear to leave, to put her home on the market and watch someone else buy it, change it.

Helen and her Edmund had purchased this house when this wasn't even Oleander Court. It was one street instead of two cul-de-sacs—Jasmine Lane—and theirs was one of few houses. Their daughters had just entered high school, and the family loved having their own woods, rolling fields. They even had blackberry bushes.

Then, in 1990, a developer had offered to buy the surrounding land, offering a price so obscene it would have been foolish not to take it. Helen and Edmund wanted to provide for their daughters, and, even with the modest level of fame Helen had achieved, she'd never be rich. Edmund was only a schoolteacher.

Helen pours her drink, recalling the deal. The ink was still drying on the check when the bulldozers came. The woods—which Helen and Edmund had roamed for hours, observing the occasional deer and listening for the tapping woodpecker or rumbling bullfrog—were razed to the ground. "What have we done?" Edmund and Helen had asked each other. Jasmine Lane stayed and Magnolia Lane was added as houses sprouted up around them like mushrooms.

They weren't houses, though. These were mansions. Oleander Court, as it was renamed during the rezoning, became a hot spot for Alpharetta real estate. *The* place to live, if you could afford it. The sticker prices on these new homes—all similar due to the same or reverse floor plans, all opulent—made Helen feel sick.

At the request of their daughters, Helen and Edmund had remodeled the house, giving it the facelift Helen had always declined for herself. The back yard gained sculpted foliage and an in-ground pool. A beautiful stone porch encircled the home. The girls' rooms were built out, expanded. Personally, Helen thought the changes made the house look the slightest bit Frankenstein-y, but she'd been the only one to voice that opinion so she'd let it go.

Helen takes a long sip of her drink. Maybe her hand had been too heavy with the vodka. Opening her door, she settles on her porch swing, surveying the neighborhood. From behind her trellis with its overgrown ivy, few can see her, not unless they're watching for her.

The new neighbors live at the left corner. Helen eyes the house, taking another drink. She hopes she hadn't made a bad impression at the book club party. And maybe her casserole had been a poor choice to bring. Do children even like tuna casserole anymore? That Nicole must be at least ten. Maybe the whole family is gluten-free and vegan like everyone else seems to be these days.

"Are you going to the party?" Pam Muenster had chirped when she'd seen Helen outside, struggling with her lawn mower. The HOA had sent her a love letter the day before, forcing her to action. A two-hundred-dollar fine for not keeping the lawn up! Imagine! When this had been Jasmine Lane, she and Edmund could let the grass grow as high as they liked.

"What party?" Helen had asked, gritting her teeth. She was well aware that Pam *was* the HOA, or at least its backbone. The lawn mower still wouldn't go, and her neighbor Tripp—an able-bodied male in his fifties—sat on his porch, glued to his laptop like he didn't notice her struggling. This was in keeping with Tripp's uselessness in general— Tripp always acts terribly solicitous, inquiring into Helen's health like it matters, but he's never once offered to do the smallest of favors. A politician, of all things, Tripp keeps a repertoire of banal comments on hand, like "A scorcher of a day today, isn't it, Helen?" and "Thank God it's Wednesday!" as if Wednesday means anything at all.

Helen has no impression of Tripp's wife, Sandy. She is literally the most boring person Helen has ever met. She might as well be a shoe.

"The book club meeting," Pam replied; and after she'd left, continuing her power walk with a flip of her short ponytail, Helen had gone inside and fired up the ancient Mac her youngest daughter had given her and forced her to learn to use. Meaning, Helen can play Solitaire and open her AOL email account. There, in her inbox, was the invitation.

As she's staring at the house with the new neighbors, the husband— Pete—comes around the corner, from the garage. He pauses to shout toward the house, and Helen's breath hitches. Is that her empty casserole dish in his hand? Is she about to have a *visitor*?

It's quite sad how excited the prospect makes her.

Oh, dear. Her glass is already empty.

Pete jogs up the sidewalk, waving to the Amazon delivery man as he passes. Likely to visit her other next-door neighbors—Marv and Bambi—who may or may not have online shopping addictions. A delivery truck stops outside their house at least twice a day, and Helen imagines a home filled with impulse purchases, half of them still encased in bubble wrap.

Pete draws up to her house, and Helen is ashamed to realize how terrible the grass still looks. In the battle between herself and the lawn mower, the lawn mower has emerged victorious.

"Helen Beecham!" Pete says as he approaches, and Helen realizes he always says her name like that: "Helen Beecham." Not "Helen," or "Mrs. Beecham." He truly is a genuine fan, though Helen hasn't produced anything to applaud in years. She hasn't even picked up a paintbrush in over three decades. "Here's your dish," he says, handing her the sparkling casserole dish as she sits on the swing. "Delicious."

"Thank you," Helen tells him, setting it aside and raising her drink. "Care for one?" Helen had refrained from alcohol at his party, as she hadn't wanted to be the silly old woman who needed to be carted home. But on her own porch, with a man who admires her, she's emboldened.

"Sure. But now I feel bad. You cooked us that casserole. I should have at least brought cookies or something." He looks around the porch, like perhaps there's a package of Oreos hiding somewhere.

"No need," Helen says, shaking the ice in her empty glass. "I have plenty in the pantry."

Pete wanders down her wooden porch steps to admire the trellis. "Boy, is that a piece of craftsmanship! We're thinking of putting one up. Who's your guy?" Pete seems to have learned that everyone in Oleander Court has a guy for everything. A guy for fixing the gutters, for patching the roof, for repairing the dishwasher. For wiping one's bottom.

"*My* guy," Helen says, feeling lightheaded. "My Edmund put that up nearly twenty years ago." It had been quite a project, taking over two months. But Edmund was retired and enjoyed projects like it. If he hadn't been a teacher, he would have been a carpenter.

"He did an excellent job," Pete calls from her yard, where he's studying the lawn mower. After her defeat, she'd simply left it where it lay. Let Pam as the HOA write her another letter. "Hey, what happened here?"

"A minor struggle."

Pete leans to fiddle with it. After a few yanks and prods, the lawn mower sputters, then roars to life. "Let me mow your lawn," Pete says. "Fair trade for a dinner."

"I couldn't let you do that," Helen protests. All she has to do is walk across the street when someone else's landscaper is at work. Ask them to mow her lawn, too. But Pete's already maneuvering the machinery over her grass, a clean stripe appearing in the overgrowth. "Fine," she mutters, taking the time to go to the kitchen for a fresh drink. She pours Pete one, too.

The whole job is done in fifteen minutes. Pete wipes his brow as he joins her on the porch, sinking into the swing. He smells like grass and man sweat, altogether not an unpleasant scent. He accepts the drink she offers and takes a slug. "Hey! That's not water!" He makes a face.

"Moscow Mule." Helen's too tired to get up. "If you'd like ice water, I'm afraid you'll have to get it yourself."

"No, this is great." Pete takes another drink, smaller this time, and it occurs to Helen that Pete has already done more for her than her idiot next-door neighbor has in ten years of sharing a property line. Pete is a good apple, one who offers to help when people need it. Naturally, reflexively.

"Hey," he says now, shifting to pull a brochure from his jacket. "Almost forgot. Brought you the old brochure for the InfoHealth apps. To give you a visual of what they do."

"Thank you," Helen murmurs as she takes it. She doesn't know what an "app" is—to be perfectly honest, her eyes had glazed over when poor Pete had attempted to explain it before—but she understands pride in a creation. "Will you look at that," she says as she squints at the brochure.

"My babies," Pete says, then smiles sheepishly. "Don't tell my kids I said that."

Helen's lips twist as she thinks of how she used to feel about her paintings. The connection was personal, deep. Indeed, they were "her babies." She misses feeling that way.

As she watches Pete study his own brochure, Helen feels a surge of gratitude for the Nobles coming to Oleander Court. They've earned their spot, have a story—unlike those who paid their first down payment with trust fund money. Those are the dullest residents of all. Just look at Tripp.

Helen should pick up and leave. She knows that. Her condo is just sitting there, collecting dust as the ocean glitters nearby. But Helen is nostalgic, and she hates the idea of leaving Jasmine Lane as what it has become. Oleander Court is the warped, untrue version of her lovely Jasmine Lane. Like a painting by Hieronymus Bosch, if one looks closely enough. Twisted, nonsensical. And, most of all—ugly.

"If you truly like casseroles made out of odd pantry items," Helen offers, "I have other jobs to do."

Pete grins. "Bring it on."

BAMBI

When Bambi finally emerges from her thousand-count pearl pink sheets, it's nearly noon on a Wednesday. Oh, well. She has nowhere to be. Bambi stretches like a cat, arms over her head as she stifles a yawn. Moving her mouth hurts after yesterday's injections, which make her lips look fuller and promote an overall appearance of youth. Or so says her cosmetic surgeon, who's overseen Bambi's Botox treatments since she turned twenty-five. He tells her where to stick and prick herself, and she listens. Then, every Christmas, he sends her a bottle of Champagne, probably to thank her for paying his mortgage.

Bambi doesn't care if that's the message. Looking young is worth any price.

Bambi pads to the kitchen in her bare feet, admiring her toenails. Before the procedure yesterday, she'd treated herself to a spa pedicure with the works. The gel polish is designed to last a month, but since Bambi is the type to treat herself frequently, the polish will be redone in a week, max.

Nothing in the fridge pleases her. Bambi doesn't often do her own shopping—that's what delivery services are for—and she's annoyed because her latest order did not include her favorite tapioca pudding. Not at herself, for forgetting to put it on the list, but at the deliveryman for not getting it anyway. It was *always* on the list. She *always* wanted it. What was the point in hiring someone to fetch if they forgot the same things you did?

Bambi's eyes stray to the Post-it Note on the fridge, the email address for that new neighbor who'd thrown that tacky book club party a few weeks ago. She'd heard all about it from Pam. Pierogies from Costco? Was she kidding?

Still, maybe it's time for Bambi to fire her deliveryman and give that Faith a go. Pam said she was a dream.

Marv must be at the country club. Technically, Marv is an executive for a chain of coffee shops in the greater Atlanta area, but that doesn't mean much considering his father is the eighty percent shareholder of the chain. It's effectively a title with a paycheck, as Marvin, Sr., had given up on affording his only son any real responsibilities years ago.

Bambi touches her lips with the tips of her fingers. They really do hurt this time. Dr. Acton had advised her to wait an additional week before this last procedure, but she'd decided to go for it anyway. She and Marv have a wedding to attend, and if Bambi looks anything less than fabulous—or older than thirty-two—she'll die.

Bambi slides open the freezer, where Isobel, her "helper"—a generic term for someone who does everything around one's house, to include cleaning, laundry, and food preparation—has neatly arranged Ziploc bags of smoothie ingredients prepared with specific purposes in mind. Bambi removes one marked "antioxidant" and dumps the contents into her Vitamix blender, flipping the switch. When it's done, she pours the smoothie into a tall glass and leaves the blender in the sink without bothering to rinse it.

Isobel can deal with it. It's what she's paid for.

Sipping on the kale concoction, Bambi wanders to the front window, where she sees that slut, Adelaide, jogging.

Bambi has no proof that Adelaide's a slut. But the actress is younger and hotter than Bambi, and married to a surgeon who *isn't* losing his hair, so she's one by default. Bambi's eyes narrow as she watches Adelaide's retreating ass, jaunty from exercise rather than liposuction.

He's not just any surgeon, either. He's *William*.

Bambi takes another pull on her straw. She's in desperate need of some shopping therapy—it can take her weeks to prepare for a social event, and the wedding is right around the corner—but her lips aren't for public viewing. With a sigh, Bambi retrieves her MacBook and pulls up her favorite tabs.

Within an hour, she's spent nearly ten thousand dollars, but she doesn't feel better at all. How can she feel better without her favorite tapioca? And where is Isobel? Isobel was supposed to be here nearly fifteen minutes ago.

Bambi retrieves her phone from the bedroom and sees the text: *Son broke leg. Will be out today and tomorrow.*

Bambi blanches. Isobel's son broke his leg? That's terrible!

Who will clean the blender?

SOON-LI

Soon-Li had purchased her elliptical machine in consideration of gym membership fees, transit times, and public embarrassment. She'd further reasoned that she was more inclined to work out if she only had to walk ten feet to do so. In weighing all considerations and options for fitness, home equipment made the most sense.

The investment hasn't panned out as she had calculated. Since the purchase last December, Soon-Li estimates she's used her elliptical a grand total of eight times. Not counting the times it's doubled as a drying rack for wet clothes.

Now, shamed at her elliptical's lack of use, Soon-Li resolutely moves her feet, watching the cruel red numbers on the screen very, very slowly count down the time remaining. She's pouring buckets of sweat, and Soon-Li wonders, again, how she can be so thin and yet so out of shape.

She has roughly an hour to pick up Lila, her only child, from violin practice after school. Lila has shown no promise as a violinist and wants to quit, but Soon-Li hasn't let her. She and Tran have never quit at anything, and now they run one of the most successful cybersecurity firms in the country. It's one of the best-kept secrets of the neighborhood, albeit boring.

Soon-Li wrinkles her nose as Pam walks by her window with her Yorkie, Buster. Pam is the reason why, when some neighbors talk to Soon-Li, they use the loud, overly exaggerated diction reserved for the deaf or the dumb. As if having English as a second language puts someone in the latter category. Buster stops at the bright pink vinca flowers lining the end of Soon-Li's sidewalk, lifting his leg. He walks a few more feet, then squats down in the unmistakable position of a shitting dog. When he straightens, Pam glances around. Then, concluding no one has seen her, she continues along.

As Soon-Li moves her feet, she considers Pam's rudeness. Allowing her Yorkie to defecate on someone's property, watching it happen (or actively ignoring it by staring elsewhere), and leaving it there. Soon-Li could put up a sign like the one Beverly Grant has, but she doesn't want to do anything Beverly would do.

Besides, Buster would probably pee on the sign.

Soon-Li powers through her session on the elliptical. She showers quickly and jumps into her white Lexus, careful as she backs out of the driveway to wait for Conner Boyle to pass. That man is a peacock, constantly strutting around the neighborhood like the women are all supposed to swoon. He raises his hand. "Good evening, Soon-Li!" Each word loud, emphasized.

"Evening, Mr. Conner!" Soon-Li calls through the open window, hearing the heaviness of her Korean accent. The elimination of the "r" in his name.

As she turns the corner out of Oleander Court, putting on her turn signal even though no one is behind her, Soon-Li lifts her hand to wave at a black Taurus entering the subdivision. Belatedly, she recognizes the driver as Laura, the host of the book club party. Soon-Li had attended it because she'd witnessed the family unpacking their first moving pod, singing off-key to '90s pop music and shouting instructions to one another. They seemed like nice people, and the daughter looked around Lila's age. Lila could use a friend.

Only Soon-Li hadn't had the chance to talk to Laura at the party. Every time she'd seen her, she'd been cornered by one neighbor or another. Soon-Li should have skipped the party.

Soon-Li has twenty minutes before she's needed at the middle school. That's plenty of time to use the McDonald's drive-through. Lila deserves a treat for being so dutiful with the violin. Soon-Li waits for the car in front of hers to move, then eases up to the intercom. The voice that greets her is garbled, staticky, but she gets the gist. Soon-Li clears her throat:

"Yeah, I'll take a number nine with a Diet Coke and two ice creams, please."

Her English is perfect, unaccented.

Soon-Li may be Korean, but she was born and raised in Philadelphia.

BEVERLY

Pam came to personally deliver Beverly's invitation to the second meeting of the neighborhood ladies' book club. Unlike certain *other* neighbors, Pam has class. She understands that invitations to an event should be hand-delivered rather than lazily shot through cyberspace.

Not that Beverly had said anything when meeting Laura, her new neighbor and sender of an Evite. Some people simply didn't know any better, and pretending you didn't see their flaws was the Christian thing to do.

"It will align with Halloween," Pam tells Beverly, looking chic in a pink cashmere sweater. "Only three days before."

Beverly glances at the invitation, which is embossed on creamy stationery. A purple glittery spider is affixed to the top right corner. "Is everyone in the neighborhood invited?" she asks, with a not-so-subtle glance next door.

"All the women," Pam says, her eyes lighting up at the hint of gossip. "Why? Is that a problem?"

"I'll deal with the situation," Beverly replies, chin held high. She won't be discouraged from a neighborhood party by someone like *Ray*.

"What *is* the situation?" Pam asks, and Beverly ushers her inside where they can't be overheard.

"From the way she's acting, you'd think I tried to kill one of those horrible dogs of hers." Beverly sniffs. "All I'm asking for is what's mine."

"Which is . . .?" Pam is looking around her living room, and Beverly feels a twinge of pride when Pam's eyes land on her built-in shelves.

They house the Fabergé egg collection amassed by Beverly's late husband George, who had collected them during his business trips around the world. Altogether, they're worth nearly a million dollars.

Beverly gestures for Pam to sit. "You're aware of that eyesore near my property line?"

"Eyesore?" Pam plays with the jade necklace at the base of her throat. "You mean the greenhouse?"

"Right. Pellegrino?" When Pam nods, Beverly retrieves two from the refrigerator, rolling her eyes when she sees that Faith has moved them from their usual location in the vegetable crisper to the door. She'll need to talk to that girl—Beverly's hired her for simple cleaning, not for rearranging Beverly's home to her own liking.

She places the drinks on the coffee table. "A few months ago, I hired a surveyor to confirm the property lines. And when he measured, he discovered the greenhouse was a full six inches over on my property."

A smile plays around Beverly's lips when she recalls that conversation. Finally, she had something on Ray Willis! She'd hated that obnoxious woman ever since she and her—*wife*, she calls Juliet—moved in years ago. With those three dogs who, much to Beverly's chagrin, have not once *actually* pooped or dug in her yard and thus triggered her right to react. And the music Ray blares from her porch, occasionally dancing with Juliet, flaunting their relationship! Like Beverly should be assaulted by their lifestyle choice.

Not that she overtly disapproves of their lifestyle. Of course not. She isn't judgmental. She merely doesn't appreciate them being so *aggressive* in celebrating who they choose to be.

"What does that mean?" Pam asks, raising her bottle to her lips.

"It means that as the property owner, I have the right to demand she remove the encroaching portion of her greenhouse from my lawn."

"But how do you move a—? *Oh,*" Pam says as she realizes what this means. "The whole thing has to come down."

"Precisely."

"What about money?" Pam asks, and for a moment Beverly worries that Pam is criticizing her approach, that she thinks she's acting too harshly. Then Pam adds, "You could make them pay whatever you want."

Beverly relaxes. Pam is on her side. "Yes, but where's the fun in that?" Juliet is a partner at one of the most prestigious law firms in Peachtree Center in downtown Atlanta. Cutting a check for eighty grand, one hundred, would mean nothing to her. Plus, turning this dispute into a simple transaction—even one where she has the other party over a barrel—would be no fun. Beverly has plenty of money already.

"Anyhow," she tells Pam, "I've initiated the court process. And my lawyer approves. He even mentioned that if I let the greenhouse stay, something called an 'easement' could apply, where she'd have the actual *right* to use my property. I'm protecting myself."

"I understand completely," Pam says, shifting on Beverly's designer couch. "Stand your ground."

The doorbell chimes. "That should be the water delivery man," Beverly tells Pam, rising. Every Monday, two jugs of triple-filtered water arrive via Crystal Springs. "Excuse me."

When she opens the door, it isn't Beverly's delivery man. It's a visibly nervous Latina girl in scuffed Minnie Mouse shoes and glossy black hair pulled back with a pink ribbon. She's holding a clipboard and has trouble making eye contact.

"I'm selling chocolates for my school," she tells Beverly's forehead, the words running together. "If you buy two boxes, it's thirty percent off. They're really good, and I'll deliver them to you when they're ready. Would—?"

"Darling," Beverly cuts her off, her voice sanguine. "What is your name?"

"Manuela."

"Manuela, do you live in the neighborhood?"

The little girl shakes her head. "My dad is Roberto." She points to the red truck parked down the street, the back filled with leaf clippings and tree limbs. Roberto provides lawn services for at least eight houses in the neighborhood and has done so for years.

"I'm sorry, dear, but you can't sell your chocolates here," Beverly tells her. "You don't live here. Your father should know better."

The sign is right at the entrance to the neighborhood: NO SOLICITORS. English probably isn't Roberto's first language, but surely he understands why it's there.

"I'm sorry," Manuela says, eyes glistening. "I didn't know."

"That's quite all right," Beverly says, closing the door gently in her face.

Beverly knows what Roberto's trying to do here. He knows Manuela won't sell chocolates in his own neighborhood, where luxury is name-brand Froot Loops. Consequently, he's relying on the good people of Oleander Court to bankroll his daughter's fundraiser.

Some people. Always looking for a handout in some form or another.

"Was that the little girl with Roberto?" Pam asks as Beverly once again joins her in the living area. "She rang my doorbell earlier, but I was just getting out of the shower. What did she want?"

"To sell me something," Beverly says, shaking her head. "My goodness. This is a neighborhood, not a charity. I feel bad"—she didn't, not at all—"but if we allowed her to go door-to-door, anyone could wander into Oleander Court peddling anything they wanted."

"Absolutely right. Good for you, setting her straight. You know, maybe I should send something out on behalf of the HOA. Make sure no one's encouraging kids like her by actually buying something."

Beverly lifts her chin. "I wouldn't bother. I should hope we all know better."

ADELAIDE

delaide's on her third loop around the neighborhood when she finds herself passing a dark-haired child in light-up Minnie Mouse sneakers. "Comin' through!" she puffs, but as she pulls up alongside she slows. The girl's crying. "What's the matter?" she asks, keeping pace. God, this child is beautiful. In a few years, it might spell trouble.

"Nothing," the girl says, staring straight ahead. She wipes at the tears streaming down her cheeks.

"Nothin'?" Adelaide asks, crouching to look into her face, to force the girl to look at her. When she does look, she starts.

"Are you . . . *Daphne?*" the little girl asks.

Adelaide wants to groan. "Daphne," her alter ego from the now-cancelled *Zombie 101*, is not how she wants to be known to America's youth. Daphne is a slutty zombie with skintight clothes and bad one-liners. And how does a child this young even know who Daphne is? She must have an older sister with Internet access. *Zombie 101* was a streaming series.

"Technically, yeah. That's me. Adelaide McKenzie." She leans closer, conspiratorially. "McKenzie's my *real* last name." Her working name is Holt.

"Wow." The girl's mouth is hanging open, exposing white lower teeth. "I've never met a movie star before."

Television star, Adelaide wants to correct her, but she's distracted by a man in a black cap and white T-shirt emblazoned with *Roberto's Lawn Services* crossing the street in long strides. "Manuela? *Cuál es el problema?*"

Damn, Adelaide thinks as he gets closer, muscles rippling under his shirt. His dark eyes piercing as he examines his own flesh and blood. Adelaide may be a happily married woman, but she can still appreciate the aesthetics of a beautiful man. He flashes her a smile before sinking to address Manuela. "Everything okay?" he asks, in English this time.

Manuela nods. "I'm done," she says, thrusting her clipboard at him. "I don't want to sell chocolates here anymore."

Adelaide's eyes narrow. She's all too familiar with the brave face, the saving of a parent's pride. When she was in grade school and Wendy Huber and her bitchy friends made fun of her for living in a trailer, her mama never, ever found out.

The man checks his watch. "Manuela, I will not be done here for an hour. There is still a whole street." He gestures.

"I'll take her," Adelaide offers. "She can hang out at my house."

"Are you sure?" He removes his cap, revealing a head of hair that matches his daughter's. "I am Roberto, by the way."

"I gathered," she says, indicating his shirt. "Adelaide. I live right there. Middle house. We'll have lemonade." She smiles brightly at Manuela, who still has tear tracks down her cheeks.

The pair head to the cul-de-sac, silent except for the occasional sniffle from Manuela. When they arrive at the door, Adelaide opens it. "You first."

"Your house is very nice," Manuela says politely as Adelaide leads her into the kitchen. "I like the flowers." Adelaide always has fresh flowers in the living room, whatever her back yard can spare. Today it's pink roses.

"Thanks." Adelaide pours them both huge cups of sugary lemonade, adding twisty straws and extra lemon wedges for good measure. Just like the lemon shake-ups at the Arkansas State Fair. Adelaide has fuzzy memories of guzzling those and funnel cakes in between Tilt-A-Whirl spins.

Manuela takes a pull on her drink. "This is good."

"It keeps me from turnin' back into a zombie," Adelaide says, immediately wrinkling her nose at her own bad joke. She's not used to children. Is terrible with them, truth be told.

"Now," she says, setting her lemonade down. "Wanna tell me what happened?" Manuela shakes her head, and Adelaide hops onto the kitchen counter, crossing her legs. "You know," she says, "when I was your age, not everyone was nice to me, either."

Manuela frowns. "Yeah, right."

"It's true!" Adelaide fishes out a lemon, biting into it. "I did beauty pageants and we were poor. Used whatever change my mama had left over after shoppin' for groceries at the Mad Pricer. There I'd be, in some dress that looked like curtain rejects and hair full of Dollar General hairspray, and other girls would have a whole entourage to zip 'em into designer gowns and do their hair nice. I'd see 'em in line backstage and they'd laugh at me. But you know what?"

"What?" the little girl asks warily, and Adelaide knows she's bracing herself for some afterschool special mantra: *I worked hard and didn't let them bother me, and now I'm Daphne-the-Zombie!*

"Fuck 'em."

"You said the F-word," Manuela says, awestruck. She seems more impressed than when she'd recognized Adelaide from *Zombie 101*.

"Well, sometimes other words don't get your point across." If Roberto calls her out for dirtying his little girl's ears, she'll apologize. But Adelaide stands by her phrasing. Manuela will remember her advice, now, won't she?

"Some people suck," she adds. "They don't *deserve* to drag you down, so don't let 'em."

How many times had she heard the term "trailer trash" when she was a kid? And later, when her curves came in, "jail bait"? It hadn't hurt her, mostly. It had pissed her off, fueled her. *I will prove these fuckers WRONG*, she'd told herself. Much better inspiration than *believe in yourself and you can do it!*

"You know," she tells Manuela, "if I'd grown up in a neighborhood like this one, where everything was easy, I might not be where I am now. Seriously," she says when Manuela's eyes flicker over the spacious kitchen. "If you have nowhere better to get, no reason to work for somethin', it's easy to be lazy."

She supposes. After graduation, Adelaide took the nearly three thousand dollars she'd saved from working at the Big Chicken restaurant and absconded to L.A., where she'd shared a roach-infested apartment with

three other aspiring actresses for two years. She'd worked waitress jobs
and starred in the odd commercial until she'd landed a role as a recurring
character on a Disney series.

Adelaide's big break had come out of *Zombie 101*, but it had nothing
to do with the show itself. It was meeting the sexy William McKenzie
when she'd begun shooting in Atlanta. They'd both been waiting for
pumpkin spice lattes at Starbucks and reached for the same one when
the barista called out the drink instead of the customer's name. It was
the perfect meet-cute, and Adelaide fell hard for the widowed doctor
(doctor!) who listened to her with respect, treated her like a queen, and
told her she was beautiful just often enough. He'd asked her to marry
him four months after he'd allowed her the first pumpkin spice latte.

"I guess that's true."

"You bet your biscuits it's true. Now, tell me this. Was it *Beverly*
who made you cry? The lady in the house with the lions?" Manuela had
been a stone's throw from her house, and Adelaide knows all about how
Beverly's treated poor Ray.

Manuela stares at the floor. "She told me I couldn't sell my chocolates
for school here because I don't live here. That Daddy should have known
better than to let me."

Other kids hawked overpriced Girl Scout Cookies and coupon books
without a peep of complaint from Beverly. But a kid from *another* neighborhood doing the same thing got treated like a panhandler?

Adelaide studies the mahogany glow of Manuela's skin. She has an
inkling what's got a bee in Beverly's bonnet. "Don't worry about an old
biddy like Beverly. She don't know what she's sayin'."

"But she lives here. She knows the rules."

"What rules? There ain't no rules." Manuela looks uncertain, so Adelaide continues. "Your daddy said it was okay, didn't he? Don't you think
he knows better than her? A man who runs his own business, has worked
in this neighborhood for years and years? Think she could handle that
kind of work, anyway?"

A smile flits across the girl's face. "Nope."

"That's right. Your daddy's smart people, and someone to be proud
of, too." Not that Adelaide can't already tell the girl worships her father.

"No one ever had to tell me what my mama was worth, neither, and she was a waitress makin' two dollars an hour servin' crappy coffee at the IHOP. Now, let me see that clipboard of yours."

Reluctantly, Manuela hands it over. "I'd only been to six houses," she says. Only two lines in the order form are filled in, one in that sweet old Helen Beecham's shaky handwriting, God bless her.

Adelaide pulls the catalog out from behind the order form. "There's nothing I love more than chocolates with coconut in 'em. Got any of those?" She nods when Manuela shows her the page. "Okay, I want six. And William—that's my husband, he's at work fixin' people—loves turtles. Six of those, too. And let's see—these are for Christmas season, right? My mama loves peppermint bark, and Don—my worthless step-daddy—is partial to candied pecans."

When Adelaide's finished, she's dropped roughly five hundred dollars on chocolates and candies that will go largely uneaten. Oh, well—it's for a good cause. If she has to, she can always give them away to delivery people during the holidays. "Check okay?" she asks Manuela, who nods.

When Adelaide's done writing it, signing her name with her typical flourish (as a girl, she'd practiced her signature), Manuela is staring at her, looking slightly dazed.

"You're helpin' *me*," Adelaide assures her as she hands her the check. "Really. I never know what to give anyone for Christmas. Chocolate's a sure bet."

She smiles, hoping she hasn't been too over-the-top, ordered too much. Maybe she didn't need so many chocolates, but she did need to make sure Beverly wouldn't dull this girl's shine.

"What?" Adelaide asks when Manuela continues to stare at her.

Manuela smiles shyly. "Can I have your autograph?"

Adelaide might never get another role like Daphne in *Zombie 101*. Hell, she might never *recover* from her role as Daphne. But as of that day, that moment, she knows she's made a fan for life. She beams. "Of *course*, sweetie."

PAM

According to Pam's crystal-encrusted Cartier watch, guests for the second neighborhood ladies' book club will be arriving in approximately thirty minutes. The cleaners have packed up and gone, and her home is spotless. She surveys the parlor approvingly, noting the plumpness of her cream-colored pillows, the colorful Kandinsky positioned behind her baby grand piano. Pam doesn't play, but it makes a nice conversation piece.

Tapas and finger foods from Dos Mundos, the area's hottest Spanish-American restaurant, are set up along the far wall, tiny plates stacked alongside. Through the glass doors leading to the backyard patio, an actual bartender waits at Pam's pool house to serve guests at her full-service bar. Although Pam hasn't so much as dipped a toe in since late July, water ripples in a rectangular pool featuring a bottom painted blue to create the illusion of the Mediterranean.

"Do you need anything, Pam?" Faith asks politely as she joins her at the pool. Hired for the afternoon so Pam can enjoy her own party, Faith is hoisting a tray of tropical fruit so heavy that Pam could barely carry it into the kitchen when it was delivered earlier. Faith holds it with ease, and Pam recalls Laura mentioning that the girl had played rugby.

That's not Pam's idea of a sport—she prefers to drink at the country club, not sweat on a court.

"Actually, I'd love a glass of wine," Pam replies. "But I'll get it from Jake here." She points to the bartender, a roughish thirty-something who flirted with her all afternoon as he set up the bar and a table with purple velvet party bags for each guest who'd RSVP'd. Each contains a miniature bottle of premium wine from Dos Mundos that was bottled and corked just that morning, a sleeping eye mask, a tiny jar of Kiehl's face moisturizer, and a satchel of bath salts.

The bags had cost a fortune. Pam wouldn't have it any other way.

Buster, Pam's Yorkie, escapes through the open doors. He snakes around Faith's legs and almost makes her drop the fruit tray. "Bad dog," Pam coos, lifting the writhing animal and holding him close. "Close him in my bedroom," she instructs Faith, who places the fruit tray onto a glass table. "I wouldn't want my little precious to escape," she says in a baby voice, staring into the animal's button-black eyes before handing him to Faith.

"That would be bad," Faith drones, and Pam purses her lips. She's not sure she likes Faith, because she's not so sure Faith likes her. Or Buster, for that matter, and who couldn't love a dog so adorable?

After a glass of sauvignon blanc and a playful conversation with Jake—he may be contractually obligated to flirt with her, but who cares?—the doorbell rings. Heels clicking, Pam crosses her marble tiles to play the role of gracious host.

Lo and behold, the first guest is Laura Noble, the now-new*ish* neighbor and host of the first book club party. Pam wonders how she'll react to a party done properly. How does one even compare a "shindig" where the guests are served heated up Costco fare to a classy event where the food is catered and each lady leaves with an individualized party bag?

"*Hello*," Pam says, kissing her on both cheeks. "Welcome to my humble abode."

"Oh, this is so nice," Laura says as she walks through the doorway. "*Ohmygosh.* Is that a Kandinsky? My husband would die." She's unabashed in her admiration, like a teenager gushing over a prom dress, and Pam wonders, again, how this woman came to live in her well-to-do neighborhood. She seems so unaccustomed to money.

Pam nods. "We picked it up in Boston. I got it in the divorce." Pam hadn't wanted it until it registered how much her husband did. Now, Pam takes great pleasure in rearranging and redecorating her living room, always posting the pictures on Facebook so her ex-husband can see. The divorce was supposedly amicable, so they're still Friends.

"And is that a baby grand piano? And the nook? That's so adorable!"

Pam purses her lips at Laura's characterization of the alcove in her parlor. The alcove isn't "adorable." It's a renovation that cost two hundred thousand dollars. The recess is eight square feet, Venetian shutters taking up the back wall. Pam retreats there on rainy days, where the unique acoustics make it sound like she's right in the middle of the storm while not exposed to a single drop. The floating staircase she climbs to get there was imported from Sweden.

"Thank you," Pam says. She raises her drink to her lips, finding it empty. "Would you like a drink?" she asks Laura. "We have a full bar in the back. And plenty of food right there." She waves her hand, her eyes sweeping her own landscape. It's not as impressive as her Christmas party, where she'd paid premium prices to enclose her entire back yard in a heated tent. Her guests had lounged in the pool while admiring ice sculptures shipped to the premises from an "ice specialist" in Raleigh. Still, it's a formidable presentation.

Laura squints at the tiny sign Dos Mundos had requested be displayed near the food. "Dos Mundos! I didn't know they catered."

"Anyone will cater at the right price," Pam informs her as she leads her to the pool area. Faith is coming through the glass doors, carrying an empty ice bucket.

"Hi, Faith," Laura says, touching the girl's arm. When Faith smiles at Laura, the smile reaches her eyes.

On the patio, something in Laura seems to deflate. "Oh. This is lovely."

Inwardly, Pam sighs. It's about time Laura noticed the superiority of Pam's party. "Jake can make you anything," Pam tells her as she leads her to the bar. "And don't forget to take your party bag."

"You did party bags?" Laura stares at the purple cloth bags, the leather tags bearing each guest's name. "That's hardcore effort. Malbec, please," she adds when Jake asks her drink preference.

"Well, I wanted to do it up right." Pam examines the tags on the bags, her fingers grazing over the one with Ray Willis's name. "Here's Ray's bag," she comments. "You've been walking together, right?" The two have crossed in front of Pam's window on several occasions, walking their dogs and laughing uproariously.

"Ray's great," Laura says, thanking Jake when he hands her a delicate glass half-full of dark red wine.

"She's very loud." Pam says it with feigned affection, as if being loud is a positive character trait instead of something she finds incredibly annoying.

"Yep. No filter at all." Laura laughs, but Pam feels the caution. Laura may be *oh, gee whiz* about money, but perhaps she isn't completely clueless.

Pam drops her voice. "I hear that Beverly has done something absolutely vile to her. Did you know she's suing her over her greenhouse? Just for spite."

"I wouldn't know Beverly's intentions. Seems like their business." Laura's brown eyes meet Pam's, and Pam feels a flicker of annoyance. Is *she* being judged?

"Hey, I thought this was going to be a Halloween party," Laura says suddenly, glancing around as if she expects an inflatable pumpkin to pop out of the bushes, for the hedges framing the pool to sprout fake spiderwebs.

Pam shrugs. "I decided to go more classic."

"We're looking forward to Halloween in this neighborhood," Laura says, taking a sip of her wine. "Seems made for trick-or-treating. Nicole's getting too old for it, but we're dragging her along anyway. And, oh— Soon-Li's daughter. How old is she? I thought it would be nice to invite her along."

The doorbell rings. "Ah! Excuse me." With a brilliant smile, Pam abandons Laura in favor of the next guest. As if there's anything to say about the Jungs, anyway. They don't even know English.

The party is a roaring success. Not one word is said about the book. Instead, the focus is on praising Pam's house, and Pam drinks in every compliment. The house is her pride and joy, each decoration hand-selected by Pam with minimal assistance from the interior designer she keeps on call year-round.

The party is nearly over by the time Pam realizes that Beverly hasn't made an appearance despite RSVP'ing. Pam checks her phone to find a text: Beverly has a migraine, and she also didn't want to be in the same room as Ray. Unfortunate for Beverly if she's lying about that migraine—Ray isn't here. Theirs are the only party bags left.

Laura's standing by the table, nursing another malbec and talking with Tracey, Conner's wife. Tracey actually looks rested today, her coppery hair hanging loose, and Pam sees how beautiful she must have been. Still is, sometimes. *Maybe if you made the effort to look like this all the time, Conner wouldn't run around*, Pam thinks, unashamed at the nastiness. Looking nice is part of a wife's job, one in which she'd taken pride. She'd also taken pride in the beautiful jewelry Kent had purchased for her over the years—a piece to commemorate every birthday, anniversary, and Christmas.

It wasn't until Kent had announced his homosexuality amidst his mid-life crisis that it occurred to Pam how unlikely it was that a straight man could choose such gorgeous pieces by himself. She still wears them—who wouldn't?—but she doesn't treasure them as many women treasure fine jewelry. In some way, they're a mockery. How could Pam not have known?

"Looks like we have two no-shows," Pam says, nodding at the gift bags.

"Bummer," Laura says, her cheeks pink from the wine. "I'll deliver them if you want. I'll see Ray later." She doesn't offer a reason for Ray's absence. *No show, no bag*, Pam wants to say, but she has no use for the extras. Besides, the miniature bottles of wine inside have each guest's name on the label in loopy lettering. Pam would feel silly pouring from a bottle of "Ray." "Fine," she tells Laura.

The party is cleared out by six o'clock, with Faith and the bartender sent home shortly thereafter. If not for the full trash and recycling bins, one would never know that Pam had entertained. She's a pro at social gatherings.

The parlor is dim, and Pam flips on the light. It's beginning to drizzle, and Pam feels the sudden bout of melancholy she always feels after a big party. She'll fix that. She pours herself another glass of wine and accesses Nextdoor, the online message board for neighborhoods and a wonderful source of validation for opinionated, strong women like Pam. People need advice, and Pam is there to give it.

Someone needs help rehoming their dog. Without reading the details, Pam comments: "Shame on you! I would never give up my Buster. He's FAMILY." Another person posted a shout-out to a restaurant. Pam comments: "Terrible service. Waited an hour for a table and it also took forever for the check." That was five years ago. Another person warns they aren't around to rake their leaves the next week. Pam comments: "How hard is it to call a service?" She misses the part of the post that cites a visit to a dying parent as the reason.

A *bum-bum-bum* makes her jump. It takes Pam a moment to place the direction of the sound. It's coming from her alcove and appears to be a shutter smacking against the house in the wind. *Bum-bum-bum.* Didn't she close that?

Pam makes a face at the floating staircase. She's had too much wine, and climbing the steep stairs—even when dead sober—is a feat to be approached with caution. Well, she'll be careful.

Lightly, Pam pads up the fifteen steps, counting as she goes and clutching the handrail. When she reaches the alcove, she finds the shutters open, rain smeared against the glass of the wide windows.

She also sees she's not alone. "Why are—?" she begins, but before she gets the rest out, the figure darts forward, shoving her in the chest and back down the floating staircase. Pam is weightless, the seriousness of the situation not registering until she connects with the fifth stair from the ground. There's a sickening crunch, a violent burst of pain.

Then there's nothing.

BEVERLY

Beverly studies the papers in front of her, a grin spreading as she drinks in the words, the meaning. "Gotcha," she says, her fingers tightening. Finally, *finally* she has the dirt she needs on her odious neighbor.

The greenhouse was small potatoes. With this, she can convince Ray and Juliet that they don't belong with normal, decent people like the ones in Oleander Court. Leave, and Beverly says nothing. Stay, and it's Beverly's civic duty to report the freaks of nature they really are.

"This calls for a celebration," Beverly says, going to her liquor cabinet. It glitters with bottles of every liquor imaginable—whiskey, vermouth, gin, vodka, brandy—but Beverly's more in the mood for a glass of wine. Unfortunately, she'd polished off the last of her malbec the night before.

Ah! Wasn't there a small bottle of something in the gift bag from Pam's party? When Laura had delivered it, she'd been positively swaying as she stood on the front stoop. Apparently, it had been *some party*. Beverly would have pushed for details, but she's aware that Laura is friendly—perhaps too friendly—with Ray. Instead, Beverly had thanked her for the bag and later perused it over a rerun of *Designing Women*.

Indeed, there is a bottle. It's a small bottle of cabernet sauvignon, perfect for imbibing in quiet celebration of an imminent victory.

Beverly retrieves a long-stemmed crystal wine glass from a hanging hook in the kitchen, watching as the dark red liquid swirls into the glass. She glances at the greenhouse through the window, but it no longer bothers her. When its owners leave, it will, too.

"Cheers," Beverly says, raising her glass and taking a long swallow, enjoying the burn of the first taste.

She takes another sip, sliding into a seat at her kitchen table. The wine is delicious, and she reaches for the bottle, reading the label. She'll have to order a case later.

Halfway through the glass, Beverly realizes that the room is moving around her. *That can't be right*, she thinks, sluggishly. She tries to wrap her hand around the glass but knocks it off the table instead, where it shatters on the floor.

Sick. The word curls in her mind. She needs help. Something. Her cell phone is in the living room. She can make it there.

Beverly takes one step and crumples to the floor. Where is she? Right, the kitchen. What was she doing?

As Beverly tries to remember, she spins into unconsciousness.

LAURA

Halloween night is almost surreal in its beauty. A bluish full moon shines behind a thin wisp of clouds that lazily skate across its surface. Watching it, Laura feels slightly off-kilter, and she snaps a picture of it with her iPhone. Onscreen, thanks to digitalization, the night sky morphs into a myriad of dark and bright blues. Eat your heart out, van Gogh.

Laura smiles contentedly as she surveys her landscape from her front lawn, where she and Pete are cutting between the hydrangeas to get to the street. Do they really live here? Laura still can't believe their good fortune. When the kids were little and she took them trick-or-treating, she had to bum along with friends who had a real neighborhood.

Now the Nobles don't just have their own neighborhood. They have THE neighborhood, the kind where you can expect full-sized candy bars at the end of every well-maintained sidewalk. Where you can trail behind your kids and not have to worry about them.

Ben and Nicole are already halfway across the street, hustling to fetch Lila at the Jungs' house. After a hint from Ray that the girl was shy and would appreciate the invite, over the weekend Laura had stopped by the house to give it.

Soon-Li had opened the door, cradling an oversized teal coffee cup. "Laura," she'd said, taking a delicate sip. "What can I do for you?"

There wasn't a trace of an accent. Hadn't Beverly said that Soon-Li barely knew English?

Laura shared why she'd come, and Soon-Li's eyes lit up, animating her entire face. "Sure," she'd said, again with perfect diction. "Can I come, too?"

"Absolutely," Laura replied, and Soon-Li had studied her over the rim of her cup, smiling softly. She tapped her fingers on the handle. "Pam," she said. "Right?"

"I don't—" Laura had begun, and Soon-Li's smile grew wider.

"No need to feel bad about it. I know she tells everyone I'm fresh off the boat."

Laura had wrinkled her nose at the term. It *did* sound like Pam, though. "It was actually Beverly," she'd admitted.

"Ah." Soon-Li had shrugged. "Those two share bad gossip like a bad virus."

"Including that you're . . . English-challenged? How'd that start?"

Soon-Li leaned against the doorway. "Pam rang the doorbell when we first moved in. I was finishing a sandwich. Chewing. She thought I didn't say anything right away because I couldn't. *Hello. Nice-to-meet-you.*" Soon-Li's nasally pitch in her impersonation of Pam was perfect. She'd shrugged. "I never bothered to correct her."

"Why not?"

Soon-Li tilted her head as if considering the question. "I suppose I didn't find her worth the effort."

Laura had admired Soon-Li's pride, her easy dismissal of Pam. What would it be like to not care what people thought?

Now, Nicole is hopping up the Jungs' steps, her legs long and graceful in their striped stockings. As she leans to press the doorbell, Laura links her arm through Pete's, pulling him closer. "She'll be a teenager next year," she whispers, her heart wrenching. It feels like yesterday that Nicole loved making Play-Doh and was unabashedly calling "wipe me!" from the bathroom. When picking out a Halloween costume was an event. This year Nicole used a slapdash witch outfit to show off her apathy to the holiday.

Ben is Darth Vader. He and Pete had researched helmet choices for weeks before ordering one. With Ben's size, he looks more like Lord Helmet from *Spaceballs*, but no need to tell him that. Let him think he's the ruler of the dark galaxy, that his plastic lightsaber looks intimidating. It glows as he marches up the steps.

There's a rectangle of light when the door opens. Lila emerges, dressed all in purple except for a helmet of her own. It's yellow, decorated like an emoji of a smiling face with heart eyes.

"What are you?" Nicole asks, appraising her, and Laura literally bites her tongue. *Be nice,* she silently warns her daughter. One look at Lila with her huge eyes—so much like her mother's, so expressive—and it's clear she's fragile.

"I'm an Emoji Pez dispenser."

Lila's so quiet, so shy, that Laura's surprised at such a fun choice. Then she feels bad for her reaction. She remembers what it was like to be the awkward kid, to sit alone along the chain-link fence at recess, listening to other conversations and wanting to interject, to say "Let me in! I have funny, interesting things to say!" But those funny, interesting things always stuck to the roof of her mouth.

Nicole links her arm with Lila's, and the girl grins as if Nicole's given her a huge gift.

Pride swells in Laura's chest. She shouldn't have questioned her daughter's kindness, her ability to recognize the need for extra tenderness. Nicole has always been special that way.

"You look cute," Laura tells Soon-Li, who is dressed as a fairy. She wishes she'd dressed up, but Nicole had specifically requested her parents not to. The aquamarine folds of Soon-Li's dress fall like water.

Next door to Soon-Li's, Stacey and Scott Denton have set up camp in their driveway. Perched on high wicker stools at a glass table, they're sharing a bottle of red wine and a cheese plate. The picture is comical—they belong on a back porch or back patio, but have inserted their image where it doesn't belong.

"Happy Halloween!" Scott raises a long-stemmed glass, his doughy face flushed—from the wine or the excitement of the holiday, Laura can't tell. "Help yourselves." Two open coolers rest at their feet, one filled with sodas and the other with beer.

"Are open containers allowed?" Laura asks, eyeing a Coors.

"You see any cops around?" Stacey asks, helping herself to more wine. "Let me know, and I'll share."

Pete reaches into the cooler and fishes out two beers. He hands one to Laura and she scrapes the ice off the top, cracking it open. Taking a sip, a small thrill runs up her spine. The naughtiness of the act. The contained world of the neighborhood. The clear, warm night. *This is heaven*, she thinks dreamily, holding the metallic liquid in her mouth before swallowing.

"What about you, Soon-Li?" Scott asks, kicking the cooler with his dangling foot. "Beer?"

"I'm fine," Soon-Li says, and Scott swishes his glass.

"Everybody's doing it . . ." he says in a sing-songy voice, and his wife hands her one. Soon-Li sighs as she opens the can. "You're both terrible," she says as she raises it to her lips.

"Mo-*om!*" Nicole calls from the sidewalk, and Stacey grins at Laura. "You're being summoned. Come back for another round."

The group crosses the street, backtracking to hit up the houses they've missed. When they ring the next doorbell, a brown-haired middle-aged woman opens it. She smiles blandly as she drops candy into bags and nods at the chorus of *thank yous*. When she closes the door, Laura forgets her face immediately.

"Now to your girlfriend's," Laura says as they make their way up Helen's cracked sidewalk. The porch lighting is dim, and they're up the steps before Laura registers the form of Helen on the swing. Behind the ivy crawling up her trellis, she could see them, but they couldn't see her.

"Helen Beecham," Pete says. "Happy Halloween!"

A huge orange pumpkin filled with Kit Kats rests on the porch mat, like an offering. Helen waves at it. "Take what you want," she says, sizing up the children. "Are you Evel Knievel?" she asks Lila.

"I'm an Emoji Pez dispenser," Lila says, and Helen shakes her head. "I'll take your word for it. *That* I know," she says, pointing to Ben's Darth Vader costume. "And you must be Pam," she says to Nicole, cackling at her own joke.

Laura notices the empty tumbler next to Helen's swing. She nudges Pete. "Do you want to . . .?" she whispers, and Pete doesn't need further prodding.

"Mind if I sit for a minute?" he asks Helen. "Get some rest, spy on the children . . . not that that's what you're doing," he adds, although it's clear that's exactly what she's doing.

"Your wife can spare you?"

"Oh, sure," Laura says. "If you'll have him."

She takes him, happily.

As the remaining group members approach the next house, Bambi and Marv Holiday hurry out the front door. "Beautiful dress, Bambi," Laura calls. Even from the sidewalk, it looks like Bambi has been poured into the black number.

"Thanks," Bambi says airily as she struts around the back of the couple's Mercedes, her eyes sliding up and down Laura's outfit. Laura had thought her sweater-and-jeans combo was perfectly acceptable, but maybe she was wrong. Nothing was designer, after all—not unless you count Old Navy.

When they turn the corner onto Magnolia Lane, Pam's floodlights are off and her windows are dark. "That's weird," Soon-Li observes, gesturing with her beer can. "There's her car." Sure enough, Pam's little red Miata rests in the driveway, covered with a dusting of dead leaves.

"Two houses in a row with no candy," Laura says. "Boo." The Holidays had also left nothing on their porch.

"Pretty sure all the Halloween cheer is centered over there." Soon-Li points. "Is Ray *trying* to get Beverly to call the cops?"

Ray's front yard had been decorated all month, spiders as the general theme. Jowls dripping with foam, neon bodies, black and hairy. Gross, if you despised spiders, but not extreme for the holiday. "It's all a decoy," Ray had told Laura. "Wait until Halloween."

Until today, the greenhouse was completely unadorned. Now, its twinkle lights are blinding even from across the street. They cast the side yard in a greenish, ghoulish glow that illuminates the trees and shrubbery and reflects off Beverly's windows. Inside, even with the curtains drawn, the entire house must be lit up bright green.

A man-sized Venus flytrap is rooted in a planter next to the greenhouse, writhing on its stem and waving tentacle-like leaves. "Feed me, Seymour!" it cries again and again, snapping its teeth. The fog pouring from a well-placed fog machine covers the grass and spills into the street, where it curls over the sewer grates. The whole thing looks like a scene from a campy horror movie.

And it's *loud*. Seymour is cranked up to the max.

"That. Is. *Amazing*," Laura tells Soon-Li as they stare from the sidewalk. "*Little Shop of Horrors*. Remember?"

"Oh, yeah."

"Wonder what the HOA will have to say about this?" Laura asks, shielding her eyes.

"Pam will be delighted to use her embossed stationery," Soon-Li intones.

"Embossed stationery?"

"For infraction notices. You haven't gotten one yet?"

As the children help themselves at a table erected at the Atkinsons' house, the garage door at the Boyle house two doors down slides open. A green gator tractor peels out, tires squealing. A scrawny boy in a Spider-Man outfit clutches the wheel, a little girl shrouded in a pink cloud of tulle beside him.

Tracey Boyle emerges from the garage, holding a stuffed bunny and her iPhone. "Gabby! The train's leaving the station!" An older girl follows, hurrying to catch up. The poor thing is big for her age, her hair frizzy. Well past the cute stage of toddlerhood and en route to awkward adolescence. The yellow bones sewn onto her black sweatsuit glow faintly in the dusk.

"Hi, Tracey," Laura says, admiring the woman's upturned nose, the smattering of freckles that complement her reddish hair. An interesting kind of pretty. "Where's Conner?"

Tracey purses her lips, her eyes following her children as they run to the Atkinsons' porch. "Running behind. He'll catch up."

"Cool." Laura wonders if she's ever seen Conner on a walk with the family. It's always just Tracey and the kids. God, she got lucky with Pete. All those carnival visits, park trips, lunches—he's always come as a matter of course.

Ray's house is next, and Ben is uncharacteristically animated as he sprints up the stairs. "I'm gonna ask if we can go in the greenhouse!" he announces as he sets off an automated spider.

Ray opens the door, dressed in tight black leather and fishnet stockings. "Welcome! Have you been a good little boy this holiday season?" she asks Ben.

"It isn't Christmas, dear," her wife tells her. As far as Laura can tell, Juliet is one of The Beatles, with long striped pants and a tucked-in paisley shirt. She looks like a Bible salesman compared to her wife.

"Whatever. Have some cookies," Ray says as she drops cellophane-wrapped treats into the kids' buckets. "They totally don't have razor blades in them or anything."

"Who are you supposed to be?" Laura asks, eyeing her friend's black lipstick. Never in a million years could she pull it off, but Ray does.

Ray stares at her. "Obviously, I am Black Cher. We're going to a costume party later." Ah, so Juliet must be Sonny Bono, Cher's ex-husband and musical partner back in the 1960s.

"Cher, your greenhouse is crazy," Soon-Li says. "Has Beverly called the police yet?"

"No!" Ray peers out the door toward Beverly's house. "I'm extremely surprised and disappointed. After all that effort." She sighs.

Juliet pats her arm. "Don't worry, dear. There's time."

"Is Beverly even home?" Soon-Li asks, and Ray shrugs.

"I think so. The light's on in her kitchen."

"Can we go in the greenhouse?" Ben asks her. "Please? Please?"

Ray smiles at him, touching the hood of his visor. "Sure, Darth. Let me grab my shoes."

After Ray zips herself into thigh-high, high-heeled black boots, she guides the group around the side of the house. "Ta-da!" she says, throwing up her hands at her creation. "Everyone nice and juicy, get inside! No reason!"

The children probably have no idea what she's talking about. "*Little Shop of Horrors* was a movie about a plant that ate people," Laura informs them. "A musical, actually."

"And a cautionary tale about being a jerk," Ray adds. She glances at Beverly's kitchen windows. "I have to say, though, not *seeing* Beverly is making me a little uncomfortable. Like all of a sudden, she'll bust out of the garage on a bulldozer and mow this whole sucker down."

"It's weird," Juliet agrees. "Not even a rustle of a curtain."

"Don't look a gift horse in the mouth," Soon-Li advises, and Laura glances again at the house next door. So silent, so still. It really doesn't seem right, especially with the green light pouring into the kitchen. It has to be annoying. Ray meant it to be.

"I'm going to ring the bell," Laura says, striding across the spongy green grass. Her chest tightens when she spots the outline of two jugs of Crystal Springs water on Beverly's dark porch. The Nobles have Crystal Springs, too, and Laura knows the delivery man comes on Monday. It's Tuesday now.

Laura rings the bell, chimes resonating throughout the house. When there's no stirring, she rings it again. Nothing—no movement, no sound. Despite Beverly's Lincoln in the driveway.

"Something's off," Laura says when she rejoins the group. The children have disappeared into the greenhouse, the gentle splashing of the waterfall audible even over Seymour. Laura's been inside the structure and knows it's beautiful, with a stone walkway meandering through tropical plants and flowers. Orchids, mainly. "Her car's still in the drive, and she didn't get her water from the porch."

"Does anyone have a key to her house?" Juliet asks after a beat.

"Pam probably has one," Soon-Li suggests.

Laura points to Beverly's kitchen, the sliver of light between the curtains. "Maybe I could check . . . ?"

Ray shrugs. "Yeah. Do that. Less effort. Less Pam."

Laura skulks across the yard, squeezing between the bushes flush against the house. A twig scratches her arm as she pokes her head up to the middle window. This will only take a moment.

When Laura peeks through the glass, it's as if the wind is knocked from her. Something on the kitchen floor glitters. A stream of red liquid snakes across the tiles, the image lit garishly green. Like a cheap trick in a bad horror movie.

Beverly is splayed out next to an overturned kitchen chair, one hand outstretched, the other pinned beneath her. One shoe has been kicked off. Laura can't see her clearly from her angle, but she can see the unnaturalness of her pose, the fact that she's not moving.

She's still not moving.

Still.

Laura opens her mouth and begins to scream.

Transcript of WAB-TV Atlanta

Aired November 1

[5:27:11] **MIRANDA ALBERS, WAB-TV CORRESPONDENT:** Hello, I'm Miranda Albers, coming at you from what used to be real estate heaven: Oleander Court of Alpharetta, Georgia. You may remember Oleander Court from its cover and twenty-page spread in *Architectural Digest*, where the magazine raved about the vision of Randy Vorstenburg, the celebrated architect commissioned to create the blueprints of those homes that would populate the up-and-coming community.

For nearly thirty years, Oleander Court has been celebrated as a vision, a dream. But now, a double murder has turned the neighborhood into a nightmare. Last night, two women, Pam Muenster and Beverly Grant, were each found dead in their homes—clearly victims of foul play.

Who's next?

[Off Camera]

MIRANDA ALBERS: I don't know. Does it sound a little kitschy?

PAUL HANSCOMB (Cameraman): A double murder in a place like this *is* kitschy.

MIRANDA ALBERS: Guess we'll roll with it. Get a shot of that crazy waterfall at the entrance on the way out, too. We'll use it as the opening image.

PAUL HANSCOMB: What about the No Solicitors sign?

MIRANDA ALBERS: Yeah, I noticed that.

PAUL HANSCOMB: Too bad there wasn't a sign that said No Killers. Could have saved a lot of trouble.

FAITH

Something's up when Pete opens the door for Faith the morning after Halloween. He's the kind of dude who always has the start of a smile on his face, but today he looks like his favorite TV show got cancelled.

"Faith," he says, rubbing at the stubble on his chin. "I'm sorry, but I completely forgot you were coming over. Laura's still upstairs. Um . . ." He trails off, looking at Faith almost hopefully, like she'll tell him what to say.

"You don't need me today?" she asks, fighting the roiling in her stomach. The night before, she and her friend Gina had stayed up way too late watching most of the *Halloween* movies in order and finishing an entire bottle of So Co along with two family-sized bags of tortilla chips.

The chips are probably the only reason Faith can stand upright. She's already thrown up twice today.

"I can go home," Faith offers, longing for her bed, her laptop with its limitless streaming television. Mostly her bed.

Ugh. Why did she let Gina persuade her to drink So Co? It doesn't even taste good going *down*.

"Nah, it's okay," Pete says as he ushers her inside. The kids' pumpkin buckets are stacked on the desk in the front entryway, candy spilling out, and Faith thinks of how she and her brother, Nick, used to run to their rooms after trick-or-treating to hoard their candy. "Like squirrels," Faith's mother would say when she came to collect, brandishing a clear, airtight container "to keep out the ants." Beth Martin was obsessed with ants.

"Is Laura sick?" Faith asks as Pete turns to her, cracking his knuckles. He never cracks his knuckles.

"No, not exactly." He shakes his head, his expression pained. "She's traumatized. I don't know how to say this, but Beverly Grant and Pam Muenster were found dead yesterday."

"*What?*" Faith asks, her stomach clenching over the roiling.

"Murdered. And Laura found Beverly."

Pete trips over his words as he shares what he knows—about Laura peeking in through Beverly's kitchen window to find her splayed out on her linoleum, how the police had gone looking for Pam when they'd figured out where Beverly had gotten the poisoned wine.

"That's, like, terrible," Faith says to be polite, even though she's not exactly *sad* about Beverly and Pam. They were old and nasty. She's more worried about Laura, who's super nice and also the kind of person to freak out over throwing a party. If she was that hyper over appetizers, finding a dead body might give her an aneurysm.

"I can totally leave if you don't need me," Faith offers again. "I don't want to be in the way."

Pete gives her a small smile. "You're never in the way, Faith. I'm sure you can find something to do."

He's right. The routine when Ben and Nicole are away is easy. The Nobles work in their offices while Faith goes through the house, cleaning and organizing whatever needs to be cleaned and organized. If the fridge needs restocking, she goes to Aldi for groceries.

Today Laura doesn't make a peep the whole time Faith's there. Faith feels bad about that. Laura's probably hunched under the covers like some kid worried about a monster under the bed. Faith would try to comfort her if she had any idea what to say.

A few hours later, after Faith's done cleaning the kitchen surfaces and rearranging the canned goods in the pantry, she taps on Pete's office door. "I'm done," she tells him, noticing that he's playing Solitaire on his computer. "Working" from home seems pretty sweet.

"Hmm?" he says distractedly, clicking at his mouse. "Oh, okay. See you later."

As Faith pads down the front porch steps, she peers down the street.

There's no sign that anything bad happened, which is crazy. You'd think that with two murders in a neighborhood this nice, the police would go all out, with lots of police cars and investigators milling around.

Or maybe it's quiet *because* it's such a nice neighborhood. Everyone wants to pretend nothing bad can ever happen in a place like this.

A breeze rustles the trees, and Faith inhales. The fresh air feels good. She isn't as nauseous as she was before. And she doesn't have anything else to do. Instead of getting in her car, Faith crosses the street and walks down Magnolia Lane.

Faith's heart pounds. She's never seen the aftermath of a murder before. Will there be yellow police tape?

There is, but that's about it. Pam's house is first, the only sign of something wrong the single piece of yellow tape across the door. When Faith walks a little farther, she finds the same thing at Beverly's house.

Faith didn't know what she expected, but she expected more than that. And she feels shady for being disappointed. Like the kind of person who cranes their head when they drive by an accident and gets bummed when there's nothing to see.

When Faith passes Beverly's house, Ray is in her side yard, balancing on a short aluminum stepladder outside her greenhouse. She spots Faith and waves. "Hey!"

Ray is struggling to remove yards of twinkle lights stapled to the wooden frame of the structure. As Faith watches, Ray yanks at a staple with a pair of needle-nose pliers, sending up a stream of curses. "Dammit!" she finishes, giving up. "They went on so much easier."

"Did you YouTube how to do this?" Faith asks, and Ray grimaces, gesturing at the plastic paint bucket at the base of the stepladder.

"Yeah. Check it out. I have the supplies of an amateur torture artist." There are half a dozen tools in the bucket, all of which look designed for pulling teeth. Except the knife. "But unfortunately," Ray continues, wiping her forehead, "the wood is stubborn. It doesn't want to give up the staples."

"Want any help?" Faith asks, and Ray scrunches up her face.

"I don't know . . ." she hedges, running a loving hand down the side of the greenhouse, and Faith knows she's imagining holes being gouged in the wood.

"I'm really good at this kind of thing," Faith tells her. "I've hung shelves and changed furnace filters and stuff. I've even fixed a ceiling fan."

Ray cocks her head at her. "At your age?"

Faith reaches for the pliers. She doesn't look at Ray as she clamps the tool onto a staple. Whether it's luck or skill, the staple slides out easily. "See? Mad skills."

"All right." Ray shrugs. "How's this? I'll pay you a quarter a staple. Throw them in the bucket and I'll count them when you're done."

A door bangs open and Ray's dogs appear from the back yard, snaking around the ladder and circling Faith as they beg for affection. Apollo steps on her foot, his toenails digging through her sneaker.

"They're so chill," Faith says, holding out her hand so they can sniff it. "They don't even jump."

"Aww, thanks," Ray says as she drops to scratch behind Hades's ears. "Good boy." She glances up as Juliet rounds the corner of the greenhouse, carrying the dogs' leashes. "I thought you could take a break," Juliet tells her wife, her eyes lighting on Faith. "Faith, what are you doing here?" She doesn't say it rudely, just Juliet-like. Unlike Ray, who can go on forever about anything, Juliet never minces words.

"I kind of crashed," Faith admitted. "Because I wanted to see what was going on after. . . you know." Faith had been waiting for Ray to bring it up.

Juliet presses her lips together. "Nothing, now. But it was a zoo last night."

"Yeah, Pete said they took your statements and stuff."

Apollo whines, and Ray rolls her eyes. "We're going, we're going. Faith, you're really okay here? Alone? You could come with us."

"It's fine. It's daylight and everything."

After convincing Ray and Juliet to leave, Faith climbs onto the ladder with the needle-nose pliers, surveying Ray's work. There are practically a zillion twinkle lights on the greenhouse, and Faith suspects the point was to piss off Beverly. It reminds Faith of how Nick used to punch her and run away, hoping to be chased. If Beverly hadn't been busy being dead, she totally would have called the cops on Ray.

It doesn't take long for Faith's arms to start to hurt. She climbs off the ladder, rotating her shoulders. There are only about twenty staples in the bucket, and Faith kind of regrets offering to help, even though she's already made five bucks for about ten minutes of work. Sure, she hadn't promised to *finish* the project, but she will. Faith always finishes what she starts.

"Excuse me."

Faith whirls to see a tall, extremely dark-skinned man standing in Ray's yard. He has perfect posture, like he's being held up with a string. Faith's mother would appreciate that posture. When her kids were little, she told them to sit up straight about a million times.

The man flashes a badge, and Faith's stomach flips when she recognizes it as a police badge. "I'm Officer Sam Kramer. Do you live here?"

One question in, and he's already being shady. If Ray and Juliet were questioned last night, he already knows she doesn't live here.

"Nope," Faith says, dropping the pliers into the bucket. She isn't sure if she should be holding a weapon around a cop. "I help out sometimes."

"What's your name?"

"Faith Martin."

The man cocks his head, recognition in his eyes. "Faith Martin? The Faith Martin who was at Pam Muenster's party on October 28?"

"That's me."

"Do you have a minute? You're on our list."

"List of what?"

"Witnesses, of course," he says, and Faith feels stupid. Of course, he wasn't going to say *suspects*. But cops always make Faith nervous. Even when she's obeying the speed limit, it freaks her out when one pulls into traffic behind her. "I'd like to take your statement," he adds, and Faith shrugs.

"Sure. Right here?"

"We could sit down if you like." She nods, and he leads her to Ray's front porch, where they sink onto the first step.

"As I understand it," he says, scratching his nose as he opens his notepad, "you helped with a party Pam threw four nights ago. Right?"

"Right."

"Did you work for her often?"

Faith scratches the inside of her wrist. The dry skin is itchy. "Not really. Maybe five times? Like, with housecleaning. But then she was having this party and she asked me to come over and help with cleaning and food and whatever."

"'This party.' Do you remember who was there?"

"Yeah. A lot of the neighbors. Do you want their names?"

"Sure." Faith lists off the people she remembers and he writes them down, his pen scratching. "I think that's it," she says.

"Was there anyone else there besides the guests?"

"There was a bartender. Jake or Jeff or something."

"When you were there, did you notice anything unusual?"

Faith grunts. "Not really." *Not unless you count Pam trying to pick up a young dude with a tongue ring.* That was so gross.

"Not really, or no?" the officer asks, his pen paused mid-air.

"No."

Officer Kramer asks her a few questions about the gift bags Pam had given out. Then he asks: "Do you remember assembling the bag for Beverly Grant?"

"Yeah, I do."

"Is there a reason why?"

Does she have to admit it? "Because I wasn't super stoked she'd be there."

"Why not?"

Faith presses her lips together. Officer Kramer has really kind eyes. She hates telling him this. "Because Beverly was always making racist comments. And she was just kind of a bitch in general. Sorry," she adds. Maybe she shouldn't curse around a cop. But this is an investigation, and "bitch" is the most accurate word to describe Beverly.

"I see."

"I think it was, like, her personality," Faith adds to clarify. "Or her background, maybe. Like, she thought it was okay to say the things she did. You know, not offensive."

"There are people like that." Officer Kramer says it like it doesn't bother him, even though it totally should. "All right. About what time did you leave Mrs. Muenster's house after the party?"

Faith shrugs. "I dunno. Like six?"

"Are you sure about that time?"

Faith reaches into her jacket pocket. "Actually, yeah. See? I went to Walmart afterwards and got a bunch of stuff. And this says I checked out at seven." The crumpled receipt she hands the officer is time-stamped, with the number "23" in bold at the bottom to record the number of items purchased. Home goods section to produce. Faith's always been a very thorough Walmart shopper.

Officer Kramer glances at the receipt and hands it back to her. "Thank you," he says, shutting his notebook and standing up. "Can you think of anything unusual you may have seen lately?" He gestures to the peaceful street. "Anything off-putting? Strange?"

Faith shakes her head. "No," she says. "Nothing at all."

Officer Kramer lowers his voice. "And what about Ray Willis?"

"What about her?"

"Ever hear her say anything disparaging about either Beverly Grant or Pam Muenster?"

Oh, geez. Why'd he ask her that? Faith's only helped Ray out with the dogs like five times, and Ray's probably said a total of fifty-seven bad things about both women—*victims*—combined.

Faith doesn't do it on purpose. It's on reflex, because she likes Ray.

"Nope," she lies.

RAY

Well, shit.

Ray had hated Beverly, but she hadn't *really* wanted her dead.

Sure, maybe she'd fantasized about it. Like the time she'd imagined smashing Beverly's face, over and over again, into the sidewalk, until it was just a bloody, pulpy mess. Or that other time when she'd noticed how easy it would be to mow Beverly over while she stood at her mailbox, right there in the street like she was daring Ray to hit her. Those were cheerful thoughts, not *plans*.

So, once Beverly was no more, Ray didn't know how to act. She couldn't act sad, because she wasn't. A world without Beverly Grant was a better, less judgmental place.

She couldn't act happy either. That would make her a suspect. Or, rather, more of a suspect. Everyone knew about Ray's feud with Beverly over the greenhouse. It would be a stupid reason to kill someone, but the world is full of stupid people.

It hadn't looked good when the police showed up on Halloween night. Laura and Soon-Li had sent the kids home with Pete so the ladies could have their statements taken at Ray's kitchen table by some nice officer with baby fat and blond hair. An older officer who remarkably resembled Liam Neeson had accompanied him, but he'd stayed silent literally the entire time.

"So, uh," the young cop had said to Ray, "when was the last time you saw Beverly Grant?"

"Yesterday afternoon, when I was walking my dogs. She was in her front yard."

"Did you say anything to her?"

"Nope."

"How far away was she?"

Ray had shrugged. "Fifteen feet?"

"But you didn't speak."

"That's what I said." She'd reached to tap his notepad. "Because I didn't like her. Write that down."

Juliet sighed. "Ray . . ."

"What? It's not like he isn't going to find out anyway." Ray had smiled. "Beverly was suing me over my greenhouse."

"You mean the thing with twinkle lights and all the fog?"

"Yep. And to be honest, her suing me over it was basically the reason for the twinkle lights and all the fog." Juliet had kicked her under the table.

Ray knew she shouldn't be so flip, but it was her go-to when she was nervous. And even if Babyface here looked harmless, Ray knew this line of questioning was only the beginning of a very serious investigation. And that Liam Neeson wasn't there as window dressing.

Now, four days after Beverly's body was found—and also Pam's, once the police figured out the source of the poison that had killed Beverly—Ray's a wreck. The police have taken more than a passing interest in her, and Ray wonders what her neighbors have told them about the greenhouse fight. And about her. God, her big mouth. She'd been so open about hating Beverly. She'd never dreamed it would bite her in the ass *this* way.

Today, as Ray walks her dogs past Pam's house, she imagines eyes on her—peering from behind curtains, peeking from the sides of second-floor windows. Far down the sidewalk, Botox Bambi is jogging toward her in her traditional skintight attire, ponytail swishing. When she spots Ray, she crosses the street in a diagonal, eyes fixed forward.

When Ray turns back toward her house, she inhales sharply. The squad car out front is black and unmarked. Inside, she finds Juliet and the Liam Neeson cop in the kitchen.

"Hi, officer," Ray says, as if it's completely normal to come home and find a police officer in one's home during an active murder investigation where you are most likely the prime suspect. "Give me a minute to wash my hands, and I'll be right with you."

"Take your time."

In the bathroom, Ray scrubs her hands with the lemon-smelling soap Juliet keeps in a shell-shaped holder. *You're okay,* Ray tells herself, meeting her eyes in the mirror. *You have nothing to worry about.*

She exits the bathroom, keeping herself composed. "Sorry about that. What can I do for you?"

Liam Neeson clears his throat. He looks at his notepad like he's checking his next line, even though Ray's sure he knows exactly why he's there. Then he opens his mouth and asks her the one question she's been dreading:

"Mrs. Willis, have you ever been known by any other name?"

BAMBI

I t's been two entire weeks, and the police haven't arrested Ray yet. Are they blind? Obviously, Ray did it. She hated both Pam and Beverly, and what do they always say? The simplest answer is always the right one.

Bambi had dropped out of college halfway through—she'd successfully obtained her Mrs. Degree, so there was no point in sticking around for a B.A.—but she's not an idiot.

Having a murderer live down the street is so stressful. It's probably giving her worry lines. Also, while she stays in bed her typical ten hours a night, she's not sleeping for all of them.

Bambi's taken to cardio. Every day, she spends half an hour styling her hair and applying the barest minimum of makeup—foundation, concealer, bronzer, eyeshadow, and tinted lip gloss—for a jog around the neighborhood. Not only does she get fresh air, but it's a chance to survey the residents. Maybe Bambi will see something suspicious she can report.

As it turns out, Bambi doesn't see anything of the sort. All she sees are people walking their dogs, or drinking their coffee on the porch, or fiddling around in their garages. No such activities appear to be an attempt to cover up a murder. Or, murders.

She does, however, see something even better. Proof that Adelaide, that trashy actress who lives down the street, is the slut Bambi had suspected she was all along. Bambi's so excited, she almost forgets about her worry lines from the Alpharetta police failing to do their job.

The first proof was the day after Halloween. Bambi had been up very early—nine thirty—and she'd figured she'd go ahead and complete her exercise routine for the day.

She had a very busy schedule ahead of her, anyway. Not only did she have five magazines to finish—she was behind on her reading—but she had to organize her closet for the change in seasons. Pairing her clothes together to avoid wearing anything twice was such a chore. She wishes she could assign it to Isobel, but Isobel knows nothing about fashion. Her own outfits look like they were thrown together in the dark.

As Bambi had come up on the cul-de-sac at the end of the street, she'd noticed someone standing on Adelaide's porch. It was Roberto, the yummy lawn man. Bambi herself uses his services, and it's not because he's good at what he does. It's for the occasional glimpse of abs as Roberto reaches to trim the lower branches of her elm, or the ripple of muscle as he carries bags of mulch.

And there was Adelaide. Looking rumpled and adorable in a pink robe, eyes bright and skin unlined as she leaned closer to Roberto. Bambi had slowed, watching Adelaide's wide smile. Watching Adelaide's fingers hook into his arm.

Watching Adelaide pull him inside.

Well, well, well, Bambi thought as she regained speed. *I knew it.*

Later, Bambi's suspicions were confirmed when she saw them a second time. Bambi had just begun her jog, her earbuds pumping out old school Britney, when she'd spotted Roberto's truck up the street. Sure enough, hanging on to the window and holding a bouquet of gorgeous roses, there was Adelaide. Had she no shame?

Adelaide had stepped backward and Bambi deliberately hip-checked her. Adelaide merely stumbled and said "excuse me" without even glancing behind her.

Bambi had turned her head slightly, taking in the sight of Adelaide and Roberto, the idling truck. In that moment, she'd felt vastly superior to Adelaide. The *gardener*. (Bambi had forgotten all about her UPS man from one year ago, a certain neighbor from three years prior, and her own lustful thoughts about Roberto.) Did William know? Who else knew?

As in, who could Bambi tell?

Bambi almost misses Pam. Pam would have appreciated this tidbit of information, which would have spread like wildfire once she got ahold of it. But alas, Pam is dead, and there's no one to help Bambi make sure the news reaches William's ears.

It takes Bambi three days to come up with a plan. It's simple. She'll have a note delivered. Anonymous, traceless. William can take it from there with whatever private investigator he wants to hire, and then he'll divorce his trampy little wife. Bambi's sure he has a prenup, and then it's back to the trailer park for Adelaide.

"What are you smiling about?" Marv asks Bambi as she bustles around the kitchen, fixing a mimosa at eleven o'clock on a Friday morning.

"Nothing," she sings.

Clearly it's not nothing, but Marv only grunts, putting his feet on the coffee table as he changes the television channel. Bambi wishes he wouldn't do that. It's mahogany, and they're not animals.

The doorbell rings, and Bambi ushers in the teenaged girl who stands there. Grace-or-Hope. When she'd run into him during a jog, Conner had made some joke about Tracey "completely freaking" over the job she'd done organizing their kids' playroom. If she was that good, maybe it was worth having her take a crack at Bambi's closet.

Ugh. Grace-or-Hope's hair is pulled back in a too-tight brown ponytail, and her yellow sweater looks polyester. Why don't high schools have a class called "Dress to Impress"? Instead, they teach garbage like geometry and civics. Those are subjects no girl needs.

At least, no girl Bambi would ever want to be.

"Conner said you're great at organizing," Bambi tells her, leading her upstairs and through the master bedroom. Bambi's walk-in closet is attached to a bathroom with a cathedral like dome. "This is my church," Bambi sometimes tells Marv as she soaks in her marble tub, generally with a drink in hand.

"So, like, you want me to put things in whatever order makes sense?" the girl asks, and Bambi wonders if she's made a mistake in hiring her for this task. Grace-or-Hope is staring in undisguised horror at her gorgeous collection of designers.

Maybe she can be directed, though. Bambi proffers a list ripped from a spiral notebook. Her handwriting covers both sides. "These are the guidelines," she tells Grace-or-Hope. "Do what you can. I'll be downstairs."

"I have a question," Grace-or-Hope says as she studies the paper.

"What?"

"What is 'D&G'?"

Bambi stares at her. "Dolce & *Gabbana*." Obviously.

"Oh. Okay."

"Just see what you can do." Bambi leaves her to it.

Three hours later, when she hasn't heard a peep from upstairs in that time, Bambi goes to investigate her progress.

"*Wow*." The closet looks amazing. Despite Faith's (*Faith*. That was her name!) poor choice of outfit, she somehow knew exactly how to arrange Bambi's entire wardrobe. There are no clothes piled on the pink carpet, no hangers askew from when Bambi had pulled off a sweater. Summer clothes, winter clothes, pants, casual dresses, formal dresses—everything has a place. And, as requested, her Dolce & Gabbana outfits occupy their own section. Bambi's walk-in closet now looks as it is intended to look—like a small high-end boutique. Faith had even located the Windex under the bathroom sink and cleaned the floor-length oval mirror in the closet's center.

"Am I done?" Faith asks. There's a sheen of sweat across her brow, and Bambi wrinkles her nose. She'd better not have sweated on her designers.

"Uh, sure." Now Bambi wishes she'd hired Faith earlier, back when she'd been irritated at her deliveryman for forgetting her tapioca. If Faith can do this, what else can she do?

"Actually, hold on," Bambi says as something comes to mind. She goes to her nightstand and removes the note for William. "You know William McKenzie? Down the street?"

"Yeah?"

"Make sure he gets this. And that his wife doesn't see it. And here." Bambi presses the envelope, along with three hundred-dollar bills, into Faith's hand. As she does, she tries not to wince at the sight of the silver charm bracelet dangling from the girl's wrist. Where did she even find something so tacky? "For a job well done today."

HELEN

"**M**om, are you sure you're okay?" Helen's daughter, Erica, asks. Erica's laptop is slung over her shoulder, her hand resting on her luggage handle. She's been asking that question for days, and Helen keeps answering the same way: *Yes, Erica. I'm fine, Erica. Go home, Erica.*

It's not that Helen doesn't appreciate the company. Truth be told, Erica—her baby at forty-five this year—has always been her favorite. Helen has treasured every moment they've spent together during this extended visit. They've gone thrift shopping and brunching, and with Erica's help Helen has finally assembled all the jigsaw puzzles that were collecting dust in her curio cabinet. But Erica has a life of her own, and Helen doesn't want to keep her from it.

"I'll be fine," Helen tells Erica. "If any killer was after me, they've given up by now."

"That's not funny, Mom."

Indeed, it's somewhat false bravado. Helen is acutely aware that she is now the sole surviving old spinster of Oleander Court. If the killer has a pattern, Helen should be worried about being next.

"Why don't you come home with me?" Erica asks for the umpteenth time. "Just for a while."

"I'm *fine.*"

Erica glances at her phone as it lights up. "My Lyft's almost here." She bends to hug her mother, tight, and Helen closes her eyes. She may not see Erica again for months.

Helen watches the gray Ford Focus hired to transport her daughter to Hartsfield International Airport until it turns the corner and is gone. Erica will be back home in Nashville in time to put her kids to bed.

Why isn't Helen out the door, too? Why does she keep hesitating? Is it misguided nostalgia? Memories of the home where she and Edmund had built their lives?

Like Erica, there's nothing here for Helen any longer. Unlike Erica, Helen's unable to let go. Maybe it's age.

To occupy herself, Helen fixes herself a drink and heads to the front porch. It's not even five o'clock, but the sky has darkened, the shadows from the trees creeping over the sidewalk. The days are growing shorter with the approaching winter. That, combined with the accompanying cold, means there is far less foot traffic for Helen to observe.

There is also no Pam. It feels strange not to see her multiple times a day, jabbering away on her iPhone while she pretends not to notice as Buster defecates in one yard or another.

Even Ray's walks are less frequent. When she does circle the block with her dogs, her gait is quicker. Head down, no dawdling.

Helen feels sorry for Ray. She knows the police have focused their investigation on Ray, but they're mistaken. Ray's too kind to be a killer. When she sees Helen on the porch, she always brings her the mail, stops to chat. The other day, she'd even wrestled a few plant covers out of the back of Helen's tool shed. Now Helen's mint supply for her Moscow Mules is safe.

Also, these deaths aren't her style. If Ray ever killed someone, it would be in a fit of rage. She'd be found standing over the body, horrified at what she'd done. Not that Helen thinks she's capable of even that.

Helen pulls her shawl tighter around her, ice clinking as she raises her glass to her lips. For the umpteenth time, she turns over what she knows about Pam's and Beverly's deaths. The officers were somewhat candid with her, likely because they assumed she was so ancient, she would forget any details the second they left.

Pam had been shoved down her floating staircase. She was found with her neck broken like a chicken bone. Beverly had been killed by some odorless poison that had been added to the bottle of wine gifted by Pam. Meaning, the logical main suspect in Beverly's murder had not only been eliminated, but she was no longer available to provide clues as to who might have tampered with the wine bottle. Very convenient. Very clever.

Tripp is dragging his garbage cans to the curb. Helen's sit at her garage door. They're not too heavy for her to roll, but she has difficulty, especially with a hip that acts out in the cold. Pete will walk Costco after dinner and do the chore for her. It will take him fifteen seconds and it will mean the world to her.

"Mom, I think that man is sweet on you," Erica had said after one of Pete's visits. He'd fixed the dishwasher and then stayed to help with part of a jigsaw.

"He happens to be an incredibly nice man. Also, he thinks I'm a great ar-*tist*," Helen replied, pronouncing it "arteest."

"You were, Mom," Erica had said, the past tense stinging Helen. When had it become past tense? If you were born an artist, a creative person, wasn't it something you simply were? How could part of yourself go away?

Maybe it could. Back in the day and after the initial flurry of excitement over Helen, her next collection hadn't been as well-received. Then she and Edmund had babies, one after another, and Helen had elected to be a full-time mother. She wouldn't change that decision for the world—those years with her sweet babies!—but it was like a train getting off track. She'd never gotten back on, even once the girls had moved away.

Helen watches Tripp as he crosses his yard. Back to his house and his boring wife, Sandy. Slouched on her darkened porch, Helen sees how he glances at her full garbage cans. How he keeps on walking.

From this vantage point, Helen has seen many glimpses like this one. Her neighbors when they think no one's watching. Their masks coming off to reveal their true selves. The distortion, the distinction between their private and public personas.

Helen stands. After topping off her drink in the kitchen, she carefully makes her way down the creaky wooden stairs to the basement. She and Edmund had never finished it, as they used it primarily for storage.

The other purpose had been devised by Edmund. "Just in case you feel like painting again," he'd said time and again.

This is her art space.

This section of the basement is as aesthetically pleasing as a jail cell. Rough concrete walls, rough concrete floor. A single rectangular window, high up. Helen never liked to paint on a sun-drenched porch to the sound of bluebirds. She could have no distractions. Only a blank slate, an empty palette.

Five years ago, on a whim during a Black Friday shopping excursion with her daughters, Helen had purchased an enormous set of paints— sixty colors. Unopened, they're likely still fine.

Helen retrieves the largest canvas in her pile and manages to mount it on the wall. As she prepares her space, a flurry of excitement passes through her. She hasn't had this urge in years.

She picks up her brush and begins to paint.

CONNER

On Sunday morning, Conner Boyle stares at his wife, wondering how the sexpot he married turned into this person. The old Tracey would have died before wriggling into leggings instead of jeans. She wore high heels instead of sneakers. She applied makeup and blow-dried her hair before leaving the house.

The old Tracey had some pride.

The new Tracey is pouring chocolate chip pancakes into the shape of Mickey Mouse, singing softly to whatever Disney soundtrack is currently on rotation. Her purple sweatshirt has a spaghetti stain on the elbow.

"Gabby! Breakfast's up!" She waves the spatula as their eldest plods into the kitchen. Nine-year-old Gabby has a weight problem, no way around it. Even as a toddler, she'd been thicker than other children, the cute baby fat quickly giving way to pudge. As Tracey heaps three pancakes onto a plate, Conner frowns from his perch at the kitchen island.

"Three, Tracey?"

Tracey darts him a warning look. "Growing bodies."

"Give her two." He lifts his coffee, studying his phone. There's a change mandatory to his Fantasy Football lineup.

Gabby looks from her father to her mother, sensing a storm brewing. "Two is fine, Mom," she says, ignoring the plate of bacon as she takes a stool next to Conner.

"I thought we'd all go to Webb Bridge Park today." Tracey's voice has an edge. "Pack a picnic, let the kids run around. The weather's high sixties today. Total fluke."

Conner feels a familiar twinge of annoyance. It's not enough that he works sixty hours a week. Tracey expects him to slough along on whatever unnecessarily complicated weekend excursion she devises for the children.

Not that he ever goes, but it's still annoying to be asked.

"Can't we hang around the house?" he asks. "What do you think, Gabby? Movie day!"

"We're not spending the day cooped up inside," Tracey snaps. "Addy! Ryan! Mickey Mouse pancakes."

Fuck your Mickey Mouse pancakes, Conner thinks as he nurses his coffee. But that's Tracey—always finding some way to look like the martyr, the browbeaten housewife. No one forced her to dirty five dishes making pancakes over the stove. The kids are fine with frozen ones.

"You know, we have a perfectly good playground outside," Conner comments just to needle Tracey. "Don't have to drive twenty minutes to share one."

The Boyle playground isn't your run-of-the-mill setup. The entire thing is wooden, a gift from Tracey's father when he came to visit from Scottsdale for a month and took it upon himself to build the fucker with his own bare hands. Designed to look like a castle, it has numerous hiding spots, a miniature zipline, swings, and even an old-fashioned seesaw.

"The seesaw's broken," Tracey says, as if the kids have ever shown any interest in the seesaw. "One of the seats came off the frame. Remember?" She's passively-aggressively reminding Conner that she'd asked him to fix it ages ago. He'd forgotten, because he had better things to do.

Also, it wasn't his fault that Tracey's father had decided to build their children a gigantic splinter factory for a playground set. One that constantly needed repairs, nails hammered in, and sanding down. Just looking at the thing pisses Conner off.

"Gotta have something to blow off steam," the old man said when he'd announced the project, and Conner had bristled. Ed had yapped about the kids needing a playground set for months before he'd built it himself. The act was his way of wordlessly communicating that he didn't expect Conner to get his shit together to buy one.

Maybe Tracey got her passive-aggressiveness from her father.

Ryan streaks into the kitchen, his coppery hair sticking up in peaks and horns. "Wow, Mom! Mickey Mouse pancakes! Can you put my syrup separate?"

"That's how it's done, isn't it?" Tracey slides Ryan's plate to the other side of Conner. "Eat up, kid. Webb Bridge Park."

"Cool." Ryan looks at Conner with his pale blue eyes. "Are you coming, Dad?"

Conner feigns disappointment. "Sorry, kiddo. Too much to do around the house." Ignoring Tracey's death stare, he spears a strawberry from Ryan's plate. "But we'll hang this afternoon, okay?" Ryan can watch the Falcons game with him.

"Cool." Ryan digs in, and Conner gives Tracey a smug smile. What would he do at a park, anyway? Sit on a bench and play with his iPhone, that's what. The kids wouldn't even fucking notice he was there.

As he knew she would—especially in front of the kids—Tracey drops the issue. "Where is that girl?" she mumbles, turning off the stove and dropping the pancake pan into the sink.

"Here, Mommy," Addy says as she toddles in, dragging her stuffed bunny.

It takes them forever to leave. Tracey packs a bag that could last them for five days in the wilderness. Juice boxes, fruit, crackers, cheese, and plenty of Pull-Ups and wipes for Addy. Ryan needs to change his shirt because it's too warm today for long sleeves. Addy's bunny is lost and then found in the couch cushions.

"If you're doing house stuff when we're gone," Tracey says, as she knows he's full of shit, "could you fix the toilet in Ryan's room?" The lid had broken earlier that week.

"Sure." Conner can feel Tracey's eyes on him as he checks his work email. She's trying to guilt him into going, and it won't work. Every Saturday, Conner is careful to carve out at least five hours of Conner Time. This generally consists of working out, a football game, and drinking a beer while playing *Call of Duty* in his office. No work, no kids. Tracey should do the same for herself. Get a manicure. Or her hair done, for Christ's sake.

Finally, Conner hears the musical sound of car doors slamming as Tracey packs the kids into their sedan. Webb Bridge Park is twenty

minutes away. If they stay for two hours—and Tracey always does—
Conner has at least three blissful hours to himself.

The first order of business is working out. Conner has his own exercise
room, which features a treadmill, an elliptical, and a squat rack. A mirror
takes up one wall for motivational purposes. The exercise room had been
designed for both Conner and Tracey, but Tracey never uses it. *Chasing the
kids is my exercise*, she always says. Well, not quite enough exercise, because
Tracey's put on at least seven pounds since Addy was born.

Across the twenty feet of yard separating Conner's house from the
one next door, Conner glimpses Adelaide McKenzie rinsing a dish in the
sink. He slows on the treadmill, angling his head to stare out of the corner of his eye. Man, she's a hot piece of ass—great rack, bedroom eyes,
glossy thick hair falling to a tiny little waist.

Adelaide never gives him the time of day. She's barely even neighborly, and they're neighbors. That makes him try harder when he sees
her—to make it a point to wave, to find something to talk about. It
drives him crazy to know she doesn't like him.

And why not? Everyone else does.

Conner wonders what Adelaide thinks about this whole business
with Beverly and Pam. Pam had hated Adelaide, Conner knows. Nice
to her face but digging at her to the other women in the neighborhood.
Typical female shit.

After Conner finishes his workout, he takes a long shower, using the
series of hair products his stylist recommended. Biotin is the key, he's
been told. No thinning for Conner. Then he dons his trackpants and
Emory sweatshirt and heads to the kitchen for a snack.

The kitchen looks nice. Ever since Tracey hired Faith to help with
some simple organizing once a week, there's been a lot less mess. The
pantry is categorized by food type, and the refrigerator isn't so cluttered.
Faith even cleaned out the mail from the kitchen drawer.

After preparing a bowl of granola and Greek yogurt, Conner exhales
in satisfaction as he enters his office. It's as much of a man cave as a place
to work. Dual screens for his computer, television mounted for *Call of
Duty* purposes. Conner switches it on, munching his granola as he waits
for it to load.

The office could do with some organizing. His desk is messy, and Conner goes to it, fingering a sheaf of papers Tracey's left there. It's the open enrollment forms for his firm, where Conner chooses the health plans and benefits for the family.

Call of Duty is still installing an update, so Conner shifts through the paperwork. Tracey's put little tabs on the pages for him to sign. If he takes care of this, it's one less thing to get bitched about. With a sigh, Conner sits down, uncapping his pen and signing his name where so indicated. Tracey's sorted through the health and dental plans to choose the right ones. Sign, sign, sign.

When he gets to the papers for life insurance, Tracey's maxed out the payout for both of them—two million for Conner, and three hundred thousand for Tracey as the employee's spouse.

Conner smirks. *Till death do us part* is a voided promise when your wife transforms into a shrieking harpy, and especially one who gets pregnant with a third kid you didn't agree on.

Also, six months ago, Conner had met Jillian. Jillian—Jill—is eight years younger than Conner and has no plans or desires for children. She works in Conner's firm, climbing the same corporate ladder Tracey had stepped off of to "enjoy the kids while they're little."

She's also an animal in the sack.

For the last two months, Conner's been moving funds and stocks to accounts that Tracey knows nothing about. To date, there's about four hundred grand Tracey will never find, not even with the nastiest of divorce lawyers and accountants sniffing around.

The fate of the kids doesn't concern Conner. They'll live with Tracey, of course, and Conner fully expects to be writing fat checks for child support. Freedom ain't free.

Conner will sign the papers. After he's out the door and that ring is slid onto Jillian's slim finger, they mean nothing. Employee benefits only go to *spouses*.

Tracey's included an addressed and stamped envelope. How thoughtful. When he's finished, Conner stuffs in the paperwork and goes to drop it all in the mailbox. The red flag creaks when Conner lifts it.

Menial paperwork is the only chore he'll complete today. Tracey can fix that toilet seat herself.

SOON-LI

month after Beverly's and Pam's deaths, Soon-Li is having trouble
sleeping at night. The police are still "investigating," still interview-
ing the residents of Oleander Court, and they seem no closer to the
truth. If they haven't found it by now, will they ever?

It makes no sense to Soon-Li that Pam would poison Beverly. Soon-Li
had observed those two cackling like hens together and knows that any
disagreement between them would be minor and shallow. Nothing war-
ranting murder.

There were also logistical problems with Pam having killed Beverly.
It was simply stupid to poison someone with something everyone knew
you'd given her. Like killing someone with a knife that has your name
on the handle and leaving it in the body.

And what about how Pam died? Assuming she'd killed herself, her
method of choice was throwing herself down a staircase? Not a chance.
Soon-Li had witnessed Pam carrying on about a splinter. If Pam couldn't
deal with the pain of a splinter, she couldn't throw herself headfirst down
a flight of stairs.

Pam didn't do this. Someone else murdered both Pam and Beverly,
and it was someone who knew them well enough to orchestrate the
double killing.

This boiled the list of suspects down to a very narrow, very concern-
ing pool of individuals: *every single person who lived in Oleander Court.*
What neighbor *didn't* know that Pam kept her spare key in that notice-
ably fake rock in her garden? Who *hadn't* heard her brag about how her

floating staircase had been imported from Sweden because it violated every U.S. fire code? What female neighbor *wasn't* on Pam's invite list for the book club party?

On a Tuesday afternoon, Soon-Li sips her coffee as she stares out her front window. Behind her, the elliptical machine is draped in wet clothes. It might not help with her heart rate, but it can dry six sweaters at once.

Across the street, Pete and Laura are raking leaves. The bus will drop the kids off from school soon, and maybe Nicole will invite Lila over again. She's a great kid, one who overlooks Lila's insecurity, who draws her out of her shell. Soon-Li continues to be thankful that the Nobles came to Oleander Court.

Still, there's something off about Laura. It's her eagerness. Throwing the first-ever neighborhood ladies' book club. Didn't she understand that by social custom, existing residents were supposed to welcome the new?

Laura's efforts had reminded Soon-Li of her own mother. Marie-Li had immigrated from Korea, taking root in Philadelphia where two cousins had opened a nail salon and offered her a job. She'd stayed within her Korean bubble until Soon-Li, her only child, started public school. Then, determined for her daughter to be "one hundred percent American," a phrase Soon-Li heard often, she'd ventured out. She joined an English-speaking church to better learn the language. She went places only to listen. All to prepare for volunteering for school events, where she hovered over Soon-Li. She wanted to ensure that her daughter was included in every opportunity, that she fit in with her peers.

But Marie-Li herself didn't fit in. The other mothers grew impatient with her halting English. When she was misunderstood, Marie-Li didn't correct anyone. She smiled hopefully as the conversation drifted around her like a stream.

Soon-Li remembers those meaningless discussions her mother had yearned to join. Gossip about other parents, exaggeration of offsprings' mediocre talents. Congratulations to Johnny for his Boy Scout badges. Everyone gets them, Mrs. Fleishman.

Marie-Li had an excuse for her attitude. It was for her daughter's future. The effort was a means to an end.

But why does *Laura* need to be so nice, so eager? What purpose does it serve?

And what about her behavior on Halloween night? One moment they'd all been talking on Ray's lawn, and the next Laura had charged into Beverly's yard to inspect for something amiss. And lo and behold, there was Beverly on the kitchen floor. Such a lucky hunch for Laura.

Or was it?

Soon-Li hates getting up twenty times in the night to check on Lila, her heart pounding every time she turns the doorknob. She hates freezing each time she hears a creak or a thump. And she hates suspecting each and every neighbor in the gruesome murders of Pam and Beverly, to include the mother of her daughter's only friend.

Soon-Li's professional occupation is to solve immensely complicated, tangled issues relating to the sources of data leaks or security breaches. She always manages to do so, but that's because she always has all information at hand, or the means to obtain it. That's not the case here. From her limited vantage point, Soon-Li only has access to a sliver of possible clues.

In her typical problem-solving fashion, Soon-Li has devised a plan to solve her local murder mystery while keeping tabs on those she finds suspicious. She has four other participants in mind. These women are smart and observant; and if Soon-Li gets them together, she may be able to cobble together the details necessary to understand what happened.

It's time to resurrect the book club, only a more exclusive version. And there's no need to inform its members of the real purpose. That might defeat it entirely.

RAY

"When do you think you'll be home?"

Ray tries to keep her voice light. For the last few weeks, she's been walking on eggshells around Juliet, and it's her own damn fault.

"God, Ray!" Juliet had exploded after the Liam Neeson officer had left after his first solo visit. "Why do you have to be so . . . flip? This is a murder investigation. Every word you say is measured, weighed. *Think* before you open your mouth."

"I know," Ray had said, and Juliet glared at her. "Sometimes," Juliet had said, "your self-destructive tendencies are hard to tolerate."

Self-destructive. Ray had pondered the word. Was she really self-destructive? Her therapist certainly thinks so, and considering how many relationships she's sabotaged throughout the years, she'd be inclined to agree—to *admit*—that she was. But going through what Ray had, who wouldn't have their guard up?

"Have you ever been known by any other name?" Liam Neeson had asked as he sat at their kitchen table, drinking the coffee Juliet had prepared for him.

"Uh . . . how is that relevant?" Ray replied, and Juliet's mouth had pursed. In a murder investigation, anything could be relevant. And what made a question more relevant? Dodging it.

The officer hadn't said anything, and Ray had drummed her fingers on the table. When the sound echoed in the silent kitchen, she'd put her hands in her lap, squeezing them together. "Yes," she'd said finally. "I was born Steven Raymond Pritchett."

"And is that something that's not . . . known?"

"It's not something I typically share, no." *Or ever.*

"Why is that?"

Ray couldn't look at Juliet. They've been together for twelve years. Juliet knew her Before, when Juliet was an out and proud lesbian and Ray was still Steven.

God, it had sucked to be Steven. Ever since Ray was a kid, she'd known she'd been born in the wrong body. It was miserable. Having gender dysphoria isn't something one chooses. As a six-year-old boy, you don't choose to only want to play with dolls and have the mean boys at school call you a "fairy" and rub boogers on you. As a thirteen-year-old, you don't choose to have the shit kicked out of you during gym because no one wants to change around a "fag." You don't choose to have your parents take you to thousands of hours of therapy to "understand" you. You don't choose to have your conservative grandmother who used to love you cut you out of her will because of who you are, and you don't choose to be lonely, and depressed, and, at your darkest, wanting to die.

"Being a lesbian is one thing," Ray tells the officer. "But being transgender is another. We live in the South. This is an upscale community. I didn't want any drama."

The officer had raised his eyebrows. "What about the drama you created with Beverly Grant?"

"That was just fun. It was so easy to push her buttons."

"Was getting sued by Beverly Grant 'fun'?" He'd placed a slight emphasis on the word.

"No. I love that greenhouse, and it was barely over on her property. On the side yard. Who uses a side yard? But she was . . . malicious about the situation."

Ray was proud of herself for the restraint. "Malicious" was generous, for Beverly.

"Were you aware that in a lawsuit to take it down, Beverly most likely would have won?"

"I'm aware."

"It looks like you don't have that problem now, do you?"

Ray had tried not to shift in her chair. "I guess not. Unless her family wants to continue the lawsuit."

"They may have other things to deal with."

Since Beverly's death, Ray has seen two different vehicles frequently parked in her driveway. Beverly had a grown son and daughter, neither of whom had visited her often. Ray wondered what they'd been told about the investigation. What they'd been told about her. When they caught a glimpse of her—working in the greenhouse, walking her dogs—did they think, *there goes my mother's murderer*?

"Did Beverly know your real name?"

Ray had snorted. "God, no."

"Why that reaction?"

"Are you serious?" Ray had asked, even though he was clearly very serious. "Beverly would have been the last one I'd have told. She was . . . I'll just say it. A judgmental bitch." There went the restraint. "If you weren't white, Catholic, and conservative, she was offended by your basic existence. She hated living next door to us."

The officer had steepled his fingers. "Are you a housewife, Mrs. Willis?"

"For now. I used to practice law."

"Not anymore?"

Liam Neeson already knew all this. "Not now. When I went through my gender-affirming surgery, the firm's atmosphere was . . . hostile. I threatened to sue. They got a full release, and I got a settlement."

Ray had fought the urge to ask, again, why this was relevant. What was he getting at?

"Pam Muenster. Did you get along with her?"

"About as much as anyone did."

"What does that mean?"

"She loved being the head of the HOA. Exploiting her minor position of authority. God, she even went after Helen, the sweet little old lady at the end of the cul-de-sac. And she never cleaned after her little yappy dog."

"Have you ever had any larger issues with Pam?"

"Nope," Ray had replied honestly.

"Why didn't you attend her party?"

Ray had glanced at Juliet. She hadn't wanted to say, to admit to the officer about her Dark Days. They come every once in a while—a sweeping depression, paralyzing—where Ray remembers life as Steven Raymond Pritchett and what she's lost in becoming Ray.

"I hadn't felt well," she'd said instead. "And I knew the whole party would be obnoxious. Pam showing off, people talking about their pools and plastic surgeries. I stayed home and watched television." Really, she'd hidden under the covers all day, crying off and on and telling Juliet to go away the few times she'd come to the bedroom door.

"Is this where you were all that day? October 28? Home, watching television?"

"Yes."

He'd looked at Juliet. "Were you together that entire day?"

Juliet had met his gaze. "Yes." She didn't offer any further details. There weren't any. In fact, even saying they were "together" was misleading.

If pressed, Juliet couldn't confirm Ray hadn't left the house. Ray had kept the bedroom door locked all day. Also, the room has a terrace, with a trellis solid enough for someone Ray's size to scale down it.

Now, as Juliet slips on her pantsuit—she has a deposition today—Ray feels guilty for what her wife has been through during the last few weeks. Juliet has given Ray an alibi she doesn't have. She's had to sit there, watching, as Ray bumblefucked her way through one interview (interrogation?) after another. She's had to deal with Ray's moodiness, to coming home to a messy house, to finding no dinner prepared because her useless wife had been too depressed to get off the couch all day.

Being questioned, scrutinized, hasn't been good for Ray. It's reminded her of when she was younger and trying to figure herself out, all the while feeling like she was under a microscope as others tried to figure her out.

Some life events make you stronger. Others, you'd just as well forget.

"It might be a late day today," Juliet says now. "There's a client in town. I might be expected to socialize after hours."

"You should!" Ray hates the false cheery note in her voice. "You deserve a drink."

Juliet cuts her with a look. "I'd rather have a drink with *you*."

"Then come home early."

"I don't have any control over that. But I'll try." Juliet kisses Ray on the forehead as she scoots out the door, travel mug of coffee in hand. "Be good."

Ray watches Juliet's car as it backs out of the driveway. She knows the real reason Juliet's been prickly these last few weeks, and it isn't because of the investigation. Not purely.

It's because, years after they first met, Juliet is still steadfast in who she is. She's been out since high school. Ray, meanwhile, still shies away from telling people her past. The only one in the neighborhood who knows is Adelaide, and Ray's still surprised the information had come spilling out. "You don't need to hide who you are," Juliet's told Ray countless times, frustrated that the advice never sinks in.

Liam Neeson hadn't asked Ray about her past for his health. There's a reason he wants to know. Something with Beverly, something not good.

What if, when this plays out, Ray's true identity becomes known? She's spent over a decade trying to forget Steven.

Steven's been dead for a long time. Yet somehow, with this investigation, he's become a Person of Interest.

FAITH

When Faith was little, it never occurred to her *not* to do what she was told. When Faith was seven and some lunch lady told her she had to eat all the million pickles she'd heaped on her plate on Hamburger Day, she did it and spent the next hour barfing in the far stall of the bathroom near the gym.

Maybe Faith should have questioned the lunch lady. Like, who really cared if she cleared her plate? It was sad about starving kids in China, who the lunch lady said would love to have her pickles, but eating every single one of them wasn't going to feed some poor kid all the way on the other side of the world.

The thing was, it was Faith's mom who had taught her to do what she was told. And Faith's mom was the best. She made cookies, and she played make-believe, and took Faith and Nick to the best playgrounds. She tried so hard, all the while working full-time as a nurse because she was a single mom. Faith could at least follow her advice and eat all her damn pickles. Even if she hasn't been able to have one since.

Faith still does what she's told. So, even though Bambi was basically The Worst (since Pam was dead and gave up the title, ha ha), Faith meant to deliver that envelope to William McKenzie and keep it away from his wife, per Bambi's instructions.

What did Faith care, anyway? Ray was all about Adelaide and *Ray* was awesome, but Adelaide totally seemed like a trophy wife to Faith.

When Faith left Bambi's house after organizing her closet, she'd walked to Adelaide's house to scope it out. Maybe Mr. McKenzie would be in the front yard, getting out of his car or something, and Faith could hand off the letter. But the house was quiet and dark, and Faith didn't want to just slide the letter under the door. Adelaide would find it since she was home way more often, arranging flowers or painting her toes or whatever it was trophy wives did while their husbands were away making money.

"Hi, Faith!" Conner had called from next door, waving big.

"Hi, Mr. Boyle," Faith had replied, mustering a smile.

Conner probably thought they were friends since he always talked to her when she was over helping out Tracey. As if acting nice made all the crappy stuff he did to his family invisible. Like when Gabby was about to take a bite of a Hot Pocket and he told her she'd be "better off" with a turkey sandwich. Gabby had turned bright red and then only nibbled at it even though the pepperoni pizza kind was her favorite and she'd just told Faith she was starving.

Faith had been at the kitchen table, sorting through the mail as Conner prepared himself a salad. "How's life treating you, Faith?" he'd asked, like she hadn't just heard him being a total dick. Then Tracey came in with a million groceries and Conner had jetted inside his "home office" and closed the door.

Now, it's a week later and Faith's relieved that Conner's not around this time. William's car is in the driveway, so there's a decent shot she can hand off the letter quickly. Even though it seems totally high school and Faith's not crazy about messing with a friend of Ray's, she'll do it. Otherwise, it would be like stealing, since Bambi's already paid her for the task.

When Faith rings the McKenzies' doorbell, though, it's Adelaide who answers. "Oh, hey!" She's holding an empty Champagne glass with bits of orange pulp stuck at the bottom. Seriously, is everyone in Oleander Court an alcoholic? "You here for Ray? Ray, you have a visitor!" she calls before Faith can reply. "Come on in, Faith."

Huh. Trophy Wife can be bothered to learn a name. *Bambi* had called her "Grace" like three times.

Adelaide nudges a pile of cellophaned-wrapped packages stacked in the entryway. It's like a Jenga game, all the pieces slightly sticking out. "Want some chocolate? I was wasteful and bought too much." Her Southern accent is thick, heavy, and it surprises Faith because Adelaide didn't have an accent on *Zombie 101*. Can Adelaide actually act?

Ray calls from the living room. "She's being modest! She bought them so a little girl wouldn't cry!"

"Yeah, I did it to compensate for Beverly." Adelaide's words are all sloshed together. "So, Beverly owes me five hundred dollars. But she's dead, so we'll call it even."

Faith can't stop staring at her. Not just because Faith has never met an actual famous person before, but because she's *so pretty*. Like, legit pretty, the kind of pretty that people like Bambi Holiday want to buy in a bottle. Snow-White-Wicked-Witch pretty.

"Hurry up, people!" Ray yells. "You'll miss Brooklyn's talent!"

"What is she talking about?" Faith asks, and Adelaide grins.

"You're unfamiliar with the world of child beauty pageants?" Her accent becomes affected, ridiculous as she moves into the house, beckoning Faith to follow. "Sugar, don't you know that's how I got my start?" The kitchen opens up to the living room, the marble countertop cluttered with half-empty jugs of juice and the kinds of snacks Faith loves (meaning they're terrible for her). Adelaide stands on tiptoe to remove a glass flute from a cupboard. "Fresh-squeezed, my favorite. Don't be shy."

Ray is sprawled across Adelaide's L-shaped couch, watching a television so huge the little girl featured on it is taller than Faith is in real life. "Help me with some math," she drawls, clearly as hammered as Adelaide. "If it costs five hundred to stay in the hotel for the pageant, three hundred for the coach, one hundred for the hair, and fifty for the entry fee, what's your net profit if you walk away with mini grand supreme and five hundred dollars?"

"You were in pageants?" Faith asks Adelaide, who is mincing across the living room, waving at a pretend audience.

"Miss Arkansas Teen USA. Money helped jazz up the trailer." She blows a kiss at the wall.

"The trailer?" No way someone this beautiful ever lived in a trailer.

Adelaide turns, her sea green eyes meeting Faith's. "Oh, yeah." For a second, she's serious. "Cozy Acres. Bedford, Arkansas. Don't tell no one, you hear?" She falls on the couch, arranging her legs over Ray's and reaching for the bowl of popcorn on the coffee table. "Okay, I'm over this trip down memory lane." She clicks the controller on her PlayStation, glancing up at Faith. "Now, I know you're only nineteen and all, but I'm not completely opposed to you fortifyin' your orange juice with a splash of Champagne. So long as your mama won't mind."

"How did you know I'm nineteen?"

Adelaide's forehead wrinkles in a frown. "Ray musta told me. She talks about you loads. Like how you've been puttin' up with everyone in this whole neighborhood." She raises her glass. "Cheers to you, for that." Faith leans to click her glass against Adelaide's, and Adelaide stops her from pulling away. She runs her finger over the ridges of Faith's bracelet. "Well, that's pretty. You know, I had a charm bracelet like that once. Lost it climbin' a tree."

Ray grabs the controller from Adelaide. "Did you need me for anything? Everything okay?"

"Everything's fine. Just checking if you needed me this weekend."

It's a lame excuse, a question she would have texted, but Ray doesn't seem to notice. "I'll think of something. I'll let you know, okay?" Ray is nice like Laura that way. Even if she doesn't need help, she'll find something so Faith will have the work.

"*I* need something from you," Adelaide says, patting the seat next to her. "I need you to sit here and watch *The Grand Budapest Hotel* with us."

OMG, is Trophy Wife serious? Faith loves anything by Wes Anderson. His movies are quirky, and fun, and plus they always have Bill Murray who is basically a national treasure. "Okay," Faith says. "If you insist."

"I do. Now, I understand workin' to get where you need to go, but Ray says *all* you do is work." Adelaide pops up, snatching Faith's empty flute from her hand and heading for the kitchen. "Just a splash," she says as she refreshes Faith's drink.

The garage door leading to the kitchen swings open, and the man who must be William McKenzie walks in. The surgeon, Faith remembers from Ray, who always stops just short of saying she doesn't like him. "Mr. Perfect," she calls him, which totally isn't a compliment. He looks younger than he is, with sandy brown hair and kind blue eyes that must be helpful when he tells someone he amputated the wrong foot. "Please tell me you're not watching *Toddlers and Tiaras* anymore," he says to Adelaide as she hops on the counter.

"You've been spared," Adelaide replies, sticking a pretzel in his mouth. She pats him on the head, lowering his forehead to hers. "How goes the garage?"

"Still a work in progress."

"You've been sayin' that since I married you."

"Hey, if that's my only vice, that's not so bad." William's eyes rest on Faith. "You look familiar."

"This is Faith," Adelaide says. "The one Ray's told us all about."

"Hi, Faith. Want a cat?"

Faith's eyebrows shoot up. "Is that, like, something you normally give out to people who visit?"

William chuckles, hoisting himself onto the counter with his wife, their shoulders touching. "Today it is. That furball won't go away."

Adelaide bumps her shoulder against his. "You love it." She crunches into another pretzel, brushing the crumbs off her pajama pants. "'Bout two weeks ago, this cat shows up on our back deck. And this softie's out there every morning, dumpin' a can of cat food and callin' out *here, kitty*."

"I'm not the one who bought it a cat house."

"It was right there on the Goodwill shelf. What was I supposed to do?"

Now Faith's sorry she'd nicknamed Adelaide "Trophy Wife," even if only in her head. Adelaide's hotness is like a trick. You see her and think, *there goes a bimbo*, but she's actually funny and observant and nice enough to take care of stray cats.

"Oh!" Adelaide crosses her legs, scrunching closer to William. "What do you think of this for Roberto?"

William reaches into the pretzel bag on her lap as he squints at the phone. "Amazon?"

"No, Home Depot. Amazon was backordered."

Faith glances toward the living room. Ray shows no sign of budging from the couch. Is it because she doesn't like William? Yeah, he and

Adelaide are so cutesy, they probably make some people want to punch them in the face, but the affection seems legit.

"Ooh!" Adelaide hops off the counter. "There he is! Here, kitty!" she croons, even though there's no way the cat hears through the closed patio doors.

"I've adopted myself a cat, haven't I?" William asks Faith, looking one hundred percent unbothered. He's staring at Adelaide like he's won the lottery. But then his phone buzzes from a pocket, and he fishes it out, making a face. "Adelaide!"

His wife hasn't heard him. Gathering the cat in her arms—a huge, buff-colored tomcat with green eyes and a clipped ear—she's carrying it across the living room. "Hi, Daddy," she says to William, waving the cat's paw, and for a hot second William's grin falters and Adelaide's face turns pink. "Are we ready for a name?" she asks. "I'm thinkin' Princess Sparklepants."

"Mini Grand Supreme!" Ray calls from the couch, and Adelaide and William exchange a look as the cat squirms.

"He *likes* it," Adelaide declares as she liberates him onto the floor. He bolts to the living room and disappears through the open patio door.

"I have to go in," William says, waving his phone at Adelaide.

"I knew we couldn't get lucky." She sighs. "I'll wait up." She stands on tiptoe to kiss him, and minutes later William's out the door.

Faith stays and watches a movie with Adelaide and Ray. Watches them, too, because they're fun to watch, how hard they make each other laugh and how they sit, limbs draped across each other like sisters and totally unselfconscious about the contact. Faith's always been squeamish about touching.

Faith knew from talking to Ray how much she loved Adelaide, but seeing them together all afternoon—she gets it. They fit, goofy and fun in their own little world like how Ray and Juliet have their own world, too. Ray and Juliet balance each other out, while Ray and Adelaide together are pure light.

"Take off your coat and stay a while," Adelaide says halfway through the movie, tugging at Faith's sweater jacket. Bambi's letter falls out of the side pocket, and Adelaide hands it back to her.

"I'm okay," Faith says as she stuffs it back inside, face burning even though there's no way Adelaide could know what the letter says. That it's probably all about her.

Hours later, after another movie and plenty of Papa John's pizza, Faith slides into her car.

She can't resist. She reads the letter, and it's no surprise. It's about Adelaide doing it with Roberto, the landscaper guy and the same one William and Adelaide were trying to find a present for. It's more high school than anything Faith encountered *in* high school. Get a life, Bambi.

And, like, hello. She has it wrong. Adelaide wouldn't be so open about being friends with Roberto if there was something going on. And anyone who saw Adelaide and William together would know they were too nuts about each other to cheat.

Faith folds the letter into a tight square and shoves it back in her pocket. A second later she's turned on her radio and is rocking out to guilty pleasure pop music, the letter already forgotten.

BAMBI

I n the week and a half since Bambi's note was delivered to William McKenzie to advise him of his wife's infidelity, not a single thing has happened. Adelaide McKenzie's happy little life appears to have gone on as normal. Bambi once even saw the two of them holding hands as they walked around the neighborhood, William's handsome face tilted attentively toward Adelaide's.

Bambi also saw Adelaide flirting with Roberto, the lawn man, in full daylight. For at least five minutes! Standing on the sidewalk outside the Everlys' yard, laughing away.

Today, Adelaide is jogging across the street to meet Roberto at his truck, which has just pulled to a stop. A little girl climbs down. When her feet hit the sidewalk, Bambi observes pink light-up shoes. As Bambi watches from her vantage point in the master bathroom, standing in the tub so she can peer out the window with her high-grade binoculars, the little girl and Adelaide walk up the street and into Adelaide's house.

Bambi can't believe it. Adelaide is probably *feeding* Roberto's daughter while poor William is away at work. Why isn't he stopping this?

"What are you looking at?"

Bambi screeches, almost slipping on the austere marble surface. "Nothing much," she tells Marv, who squints at her.

"You're standing in the tub."

"It's the best way I can see out the window. Look!" She extends the binoculars. "Adelaide McKenzie is having an affair."

Marv doesn't take them. He yawns, scratching his belly. "Who?"

"Adelaide McKenzie, at the end of the other cul-de-sac on Magnolia Lane."

"Oh, yeah. The hot one," Marv replies, which infuriates Bambi.

"She's not hot, she's cheap."

"Okay, honey," Marv says agreeably. "Do you want to order Italian for dinner?"

"Are you insane? I can't eat carbs." For the last six days, Bambi has subsisted on nothing but grilled chicken, kale, and grape tomatoes. She and Marv are going to Bermuda for Christmas, and she's already bought three size two bikinis.

"Maybe you should. Could make you less irritable."

"Shut up, Marv," Bambi grumbles, picking up the binoculars again. She'll be a lot less irritable once she can squeeze into that size two. And once she sees Adelaide's possessions tossed onto the lawn.

"Well, I'm getting the chicken parm."

Bambi smothers a grunt of disgust as her eyes rake over Marv's body—the paunchy stomach, the skinny legs. He wasn't much to look at when she married him sixteen years ago, but his bank account sure was. Bambi had figured looks were a tradeoff for the life she deserved: trips abroad, designer clothes, a home where she never had to lift a finger. She never worries she made the wrong choice, but that doesn't make Marv easier to look at.

"Maybe you should try a salad," she says, not able to resist the dig.

"Maybe you should try some water." He gestures to the clear glass resting on the window ledge. He knows it's vodka.

Marv leaves, and Bambi folds herself onto the window ledge, resting her forehead on the glass as she stares toward Adelaide's house. She hates being fixated on Adelaide. Adelaide was the kind of girl Bambi could make miserable in high school. Like Peyton Fairbanks, whom Bambi had hated for how she'd bewitched boys without even trying. Lips that only needed Chapstick to be beautiful, glossy hair without salon effort. Walmart clothes she rocked.

Sophomore year, Peyton had wanted to be a cheerleader, and, as an upperclassman and co-captain of the squad, it had been Bambi's right to haze Peyton into realizing she didn't belong. During a blindfolded exercise in the dead of night, Peyton had lost most of her hair to Bambi's razor. Then the squad "accidentally" left her tied up on the football field until morning.

Bambi had promised Peyton this was the last test before the squad list went up with her name on it, but Peyton should have known better. Down the hall, surrounded by her friends, Bambi had watched Peyton's face crumple as she surveyed the paper Bambi herself had tacked up next to the athletic department office.

Bambi had to do it. She had to protect her status. Letting Peyton climb the ranks was dangerous. And unnatural, too. Peyton used *generic* shampoo.

It was kind of a shame, though. Peyton was one of the few girls who could do a back aerial.

According to Facebook, Peyton Fairbanks is still tight with her high school best friend. That dorky, arty girl Malorie, who apparently lost a significant amount of weight and isn't a cow anymore. In fact, if Bambi were being honest, she's actually pretty. And Peyton is married to a *hot* guy, and has two children she appears to adore. Bambi can't gauge how rich she is based on her Facebook profile, but the bitch sure seems happy.

To be fair, according to Bambi's own Facebook page, she's more than happy. She's fan-fucking-tastic. And she's still BFFs with the crew who helped her torture Peyton, even though she hasn't actually seen anyone in years. Only their Facebook walls.

Bambi takes another sip of her drink. The ice has melted, watering down the vodka. At this point she's numb to the alcohol anyway. A dark haze has settled around her, and Bambi broods about how unfair life is. Why does she have to get old? Why can't she stay young and hot forever?

Unfolding herself from the window ledge, Bambi steadies herself against the side of the tub as she climbs out. She's not that drunk. She'd prefer to be drunker. To forget about Then versus Now and how a woman—girl, really—who lives down the street reminds her of who she used to be. How she *used* to be the envy of all other women.

And why hasn't Bambi been able to take Adelaide down a peg? Has she lost that much of her old self? If this was twenty years ago, Bambi would have made Adelaide miserable with ease. Instead, she's staring at her through binoculars, searching for nonexistent signs of distress.

Rage flares through Bambi. How dare Adelaide make her feel this way! She goes to her walk-in closet, wriggling out of her skinny jeans and cashmere sweater in favor of her tightest workout outfit. She'll sweat out the booze while showing off her hot body to the whole neighborhood. She can still make heads turn.

In only ten minutes, Bambi's out the door in black-and-pink spandex, Britney's *Oops . . . I Did It Again* motivating her as her feet thud against the sidewalk. This song was huge the year Bambi won the title of prom queen, and Bambi recollects the girl she was as the crown was placed on her head. Shiny hair, perky tits, unlined face.

Bambi runs faster.

As she turns the corner, Roberto's truck is still parked along the street. The ebbing light casts long shadows of the landscaping equipment as Roberto and another man load them into the back of the truck. They don't even look at Bambi as she sails past, even though she sucks in her stomach and sticks out her chest.

They don't even look at her.

Bambi does two loops around the neighborhood, hoping it will calm her. It doesn't. The blood rushes through her head, and inhaling the cold air makes it feel like something's scraping at her chest, but fury pulsates through her. *It-isn't-fair, It-isn't-fair, It-isn't-fair.*

Bambi is approaching Adelaide's house on her third loop when the door opens. There she is, the whore herself, with that little girl. And shit—she's going to be beautiful one day, too.

Bambi glares as they make their way down the walkway, the little girl jumping to land on each crack. Adelaide carries a large plastic container. They reach the sidewalk as Bambi passes. Adelaide is distracted by the little girl, who's now using the stone ledge that runs parallel to the sidewalk as a balance beam. Maybe she'll want to be a cheerleader one day. Fabulous.

The blood boils in Bambi's veins. She veers to the right, connecting with Adelaide and sending the plastic container flying. It cracks open as it hits the sidewalk, scattering cupcakes. Cupcakes! Bambi hasn't had a sweet in over two weeks. She pictures Adelaide licking the spoon, not even concerned about what it might do to her ass.

"Whore." The word whooshes from Bambi's lips.

Adelaide pushes her hair back, shaking her head at the scene. "Aw, shoot. Well, Manuela. I'm invokin' the five-second rule." She picks up a cupcake, her face scrunching as she observes the dirt embedded in the white icing. Then she looks up at Bambi. "What was it you said to me?"

The kid blinks at Bambi, biting her lip. *She* heard.

"I said sorry," Bambi says, not moving to assist. Britney's breathy singing voice is still in her ear. Adelaide doesn't deserve her full attention.

Adelaide studies her from where she's kneeling, tossing the ruined cupcakes back into their container and licking the icing from her fingers. Trailer trash manners. "That's what you said?" she asks quietly, picking up the last cupcake and standing. She's shorter than Bambi. "You know, runnin' into someone ain't easy," she adds. "Interesting you've done it twice now."

Bambi doesn't like this—Adelaide calling her out. Girls like Adelaide don't call girls like Bambi out. They absorb abuse, and pretend it never happened to save face. Also, Bambi hasn't had a confrontation in ages, and never without an entourage.

"Maybe you have the habit of getting in my way," she says, standing tall over the other woman. An inch shorter and how much lighter? Bambi tries not to think about it.

Adelaide's eyes are green. A beautiful sea green, with long lashes. "I'm not in your way." She cocks her head. "Nice to meet you formally, though. *Bambi*, right?" When Bambi doesn't respond, Adelaide shakes her head. "All right then. Come on, Manuela. Let's go give your daddy a dirty cupcake."

"I bet you give him more than that, don't you?"

Adelaide's eyebrows shoot up. "Wow." She steps so close that Bambi can smell her lemony shampoo. "Watchin' people, makin' up stories, huh? Though I guess it makes sense for someone with nothin' better to do." There's mirth in Adelaide's eyes as she steps around Bambi. As if she's figured her out. As if what she thinks doesn't even matter. Bambi grabs her arm to stop her, digging in her fingernails.

"Let go of me." Adelaide's voice is steel.

Bambi releases her, her heart pounding. "Shameless."

"You don't even know me." Adelaide puts her hand on Manuela's back to guide her away.

"Enjoy your *lawn man.*"

Adelaide turns around. "What's wrong with bein' a lawn man? Workin' for a livin'?"

Bambi sneers. "A lawn man and trailer trash. Should have—"

Her head snaps back as Adelaide's palm connects with her cheek, hard. Bambi grabs her stinging face, her eyes watering. Shit, that *hurt.*

"There's nothing wrong with being a lawn man *or* from a trailer." Adelaide whirls back around and hurries Manuela down the street. She doesn't look back.

Bambi holds her cheek, gasping. Did that really happen? Maybe Bambi should call the police. But then that slut would tell them about the ruined cupcakes, turning an innocent hip-checking into an assault. The girl would back her up. Instead, Bambi re-inserts the earbud she'd lost *when she'd been slapped* and jogs home.

Marv doesn't look up when she bursts through the door. *Ted Lasso* is on the television, and Marv's feet are on the coffee table, again. "I'm taking a bath," Bambi announces, scaling the staircase two stairs at a time.

"Okay, honey," he says as he takes a huge bite of chicken parm. Probably two hundred calories of cheese and carbs per forkful, the bastard.

"Alexa! Play soothing music!" Bambi barks at her voice-controlled sound system once she's in the bathroom, slamming and locking the door behind her. Rushing to the medicine cabinet, she grabs the extra bottle of Percocet she'd wheedled her doctor into prescribing after her last liposuction, shaking two into her palm. They'll make her forget what happened in no time.

In the mirror, her cheek is red and splotchy from the slap. It still stings. Damn, that whore packs a wallop.

Bambi averts her eyes as she gulps water from the sink to wash down the narcotic painkiller, willing it to take effect. She loves how Percocet makes her feel, which is *un*-feeling.

Bambi inserts the plug in the bathtub and turns on the water, which gushes onto the clear marble. She shakes in a generous dose of bath salts before adding the bubbles, watching them foam. When the water—scalding hot, the way she likes it—is high enough, she turns on the jets.

Climbing into the tub, Bambi notices her empty glass on the ledge and wishes she'd topped it off. Oh, well—it's probably better not to mix a painkiller with vodka, not that Bambi hasn't done it before. And, in fact, is doing it right now—those three vodka shots aren't out of her system.

Ah, there comes the Percocet. Bambi tries to empty her head as the painkiller kicks in, creating a welcome euphoria that dulls the edges of her entirely bizarre and unpleasant encounter with Adelaide McKenzie. She dips her hand in the bubbles, inhaling the relaxing scent of lavender.

Maybe she's not actually having an affair, a tiny voice suggests in her head, and Bambi frowns. Only happy thoughts are allowed in the bathtub.

Within minutes, Bambi's entire being is completely relaxed. God, Percocet is amazing. It's too bad she only has fourteen capsules left. It's time for a follow-up visit with her doctor.

The jets are loud, but the steady, humming sound always puts Bambi to sleep, or near it. She closes her eyes, allowing herself to drift.

Bambi doesn't notice as the door to the master closet, which was slightly ajar, slowly eases all the way open.

She doesn't notice as a familiar figure skulks from the closet, carrying an item tethered to an electrical cord. They stop at the foot of the tub, studying the woman submerged in the bubbles. Some people would sense being watched, even under the influence of Percocet, but Bambi doesn't.

The figure doesn't hesitate beyond this cursory examination. With a flick of the wrist, the item in their hand—including the cord, which is plugged into one of several outlets housed in Bambi's glorious walk-in closet—disappears into the bubbles.

Bambi's eyes fly open. "Yah!" It comes as a slur, her eyes meeting those of her killer as her body twitches and flails. The pain is exquisite—like being bitten by a million red ants all at once. Pinned beneath the bubbles, a new heat pulsates through her, and Bambi stares at the water, dimly surprised it isn't running red with her blood. Muscles spasming, she gasps, her foot hitting the metal, cylindrical item that doesn't belong.

The item that's killing her.

It doesn't even take a minute. Bambi's body—the one she'd so carefully pruned, exfoliated, and manipulated over the years—gives one last violent shudder, and her eyes stay open, staring sightlessly at the cathedral ceiling.

The tub jets drown out the sound of her killer's footsteps as they retreat into the master closet. Silly Bambi—she never bothered to latch the double window at the far wall, and most anyone could scale the trellis. Planning this one wasn't difficult.

The killer smiles as they hook their leg over the window ledge, allowing one last glance at the plug leading to the curling iron at the bottom of Bambi's tub. It had been procured for three dollars at Goodwill. Not even a name brand, it lacked all the safety elements and features of Bambi's own four-hundred-dollar curling iron.

And Bambi will be caught dead with it.

Transcript of WAB-TV Atlanta

Aired November 17

[6:35:11] MIRANDA ALBERS, WAB-TV CORRESPONDENT: Hello, I'm Miranda Albers, coming at you from the once-peaceful neighborhood of Oleander Court, where the community is still rocking from the untimely and grisly death of bambi Holiday, a former Miss Fulton County and the beloved wife of the heir and board member of the Atlanta Beans Coffee Company, Mr. Marvin Holiday, Jr.

Just last night, Mr. Holiday found his young wife's body in the bathtub of their beautiful home in Alpharetta, Georgia, the open window in the walk-in closet creating a chill in the air and a clue as to the killer's way in.

Police are baffled by this latest in a series of murders which also claimed the lives of Pam Muenster, president of the Homeowners Association and popular neighborhood socialite; and Beverly Grant, active member of the Lutheran Community Church. On Halloween night, Mrs. Muenster was discovered crumpled at the bottom of her staircase, and Mrs. Grant was found poisoned.

Officer Moskowitz, I understand you're in charge of the investigation into these grisly crimes. Tell me, do the police have any leads?

OFFICER JOHN MOSKOWITZ: Well, there are still a number of angles we're exploring. As this is an active case, I can't say too much without compromising the investigation.

MIRANDA ALBERS: Can you tell me if an arrest is on the horizon?

OFFICER JOHN MOSKOWITZ: [*Long pause*] It doesn't look like we're quite there yet.

MIRANDA ALBERS: Do you have any message for the other residents of Oleander Court? Ones who fear they may be next?

OFFICER JOHN MOSKOWITZ: Nothing that isn't obvious, but bears repeating. Avoid being alone. Be aware of your surroundings. Keep your home secure—window latches, door locks. If you don't have one, invest in a security system and use it. In Mrs. Holiday's case, her Ring system for the back porch was never set up. It could have saved her life.

MIRANDA ALBERS: Simple yet effective advice. Thank you, Officer Moskowitz. Now, let's cut to the reaction of some of the neighborhood residents of Oleander Court. Tell me, Mrs. Beecham, were you close to Bambi Holiday?

HELEN BEECHAM: She lived next to me for eight years— [CUTAWAY]

MIRANDA ALBERS: Mrs. Womack, you were on the Homeowners Association Board with Pam Muenster, correct?

BRANDY WOMACK: Yes, and it's crazy to think she won't be at the next meeting! Pam basically *was* the HOA! No one cared as much as she did about this neighborhood. It's utterly tragic.

MIRANDA ALBERS: Mr. Everly, Beverly Grant was your next-door neighbor. Did you suspect anything was wrong on Halloween?

RICK EVERLY: We were actually out of town for the holiday. When we came back, it was like a real-life Halloween movie.

MIRANDA ALBERS: There you have it, folks. Horror can strike anywhere. Hopefully this terrible story has come to a close for the good people of Oleander Court, but who knows? The killer's still out there, and he or she may be plotting their next move.

You heard it first, from WAB-TV Atlanta. I'm Miranda Albers, and now back to the studio.

[END OF TRANSCRIPT]

[UNAIRED FOOTAGE]

HELEN BEECHAM: —but I couldn't tell you the color of her eyes. Avoided me like the plague. I suspect she thought old age was catching.

STACEY DENTON: That woman had so much plastic surgery, she could blink her lips. Oh, geez, that was mean. I didn't even say it. My husband did. But Bambi didn't have much of a personality, really. The only thing that sticks out to me is the plastic surgery.

MIRANDA ALBERS: Mrs. Willis, Beverly Grant was your next-door neighbor. Did you suspect anything was wrong on Halloween?

RAY WILLIS: [*Sighs*] I guess I have to say I have no comment. My wife would kill me if I shared what a bitch I thought she was. Oops, guess I said it anyway.

MIRANDA ALBERS: Mrs. Winslow, will Beverly Grant be missed in Oleander Court?

PAIGE WINSLOW: Define "missed."

MIRANDA ALBERS: I understand you worked for all three women to help save up for college. From your observation, did the victims have anything in common?

FAITH MARTIN: Um . . . honestly? They were all kind of awful.

MIRANDA ALBERS: Do you have any advice for any of the neighborhood residents?

FAITH MARTIN: Maybe, like, not be such awful people and someone might not try to kill you off?

MIRANDA ALBERS: Be serious.

FAITH MARTIN: I am serious.

[OFF AIR]

PAUL HANSCOMB: Good thing you weren't live.

MIRANDA ALBERS: You're telling me. Geez, how am I supposed to paint this as a tragedy if their own *neighbors* don't give a shit?

TRIPP

The house is spotless, the glossy chestnut furniture gleaming with lemon Pledge. Fresh-cut white roses are centered on the accent table against the front wall, the blooms doubled by the gilt-framed mirror behind the square vase.

Tripp straightens his tie in the glass, tapping on his iPhone to check the time. It's 6:59 PM.

"Sandy! He'll be here any second!"

"They're almost ready." Sandy is an excellent cook and baker. Her beef stroganoff really is quite spectacular, and she's aware that the most effective means of drawing out her husband's best mood is to pair it with tender broccoli and buttered rolls. This was the exact meal she'd prepared tonight, subtly glancing at Tripp when she thought he wasn't looking to study his expression as he ate.

At this moment, Tripp's wife is inspecting the cookies baking in the oven. They permeate the home with the cozy, inviting smell of sugar, reminding one of the nearing holiday season and associated fuzzy memories. As the oven door closes, the doorbell rings. Tripp goes to the foyer, pasting on the smile that has won him local elections, charmed juries prone to disliking large pharmaceutical and cigarette companies, and earned forgiveness for sending meals back in extravagant restaurants.

"Officer Moskowitz," he says warmly, greeting the man like an old friend. "Thanks for coming."

He hopes this visit is worth it. Is it possible? *Does* he know something that may put an end to this horror? Three of his neighbors—murdered. It's too terrible to contemplate.

"Lovely home," the officer says politely, allowing Tripp to lead him into the sitting room. It's a Pottery Barn dream—Sandy loves that garbage—and Officer Moskowitz takes a seat on a beige sofa next to a beige pillow accented by a beige throw.

"Thanks," Tripp says, glancing toward the kitchen. Sandy appears, heels clacking as she goes to slide a plate of star-shaped warm cookies onto the glass table. After greeting Officer Moskowitz, she makes a show of adjusting the plate. "Would you like anything to drink with this? Tea? Coffee?"

"Coffee, but only if it's easy. Don't go to any trouble."

"No trouble!" Sandy bobs her head. "It'll only take a minute."

"No. Really. Water's great. I won't be here long, anyway."

Tripp gives Sandy a look she knows well. "All I have to do is click the button," she gabbles. "Give me five minutes." She retreats into the kitchen, where a moment later Tripp hears her dragging the coffee pot out from under the kitchen counter. The Schulmans are tea drinkers.

Tripp watches as Officer Moskowitz takes a polite bite from a star cookie. "I could eat the whole plate," his guest says, patting his stomach, and Tripp commends himself on choosing the star cookie cutter. Non-denominational. Tripp doesn't want to serve Christmas cookies to a Jewish officer, now, does he?

"I bring these to city council meetings," Tripp says, and the officer bobs his head. Encouraged, Tripp continues: "I've been on the board for five years now. Public service is my passion."

"Is it now." The officer takes another bite of his cookie. "I understand you're an attorney, too. Read your verdict in the paper a few weeks ago."

Tripp doesn't have to rack his brain to know what he's talking about. He's referring to his big win for a diet pill company. The plaintiffs had alleged the pills caused birth defects. They'd walked away with nothing but legal costs. "Ah, yes." Tripp clears his throat. "But, you know, public service doesn't pay the bills."

"Right." Officer Moskowitz shifts on the couch. "Now, what can I do for you?"

Tripp had been vague when he'd talked to the officer earlier. He hadn't decided upon how involved—how visible—he'd wanted to be. "City Councilman Living on Murder Avenue," he could see splashed across the front page of the same *Alpharetta Times* that includes the announcements for garage sales and craft fairs. Now he regrets being cryptic. Lives are at stake.

The idea of glory is attractive, too. Who wouldn't want to be a hero? A real one, too, and not like that Jade Coleman. She's launched a website detailing what it's like to survive "Murder Avenue." It's a counterfeit undertaking considering *she hasn't been part of the neighborhood for years.* Jade left for Emory nearly a decade ago, and her parents, the actual owners of the Coleman house on Jasmine Lane and payers of the mortgage, have been in Tampa for at least six months now.

"Isn't this your neighborhood?" Tripp's assistant, Melinda, had asked Tripp that Monday, brandishing her iPhone. "Oleander Court, right?"

Tripp had been horrified to scroll down, to see familiar image after familiar image of the peaceful neighborhood he's called home for years. *It can happen anywhere,* was the tagline, with which Tripp disagreed. Places like Oleander Court were supposed to be shielded from crime. These happenings were an anomaly.

All the articles were linked to Jade's Instagram account, which revolves around promoting organic health products. The fraudster is sensationalizing, *sexyfying* this terrible crime spree to sell things. Disgusting.

"I saw something suspicious the night Bambi Holiday was killed," Tripp says now to Officer Moskowitz, leaning forward slightly, his hands clasped together. It's the way he delivers important information to a client. *Sit up and listen,* his body language says, and it works because his guest does sit up the slightest bit straighter.

"What did you see?" Officer Moskowitz glances at Sandy, who's hovering in the doorway. Tripp cocks his head to the right, indicating that she should sit, and she does, crossing her ankles and keeping her back straight like a girl being tested at charm school.

"I came home around 6:30 that night. And as I was turning onto our street, I witnessed Adelaide McKenzie and Bambi Holiday arguing."

"You're sure it was Adelaide McKenzie?"

"I'm sure. She's hard to mistake. She was outside her house—and she had a little girl with her."

"How do you know Mrs. McKenzie and Mrs. Holiday were arguing?"

"Posture. They were in each other's faces. And then Adelaide hit Bambi."

Officer Moskowitz pauses from scribbling in his notebook. "What do you mean, hit her?"

"I mean, she hauled off and hit her." Tripp mimes the slap he saw. "Sprang forward and socked it to her. It was just a glimpse, two seconds, as I was turning onto Jasmine Lane."

"Did you see what happened then?"

"No, once I turned, I couldn't see them anymore. But I'm sure about that slap." He glances sideways at Sandy. "Do you want to add anything, honey?" They've discussed this before, but Sandy flushes, uncomfortable with the rare moment of attention. She uncrosses and re-crosses her feet, fiddling with an earring.

"I saw something a few weeks ago," she says finally. Mouse-like, meek, and Tripp tries to ignore the ripple of annoyance that flickers through him. God forbid his wife should utter a single declarative sentence.

"It was a few weeks ago," she continues. "I was on the back patio, and I saw Ray Willis in Helen Beecham's back yard. Next door." She gestures vaguely.

"What was Ray Willis doing in Helen Beecham's back yard?"

"She was doing something with the outdoor equipment shed."

"Why did that stand out to you?"

"Because she was just standing there, with the door hanging wide open. Staring up at the Holiday house. At the back windows."

"The back windows?"

"You know. Where the killer broke in." Sandy shrugs, helplessly, like she's said something stupid rather than shared a potentially valuable clue. "It looked like she was staking out the place."

"Do you know if Ray Willis would have any reason to harm Bambi Holiday?"

Sandy shakes her head. "No. But what about for Adelaide? Ray Willis and Adelaide McKenzie are close. Maybe there was something between

Adelaide and Bambi all along, and Ray took care of her. And Ray and Beverly hated each other, so Adelaide returned the favor." She exhales, like espousing the theory has exhausted her.

"Right." Tripp nods. "Like in that movie, *Strangers on a Train*." In *Strangers on a Train*, two strangers plot to kill the other's nemesis. Eliminate the motive, eliminate suspicion.

"And the book by Patricia Highsmith," Officer Moskowitz says, and Tripp doesn't miss the indulgent tone. The officer sees them as dreamers, self-imagined sleuths. Where the police have failed, they'll solve their local mystery using the efforts of their superior intellect alone.

Sandy jumps up. "The coffee!" The house may as well be on fire, she sounds so upset.

Officer Moskowitz holds up a hand. "Appreciated, but really, not necessary." He rises. "I appreciate you telling me about this . . . altercation . . . between Mrs. McKenzie and Mrs. Holiday. I'll look into it." He adjusts his belt as he heads for the front door. "Thank you for your time tonight."

"Oh, absolutely," Tripp says, flashing his caps. "It's what a good citizen does, right?"

After the officer leaves, the smile drains from Tripp's face. "Fuck," he mutters, ignoring Sandy as he storms to the kitchen to pour himself a glass of Pinot Grigio, the liquid *glug-glug-glugging* in his haste. The smell of coffee hangs in the air. His wife follows silently, re-opening the cabinet as he closes it in order to remove her own glass. He carries the bottle into the sitting room—beige, beige, *beige*—and she trails behind with her empty glass.

"It'll be fine," Sandy offers as Tripp clunks the bottle onto the coffee table. Warily, half-heartedly—she knows how Tripp is when he gets in one of his moods.

Which is why she should know to stay away. "Shut up, Sandy," he snarls, downing the acidic liquid and pouring himself a new glass. Sandy's is still empty.

What if the culprit isn't Adelaide? What if this continues—with another murder, then another? Tripp can't live on *Murder Avenue*. What will his constituents think? Re-election time is fast approaching.

And what about home values? Even though he knew it wouldn't be reflected on the sites so quickly, the day the news covered Pam's and Beverly's double homicide, Tripp had gone on Redfin and Zillow. His home's value is still where it was a month ago. But before this had all gone down, Tripp had looked forward to upgrading his inground pool and pool house and watching the numbers climb a few hundred thousand dollars.

Every day—actually, numerous times a day—Tripp refreshes his home's listing on Redfin and Zillow. Same value, always. But what happens with another murder? When there's been time for the news of the three deaths to sink in, be factored in?

Sandy doesn't attempt any other pearls of wisdom. She pours her own glass of wine and flees upstairs. Probably the smartest move.

Tripp turns to look out the window. For a moment, he sees only his reflection—the veins in his neck bulging, the worry lines creasing his high forehead. The widow's peak that continues to creep into his hairline. Then his gaze focuses outward and he sees Helen, gently rocking in her porch swing as always, face turned toward the street with a peaceful look of contemplation.

Snorting, Tripp takes another sip of wine. Helen reminds him of one of those fuzzy, funny-looking targets set up to be knocked down at carnivals. She may as well be wearing a sign that says *come and get me*.

Still, Tripp hopes for Helen's safety. Tripp doesn't want another murder of a neighbor. He wants these crimes to stop, for Oleander Court to be safe once more. That was, of course, the reason he'd invited Officer Moskowitz into his home:

Tripp doesn't want the murders to drop his home value.

ADELAIDE

A delaide feels like she's on a reality show—the kind where people with nothing in common are forced together for the jollies of others. Or maybe that's on her mind since her agent recently called to offer her a place on that kind of show. When he'd rattled off the names of the other participants, the message was clear: all child stars, has-beens, and almost was-es.

"I ain't starvin' yet!" she'd snarled, hanging up on him. Though she had to give Lance credit. He'd called with a number of suggestions recently, boneheaded as they might be. At least he's trying.

Adelaide shifts on Soon-Li's couch, leaning to claim a shortbread from the coffee table. As she does, she checks her iPhone for the time. Oh, Lord, wasn't it 5:05 ten minutes ago?

Laura Noble is sitting next to Adelaide, staring and pretending she isn't. Adelaide would be worried about Laura sneaking a picture and putting it on Instagram—#afternoontea, #DaphneLives, #girltime—but she doubts Laura would dare. As Adelaide's mama would say, Laura's got stars in her eyes, and Adelaide half wants to turn to her and tell her that portraying a zombie slut does not entitle someone to adoration.

Helen and Soon-Li are on the opposite couch, the old woman merrily crocheting a scarf while she yammers on about the weather. Helen knows it's going to rain because her hip hurts, but it's a tradeoff to hear the droplets pelting against the window. Laura is the only one making any effort to appear interested, mustering "oh, no" and "you're right" and "uh-huh" in all the right places.

Ray talked Adelaide into this, and she isn't even here yet. Ray told Adelaide that Soon-Li wanted to invite a few people over to "revive" the neighborhood book club, adding pointedly that if Adelaide planned on staying in Oleander Court, she might as well try to make friends. It was a fair point, and Ray's heart's always in the right place, so here she is.

The doorbell rings and Soon-Li rises to get it. Ray's there, toting a cloth bag. She pulls out two bottles of Champagne. "Who's thirsty?" she asks, waving them like a prize before heading to the kitchen like it belongs to her.

In a few minutes, Adelaide feels much better with a glass in hand. She watches the Champagne bubbles fizzle in her mimosa, thinking of the cheap Boone's Farm wine she used to throw back in high school.

"Soon-Li, you're in charge," Ray says as she settles into the couch, pulling her feet up under her. "What's up?"

Soon-Li is sitting cross-legged, black hair shining, and Adelaide wonders if Soon-Li knows how pretty she is. If she even gives a hoot. Adelaide reckons Soon-Li's never had to use her looks to get anywhere. Ray told her some story about how when Soon-Li was thirteen, she'd built her own radio from scratch. With a brain like that, who cared about anything else?

"It's been a rough time for the neighborhood," Soon-Li says. "I thought it would be a nice way to take our minds off everything."

"The book you picked is perfect for that," Laura tells her. "Like literary cotton candy." She removes her copy from her handbag, and Adelaide wants to check for colored tabs since if Laura's anything, she's certainly an eager beaver. Like Kelly Weaver in seventh grade, who spent ages decorating buttons proclaiming her the best candidate for Student Council. Handing out candy to seal the deal.

"Did you like it?" Laura asks Adelaide, which probably means "did you *read* it?" Most people assume Adelaide is smart as bait because of how she looks. If they knew her S.A.T. score, they'd have themselves a heart attack. Her school counselor almost had. "Um," he'd said, staring at the test results and looking plumb confused, "this may open some doors." But Adelaide had her heart set on Hollywood. And besides. If college cost more than free, she couldn't afford it.

"Yeah, I read it," she tells Laura now. "But it was a while ago."

"I only got through two-thirds," Laura says, apologetically.

"I didn't read it at all," Helen says, cheerfully. She's probably thrilled to be out of the house. "I've been busy."

"With spying?" Ray asks. Her Champagne flute is already empty. "Don't think we don't see you, staring through the trellis from your porch swing. You're our neighborhood gargoyle."

"We may need a neighborhood gargoyle," Helen says, somber. "I can't begin to wrap my head around what's happened."

"Those poor women," Laura says, helping herself to a chip from a bowl on the coffee table. "And Bambi—so young."

Adelaide lifts her drink again, feeling the flush that heats her cheeks. She can't believe the woman she'd argued with had kicked the bucket that same night. That she'd *slapped* that woman—touched warm, live flesh that had turned cold not long afterwards.

Bambi deserved the slap, but she didn't deserve to cook to death in the bathtub. What a terrible, ugly way to go.

"Did anyone see anything unusual that night?" Soon-Li asks. She hasn't touched her own mimosa. "What about you, Helen?"

"I never went outside."

"Helen, you're *always* outside. Not even for a little while that night?"

Helen crunches into a chip, chews. "Not even for a little while."

"Well, that's bad timing," Ray observes, helping herself to the second bottle of Champagne. It opens with a satisfying *pop*, and she tops off Adelaide's drink when she extends it.

"Maybe it's good timing," Soon-Li says. "For someone."

"We all have security systems," Laura muses. "I don't understand how no one's seen *anything.*"

"Pam didn't have one," Ray tells her. "Just the ADT decoy sign in the yard."

"What about Bambi?" Soon-Li asks her.

"They only had Ring set up at the front door."

Adelaide's phone buzzes. She pulls it out of her purse, swiping up to read the text from William: *Can you come home? Police are here.*

Oh, biscuits. She should have come clean on the slap. That's probably the reason for the visit. And now they'll wonder why she didn't say anything up front.

Adelaide struggles to free herself from the low couch. "I'm real sorry, but I've gotta scoot," she tells the group. "Emergency at home."

Ray eyeballs her like she thinks she's full of beans, that the call's fake. But she holds her tongue. "Fine." She knocks back the rest of her mimosa. "As penance, you're hosting the next meeting."

At home, Adelaide finds Officer Moskowitz, the officer Ray has unflaggingly referred to as "the Liam Neeson cop" despite no resemblance between the two men whatsoever. He's in the living room with William, drinking coffee like he's there for a regular chit-chat.

"Hi, officer." Adelaide keeps her tone friendly, not too bright. "What can I do for you?"

"Sorry to tear you from your book club," he says, and Adelaide waves her hand. "It's fine. Mind if I fetch myself some coffee, too, though?"

In the kitchen, Adelaide wills her hands to stop shaking. She's only been arrested once before—for public indecency when she was a high school senior too proud to turn down a dare—but the memory still stings. She'd spent a night in county lockup and hadn't slept a wink. Ever since, Adelaide's stomach twists an extra turn at a man in uniform.

"I'm here to ask you a few questions about Bambi Holiday," Officer Moskowitz says after she's sitting, coffee in hand. "Is that all right with you?"

"Sure is." Uh-oh. Adelaide's Southern accent thickens when she's nervous or drunk. She's definitely nervous, *and* she'd downed those mimosas right quick. Adelaide takes a quick sip of her coffee, scalding her tongue.

"How well did you know Bambi Holiday?"

Adelaide takes a deep breath. *You're an actress,* she tells herself. She can handle this dinky little interview, especially if the role is herself.

"Not much at all. I saw her around the neighborhood. Both of us jogged."

"When you crossed paths, did you interact? Say hello, make conversation?"

"Not really. She wasn't real friendly. One of them girls with a stick up her butt."

"Stick up her butt?"

"You know, nose in the air, look forward and pretend she didn't see you. Take up the whole sidewalk so you have to run in the grass." The more candid Adelaide is, the more believable she'll come across. Like her mama's harped her whole life, *honesty's the best policy.*

"Did you ever interact with her? Speak with her?"

"Just once. The night she died. I'm sorry to say I reacted to an insult with a slap."

William stiffens next to her. "I'm sorry I didn't tell you, honey," she tells him, wishing she didn't have to say it in front of the officer. "I was embarrassed. Hittin' someone ain't exactly classy."

That wasn't the reason, though. Bambi's slur was a barb that tore right through Adelaide's hide. *Trailer trash.* She hadn't wanted William hearing it and her name in the same sentence. To get him thinking, considering—how did a girl from a trailer end up with someone like William? His former wife, Liddy, was a pediatrician before cancer raised its ugly little head. They were equals. Quickly, Adelaide recounts the incident, starting with the hip-check and ending with a paraphrased version of what was said. Omitting that nasty term from the narrative.

"Where did you go after the incident?" Officer Moskowitz asks. What he's really asking her for is her alibi.

"Home. Talked to my mama for about half an hour and then watched an episode of *Only Murders in the Building.*" Adelaide bites her lip. Not the best choice of show. "I've always loved Steve Martin," she adds.

"Personally, I find it's Martin Short who steals the show." Officer Moskowitz smiles, showing off nicotine-stained lower teeth, and Adelaide reminds herself to tread carefully. He isn't here to talk comic legends. He's here for information. Did he get what he needed? And what will he do with it?

After the door closes behind him, William waits a few beats before turning, hands on his hips. "Why didn't you tell me about this before?" he asks Adelaide. "Or the police? Why did you wait for it to come up?"

"I know, I know. I shoulda said something right away." Adelaide wanders back to the living room, folding herself into the middle corner of their L-shaped couch. "But like I said, I wasn't exactly proud of it."

William follows, sinking down next to her. "The timing of it, Adelaide." He runs his hand through his hair. "Right before . . . you know. I don't like it. I don't want them to have any reason to bother you. To suspect you. Which would be insane, but so is everything else that's happened around here lately."

Adelaide squeezes his hand. It's sweet that he's so concerned. "I hear you. But they can't really suspect me. Think about it. I slap the woman because she says something fresh, and I'm so upset I follow up with flat-out murder? And how would I pull that off? I've never even been in her house."

Hearing that cuckoo logic out loud helps Adelaide feel better, too. They can't *truly* suspect her, can they?

"I can't believe you slapped her," William muses, leaning closer. "You must have been in a mood."

"I was," Adelaide agrees. "That was one of the days Lance called." Her agent. "This time with the advice that if I just wait ten years, I can re-start my career playing 'the mother.'" She makes air quotes. "Great advice, Lance."

William gives her a lopsided grin. "Terrible advice. Why wait ten years to play a fake mother when you could play a real one right now?"

Adelaide pulls him to her so she doesn't have to respond. This isn't the first time he's raised the issue. William's almost forty, and he loves her. He wants a family.

William doesn't know that eight months ago, Adelaide threw away her birth control. That every month, when a certain week rolls around, she's on edge, waiting to see if she can finally schedule that appointment, to surprise William with the news he's been waiting for. She'll come up with a clever way to tell him, something with a baby theme.

Adelaide wants that baby, too. She does. It's one reason she's been trying so hard with Manuela. She needs to learn how to act around kids. To have patience, empathy. She knows she's doing a good job with Manuela, and it pleases her to see how effortless it is. Adelaide adores Manuela all on her own. Sometimes, when drawing in chalk with the girl, or baking with her, Adelaide has a flash of what it would be like to do such things with her own daughter.

It will be a daughter. Her head is filled with pink, pink, pink. Adelaide's begun to eye the spare room, contemplating the nursery.

It's been eight months, though. Eight months of waiting, of taking vitamins, of following her doctor's advice. Now she only has alcohol once a week.

As the months tick by, Adelaide worries. Her friends from high school got pregnant from looking at boys cross-eyed. Heck, Carly got pregnant when she'd lost her virginity, which was awful luck if it was true. Now she has four boys.

William's given Adelaide everything. He's provided love, shelter, comfort. He makes her feel secure just by looking at her right. He's taught her how to trust. He looks at her like he really sees her.

What good is Adelaide, if she can't give him this one thing in return?

LAURA

aura's counter is cluttered with spices, flour, and sugar, and her floor is gritty underfoot. She hasn't bothered to sweep. She'll only spill more later, so why bother?

On the television, *Bad Santa* is playing. Before that, it was *National Lampoon's Christmas Vacation*, and, before that, *A Christmas Story*. The Noble family watches the same movies every Christmas season, and there's comfort in the familiarity. Especially when there's a murderer loose in your own neighborhood, threatening to ruin the festivities.

The molasses and snickerdoodle cookies are probably cooled off enough. The chocolate chip ones have been on the kitchen table for an hour, though the other Nobles have been pecking away at them. Ben has helped himself to at least three, each time swooping in with a bored look on his face. As if he's not even aware he's taking a cookie, that his hand acts of its own volition.

"Mom, it's almost four," Nicole tells her as she appears in the kitchen, dropping her overnight bag by the fridge. She's wearing glittery purple eyeshadow, which Laura decides to ignore.

"Four's not late," Laura says. "Help me with the boxes." The day before, she'd purchased a stack of buildable pastry boxes from a party supplies store. The label claimed they were easy to assemble, which was not untrue. The issue was they *un*-assembled as soon as one put them together, the tabs popping out of their slots. Somewhere, the label maker was laughing.

"I can't help," Nicole tells her mother. "I told you. I have to be there at four."

Laura sneezes into her shoulder. Is she allergic to nutmeg? "Where?" Laura told Nicole days ago that on Saturday they were delivering home-made cookies to the neighbors. Today is Saturday. So why is Nicole now claiming she needs to be somewhere else?

"Remember, Maddy invited me. Ice skating, and then we're all spending the night at her house."

Laura shoves the cinnamon and cream of tartar back into the spice cabinet. "Who's 'we'?"

"I don't know." Nicole bypasses the cookies and takes a banana from the fruit stand. "Just a bunch of us from class. I told you," she says again as she starts to unpeel it.

Laura's sure Nicole had not. If she had, Laura would have adjusted her cookie delivery plans so the whole family would be present. "Can't you go later? This won't take long."

"They have a reservation," Nicole says. "Why can't we do it tomorrow?"

"Because the cookies are fresh-baked *today*." Laura's literally been slaving over a hot stove for eight hours. After that effort, the cookies are getting delivered *today*, dammit.

Pete wanders in from his office. He puts his hands on Nicole's shoulders. "Nicole, listen to your mother. She knows what she's talking about."

"You don't know what's going on," Nicole complains, tossing the banana peel and lifting her bag again.

"Nope. What's going on?" Pete asks as he moves to liberate a molasses cookie from the stovetop. Costco's toenails click on the hardwood as he comes into the kitchen, searching for scraps. He always gets scraps. The dog is getting fatter by the day.

"We're supposed to deliver the cookies as a family, but Nicole has more important plans." Laura tries to say it lightly, but she can't keep the hurt out of her voice. Nicole used to beg to tag along to the grocery store, to help with chores like unloading the dishwasher.

"They're not more important, Mom," Nicole says, patiently. "But I told them I'd go, and Maddy's mom has already paid for everyone."

Pete looks at Laura, and Laura knows she's lost. It's important that Nicole has friends, a social structure. "Okay, fine," she relents. "But will you take a box of cookies to remember me by?"

Nicole rolls her eyes. "I'll take a box of cookies to thank Maddy for having me," she says. "And tomorrow, we can watch that sappy Christmas movie you love so much."

There are a few options. Laura loves them all, even the Hallmark Channel ones. "Hrumph," she grumbles as she hears the front door open. "I suppose that's acceptable."

Pete grabs his keys from the wall hook. "Be back soon. And the remaining elves will help distribute."

Nicole and Pete leave as Faith comes into the kitchen, unwinding her scarf from around her neck. "You went all out," she tells Laura, who swallows against the lump in her throat.

She shouldn't be upset, she tells herself. Nicole is twelve, the age when kids start putting their friends first. But knowing that doesn't make it hurt less. What's next? No more Sunday brunch?

"Thanks," Laura says, shoving aside items in the pantry to fit the sugar and the flour. She sweeps the excess granules into the sink. "Here, help me with these boxes. I want them delivered by dinnertime."

"Delivered where?" Faith asks as she expertly folds the corners upwards, tucking the tabs into the designated slots. For Faith, they stay put.

"To the neighbors," Laura says. "Holiday cheer."

"Really? You're giving them all away? But didn't they take, like, forever to make?" Faith surveys the disaster of a kitchen.

"Kind of. But everyone's having such a tough time." Laura runs her hands under the faucet, scrubbing vigorously. Flour has lodged under her fingernails.

"Yeah, but you are, too. And you have two kids. And a job."

Laura shrugs. "So?"

"I dunno. You just don't always have to be the good person, I guess." Faith leans to pet Costco, who still hovers. Shoot, Laura had meant to make him dog cookies. She'd found a great recipe with only four ingredients. Leaning across the dirty dishes, she retrieves a Milk-Bone from his cookie jar before turning back to the job at hand.

"I'm not trying to be a good person. Just . . . neighborly, I guess." Laura uses a spatula to pry molasses cookies from the sheet, carefully depositing them into a box. They're still warm. "Since I thought of the cookie idea, I figured I'd carry it out. Even though Nicole jumped ship after promising she'd help with the delivery."

"It's nice, for sure. Like something my mom would do."

"Not by herself, I hope." Laura wrinkles her nose. "I'm overreacting. But lately Nicole's been acting more like a teenager and less like a kid and . . ." *And it breaks my heart.* She can't say that to Faith.

"You know, we're having a Christmas Eve dinner," Laura says instead. "Nothing special, but it'll be fun. Your mother's welcome to come. Your brother, too."

"I'll ask," Faith says. "We kind of have our own traditions."

"Like what?"

"My mom's really big into Christmas lights. We drive around staring at them. She knows all the good neighborhoods."

"Sounds nice."

"It's the most boring thing ever."

"Or that."

Faith's lips twist in a smile. "Hey. Don't worry about Nicole bailing on the cookies. She'll outgrow being . . . whatever. Like, with my mom's stupid Christmas lights? I totally complained about them until a few years ago, but then I got over it. My mom did stuff for me all the time. The least I could do was drive around with her a little bit." Faith pauses. "This year, I'll probably drive around for hours."

Laura steals a sidelong look at Faith. Faith is generally a closed book. She may share an anecdote now and then, but nothing too personal.

"I hope you're right about Nicole," Laura says carefully, and Faith shrugs. The moment is gone, but it was there.

The boxes have been filled with cookies and fastened closed. All that's left to do is load them into Ben's wagon to distribute them to the neighbors.

"Want me to get Ben?" Faith asks. "He might come down the stairs faster." In general, Ben cooperates more for Faith, likely because she is not an immediate family member and therefore not obligated to love him unconditionally.

Laura nods her assent, opening the kitchen drawer for her keys. As she rifles for them, a sheaf of papers falls from the drawer—a computer printout and a letter she thought she'd thrown away ages ago. It must have gotten wedged against the front of the drawer.

Laura doesn't have to open it to know what it says. Bearing the letterhead of the Oleander Court Homeowners Association on creamy stationery, it reads:

> Dear Laura and Peter Noble:
> I know we're all invested in ensuring high property values in our beautiful Oleander Court by keeping unsightly items from view. Towards that end, all garbage cans must be kept out of sight except for trash collection purposes. Please comply by the end of the month or the next notice will be accompanied by a one-hundred-dollar fine in accordance with the HOA bylaws. Thank you and have a blessed day!
> Sincerely,
> Pam Muenster
> HOA President

"What's the matter?" Faith says.

Laura unfolds it and hands it to her. The letter had arrived the day after Pam's body was discovered. When Laura had opened her mailbox to find it, it felt like a ghost had run its bony finger down her spine.

Also, she'd felt annoyed. She'd had no idea the trash cans were required to be kept in the garage. If that was the case, and Pam was offended, why not tell Laura directly? She saw her around the neighborhood, all the time. She could have saved a stamp and a piece of that pretty stationery.

Then Laura had felt bad. The woman was dead, after all.

"Oh, geez. Guess no one's getting these anymore, huh?"

Laura crumples it up, mustering a smile. "Not with Stacey Denton in charge." Stacey, the acting President of the HOA, is Pam's polar opposite. According to Ray, when she and Juliet had left their dead leaves piled up in the gutter, all she'd done was saunter over and inquire, "Ladies, you know what a rake is, right?"

Faith picks up the computer printout that had fallen out with the letter. "Thinking of going to France?"

"Somewhere like that," Laura says. "We've never been abroad as a family, so we're looking into it. Maybe for the summer."

"You should." Faith hands her the papers.

"You ever been abroad?" Laura asks, shoving them back in the drawer and shutting it.

"Nah. But I always promised my mother I'd go to Greece with her."

"Why Greece?"

"Not just Greece—Athens. She's read everything about it—the history, the architecture, the culture. Says it calls to her."

"That's lovely."

"Yeah, so our big plan was always to go the year I graduated college." Faith turns at the sound of the garage door rumbling. "Guess Pete's home. I'll get Ben."

The cookie delivery is finished in fifteen minutes. Half the neighbors don't even open their doors, so they leave the box on the doorstep. Laura tells herself it doesn't matter that they won't know who it's from, that she didn't expect *credit* for her good deed, but it's still somewhat of a letdown. A thank you is always appreciated.

At Ray's house, Juliet opens the door. She's so thin, Laura wonders if she'll even touch the cookies. She looks like the kind of person who forgets to eat.

"Where's Ray?" Laura asks, and Juliet lifts one shoulder. "In bed," she says. It's not even five. "Sick."

Laura had seen Ray walking the dogs earlier, chin set. She doesn't push the issue, though. "Well, tell her we hope she feels better."

In the side yard, Ray's greenhouse is dark and unlit. Next door, at Beverly's, a FOR SALE sign is staked in the front yard. Small, almost apologetic. Who would pay for a house where the previous owner was found dead in the kitchen?

As the group continues the home stretch—only a few more houses to go—something eats at Laura. A piece of information she'd shared with Officer Moskowitz, which maybe he's taken seriously. Everyone knows the police are looking at Ray.

After Pam's party, Laura had delivered Ray and Beverly their gift bags. She'd gone to Ray's first, where she'd asked to use the bathroom. Leaving Ray alone with Beverly's bag.

Before, Laura had thought the idea of Ray tampering with it was ridiculous. There simply wasn't enough time. And who has poison lying around?

Now, as the police seem no closer to solving the murders, Laura wonders if the notion's so crazy. As Laura had sat at the kitchen table, Ray had sorted through the items in her own bag. She would have known that Beverly's also contained a miniature bottle of wine. Then, Laura had excused herself for the bathroom. She'd been tipsy, taken longer than usual. Admired the uneven shelving on the walls, the couple's collection of ceramic figurines. Unique, just like Ray.

If she'd acted quickly, and had something to use, Ray absolutely could have poisoned Beverly's wine.

It wasn't just that. When Laura had set Beverly's bag down on Ray's kitchen table, she'd noticed the bottle sticking up from the left side, peeking up from the pink tissue paper nestled in the purple velvet bag.

When she'd picked up the bag to carry it next door, the bottle had been on the right.

She was sure of it. And she'd told Officer Moskowitz.

HELEN

Helen keeps forgetting to eat, to take care of herself. An entire day will go by before she realizes all she's consumed is the cup of coffee she'd swallowed in the morning before hurrying down the basement steps. Or that she's still wearing her pink nightgown and purple slippers. It's only when dusk arrives—and she realizes she'll soon see Pete during the route of his evening jog—that she hurries to heat up a can of Campbell's soup and to navigate in and out of the shower.

There are times when Helen steps back from her painting, a euphoric feeling spreading through her, and she thinks to herself, *My God, where have you been all of these years?* The paintbrush moves of its own accord, propelled by a creative spirit that had left Helen long ago.

It has returned.

On a weekday evening—Helen doesn't know which, she's lost track of days—Pete is huffing and puffing as he rounds the bend in the sidewalk. Helen has only recently positioned herself on the porch swing, and she feels like a naughty student sneaking into the back of the class and hoping the teacher assumes she's been there since the ring of the bell.

Pete raises his hand in greeting, his feet shuffling against the sidewalk. He's moving so slowly, he's barely moving at all, poor dear. "Didn't see you before," he says, and Helen moves the swing by pushing the floorboards, the ice clinking in her drink. "Refresh," she says, raising her glass.

In truth, it's the first drink Helen's had in days. She hasn't wanted to be impaired, to cloud her vision. Now she sips tea on her front porch, not Moscow Mules.

"It's chilly," Pete says as he joins her, his hair wet with sweat. He shivers, pulling a knit cap from his pocket. "You sure you're bundled up enough?" Everyone always assumes the old are freezing, and they're right. Helen is cocooned in three layers of blankets.

"This will help." Helen takes a sip of her drink. "But you'll need to make your own. I'm too comfortable."

Pete taps her on the shoulder as he goes inside. As the door slams, movement to the left catches her eye. The kitchen light is on in the Schulman house, and Tripp passes by the window—gesturing animatedly, angrily. Trailing behind is Sandy. Cowed, apologetic.

"Hmm." Helen keeps the glass to her lips, letting the liquid tease her before opening her mouth.

"Used the last of your lime," Pete says as he returns. "Hope you don't mind."

"That's what it's for." Helen clinks her drink against Pete's. "Cheers."

The garage door next door rattles, and a moment later Tripp's car backs from the space. Helen's aware of his lone bumper sticker—*St. Vincent's Church*. That's Tripp, always careful to let the world know what a wonderful Christian he is. Pete and Helen lift their hands in a wave, and Tripp waves back.

After Pete is gone, Helen washes the glasses in the sink. She hates seeing dirty dishes, even if only a few. After, she holds tightly to the banister as she makes her way down the stairs. Easy, easy. The drink she'd consumed had made her the slightest bit loopy. Particularly when combined with the one that came after it.

Helen reaches the uneven cement floor and goes to admire what she knows, already, will be her true masterpiece. She had never before attempted something so fearless, so daring.

The amusing thing is knowing this piece required neither fearlessness or daring. The images simply came to her. Images capturing the neighborhood, the terror sweeping its residents.

As Helen studies the work, her forehead creases. She takes another sip, her teeth biting the cold glass. Among the colorful, vivid swirls, a pattern of selection has emerged that any fool could see. If there's truth to this pattern, the killer isn't finished.

Not even close.

CONNER

Tracey and the kids are in Arizona! Conner's so thrilled, he finds himself doing one of those *Risky Business* moves after he thuds down the staircase—sliding across the floor in his socks, miming some air guitar.

He'd acted sad to see them go. "Are you sure?" he'd asked, trying his best to look abandoned. "I could arrange a sitter for the kids . . ." He'd trailed off, fully aware the option was a non-starter. Tracey wasn't going to depart for their planned Christmas in Arizona five days early—her sister had broken her ankle and could use the help—and leave the children in Conner's care. She knew what would happen. Conner would either park them in front of screens in lieu of interacting with them, or he'd hire a sitter who couldn't be trusted to give them the level of attention Tracey found necessary for their eventual achievement of self-actualization.

Yes, it made far more sense for the children to fly to Arizona with Tracey, and for Conner to follow as planned. Besides, Conner had that important client meeting coming up on Tuesday. He couldn't miss that.

Unless, of course, the meeting had been canceled because the client was hospitalized with pneumonia. Conner had nothing big on his plate through the end of the year.

Tracey didn't need to know that. She could fly the kids to Arizona and spend the week exploring every playground in the greater Scottsdale area with the kids. Crafting and baking when she wasn't busy pushing one kid on the swings or wiping the ass of another.

As Conner prowls through his home, breathing in the smell of Pine-Sol—Tracey's the type to clean the house *before* she leaves it—his five days of freedom stretch endlessly in front of him. Already, Conner's had the in-ground heated pool treated and ready, the hot tub switched on. A case of premium wine rests on the dining room table, next to the poinsettia Tracey had carped at him to water while she was gone. It's already looking thirsty, since he hasn't.

Jillian will be here in an hour and a half. Luckily, Tracey had opted to park her own car at the airport, so there will be plenty of room in the garage. Conner can't have the neighbors ringing the adultery alarm for Tracey. He's so close to the finish line, and from past experience he knows how easily, and how quickly, one may observe a transgression.

It had been over three years ago, right before Adelaide came into the picture for William. Conner had gone to the back yard to check the pool chemical levels and seen, right through the slats of the fence dividing his yard from William's, William's naked ass grinding into a woman reclined on a lounge chair. Feet tangled, passionate moans—the whole bit.

The sexual nature of the act had barely registered before William's head had moved and Conner identified the woman getting pounded. It was none other than Bambi Holiday. Just that day, Conner had stopped at her yard during a jog to discuss the merits of his new exercise machine with Marv. It looked like his wife was getting a different kind of exercise—heh, heh.

Before they could see him, Conner dropped to check the chlorine levels, then turned around and walked smartly back to his house. The microwave clock had read 3:17 when he'd gone out to the yard, and it was now only 3:20.

Two months later, Conner had observed Adelaide for the first time as she and William had drinks at his tiki bar by the pool. He'd never seen Bambi with William again.

Or had William simply been more careful?

Conner's face scrunches in concentration as he works a corkscrew into a bottle of cabernet sauvignon. Adelaide was a step up from Bambi, no doubt. But maybe William couldn't resist playing around. Just because he could, for the thrill.

Could Adelaide have found out? That little hellcat clearly has a temper—Conner once saw her hurl a cup at a wall. She'd been at the kitchen window, chewing her lower lip and frowning as she washed dishes, the phone wedged under her chin. Apparently, the conversation had disagreed with her.

Conner's iPhone lights up with a text. From "Charles Bentley," Jill's alter ego. Anyone who read their text exchanges would think they were work colleagues discussing due dates and the like. It was all code, of course. *Have it to you by 8:20,* the text reads.

As Conner splashes wine into a glass, he thinks of how Tracey reacted to Conner mentioning Bambi's affair with William. *It's none of our business.* A martyr, always.

Even two thousand miles away in Scottsdale, Tracey still pisses him off.

Conner fixes himself a salad from the many options available in the refrigerator. Thinking they had nearly a week left at home, Tracey had recently restocked. He layers beets, chickpeas, and artichokes on top of mixed greens, topping it off with a splash of balsamic. Taking it to the living room, he flicks on the television.

There's no one there to nag at him, to whine at him, to pull at him, to ask him to *see this, do this, open this.* He's all alone in the magnificent home he's earned by clinging to the corporate ladder and never letting go.

As Conner's eyes rake over the vaulted ceiling, the leather couch next to the fireplace, he feels a twinge of regret. It's true that the high-ceilinged condo in Midtown he and Jill have their eye on is sleek, sexy, and modern, but it also boasts a third of his current floor space. There's no back yard, and the pool on the fifteenth floor is shared by the other residents. Meanwhile, Tracey will have this entire house— the one paid for by his blood, sweat, and tears—to herself. "Equitable distribution," her lawyer will call it. Yeah, right.

Closing his eyes, Conner repositions himself on the couch and drapes the crook of his elbow over his eyes. He hasn't slept for crap lately— too much stress thinking about the finances, logistics, and Tracey's reproachful face—and he should be on his game when Jill arrives.

Conner awakens with a start. Shit, what time is it? He hadn't opened the garage for Jillian. He grabs his iPhone from the coffee table and relaxes. He barely had a catnap. Yet he feels *great.*

Discarding his salad bowl in the sink, Conner helps himself to another glass of wine. He's deeply relaxed, the edges of the world softened by the alcohol, and suddenly the concept of giving up the house doesn't bother him. No more bitching by Tracey for him to handle its various maladies, both substantive and who-gives-a-fuck. No pool to monitor, no yard to worry about, no getting yelled at to keep off the floors because Tracey had mopped or sponged or Swiffered yet again.

Conner extends his glass to the empty living area. "Cheers, house." He takes a sip, wandering to the glass sliding doors that lead to the pebbled patio.

As he slides them open, goosebumps prickle his arms. Steam rolls off the heated pool, the cloud-like atmosphere obscuring the patio furniture, the pool house, and trees lining the far side of his property in the dark. The castle-like playground hulks in the night, a refuge for ghouls and ghosts if there ever was one. Seeing it reminds Conner that he still hasn't fixed the seesaw seat, not that it matters.

Good thing I'm not a chick, Conner thinks to himself as he circles the pool in his Crocs. With this atmosphere, if Conner possessed a vagina and a pair of tits, he may as well have strapped a MURDER ME sign on his dumbass back. But luckily for Conner, the killer—if they're still out there and looking for business—obviously only has it out for women.

Maybe, when the family returns from vacation, Conner can persuade Tracey to take a night swim.

Cackling at his own joke, Conner leans to dip a toe into the water. As he does, he hears a rustling in the bushes lining the fence separating his property from the McKenzies'. He freezes, cocking his head.

"Meow."

It's that mangy cat both Adelaide and Tracey have been feeding—a cream-colored beast with unsettling green eyes and a chunk missing from its right ear. It goes to rub against Conner, and for a moment he contemplates grabbing it around its scrawny neck and holding it underwater. It wouldn't take long. But then he'd have to hear Tracey and the kids whine about where it had gone. "Custard," they called it.

"Scram," Conner says, pushing it away. Tracey usually keeps tuna for the cat on the patio, but Tracey's not here.

"Meow," the cat says again, its green eyes meeting Conner's, holding his gaze. Conner's pretty sure the word translates to "asshole" in Human.

"Fuck off," he says with a jerk of his hand, and the cat does, disappearing through the hole in the fence that serves as its egress between the two houses.

Conner rises, shaking droplets from his hand. The pool water might be too cold for swimming, but that's fine. He'd planned on spending the evening in the hot tub, anyway, which was out of view from any peeping neighbor and an excellent venue for screwing the soon-to-be new Mrs. Boyle. He's hard just thinking about the night that awaits him.

Conner turns, and he's caught by surprise when something solid connects with the side of his head. He stumbles for balance, his head feeling like it's exploding, his fingers going to where the object landed. There's something sticky there, and when he pulls his hand away, it's bright red. Blood.

He's struck again, and this time he manages to look at his assailant. "Why—?" he chokes, his gaze falling to the patio surface. The blood, the . . . matter. *What* is *that?* what's left of his brain inquires as his killer gently pushes against his chest. Conner's arms pinwheel uselessly, his eyes fixed on the murder weapon as his body splashes into the water, instantly clouding it red. It's the rotted seat to the seesaw, the one he'd neglected to fix for weeks despite his wife's incessant nagging.

Not getting to it had mattered after all.

RAY

lashing blue lights illuminate the popcorn texture of Ray's bedroom ceiling, the distant whoop of a siren intensifying. She shakes her wife awake. It's not even eight thirty, and already Juliet had passed out over her book. The long hours at work are getting to her.

"Oh, my God. Juliet. Something's happened. *Juliet!*"

Juliet's eyes widen when she sees the police lights. "What time is it?" She untangles herself from the bed, lightly stepping over a sleeping dog—Apollo always insists on sleeping on the rug on her side—and pulls on her robe, cinching it closed.

"Eight twenty." Ray's heart thuds—slowly and painfully—as Juliet fumbles for her boots. Through the gap in the curtains, at least five police cars and an ambulance are assembled at the end of the cul-de-sac.

Remembering her phone, Ray grabs it and texts Adelaide. Then she hits the call button, but it goes straight to voicemail. When did Adelaide's plane arrive from L.A.? Maybe it was delayed.

Shoving the phone in her pocket, Ray zips up her quilted jacket and jams her feet into her fur-lined slippers. "Come on," she says to Juliet, finally saying the words out loud: "What if it's Adelaide?"

"It's not Adelaide," Juliet says, placing her hand on Ray's forearm. Ray shakes her off. She doesn't want to be touched, or comforted.

"I couldn't take it," Ray says, her voice breaking as she looks at her phone again. Still no reply to her text. She hits the call button, and again it goes straight to voicemail.

"Sorry for trying to help," Juliet says icily, and Ray musters a smile. "I'm sorry. It's just—you know how I get."

"Yeah. I know how you get." Juliet pulls the door behind her and locks it, which is not something she would have done a few months ago. "Wow, everyone's out."

It appears the entire neighborhood had noticed the commotion at the end of the street. If they aren't at the scene itself, they're hurrying toward it. If one didn't know any better, considering the soft glow of Christmas lights illuminating the palatial homes, they'd think the focus was on a neighborhood Santa sighting or a holiday parade. Not the aftermath of what was surely a fourth grisly homicide.

A news van is stationed at the side of the road. Ray recognizes the Miranda woman who'd interviewed her after Bambi's untimely demise. She's testing her microphone and chatting with a burly cameraman.

As Ray and Juliet hurry down the sidewalk, a female voice rips through the air: "Ray!"

Ray's head snaps in that direction. "Adelaide?"

Adelaide pushes between Scott and Stacey Denton at the fringe of the crowd. "Ray! Did you—?" She cuts off as Ray catches her in a bearhug, lifting her off the ground.

"I thought—" Ray sputters. "I thought—" The relief is so great, she feels as if she's melting, her muscles quivering.

"It wasn't me," Adelaide says into Ray's ear as Juliet stands there, hands shoved into her robe pockets. "It was Conner."

"*Conner?*" Ray begins before she realizes she's being filmed. The burly cameraman had slithered his way over, and Ray turns to find herself staring into the black eye of his equipment, red recording light shining. "Don't you people have any shame?" she snaps. "A man is dead. We're all terrified. Leave us alone."

"Mrs. Willis," the reporter interjects, Christmas festive in a bright red peacoat. Her cheeks are pink. Probably more from excitement than the cold, the vulture. "Your concern for your friend is extremely touching. Tell me—why did you fear she was today's victim?"

Miranda Albers is good, Ray will give her that. She'd even remembered Ray's name. "Oh, I don't know—because of the ten police cars parked outside her house?" Up close, Ray now sees that Conner's house is the focus. The ambulance is parked right across from the front door, clearly waiting for the officials to complete their examination before carting away the deceased.

"Excuse us," Ray says, and Miranda pivots to accost Laura, the latest arrival to the scene. Her face is pasty, eyes huge. She'll be the perfect reaction shot.

"Are they sure he's dead?" Ray murmurs to Adelaide, who nods. "His mistress found him. I saw her."

"You *saw* her?"

Adelaide leans over so both Juliet and Ray can hear. "I was in the bathtub when I heard the sirens. And when I peeked through the window, there was some blond woman tearin' her hair out and makin' a fuss. And not in a sisterly kinda way."

"That's awful," Juliet murmurs. "Tracey loses her husband *and* finds out he was having an affair?"

Adelaide nods gravely. "I suppose so. Oh—!" she says as William appears with two steaming mugs of coffee. "Thanks, honey."

William looks as chipper and perfect as ever, his cheeks pink from the cold. "Would you ladies care for something?" he asks, and Ray shakes her head. "No, thanks. My stomach's in knots."

"I can't believe it was Conner," William says. "I talked to him just this afternoon. About . . . skiing, I don't know. Mundane stuff. And now he's gone."

"He's dead," Ray corrects. "Not gone. Dead."

Adelaide shoots her a quizzical *what's your problem?* look, but Ray ignores it. It bothers her that William—anyone—would sugarcoat the situation. Four people have been *murdered* in their neighborhood, more surely to follow.

In a few moments, the crowd gasps when a body on a stretcher is carried out through the fence door. It's completely shrouded in white cloth, leaving nothing and everything to the imagination. Two white-garbed medical personnel march it up the driveway and directly into the ambulance, where they slam the doors and drive away.

No siren. No need.

"I feel sick," Juliet says. "Is this really our neighborhood?"

Ray studies her. "Babe, you *look* sick." She brushes her hand against her forehead. "You're burning up! Let's get you home."

When they arrive, it feels like the middle of the night even though it's barely nine o'clock. "I'll get the thermometer," Ray says once she's guided Juliet upstairs. After she grabs it from the kitchen medicine cabinet, she comes back upstairs to find Juliet pacing their bedroom, her robe thrown across her rocking chair and nightgown sleeves pushed up. Definitely fever.

"I don't think I can stay here," Juliet says, her sinewy hands twisting together. "We should leave. Lisa said we could stay at her cabin in Asheville."

"You already asked her? Isn't that something we should discuss together?"

Juliet shrugs. "We were talking, that's all. I wasn't planning behind your back."

"It's Christmas, though."

"So? It's just us this year. We'll bring Christmas with us. And the dogs."

Ray drops onto the unmade bed, playing with the thermometer. "What about your work?"

"I believe these extenuating circumstances give me the right to work remotely."

"We can't stay away forever, hiding. Especially in some mountain cabin. You called it a closet last time. And the Wi-Fi's terrible."

"Then we'll go someplace else. God, Ray! There's an actual killer out there."

"Get in bed," Ray tells her. "You're sick. We'll discuss this tomorrow, I promise."

"No, we'll discuss it now." Juliet takes a deep breath. Her cheeks are mottled. "You were so worried about Adelaide tonight. *Terrified* to lose her. Ray, is there something going on there?" She can't even look her wife in the eye. The answer clearly terrifies her. Still, it takes Ray a moment to process what Juliet's asking.

"What? No! I love her dearly. As a *friend*."

Juliet rubs a hand over her face. "You wouldn't lie to me, would you?"

"God, no." Ray's never thought of Adelaide in that light. Maybe that's why Ray has never filtered what their friendship means to her. How important Adelaide's become. "I can't believe you'd even ask that," Ray says to Juliet, hating how her voice breaks. "You know me. I would never—"

Juliet crosses her arms. "You should let me take your temperature," Ray says, but Juliet shakes her head.

"Today when . . ." Juliet takes a deep breath. "When you found out Adelaide was fine, I had to wonder—would you have reacted the same way for me?"

Ray is dumbstruck. "You can't be serious."

There's a sour taste in the back of her throat. Juliet sees her as she truly feels—the dark, the empty. Ray hides nothing from Juliet, and while it's a testament to how she feels about her wife, she understands how it might seem.

How would Ray feel if Juliet gave the best of herself to someone else?

"Make it up to me," Juliet says softly. "Come to Asheville."

Ray almost says she will. She wants to give her wife—Juliet, who's given her everything, oftentimes receiving nothing in exchange—something. But that would be giving in to who she used to be. To Steven Raymond Pritchett. The cowardly, the confused.

She's not that person anymore. She's Ray Willis, and Ray Willis is a fighter, a doer. She doesn't run away from a killer on the loose.

"Give me time," she tells her wife, but Juliet shakes her head softly. "I've given you time."

Transcript of WAB-TV Atlanta

Aired December 22

[6:35:11] MIRANDA ALBERS, WAB-TV CORRESPONDENT: Hello, I'm Miranda Albers, again coming at you from Oleander Court, an affluent neighborhood in Alpharetta that has fallen victim to a string of murders seemingly aimed at the residents. The victim this time? Hedge fund manager and family man Conner Boyle, whose neighbors often saw him jogging around the neighborhood or out working in his yard. Mr. Denton, you say you knew Conner Boyle?

SCOTT DENTON: Yep, I saw him about once a day as he passed in front of my window. He was the reason my wife always told me to take better care of myself.

MIRANDA ALBERS: Can you think of anyone who might have targeted Mr. Boyle? Or any of the other victims, for that matter?

SCOTT DENTON: I can't imagine. It's murder. Whatever beef someone had with them, that's never justified.

MIRANDA ALBERS: What kind of "beef" do you mean?

SCOTT DENTON: I dunno. Don't listen to me. My wife always says I don't know what I'm talking about, anyway.

MIRANDA ALBERS: Mrs. Atkinson, you said your sons are good friends with Mr. Boyle's eldest son. Is that right?

KATIE ATKINSON: Right, they're always over at each other's houses. This is such a shame! Poor Tracey.

MIRANDA ALBERS: And Conner? Did you know him, too?

KATIE ATKINSON: Well . . . he was so busy. He worked so hard for his family.

MIRANDA ALBERS: The murders plaguing Oleander Court have left many residents fearing that they or their loved ones might be next. The following is emotional footage as Ray Willis realizes the victim was not Adelaide McKenzie—working name Adelaide Holt—Mrs. Willis's close friend and also the star of the recent streaming hit, *Zombie 101*:

[Camera side view of street, ADELAIDE MCKENZIE pushes through crowd]: Ray!

RAY WILLIS: Adelaide?

ADELAIDE MCKENZIE: [*Runs across the street*] Ray! Did you—? [*Ray catches her in bear hug, lifts her off the ground*]

RAY WILLIS: I thought. I thought— [*Turns around. Glares at screen*] A man is dead. We're all terrified. Leave us alone.

MIRANDA ALBERS: Like Mrs. Willis, most residents of Oleander Court have the same mindset: terror, confusion, and sadness at the loss of those they've lived next to for years . . .

WILLIAM MCKENZIE: [*Addressing someone off-camera*] I talked to him just this afternoon. About . . . skiing, I don't know. Mundane stuff. And now he's gone.

MIRANDA ALBERS: While the local police continue to work closely with Oleander Court residents, they appear no closer to solving this mystery. If there can be any silver lining in the death of Conner Boyle, it's that the killer may have left some clue to lead law enforcement in the right direction. This has gone on long enough.

[END OF TRANSCRIPT]

[UNAIRED]

MIRANDA ALBERS: Did you notice? No one seemed upset about the dead guy.

PAUL HANSCOMB (Cameraman): Could be trauma.

MIRANDA ALBERS: Whatever. I've seen people more upset over losing a water bottle.

PAUL HANSCOMB: Well, maybe he was an asshole. That crying chick in the cruiser? Not his wife.

MIRANDA ALBERS: Shit, are you serious? Why didn't you tell me?

PAUL HANSCOMB: Thought maybe the widow had enough to deal with.

MIRANDA ALBERS: [Pause] You're a good guy, Paul.

PAUL HANSCOMB: Yeah. Don't think that Conner was.

JADE

Jade Coleman's not sure how welcome she'll be at the neighborhood watch meeting at Ray Willis's house held three days after Christmas. Oleander Court hasn't been her home for years. Just because her parents still pay the property tax at 125 Jasmine Lane doesn't mean she's a resident. Jade's lived in Boston for the last five years. And if she's not a resident, the others will ask, what is she doing there?

Four murders. How could Oleander Court come back from that? The headlines across the country are already calling it "Murder Avenue."

Jade knows she hasn't helped its reputation. After Bambi Holiday's untimely demise, and during yet another sleepless night, Jade had made a pot of coffee and opened her laptop, a seed of an idea sprouting. *It can happen anywhere,* Jade used as the tagline on the new website she created, starting it off with a series of posts about the storied history of Oleander Court. The charmed lives of those who lived there. It wasn't a gated community, but it might as well have been. Exclusive, elite. Maybe not everyone would find it interesting, but it was interesting to Jade.

"Is that Jade Coleman?" Stacey Denton accosts her almost as soon as she walks in the door at Ray Willis's house, ushered in by a bear of a man she didn't recognize. "Look at you! You're so exotic!"

Jade had always liked Stacey. She was one of those people who was open, warm. Jade used to babysit her son Brandon back before he was a six-foot-four college linebacker. "Thanks, Stacey." Jade fingers the hoop earrings that dangle from her ears. Lately she's leaned into her

Colombian roots, in part because they complement her Instagram persona. Worldly, earthy. Zen-like.

Insomnia? Anxiety? Her two hundred thousand Instagram followers have no idea.

"Are your parents loving retirement?" Stacey asks, moving sideways so someone can pass. She's holding a red Solo cup, like this is any other party, "Stacey D." written on the side in black lettering.

"God, yes." Jade had stayed with them all last month at their new condo outside Tampa. "Dad's at the fish market every day, haggling. Badgering the locals."

Pat Coleman won't be retired for long. He can't be idle. When he'd announced that he was selling his restaurants and moving to Florida, everyone thought he was kidding. Jade estimates it won't be six months before he opens a new venture. While visiting in Tampa, she'd seen the gleam in his eyes when he presented dinner. Tilapia with a twist. Mussels. Soft-shell crab. As a chef, her father was always branching out. Or, as her mother put it, "showing off."

Stacey waves at someone on the other end of the room, and Jade turns to see Scott Denton gesturing to his wife. "It appears I'm needed," Stacey tells Jade.

Stacey can't leave her. Jade has no one else. "Let me follow you. I'll grab some food."

Ray's kitchen connects to the living room. Like every house in Oleander Court, the floorplan is one of open space, high ceilings. On the island dividing the living room from the kitchen, paper plates and napkins are stacked next to an array of vegetables, desserts, and bags of chips.

Bags of chips! Jade had totally forgotten. She only has until five tonight to post a reel on Instagram for Chickpea Heaven. It's four thirty now, which basically means it's now or never.

Jade needs a volunteer. But considering the seriousness of the gathering's purpose and the fact that no one has seen Jade in ages, she doubts anyone would appreciate the ask. Then a girl in a green zip-up sweater walks up to the food and grabs a paper plate. Perfect.

"Hey!" Jade moves closer, her voice low. "Would you mind helping me with something? It'll take thirty seconds, I promise."

The girl turns her head. "Sure. With what?"

"This might sound weird, but I need to post something on Instagram," Jade says, rummaging through her shoulder bag and pulling out a bright green package.

"Oh. Why?"

"I'm commissioned by different companies to market their products. And I'm on a deadline. Chickpea Bites from Chickpea Heaven." Jade waves the package. "Eleven grams of protein per serving. A healthy alternative to garbage like Doritos."

"I love Doritos."

"Well, did you know that Doritos are fried in oils and full of trans fat? People eat Doritos because they're not aware of healthy alternatives like Chickpea Heaven."

"No, people eat Doritos because they're awesome."

The girl's eyes shift. Jade's losing her. And by now, a few people are listening. Jade doesn't recognize them. She doesn't recognize almost anyone. When her mother forwarded her the HOA email about this meeting, she should have stayed home. If it wasn't Jade's invitation in the first place, shouldn't that have told her something?

She's about to let it go when the girl takes mercy on her. "Okay, fine. Tell me what to do."

"We have the perfect backdrop. A lot of snacks, none of them good for you." Jade nudges the vegetable tray so it's out of frame. "And you ignore all of them to grab Chickpea Bites." She places the bag in the middle of the selection, arranging it between a bag of Fritos and, of course, Doritos. "Ready." Picking up her phone, she zeroes in on the girl, who reaches to snap up the bag.

"Got it." Jade uploads the two-second video, which plays on repeat on her Instagram feed. Again and again, the hand chooses Chickpea Heaven over the other brands. #healthyeats #ChickPeaHeaven #livingwell #fightfat. Done.

"That's all?" asks the girl.

"Yeah. See?" Jade raises her phone to show her the post. "Thanks, I really appreciate it." She reaches to take the bag, but the girl holds it out of reach. "Since I endorsed it, shouldn't I at least try it?"

"Absolutely." Jade bites her lip as the girl pops open the bag and helps herself to the product. A chickpea barely touches her tongue before she spits it out on her plate.

"Gross! What *is* that?"

A mousy brown-haired woman has come up in the line behind the girl. "I'll try it."

"Why? It's like eating dried toenails."

"It can't be *that* bad," the woman says.

"Is that a reason to try something? That it's not *that* bad?" Wrinkling her nose, the girl extends the bag. "You'll regret it."

The woman takes a single chickpea. She spits it out, too.

"Oh, wow. That has a . . . *bite* to it, doesn't it?"

"The barbeque isn't for everyone," Jade tells her. *Or anyone.* "You could try the wasabi flavor." *Shouldn't.*

"No, thank you." The woman smiles at Jade. "You know, I don't recognize you. And I thought I knew everyone in the neighborhood by now."

"I'm Jade. Jade Coleman," Jade replies, and the woman cocks her head.

"From next door! I'm Laura Noble. We moved into the Garlands' house last July."

"Oh, yeah. My mother told me when it sold." It had only taken a week. It wasn't long ago that Oleander Court was the hottest real estate in Alpharetta.

"This is Faith," Laura says, nudging the girl. "She helps out around our house. Around the neighborhood, too."

"Not so much recently." The girl—Faith—opens and closes her mouth like a fish. "Ugh. Will that taste ever go away?"

According to the market research, no. "Absolutely." Jade reaches into her shoulder bag. "And to help wash it down, I have this new acai berry drink that—" she begins, but the girl interrupts her mid-sentence.

"Nope. I want Coke. Chemical-filled, dyed, toxic Coke. And gum. The kind with artificial colors and, like, fructose corn syrup." Faith roots in her jacket pocket, but all she pulls out is a folded envelope. She tosses it into the recycling bin without looking at it before digging farther. "Yay, gum," she says as she pulls out a crinkled package. "Seriously," she tells Jade as she unwraps a piece. "That was like the worst thing I've ever had. Ever."

"We're starting!" Ray Willis calls from the living room, and Jade gravitates in that direction with the rest of the crowd. She feels like apologizing to her test subjects—Faith and Laura—but maybe it's best to play it cool. To act like she doesn't know that the product she's promoting does, in fact, taste exactly like dried toenails.

Standing at her fireplace, hands on her hips, Ray is a formidable force. Pretending to scratch her forehead with her phone, Jade snaps a picture of Ray. #toughasnails, she thinks. Then she notices an Asian woman staring at her. Jade hadn't been as surreptitious with the picture as she'd thought.

Jade deletes it. It's in poor taste. And the last thing she wants to do is immediately piss off the entirety of Oleander Court by posting pictures of a supposedly closed meeting.

"Everyone knows Officer Moskowitz by now," Ray says to the group. "He's here to tell you about our neighborhood watch."

The man who had opened the door for Jade edges closer to Ray. His eyes scan the room, landing only briefly on Jade but searing right through her. "The police will have someone stationed in the neighborhood 24/7 from now on," he says. "And we're relying on all of you to report anything unusual. Anything at all. We're also strongly recommending that each house have a security system installed at any point of entry."

The Colemans don't have a security system. Maybe coming back here, to what Jade herself has called "Murder Avenue," was a horrible idea—the kind of poor judgment you'd expect from the first victim killed in a horror movie. The big-breasted blonde who calms her nerves at a bump in the night by taking a shower instead of locking the doors and calling a friend for safety in numbers.

"I do not understand," her mother had sputtered when Jade had told her about returning. "Your lease is up, you come to Florida. We pay for storage. You do not stay on Jasmine Lane!" Then she launched into the rapid-fire Spanish she always used when she was truly upset.

Jade didn't know how to explain her decision—at least not in a way to make it resonate with her mother. There are stories here, and Jade wants to find them. To tell them in her own way. To be brave in a way she hadn't been at twenty-two. She'd been a coward, and, as a result, six years later she's still trying to find herself. To understand what would make her happy.

She could also never tell her mother *she's* the reason Jade's been so lost. Her mother would understand that even less.

When Ray and the officer have finished their spiel, Jade is one of the first out the door. As she walks home, reveling in the light jacket weather of an Alpharetta December (in Boston, Jade would be frozen in winter gear), she scrolls through her Instagram feed, wondering if it's possible for her to go without her phone for longer than five minutes. Even during a discussion about murder, she couldn't resist peeking at her Instagram. Her post of the girl has nearly a thousand "likes" already. Jade's done her job for Chickpea Heaven.

Jade unlocks the door and double-bolts it behind her. Her stomach, which hasn't been fed since lunch, audibly grumbles. Flipping on the light as she trails through the foyer, Jade makes a beeline for her walk-in pantry.

As the door opens and she examines the contents of the five shelves on all three sides, she sighs happily. The pantry is stocked with enough sweets and treats to satisfy a high school football team: chips, chocolate bars, gummies, licorice, and soda galore. Jade pops open a warm Sprite and grabs a bag of her favorite snack—Doritos. Her mouth waters just thinking about the fine orange powder which she considers one of the world's most marvelous creations.

On Instagram, Jade may be Miss Granola, fooling the masses into buying "snacks" that do, indeed, taste like dried toenails. It's a part she plays, an image she creates to lucrative results. In the privacy of her pantry, however, Jade can eat whatever she wants. Processed, gluten-filled, synthetic, corn syrup—anything.

If it doesn't get posted, it never happened.

SOON-LI

Soon-Li's mother taught her to be thrifty. Growing up in Philadelphia, the two spent every weekend morning—those when Soon-Li wasn't engaged in an academic extracurricular activity—wandering the streets and picking up aluminum cans for recycling. Her mother let her keep the money they earned. Marie-Li also bought everything off-brand, and she regularly checked the cans in her pantry to make sure they weren't on the edge of expiring. "Waste not, want not," she'd said time and again—and, indeed, the family never did either.

Being "thrifty," however, did not equate to dumpster diving. Soon-Li and her mother never went through other people's trash, even when it was on the curb and something good was right on top. There was a line.

Now, as Soon-Li skulks down the street of her neighborhood, her breath coming out in puffs in the early morning air, she finds herself thinking of her mother. She's been gone for five years, and Soon-Li misses her. With every milestone in her business, every birthday for Lila, Soon-Li wishes she was there. Soon-Li would have none of her blessings without her mother pushing her along, encouraging her. Having an Asian mother came with its drawbacks—the stereotypes were true—but Soon-Li always knew how fiercely proud her mother was of her. Marie-Li never accepted less than Soon-Li's best from the truest of intentions.

The neighborhood is eerily still, the sky gray, with not a whisper of wind to stir the trees. At the end of each driveway, the residents have pushed their trash cans—blue for recycling, brown for regular discards—to be hefted up, the contents compressed and swallowed by the garbage truck. Soon-Li moves her wool scarf away from her face as she comes to the end of the Willis driveway, glancing toward the house. Ray has Ring, and Soon-Li knows the camera view stretches all the way to the end of the driveway. Ray told her.

As Soon-Li studies the cans in front of her, she remembers the time she and her mother had found a doll in a trash can. It appeared perfect, and Soon-Li had reached for it. Marie-Li smacked her hand away: "Bah! You don't know what kind of germs!"

Soon-Li flips open the lid to Ray's recycling, lifting out bags until she spies the one filled with empty cans and red Solo cups. She grabs it, flips the lid closed again, and hustles back down the street to her home, where she presses the button on her car keys to unlock her trunk. She flings the bag inside, no longer worried about being spotted as the trunk slowly closes.

As Soon-Li heads into her home, she checks the time. It's not even six o'clock, far too early to make the delivery she's planned.

This was all Ray's idea. Ray had turned up on her stoop the day before her neighborhood watch meeting. "You're going, right?" she'd asked Soon-Li, her hands thrust deep into the pockets of her UGA hoodie. It made her look oddly childish despite her large frame.

"Absolutely," Soon-Li said, ushering her inside. She was making pumpkin cookies—Lila's favorite, an apology for subjecting her to the school holiday musical recital where it was confirmed that Lila, indeed, was still terrible on the violin. "Neighborhood watch. That's very . . . neighborly of you."

"You can't tell I'm full of shit?"

"What do you mean?" Soon-Li asked, sliding the last of the cookies into the oven.

"We don't need a neighborhood watch. Everyone's spying on everyone anyway. And why wouldn't they be? Four murders, for God's sake."

"Then what are we doing coming to your house?"

Ray glanced up Soon-Li's stairs. "Is Tran home?"

"No, he's playing golf," Soon-Li said, then laughed. "Or trying to." Tran had been thrilled at the invite from the programmers with his company, blowing wads of money on new equipment. It would probably be as good an investment as his wife's elliptical machine.

"What do they always say about criminals?" Ray asked.

"I don't know, what?"

"They sniff around the crime scene, assessing what the police know. Showing up for the funeral, making casual conversations with witnesses to figure out what they saw. Don't you think they'd come to a neighborhood watch meeting, too?"

Soon-Li pursed her lips. "Would they be that stupid?"

"It's not stupid. They have a cover. Their community is dangerous. Why wouldn't they participate in a neighborhood watch?"

"So, what's your plan? Check to see who's acting shifty?"

Ray shook her head. "The police say they haven't found any fingerprints. That's a crock. You know they're sitting on fingerprints, but they can't do anything with them until they have probable cause to arrest someone. They can't just go around requiring people to submit to fingerprinting. And if no one in the neighborhood has a criminal record, their fingerprints on file, there's nothing to match them to. Here's what we're doing—"

"What *we're* doing?"

"Yes, *we're*. You and I. Soon-Li, don't you think I know what you're doing with that 'Hey, let's re-start the old book club' thing? 'Oh, and while you're all here, why don't you all tell me anything shady you've seen going on in the neighborhood lately?'"

Soon-Li had felt her face redden. "I don't know what you're talking about."

"Yes, you do. You're completely transparent. Why would *you* start a social club?"

Ray said it matter-of-factly, and Soon-Li had remembered the day she'd first talked to Ray. Soon-Li had been unloading groceries from her car, and as Ray was passing during a walk with her dogs, the bottom of a paper bag had burst open and a jar of pasta sauce smashed on the ground, spraying orange sauce all over Soon-Li's favorite sandals. Ray had stopped, commanding her dogs to stay while she helped Soon-Li carry her items into the kitchen.

"If you need pasta sauce, I have extra," she'd offered as she surveyed the array of herbs and pasta Soon-Li had purchased. Italian was clearly on the menu for dinner.

"It's fine. I have others in the pantry," Soon-Li had replied, and Ray stared at her. Then she'd thrown her head back and laughed. "Genius!"

"Why are you laughing?" Soon-Li had asked guardedly, and Ray snorted. "Because I've talked to Pam. And I understand *you* don't have to. Faking a language barrier to get out of talking to her. Wish I'd thought of that." She snorts again. "*No comprendo, lady.*"

"It was an accident," Soon-Li protested. She truly hadn't meant to trick Pam. When Pam had rung the bell those months ago, all Soon-Li had been trying to do was finish a sandwich. But then she'd seen how Pam's eyes had slightly widened, reflecting misguided understanding as Soon-Li tried to swallow. "We are glad you are here," Pam said loudly, carefully. "We hope you enjoy the neighborhood." Later, she went to work spreading the rumor that the Jungs were English-challenged.

What was Soon-Li supposed to do? Talk to as many neighbors as possible to prove her language skills?

The encounter with Pam had reminded Soon-Li of an unpleasant memory from elementary school. It was one of those moments that, while she hadn't realized it at the time, Soon-Li now understands was formative.

It was during a bake sale, one of Marie-Li's many efforts to bond with the other school mothers. "Did you hear about that Vietnamese girl?" Soon-Li and Marie-Li had overheard one mother saying to another. "She's taking college courses." Marie-Li had beamed with pride, but then the other mother responded: "I don't understand how. Her mother's not exactly the brightest lightbulb."

Soon-Li saw the realization dawn on her mother's face. Her smiling, her friendliness, her *niceness*—it was all for nothing.

Marie-Li stopped trying. She didn't need to anymore, anyway. Soon-Li was already in the most advanced classes, was the top student— the top everything. That was exactly what Marie-Li had wanted for her, so who cared what the other mothers thought?

Soon-Li had never been prouder of her mother. Marie-Li hadn't given up. She'd realized the other mothers weren't worth the effort. Soon-Li had never articulated this to her mother—especially as she was too young to truly process the insight—but something had shifted. Never again, when her mother spoke to her in Korean at school, did Soon-Li respond in English.

Pam was just like those other mothers, the ones not worth Marie-Li's time. So, let her think Soon-Li was beneath her. Soon-Li knew the score.

"See, under criminal evidentiary rules," Ray continued now, "police can't take fingerprints without consent or without properly arresting someone first. But they can use fingerprints from items *donated* from a private party. Doesn't matter how they got them. Not their problem.

"So, during this meeting, I suppose I'll be expected to serve refreshments," Ray had continued, raising her eyebrows. "Maybe I'll use red Solo cups. Have everyone write their name on theirs. Don't want to spread any germs."

Soon-Li had leaned against her counter, fiddling with the band of her watch. "Why do you need me?"

Ray shrugged. "I could turn the cups over myself, I guess. It'll be my trash, after all." She paused. "But—" She'd swallowed, rubbing her hand over her face. "I feel like I'm in this alone, you know?"

"In what alone?"

"The police have questioned me *six times*. Did you know that? And Juliet's in Asheville, and God knows when she'll be back."

"What about Adelaide?" Ray was much closer to Adelaide. Why wasn't she asking her for this favor?

"She's got her own shit to deal with." Ray had looked like she wanted to say more, but she'd stopped herself. "Look," she'd said. "Do you think I'm the murderer?"

The directness of the question took Soon-Li aback. "No," she'd said, realizing as she said it that it was true. Even though she had no evidence to back up her intuition.

"Well, the police seem to disagree. But if you show up with your bag of cups, saying you took it from the curb and asking them to at least *consider* it's not me, maybe they'll play a matching game."

"Am I allowed to take your trash, though?"

"It's at the curb, isn't it? Sounds like fair game to me." Ray's voice was strong, but her chin gave her away. It wobbled.

Ray needed her, and Ray has never been anything but kind. So now,

Soon-Li is standing under the harsh florescent lights of her kitchen, contemplating the plastic bag of recyclables in the trunk of her car and remembering her mother.

Is it possible? Could Ray be the killer? Soon-Li hates to even think it, but the reality is that the scant evidence does point to Ray. And Ray's right—the guilty tend to assert themselves into investigations, to try to throw the police off their scent. That could be exactly what Ray is doing here.

In Soon-Li's heart, Ray as the culprit doesn't feel right. Ray isn't capable of this, period. Still, she doesn't *know*. It's the not knowing that's eating at her, that's slowly driving her mad. Soon-Li is used to answers, a path to a solution. And she's used to having control over problem-solving.

She has no control over this.

TRIPP

Tripp's been in a foul mood all day. It was one of those days where nothing went right, beginning with waking up twenty minutes late because he'd inadvertently set the alarm on his phone for Thursday morning instead of Friday. Tripp is calmed by order, routine, and it irritated him to no end that his shower was cut from twelve minutes to six, that he had no time to linger over his tea while listening to exactly fifteen minutes of his current podcast.

Then, because of an accident on GA-400, he'd crawled—when he was able to move at all—to his office, only to find that his computer had crashed during the night and wasn't available for immediate use. Tripp had organized his physical files while Dan from IT fiddled with his computer, clicking and typing until he'd announced it was "all ready to go."

At the end of the day, another accident makes the drive home unpleasant as well. By the time Tripp pulls into Oleander Court, his hands ache from gripping the steering wheel and a headache throbs at his temples.

As Tripp coasts along his street, slowing at the speed bump, he notes Officer Moskowitz's squad car parked next to the Willis home. Again.

Tripp breathes out shakily, anger rising in his chest. He's a taxpayer. A city councilman. And yet he's forced to live in a neighborhood where there hasn't been a single arrest following a string of murders. What are the police doing with their time? Racking up speeding tickets so they can upgrade their facilities?

Meanwhile, while trapped in traffic on the interstate, Tripp had refreshed his home's listing on Zillow. His eyes bugged out of his head when he saw the new Zestimate. Down thirty thousand dollars. Finally, the notoriety of the neighborhood was costing him, literally.

Who knew what the value would be if the killer was never caught? That seemed likely, considering the lack of headway the police were making. Especially considering the information Tripp had recently procured from inside sources.

But, wait—what's going on? As his eyes flick toward the Willis house, the door opens and out comes Ray, flanked by Officer Moskowitz and that tall African-American officer. As he turns down his cul-de-sac, Tripp slows to watch them in the rearview mirror.

To his surprise—even though he's been waiting for a moment like it for months—Ray walks to the squad car and gets in the back. *Ray Willis is getting arrested.* Holy shit. Tripp jabs at the garage door opener, adrenaline pumping through his veins.

"Sandy!" he bellows as he bursts through the kitchen door. "Sandy!"

Sandy drifts in from the beige living room. "Dinner will be ready in fifteen minutes," she says, her voice low.

"I don't care about dinner," Tripp says. "Ray Willis got arrested!"

"Oh?" Sandy reacts as if Tripp had reported the weather. "Are you sure?"

"I saw her getting into a squad car."

"Wow. Well, that's something." Tripp waits for her to say something else—anything of substance, anything at all. As always, Sandy has nothing to contribute to the conversation.

"*That's something. That's something,*" he mimics her, glaring. "Nothing of your own to add?"

Sandy and Tripp had been college sweethearts—in fact, Tripp was Sandy's first boyfriend. Sandy had been a cheerful, affable girl then, an easy disposition considering the comfort provided by her family's inordinate wealth. Never going to set the world on fire with her own ambitions, but happy to support Tripp in his many accomplishments.

As a young law student who enjoyed being told he was brilliant, Tripp had found such a girl perfectly suited to him. Now, as a middle-aged man, she bores him, and has bored him for years.

Also, no one triggers his temper like Sandy. She barely has to do anything at all.

She knows that, too. "What is there to add?" she says nervously. "You're the one who saw it happen."

Tripp shakes his head, striding into the kitchen for a glass of wine. He stops, sniffing the air. "I thought we were having mushroom chicken for dinner."

"Oh. I didn't have mushrooms."

"Isn't there a Publix a mile away?"

Sandy pulls at her earlobe. "I made eggplant lasagna instead. You love that."

Tripp moves close to her. She flinches when he grabs her arms. Squeezing. She won't cry out. She never does. "I wanted chicken," he says softly, his grip tightening.

"I'm sorry." Her eyes are wet. "I'll make it tomorrow, I promise."

"Good girl." He releases her, and she rubs her arms. There may be bruises there tomorrow, but it's winter. No one will see. No one ever sees. Even in the summer, Sandy is prone to wearing long sleeves.

"So." She follows him into the kitchen, still trying. It grates on him. Sandy should quit while she's behind. "Ray Willis. I'm surprised, aren't you?"

"Why are you surprised?" Tripp asks, glancing at the timer on the microwave. As his wife had indicated, dinner will now be ready in twelve minutes. His stomach growls when he thinks of the layers of cheese and tender eggplant. In actuality, Tripp prefers eggplant lasagna to mushroom chicken. He also knows it takes much more effort to make.

But he'd told Sandy to make mushroom chicken.

"It seems too . . . obvious, doesn't it?" Sandy trips over the words, unsure of herself. "If she was going to do it, you wouldn't think she'd be so open about hating Beverly. And what did she have against Conner or Bambi? Other than them being—"

"Being what?" Tripp is distracted as he studies the labels of the bottles on the counter. They need a nice red to go with the lasagna.

Sandy shrugs. "Never mind. Nothing in particular."

Tripp rolls his eyes. It used to be cute that Sandy had no opinion but his own.

"I learned something else interesting about the case today," he says. The sharing isn't so much due to an urge to continue the conversation as it is the need to unload the information.

"What?"

"A friend of mine got a look at the case file," he says as he screws open an aged cab with his Rabbit corkscrew.

The "friend" was a law school associate at a prestigious criminal defense firm for white-collar defendants. In exchange for a referral, as Tripp's clients did admittedly sometimes border on criminal, the associate had obtained a photo of the case file notes from a cop who occasionally fed him information for a price.

Tripp has no qualms about his source. He's entitled to the intelligence as a concerned citizen and interested party. Bambi Holiday had been killed less than two hundred feet from where he and his wife were eating dinner that night. Pork chops, if his memory serves him.

"What did the case file say?" Sandy asks.

Tripp takes a while to answer her, pouring a stream of liquid into his glass and swishing it in a circular motion. He takes a sip, unimpressed with the experience.

"According to the file, the killer's also a thief. Beverly had a collection of Fabergé eggs that were worth a small fortune. When they did inventory for the insurance, one egg was missing."

"Why would someone take just one?"

"Maybe because it was the most valuable one. Over two hundred thousand dollars, and she had it just sitting on a shelf in her living room." The concept is horrifying to Tripp. Who keeps their most precious items unprotected?

"That's crazy."

"And with Pam, her sister looked through her jewelry. She swears a diamond necklace is missing. Said it had distinctive blue gems. When the cops talked to her ex-husband, he said he got it for almost fifty grand fifteen years ago and it was one of a kind. It's worth more now."

"Did the killer take anything from Conner or Bambi?"

"Not from Conner. It looks like the killer didn't go inside. And they can't tell with Bambi. Marv had no idea what she had in her closet."

Sandy bites her lip. "That doesn't tell us much." When Tripp looks at her sharply, she hastily amends, "It's interesting, of course. I only mean I don't see how that helps the police."

"Well, it's a good thing you're not a criminal investigator, isn't it?"

Tripp doesn't know what to make of the information either, though. Theft can be a motive, but that doesn't seem to be the case here. Especially because everyone in Oleander Court has something worth stealing.

"I'll get us a decent wine," Tripp says, brushing past his wife as he heads for the basement stairs. He'll return in fifteen minutes—enough time for Sandy to remove the lasagna from the oven and let it cool for a few minutes. Enough time for her to set the table and slice up the bread.

The stairs muffle Tripp's footsteps as he pads to the basement, heading for the narrow hallway off his movie room. It opens into a perpetually cold cellar lined with brick on all sides and a stone floor. A wine rack takes up the left wall, and Tripp studies the selection, finally choosing a bold red that will pair nicely with pasta.

When he's finished, Tripp reaches to pat the top of the door frame, fumbling for a small metal key. When he doesn't find it, he looks down. The damn thing is always falling off the narrow ledge, and sure enough, there it is on the brick. He'd stepped right on it without noticing.

With a sigh of anticipation, Tripp scrapes the metal piece off the floor and turns the lock in the door behind him. He clicks on the light, cradling the wine bottle as he scans the heirlooms inherited from his grandfather, a decorated war veteran. If the killer's motive was theft, Tripp should be high on his or her prospective victims list.

Paraphernalia and wartime posters in excellent condition cover the far wall. In a glass case on the left shelf, a Walther P38 pistol is displayed along with insignia and badges. It had taken a while for Tripp to get them just so.

At the center of the room, Tripp's grandfather's uniform, including its red armband and black tie and white dress shirt, hangs on a faceless dress mannequin. The matching hat rests atop. It looks like new because Tripp refurbished it himself.

A medal bearing the symbol of the territory Tripp's grandfather had represented is enclosed in a separate case, by far and away the most valuable of Tripp's pieces. Not that he'd ever sell it. It's worth far too much to Tripp, to his family. Tripp's eyes glance over it one last time as he closes the door behind him. At the sharply drawn corners of the symbol standing for a fallen empire.

The symbol is a swastika. Tripp's grandfather was a Nazi State Inspector. Almost a National Inspector, but the Third Reich had ended and Fritz Wendt had chosen the honorable death of suicide upon the demise of Adolf Hitler.

Tripp takes one last look at the memories of his grandfather, the war hero, and closes the door.

HELEN

"No, really. Not another one. Seriously." Pete grabs his stomach, shaking his head as Helen holds out the plate. "You're making me fat."

"Nothing wrong with a little padding," Helen says as she inserts a shortbread into her mouth. "It keeps you warm."

"A sound argument." Pete reaches for another one, as Helen knew he would. Pete has no willpower at all. Helen feels somewhat guilty taking advantage of that, especially considering that his visits always follow a run around the neighborhood. Her treats undo his efforts, so much so that his waistline would benefit if he avoided his nightly exercise routine altogether.

Still, Helen can't help herself. Helen adores Pete, adores sending cookies and cakes home with him and receiving a clean plate and repaired appliance or fixture in return. To be invited over for dinner on occasion, to have the Noble family fuss over her. Her relationship with them makes her feel loved, purposeful.

She's even grown close with Ben. He seems to find it amusing how little she knows about iPads and iPods and iBots and is trying to educate her. Pete bought her a Kindle as a Christmas gift, and it was Ben who showed Helen how to upload ten thousand books to that one little device.

Ten thousand! Imagine! Ten thousand books would more than fill an entire room. Helen knows this because she still uses her spare room for a library, the majority of books Edmund's. On a lonely day, Helen will take down *The World According to Garp* and turn to the pages stained by her late husband's fingers. Holding a well-worn, well-loved volume makes her forget he'll never again sit in his reading chair, glasses perched on his nose, feet crossed as he loses himself in the written word.

Pete checks his iPhone. "It's getting late. I told Nicole I'd help her with her science project." He stretches as he stands, picking up his mug. Pete is such a gentleman—always cleaning up after himself. "Thank you, as always."

After Pete goes, Helen sits on the porch for a moment longer. Next door, at Tripp's house, the kitchen light is on. Helen has been spying on the couple more lately, mostly because they give her a reason to look. Every single time Helen sees Tripp through the window, he's angry, gesturing. The movement catches her eye.

Finally, Helen rises, her knees creaking. Her right one has been bothering her more lately, but she's avoided going to the doctor. She's old; she doesn't need a doctor to tell her that. She gathers her empty plate and mug and shuffles into the house.

Once inside, Helen's heartbeat accelerates. She finds herself hurrying as she locks the door behind her, placing her few dishes near the sink. She'll get to them later. It's more important that she go downstairs. She's almost done with her project, which has bloomed and bled onto the canvas. Color fills every inch of the triptych.

What will she do with it once she's done? Perhaps nothing. She might cover it up, place it in storage to be found after she's passed on. Her daughters can decide what to do with it.

Sometimes, when Helen's imagination runs away with her, she imagines the painting selling for millions of dollars, articles in art journals analyzing the work, pontificating on meaning and technique. Solidifying her legacy.

More often, Helen considers the painting as just for her. Her children are comfortable. They don't need more money. And this one is *personal*, capturing so well how she feels about Jasmine Lane and its transformation into Oleander Court. She might not want to share it.

It's dark, too. Ugly. Her other paintings were never ugly. What does the darkness of this one say about her, her evolution from a young painter into an elderly one?

Helen treads down the stairs, careful on the uneven ground. Goodness, her knee hurts. She might make that appointment after all. At least the doctor would prescribe something.

She's all the way downstairs when she hears it. A creak, in the kitchen. This isn't unusual, as Helen's house is older and often creaks and cracks as the foundation settles, but it's still unnerving considering recent events. What if someone's inside the house?

Slowly, slowly, Helen creeps back up the stairs, avoiding those that creak and wincing every time she puts weight on her right knee. She tries not to breathe audibly, her stomach turning as she eases open the door at the top of the stairs, which is prone to closing on its own.

Nothing. Helen inspects every room, even getting down on her hands and knees to look under her bed. The windows are all closed, locked from the inside, and the double bolt on both doors—front and back—is securely fastened.

Helen breathes out. She'd feel foolish if she didn't have a solid reason to be frightened. With what's happened in the neighborhood, there's no such thing as being too cautious.

She almost pulls on her coat to make the short walk to Pete's house. "I'm frightened," she'd say, and they'd understand. They'd fix up the guest room for her, and she'd wake to the comforting sounds of a family making breakfast together. Nicole and Pete finishing up her science project, Ben asking Laura to help him find a lost school item. Togetherness. Safety.

It's a tempting thought, but it's fleeting. Helen wants, *needs* to finish the painting in her basement. Just today, she's likely spent ten hours in front of the canvas. Not even actively working for the most part, but looking. Contemplating. Is it truly nearly done? Yes, after just the smallest bit of shading in the right panel. Maybe not even that.

Ten hours standing. No wonder Helen's knees hurt so badly. She hasn't been on her feet so long, all day and every day, since she was much, much younger.

It's drafty in the house, and Helen pauses in the kitchen to microwave a mug of water for tea. Chamomile will soothe her nerves. As soon as she submerges the tea bag, she makes her way to the stairs again.

No one here, she tells herself, reminding herself of the bolted doors, the locked windows.

Holding tightly to the banister, Helen inches her way down. Goodness, that knee hurts. How did this flare-up happen so suddenly? Then again, that's the nature of a flare-up. She limps as she maneuvers downward, wincing from the effort. Five more stairs to go.

The door creaks open behind her, and she whips around. Tea sloshes over the cup's rim, burning her hand. "Ouch!" she cries, dropping it. The hot liquid splatters over her slippers as the cup shatters on the step below.

Helen strains to see the top of the stairs, but she slips first, grabbing for the banister but not gaining purchase. Down she goes, a terrible pain shooting up her entire leg as she lands hard on her left knee—her good knee, until now. She rolls down the stairs, crying as a shard of porcelain cuts into her. She bangs and bumps her way down until her left knee connects with the concrete with a sickening crack.

The pain is so awful that Helen gasps, for a moment thinking she'll be sick. Still, she struggles to pick herself up, to turn her head. Who's there? Are they coming?

The room is already fading away, the edges darkening and closing in. Before Helen can look behind her, the darkness takes her.

RAY

"**A**m I really only allowed one phone call?" Ray asks after she's been fingerprinted and booked at the police station, which was much less interesting than as represented in the *Police Academy* movies Ray had loved as a kid. Fluorescent lights, neutral colors. The entire experience is surreal.

She's about to be booked for *murder*.

At least the police hadn't insisted on handcuffs when they removed her from the neighborhood. Since they're old friends by now, Officer Moskowitz told Ray there was no need, as long as she came willingly.

"That's a Hollywood myth," Officer Kramer tells her now, about the phone call. "You can call whomever you want." He leads her to an unadorned, windowless office. A landline phone sits at the center of a desk with a wooden chair. "Help yourself."

Juliet's is the only phone number Ray knows by heart. *Please pick up, please pick up*, she chants silently, at the same time hoping she won't. She doesn't know how to tell her wife where she is even though they've both been waiting for this to happen for months.

"Babe?" Juliet asks when she answers, sounding breathless, as if she's run for the phone. Ray leans her elbows on the desk, looking down at her navy jumpsuit. Prison garb. It's surprisingly comfortable, like wearing pajamas. "Are you okay?" Even from hundreds of miles away, Juliet knows she's in trouble, and suddenly Ray misses her wife so much it feels like her heart's been carved out of her chest.

"Not really." Ray fastens her eyes on the file cabinet to avoid looking at Officer Kramer, who stands obtrusively in the doorway. "I've, ah—been arrested."

"*What?*"

"For murder." Ray's voice is flat. "Pam, Beverly, and Conner."

"Have you been read your rights?"

"Yes."

"*Do not* say anything until you have legal representation. I'll find someone. You hear me, Ray? *Do not say anything.*"

"Okay," Ray tries to say, but it comes out as air and she has to clear her throat and try again. "Okay."

"I can be there in four and a half hours. I just need to clean up the cabin. And I'll post your bail. What is it? Or are you being released on your own recognizance?"

"I don't know. They haven't told me anything. But it's three first-degree murder charges, Juliet. We're going to need bail, and it's going to be a lot."

Juliet inhales sharply, and Ray grips the phone, tears pricking her eyes. "I can't stay in jail, Juliet. You know that." She doesn't say it aloud because she doesn't want Officer Kramer to hear: *I can't be a transgender woman in the general population.*

Her blood runs cold. What if Georgia won't recognize her as a woman? What if the "general population" she joins is the male population?

"We can't get the money tonight," Juliet muses. "We have to go to a bond company, right? It's already after work hours."

The evening hour hadn't registered to Ray. Time had ceased to exist once she was informed she was under arrest for murder.

Murder. Murder. *Murder.* The ugly word keeps churning in Ray's head.

Officer Moskowitz isn't a buddy, after all. If he'd had the decency to arrest her in the morning, or even by early afternoon, she wouldn't be spending the night in jail.

"A lot of bail bondsmen work after hours," Juliet continues. "I think. But you have to show up personally to make arrangements?" The end of the sentence rises in a question. This situation is a first for them.

Ray blows out through her teeth. "You won't be in the area until midnight."

Juliet's silent for a moment. "I'll find someone else to post your bond."

That "someone else" will be Adelaide. Who else?

"I'm sorry."

"Don't be. I'll get on finding a lawyer."

"Can you call Faith? Maybe she could dog sit."

"Absolutely not." Juliet's tone is horrified. "I'm not asking a child to sit alone in an empty house on Murder Avenue."

Ray feels chastened. She should have thought of that. At the same time, Juliet's words and tone give her strength. They assure her that Juliet thinks the murderer is still on the loose, not soon to be safely locked away for the night. That Ray is innocent.

"I'll get you out of there. Sit tight and wait for the lawyer, whoever it might be. And *don't say anything.*"

After Ray hangs up, she pushes her shirtsleeves over her hands. It's cold in the office, possibly intentionally. "We'll post bail," she tells Officer Kramer, who nods.

"That can take a while," he says.

"What's 'a while'?"

"Officer Moskowitz will fill you in. He'll be back any moment."

"What happens now?"

"You wait."

"Where?"

"We have an open jail cell."

"Right."

"Unless you've changed your mind about not wanting to talk." He says it conversationally, as if he's asking if Ray's changed her mind about not wanting a glass of water or a cup of coffee during a social visit.

She shakes her head. "Nope. Looks like you'll have to show me to my accommodations."

"As you wish," he says, bizarrely bringing the movie *The Princess Bride* to Ray's mind. Isn't that what Westley always said to Princess Buttercup? *As you wish.*

Officer Kramer leads Ray down a labyrinth of hallways until they reach a series of rooms. Cells. They're all empty, reflecting the nonexistent crime rate in Alpharetta. They almost look like college single dormitory rooms, with a bed attached to the far wall and a desk bolted to the adjacent wall. The big distinction—other than the bars, of course—is the standalone toilet in the corner.

Officer Kramer slides the gate open and indicates for Ray to step inside. When she does, she tries not to jump at the harsh squeal of the metal tracks, the clicks as he secures both locks.

"He'll be with you in a minute," Officer Kramer says, his shoes echoing in the empty hall as he leaves her.

Ray surveys her surroundings. The toilet looks freezing, the bed pillow flat, and the blanket thin and scratchy. Ray also can't determine the purpose of the desk considering she has nothing to write with or read. Sitting gingerly in its chair, she drums her fingers on the table, singing softly to herself.

It will be all right. Juliet will find a lawyer to talk to her, to tell her what to expect. And Adelaide will come with the bail money. Although, now that Ray thinks about it, she's not sure how Adelaide will come with the bail money if she doesn't know how much it is. It's also after bank hours.

After what feels like an eternity, footsteps tap. Ray sits up straighter, smoothing her hair. She'll stay calm and collected. And, like Juliet advised, *not say anything.*

Officer Moskowitz is on the other side of the bars, his mouth turned up in a grimace. "Hi, Ray."

"Hi, officer." She stands, folding her arms in front of her. "My lawyer should be here soon. And my bail . . . how much is it?" She'll need another phone call so she can help Adelaide make arrangements. Or the attorney will take care of it, she supposes.

"Bail hasn't been set yet."

She stares at him. "If bail hasn't been set yet, how do I get out of here?"

"You won't. But you can talk to your attorney about that." Officer Moskowitz's pocket buzzes, and he extracts a cell phone. "Excuse me," he tells Ray, turning away. "Okay. Escort him down." He hangs up the phone and nods at Ray. "Your wife works fast. Your lawyer's here."

In minutes, a stout female officer with her hair pulled back approaches with a tiny silver-haired gentleman in tow. He's wearing a crisp blue button-down shirt and black dress pants, which make Ray more aware of her prison garb.

"Evening," he says curtly, with barely a glance at the cop holding Ray hostage. "Phillip Goldstein. Ray. Nice to meet you."

"Uh, thanks." *Who* is *this man?* she thinks, sizing him up and down. She'd figured Juliet would choose a woman, not this dapper fellow.

"May I have a moment with my client." Mr. Goldstein doesn't pose it as a question, and Officer Moskowitz nods his head. "I'll be back in ten minutes," he says as he unlocks the cell and draws it open.

"I'll tell you if we need more time." The man may be small in stature, but Ray likes the way he talks, how he calls the shots and handles himself in a way just short of being rude.

"Thanks for coming," Ray says once Officer Moskowitz's footsteps fade away. She plops onto the bed, wincing when it doesn't yield. It's hard plastic beneath the flimsy mattress.

"Juliet's a good person. I'm glad to help her out."

"How do you know her?" Ray asks, and he shakes his head like he's dismissing the small talk. "From volunteering with ATLA." The Association of Trial Lawyers of America. "I'm from Troutman, Bing, and Peabody," he says, naming one of the biggest and most expensive criminal defense firms in the Atlanta area. "I'm not saying I'll take your case, but I can at least get you through the initial proceedings. Is that agreeable to you?"

"Sure." Ray's palms are sweaty, and she wipes them on her navy pants. "Can you tell me what's going on? When can I pay bail and get out of here?"

Mr. Goldstein presses his lips together. "They haven't told you? In Georgia, bail for murder cases is only set by a superior court judge. They need to take you to Fulton County Superior Court for that."

"When can that happen?" Ray asks, her heart sinking.

"First you make your initial appearance before a magistrate judge here at the jail. They'll read your charges and ask if you have an attorney. But since a magistrate judge doesn't have the authority to set bail—not for murder—we file a request for a bail hearing before the superior court judge. I've been able to get bail hearings in four days."

"*Four days?*"

The lawyer nods, pressing his lips together. "That's for my typical type of client. Rooted members of the community charged with white-collar, non-violent felonies."

Ray drops her head into her hands. "Murder," she murmurs, tasting the word. "*Murder*." No superior court judge is hearing her case soon. She's been accused of three extremely violent crimes. They'll make her wait. "It could take as long as two weeks," Mr. Goldstein says through the roar in her ears.

She looks up. "Will I stay here the entire time?" She gestures to the cell. She'll go crazy with boredom and anxiety, but at least she's safe here.

A frown creases his forehead, and Ray imagines him with Juliet during a volunteer activity with their bar organization. Passing out folders of materials, joking. Ray knows so little about Juliet's professional life and what she does. She doesn't like to ask questions because she feels so badly about her own career.

Selfish, she thinks now. It's not all about her. Why shouldn't Juliet have pride in her success? God knows she's worked for it.

"I'm hoping so," he says. "It's that or you go into the general population."

It's exactly what she'd feared. She gulps. "Male or female?" she asks, and from his confounded expression she knows he doesn't know. She'll have to say it.

"I was born physically male," she tells him. "I legally changed my gender type after gender-affirming surgery. If they put me in with the regular jail population, it has to be female."

Goldstein doesn't react. "If you're legally recognized as female, you'd have the same rights as any female accused."

Ray closes her eyes. "Can you check?"

"I don't need to check." The softness in his voice makes her open her eyes again. "I have a sister like you. We've gone to the mat plenty of times before. Though not under these particular circumstances."

Great, so your sister's never been accused of murder. Ray bites back the sarcastic reply. She likes this man. He's a superhero with conservative clothes on the outside and rainbow tights and a pink leotard underneath. Now she understands why Juliet chose him.

Footsteps tap again, and this time Officer Moskowitz returns with Officer Kramer. "I know it's late, but considering counsel is present, we'd appreciate taking Ray's statement."

"Didn't you do that the six times you came to my house?" Ray asks. She's not trying to be smart; she genuinely wants to know. What else could there be to cover?

"In light of additional evidence we've obtained, we'd like to ask you a few more questions."

Additional evidence? What the fuck did that mean?

Mr. Goldstein glances at Ray. "For now, my client's invoking her fifth amendment privilege." Ray took only a handful of criminal procedure classes in law school, but she knows a defendant can refuse to make a single statement to the police, even up until trial. To stop herself from speaking, Ray bites her lip, deferring to the nice man who has shown up on no notice to defend her.

"That's your right," Officer Moskowitz says, checking his watch. Time actually matters to him because his life isn't the four corners of a jail cell. "But," he says, "while you sit here, maybe you could think on something for me?"

"What's that, officer?"

"If you have an accomplice—and we have reason to believe you do— think about what you're willing to share with us. Plea bargains can be very valuable in Georgia." Officer Moskowitz's Adam's apple twitches as he leans in toward the bars.

"Because, Mrs. Willis—Georgia has the death penalty."

LAURA

"What's the matter, babe?" Laura asks when she notices Pete in the doorway, his forehead creased. Her hand is halfway toward her Scrabble tiles, where she plans on *t-r-y-s-t* in her battle against Nicole. Not her best effort, but it's a double word score.

"That's the second night in a row," Pete says, sloughing off his knit hat and twisting it in his hands. "That's weird, right? Where could she be?"

Nicole casts her mother a dark look across the coffee table, and Laura's worry antenna perks up. "Helen? You didn't see her last night, either?"

"The porch light was off when I got there. I didn't tell you?"

Laura picks her brain. "I guess not." She'd had to run the kids to Target during the late evening—supplies for some school project for Ben. When she'd gotten in, Pete had been snoring in front of the television.

"Want me to go with you to check?" she asks now, feeling guilty that it's the last thing she wants to do. What if there's something awful to find?

"I'll go," Pete says, and Laura shakes her head. "Nope. Together." Then, "Oh, shoot. What about the kids?"

"Text Ray," Pete suggests. "She'll come over."

"Sure." Laura complies, but as she does, she realizes she hasn't heard from Ray in two days. Not even a reply text yesterday about taking a walk. After Laura hits "send," she calls Ray outright and gets her voicemail. "Huh. Maybe Soon-Li?"

"Do it."

In five minutes, Soon-Li is through the door, Lila in tow. "I brought my bracelet stuff!" Lila beams, brandishing an opaque plastic box. For Christmas, Lila was gifted with several bracelet-making sets consisting of brightly-colored threads and plastic lanyards. The girls have spent hours making matching jewelry. Friendship evidence.

"We'll be back," Laura says as she pulls on her coat, then wrinkles her nose. That's exactly what horror movie victims say when they leave, off to be hacked into tiny pieces.

"Text me," Soon-Li says, her eyes meeting Laura's. The fear that's already coursing through Laura's chest flares. Now she remembers walking Costco today and yesterday—seeing but not really seeing Helen's empty porch.

The air has a nip in it, a breeze scuttling the January leaves across the sidewalk. It reminds Laura of the dead leaves that had covered Pam's Miata in the days before her body was found. Was that really only months ago?

As they pass Jade's house, Laura squeezes Pete's hand. Laura's aware from Stacey Denton that Jade's parents have a lovely new condo in Tampa, one with a spare room kept for their only child. Jade also likely has her own place to stay. Yet she's come back to Oleander Court, where she's blogging and Instagramming about its recent tragedies. It makes no sense to Laura.

Others have been far less charitable in appraising Jade. "She took a picture of Ray," Soon-Li told Laura. "At the neighborhood watch meeting. We're all trying to figure out how to stay safe and catch the killer, and she's probably dreaming about a book deal. *My Life on Murder Avenue.*"

The porch light is on at the Schulman house. Pete purses his lips as he passes. "Ass."

"What?" Laura asks, surprised. The slight is unlike Pete.

"That guy. He's like a robot. 'Hey,' 'How are you,' 'Fine weather we're having,' etc. But if a neighbor needed something, he'd never lift a finger. Helen says he's never once helped her with anything."

"Ah." Of course this is about Helen. Pete is completely under the woman's spell, and she doesn't have to do anything at all.

"A different next-door neighbor would have noticed earlier that something was wrong. *If* something is wrong," he clarifies, his Adam's apple jerking.

They shuffle up Helen's sidewalk. It's dark, leaves concealing any bumps in the concrete. The sagging stairs are crumbling, clashing with the new wooden handrail Pete had installed. Laura's heart softens as she thinks of her husband sawing and hammering to make an old woman safer.

The porch is empty of life—no Helen on the swing, no empty tea cup or glass with melting ice. When Pete rings the doorbell, the house remains still.

Pete jabs at the doorbell three times before crossing the porch to reach for the wooden birdhouse hanging from a tree branch. Extracting the key hidden within, he returns to insert it in the lock. "Helen?" he calls as the door swings open. "Helen, are you in here?"

The house feels like a sauna. Sweat instantly pricks Laura's lower back. "The old gal doesn't like the cold, huh?" Laura asks as she shrugs out of her jacket, draping it over a love seat.

Pete grunts a response, his worried eyes taking in the dishes at the sink. "That's my mug," he says.

"Your mug?"

"She always gives me tea in the same Snoopy mug, that one right there. I'm the only one who uses it."

The words hang in the air. If Pete's mug is still sitting, dirty, at the sink, it means Helen hasn't washed dishes in the two days since Pete visited.

"Helen!" Pete moves through the house, flipping on lights and entering rooms far enough to scan for Helen. Laura trails behind, her stomach twisting, mouth dry. She both wants and doesn't want to find her. Doesn't want to see.

A faint light gleams from a door ajar at the end of the hall. Pete yanks the door open. "Helen!" he calls again, then glances down. "Helen! Oh, God!" Laura's stomach flips. He's pounding down stairs, barking over his shoulder: "Call 911! Now! Helen, can you hear me?"

With shaking hands, Laura unlocks her phone and obeys. "911, what is your emergency?" the operator chirps on the other end, sober and calmly reassuring.

"I'm not sure yet," Laura stammers as she comes to the door. She gasps as she catches sight of Helen at the bottom of rickety wooden stairs. Curled up on the floor, her face is gray. She looks like a toppled statue. Or—

Laura won't think of it. This isn't Beverly. This is Helen, and maybe it isn't too late. "My husband and I went to check on our friend we hadn't seen for a few days—she's older—and we found her at the bottom of the stairs. Maybe she fell?" *Or was pushed.*

"Okay," the operator says as if she's gotten a hundred calls like this before. "I need you to do something for me. Can you check for a pulse?" Pete's already doing so, his fingers against Helen's neck. Laura's stomach clenches when he frowns, adjusts his position.

"I don't think—" Laura begins, but then he hollers:

"I've got one!"

"She's alive," Laura breathes, tears pooling her eyes. "Oh, thank God."

After the operator takes Helen's address, promising to send an ambulance, Laura eases her way down the stairs. How did Helen manage these? They're narrow, bowing and sagging under her weight. They have the feel of something abandoned, unused.

And *why* did Helen use them? What did she need in the basement? It's cold and clammy, unfinished. The storage items look ancient.

As Laura reaches the bottom, Helen's eyes flutter open. They dart from Pete to Laura. "Erica," she rasps, and Laura's heart sinks. Doesn't she recognize them? "Call Erica, my daughter." Thank God. "My phone's in the bedroom."

"Be right back." Grateful for something to do, Laura races upstairs, her hand skimming the banister. She finds an ancient Samsung on the nightstand. There's no security. Laura goes to Helen's contacts and finds Erica as the only "E." She hits the call button, and a second later a pleasant voice greets her. "Hi, Mom."

"Um, it's not Helen. I'm Laura, a neighbor."

"Is everything okay?" The voice shifts to alarmed.

"Helen fell down the basement stairs, we think. Maybe some broken bones, but she knew who we were—my husband and me—and to ask for you. An ambulance is coming."

Erica sucks in her breath. *"Dammit*, Mom." There's rustling, a man's voice murmuring in the background. "I'll be there as soon as I can." She swears again. "The basement—what was she even doing in that dungeon? God, I'm so glad someone went looking for her. What if—?" Her voice is wobbly.

"My husband visits her about every day."

"Oh, you're *Pete's* wife," Erica says as she makes the connection. "Mom loves him." She makes a strangled sound. "Oh, that woman. Always says she doesn't need help. Doesn't accept any, so all I can do is worry. But now that she's broken, she has no choice but to come home with me. For *supervision*." Erica says it jokingly, but concern seeps into the words.

And love. Nicole would react the same for an older Laura. Dropping everything to care for her, insisting she stay with her. She'd know what to pack on her mother's behalf.

After the ambulance leaves, siren wailing, Laura and Pete wander into Helen's home again. "I'm just glad she's not dead," Pete says shortly, echoing Laura's thoughts. "I thought—"

Laura slips her hand into his. "I know."

"What the hell was she doing in the basement anyway?" Pete asks.

"Her daughter asked the same thing."

They exchange a glance. Without a word, they make their way down the hallway to the basement door, easing it open. The stairs creak as they descend, single file.

The hair on Laura's arms raises as the temperature drops. Hugging herself, she glances at the shelving crammed with indiscernible junk, the file cabinets pushed against the walls. Nothing about the basement is inviting.

Pete leads them around the hulking cabinet in the center of the room. He stops so suddenly that Laura almost runs into him. "Holy—" he begins, then falls silent.

The ground is draped in drop cloths spattered with paint. Bright colors, dark colors. Mostly dark. A canvas larger than the Nobles' television hangs on the far wall. Divided into three panels, the artwork is so busy and detailed that Laura has trouble taking it in. When her senses sharpen, the awesomeness and terribleness of it all hits her like a punch to the gut.

In the left panel, Helen has painted Oleander Court when it was Jasmine Lane, the imagery a distorted Disney cartoon of earlier years. The vast majority of the panel is woods and foliage, meandering gravel drives leading to a handful of modest homes. One features three little girls running through a sprinkler system, the parents in silhouette on a wooden front porch. The tranquility of the neighborhood is underscored by the cool tone of its pastel colors, the relaxed posture of the few individuals featured.

A bulldozer is at the far right. Its blade fells a leafy tree dotted with flowers vibrantly pink at its base but ebbing in color—shriveling, deteriorating—as it crashes into the middle panel. As the tree lands, green money bills shake loose instead of leaves. They dot the middle panel like Easter eggs—caught by the wind, papering a car, substituting for a rolled newspaper.

At first glance, the middle panel seems almost humorous. Surreal and bold, it caricatures the opulence of Oleander Court. Everyone and everything is glossy and shiny, from the lipstick on the women to the paint on mailboxes and shutters. Out of scale, Helen has drawn the general outline of the neighborhood, each house comically mirroring all others save for a minor detail such as a water fountain raining coins, a koi pond with fish with dollar signs for eyes, a Mercedes-Benz with a price tag affixed to the side mirror. Empty wine bottles litter the panel, along with red apples in various stages of decay.

The figures swarming the middle panel are identifiable. There's Conner Boyle on his running loop, and Bambi, too. Perfect specimens in spandex. Tripp flashes a white-toothed smile, taking up a cartoonishly small porch. Pete rakes leaves in the Nobles' front yard. Stacey and Scott Denton click oversized wine glasses by their pool.

As Laura looks closer, the images become multi-layered. Bambi's body is perfect, but her face is ghoul-like. Conner's children run nearby, desperately trying to reach him. Tripp's smile is a grimace.

Laura's heart beats faster as she scans the images, looking for her own. How does Helen see her?

There she is, hands pressed to her upstairs window. Smiling, maniacally almost. Hopeful, pained. Looking out from the inside.

It's just a painting. But as Laura studies the small image of herself, captured so perfectly in only a few brushstrokes, she wants to cry. Regardless of her professional achievements, her money, her efforts, she'll never quite belong to a place like Oleander Court, will she?

"God, look at that." She jumps at the sound of Pete's voice, even though he's been standing right by her all along. He points to an image in the right panel, which captures the neighborhood as if caught in a terrible storm. The imagery is dark, and Laura squints to see that the pelting rain isn't rain at all but extravagant items—jewelry, a baby grand piano, laptops.

Pete is pointing to a pair of legs sticking out from underneath a staircase that resembles a jagged bolt of lightning. Drawn in outline only, the staircase is filled with conversation bubbles.

One foot is bare, a stiletto clinging to the other in clear homage to *The Wizard of Oz*. Pam.

A blond woman in a shiny pink dress has her back to the viewer, preening in front of an oval floor mirror. It's Bambi Holiday, proud in her Ms. Fulton County sash and tiara despite being nothing but a skeleton in the reflection.

Laura doesn't look for Conner or Beverly. She feels sick. "Helen painted all this?" What she really wants to say is, "*This* is what she sees?" That nice old woman, behind the trellis.

"At least I'm just raking the leaves," Pete says, his jaw slack as he examines Helen's creation. "This is . . ."—*terrible*, Laura expects him to say—"extraordinary," he finishes. "Who knew the old gal had it in her?" He takes Laura's hand. "I have actual goosebumps."

Laura stares at him. "You have to be joking. You're in *awe*? That's your reaction? Looking at this makes me feel physically ill."

"It makes you feel sick," Pete says softly, "because of its honesty. And—God. Could Helen be right?"

"About what?" Laura asks, although she already knows. The painting isn't exactly subtle.

"If Helen's right, the Oleander Court killer is carving out the rot. Every single victim— they symbolized what's wrong with the neighborhood. Why it's not beautiful anymore."

Helen's Jasmine Lane. They've both heard her speak of it many times.

Laura forces herself to look at the middle panel again. She doesn't understand the images associated with Ray. She's in her front yard, standing tall with her dogs guarding her like sentinels. Her back yard is overgrown with thorns and weeds. While the top of her home is rainbow-hued, the colors end halfway down the structure. Abruptly, as if Helen had run out of paint.

"If someone is carving out the rot," Laura says, "at what point do they stop?"

ADELAIDE

Adelaide can't sit still. William will be home early tonight, and she's planned a meal he'll never forget. She's even using the antique silver serving tray with the dome cover, the McKenzie family heirloom William always cheerfully agrees with her is as useless as buttons on a dish rag.

Adelaide keeps erupting into fits of giggles as she eyes it on the kitchen counter, the silver gleaming. She can't wait for William's reaction when he sees what she's fixed for supper.

It's not even four, though. William won't be home for at least an hour. Sixty whole minutes for Adelaide to sit and stew on her own. Adelaide turns on the stereo and hops up the stairs to her bathroom, where she busies herself by sorting through her various creams, moisturizers, and nail polishes. No use sitting there like a tree stump.

If she did, she might think about Ray. Adelaide's trying hard not to. The night before, she'd hardly slept a wink thinking about her dear friend in that cold, bare cell. How was Ray dealing? How scared was she? But there's only so much worrying and fretting one person can do, and Adelaide going to pieces won't do Ray any good.

Right now, according to Juliet, Ray's awaiting her bail hearing at the superior court. Some judge will decide how much Ray has to pay to have her freedom as she awaits trial.

That's the biggest load of bullshit Adelaide's ever heard. What happened to being innocent until proven guilty?

The Alpharetta folk don't seem to understand the notion either. Early that morning, as Adelaide took her morning jog, she'd stopped short at Ray's house. Someone had spray-painted KILLER across the garage door, in a garish red that looked like lipstick. Adelaide had turned around to fetch some Dawn and a scrub bucket and spent the next twenty minutes scraping and grunting away any trace of the ugly word.

Adelaide barely stopped herself from knocking on the door to tell Juliet about her good deed. She'd love for Juliet to outright like her, versus put up with her. But Juliet has enough to worry about without adding Adelaide's feelings to the list, and Adelaide gets it, anyway. Adelaide's never been in this *exact* situation, as Bedford was fresh out of lesbians, but consorting with anyone's spouse as they're away working long hours is always bound to rub them the wrong way.

The doorbell rings as Adelaide's hand is deep in a bathroom drawer, trying to extract something stuck at the back. "Comin'!" she hollers as she straightens up, slamming the drawer. Eyeing her profile in the mirror, she rushes across the landing and down the stairs, pausing to peer through the peephole.

Oh, shoot. It's that same officer who'd arrested Ray. Adelaide wishes she hadn't been so noisy coming down. He knows she's home. "Hi," she says as she opens the door, crossing her arms. "Can I help you?" Being as mad as a wet hen has its benefits. She's not scared of him this time.

"May I come in?" Officer Moskowitz says, polite as can be. "I have a few questions for you."

"Lookin' for more ways to hang Ray?" Adelaide asks, but she moves aside. She's probably legally required to do so. "You know, you could be using this time you're wastin' to catch the real killer."

"I'm sorry you feel that way," the officer says as he follows Adelaide to the kitchen. She drops into one of the island's stools, gesturing for him to do the same. He eyes the silver platter and she's glad when he doesn't comment. It's none of his beeswax.

He pulls out his ratty little writing tablet as he sits down across from her. "The more this investigation develops, the more questions it raises."

"What do you mean?" Adelaide glances at the clock on the microwave.

"You didn't really know Bambi Holiday. Is that right?" he asks as if he doesn't remember her prior statement.

"Right," Adelaide says, waiting to see where he's going with this. "I'd only seen her around. And there was that one incident." *The one where I slapped her silly.*

He nods, as if she's jogged his memory. "Right. Right. And is the same true for your husband?"

"What do you mean?"

"Did your husband know Bambi Holiday?" He's eyeing her the same way Adelaide's cousin Buck stares down his poker buddies. Like he knows their cards.

"I-I don't know," Adelaide replies, ignoring the slithering feeling in her stomach. Why is he asking her this? "She lived on the other side of the cul-de-sac. But they probably met at some HOA event or somethin'. It's not the biggest neighborhood."

"You're not aware of any *romantic* relationship between your husband and Mrs. Holiday?"

Maybe he's playing her. Maybe their latest cockamamie theory is that Adelaide offed Bambi because she suspected William was fooling around. She folds her arms and leans over the counter. "Tell you what," she says coldly. "Let's make it nice and easy. You ask a direct question, and I'll see if I have an answer for you."

"Fair enough." Officer Moskowitz shifts in his chair, and it's on the tip of Adelaide's tongue to offer the man a cup of coffee. Engrained Southern hospitality. "Are you aware," he clarifies, his eyes meeting Adelaide's, "that your husband and Mrs. Holiday were engaged in a romantic relationship?"

Adelaide feels her lightheadedness from earlier in the day returning. She may need to lie down again. "No, that isn't right," she manages.

Officer Moskowitz's lips twitch. "I don't mean *recently*," he says, and now she knows the vague phrasing was purposeful. To gauge her reaction.

"Even so. He would have told me."

Officer Moskowitz raises an eyebrow. It's either an infuriating *Oh, honey, don't you know that men lie?* look, or it's an *I know you're full of shit* look. "We've interviewed everyone in the neighborhood. To gather perspectives, to understand the different relationships and . . . motives . . . at play." His voice drops on the m-word, and Adelaide squirms despite herself. "And several individuals commented on suspecting a relationship—"

Oh, thank Jesus. "*That's* your evidence? Gossip?"

"—while one neighbor relayed how their spouse had actually seen them in the act."

Adelaide stares at him. "Act of what?"

Officer Moskowitz's eyes shift the slightest. "Of intercourse."

"When?"

"Some years ago."

Adelaide's already thrown up once that day, but she could do an encore performance. "They're lyin' or mistaken," she says, though she clings to the word *years*. Maybe the affair hadn't overlapped with their relationship.

Still, why hadn't he told her? Adelaide had never opened up to a man the way she had with William. Confessing her past relationships despite the embarrassing and sometimes traumatizing nature of the details. "It's fine," he'd told her, pretending not to see the tears sliding down her face as he kissed her. "It doesn't matter where we've been. Only where we end up."

When it came to divulging his own past, William's was as uneventful as it could be—only a handful of serious relationships before he'd married his first wife, Liddy. Only a few dates after. He hadn't been ready to move on, not until he met Adelaide. Or so he said.

"Why would it matter?" Adelaide lifts her chin, hoping the officer doesn't notice it trembling. "Even if it's true, why would I kill Bambi? Motive, you said. You think women go around, killin' their husbands' ex-lovers out of insecurity? Makin' sure they can't go back on old options?"

"We don't know if it was an old option."

Adelaide's stomach drops, but she hides it. "What do you mean? You said the relationship was years ago."

"That was when it was last confirmed." He pauses, letting the suggestion hang. The last time William and Bambi were *seen* together wasn't necessarily the last time they'd *been* together.

"William had nothin' to do with Bambi," Adelaide says.

"See, that's where we're confused. Because it appears that Bambi sent him this." Officer Moskowitz reaches into his front shirt pocket, extracting a folded note. "You can keep that," he tells Adelaide as he hands it to her. "It's a copy."

Adelaide's eyes tear through the words. *Roberto . . . affair . . . seen them . . . our history.* Her face prickles in shame even though she hasn't actually done anything wrong.

"Where did you get this?" she asks him, and his forehead knits.

"You don't know?"

"If we're going to keep playin' Twenty Questions, this visit's going to take a lot longer than it needs to," Adelaide snaps.

"It was found in Ray Willis's recycling, after her neighborhood watch meeting. Remember that?"

"Yeah, I was there." Adelaide shakes her head. "You're telling me someone threw it away during the meetin'?"

"Actually, we have reason to believe *you* threw it away."

"But I've never seen it before!"

"Then why did we find your fingerprints on the envelope it came in?"

"What?"

"Your fingerprints were on the envelope it came in," he says again, slowly. "We matched them when we ran them with prints on file."

"On file," she repeats.

"From a prior arrest."

Shit. Shit, shit, *shit.* Adelaide remembers her arrest in that dinky little sheriff's office in Bedford, the bright lights as they took her picture. She'd had dark eyeliner all around her eyes, smudged. Matted hair. Her lips slightly parted, catching her talking back.

"Public indecency," Adelaide says through numb lips. "They dropped the charges."

"But they still arrested you," Officer Moskowitz says helpfully. "So we have the fingerprints."

"I—" Adelaide's phone chimes. The text is from Juliet:

Saw M.'s cruiser outside your house. You don't have to tell him anything unless it's a custodial interrogation. Ask, and if not, get rid of him!

Adelaide swallows when she reads it. How much damage has she done during this ten-minute conversation? "Is this a custodial interrogation?"

The term feels foreign in her mouth, like having bad lines fed to her offstage.

"Why, no," Officer Moskowitz says, smiling. "This is a conversation. At this stage, we're merely trying to understand what this letter means."

At this stage. A threat if there ever was one. "Then I'll have to ask you to leave. I'm expectin' my husband for supper."

Officer Moskowitz rises. "Appreciate your time, Mrs. McKenzie."

"Yeah, it's been a real pleasure." Adelaide can't bite back the sarcastic tone in her voice. But like her mama always says, *don't feed me shit and tell me it's sugar.* Hadn't she taught Adelaide better? Adelaide should have kicked him out as soon as he started pontificating on indiscretions of the dead.

"Word of advice, though, Mrs. McKenzie?" Officer Moskowitz says as he pockets his notebook.

"Yes?"

"If you haven't done anything wrong, come clean about the letter. Could reduce your stress level."

As the door closes behind him, Adelaide presses her back against it, sinking to the floor. Burying her face in her knees, she tries to control the dizziness sweeping through her. She's had her share of it lately, and Officer Moskowitz's house call has her feeling like she's spent too much time on the Tilt-A-Whirl.

Was this why William had seemed so concerned during the questioning about the slap? William knew she had a motive. The oldest one in the book—jealousy. Provided she knew what she needed to know, only she hadn't.

And that motive would be even bigger if the affair was ongoing.

William loves me. Adelaide knows it's true. But she also knows that men are made to bend the truth. Her mama said it was part of their DNA, which was why she overlooked Don's tall tales about his high school football glory days and pretended not to smell cigarettes on him when he came home from poker night.

But those are white lies that hurt nobody. This is in a whole other category. This is carnal knowledge of another woman despite coming home, kissing on Adelaide and professing his love. That's not adding yards to old football throws or spraying on gas station perfume after a smoke.

And what about that letter? How did her fingerprints get on it? And how did it wind up in the trash at Ray's house?

Headlights wash over the now-dark kitchen, and Adelaide snaps to. William is home. Rushing to the kitchen counter, she grabs the domed serving tray and dumps the contents into the trash. By the time William comes through the garage, Adelaide's at the fridge, discarding a second layer of old food on top of the items she'd so carefully arranged on the tray.

"Cleaning out the fridge, huh?" William asks, his eyes lighting on her like it's any other day. As if everything hasn't changed.

"Keepin' busy," Adelaide manages, her heart lurching when she looks into his face. She really does love him.

This is why it's so hard, why she's so confused. She'd been beyond excited about tonight. When she'd found out, she'd known it was right. That this was what she wanted, more than anything.

"You look nice," he says, leaning in to kiss her cheek as he goes to the Keurig. Adelaide glances down at the slinky sweater dress she'd pulled on. It was one of William's favorites. Each time she wore it, he complimented her like he'd never seen her wear it before.

"Thanks," she says, her stomach twisting as William grabs the open bag of candy she'd stashed next to the Keurig.

"Oh, man. Baby Ruth. I haven't had one of these since I was a kid."

Adelaide straightens up, bumping the fridge door with her hip to close it. "Me neither. Guess I was feelin' nostalgic."

William unpeels the wrapper from his candy and steps on the trash can pedal. As the lid opens, Adelaide looks at the pile of refrigerator discards, swallowing around the lump in her throat. Underneath expired yogurt, old soup, and moldy oranges is the supper Adelaide had prepared for William, the real one to follow after a call for take-out.

The supper is baby carrots and miniature Baby Ruth bars. They spell out SEPTEMBER 20 on the silver tray. Adelaide's due date, as confirmed this morning. She's pregnant. She couldn't wait to tell William.

Now Adelaide wonders if she should tell him at all.

JADE

Jade lifts her no-foam soy latte to her lips as she pulls into the neighborhood, taking a small sip to make it last. Six dollars for specialty milk and two shots of espresso. Six-fifty once Jade added the tip "suggested" on the credit card payment screen.

Jade justified the luxury by her need for a little pick-me-up after running her errands and visiting her uncle's family nearby in Roswell. Uncle Jack is her father's brother, and his effortless ability to get under her skin has existed for as long as she can remember:

Jade, you have a boyfriend?

No, not yet.

Jade, you make the tennis team?

No, but it was really competitive.

Jade, you get a 30 on your ACT like you wanted?

No, but 29 is good.

Uncle Jack has never been the most verbose individual, but he's always known exactly what to say and what to ask to make her feel like crap.

Especially now, when Jade has reasons to feel like crap. She's been "floating" ever since the lease on her apartment in Boston expired, a term her friend Amy generously employed when she'd offered to store Jade's belongings in her basement. "Homeless" could be another word for it, but that doesn't feel accurate considering that Jade does have income and her parents have an entire guest room waiting for her in Florida. "Drifting" might be a better term, considering Jade's lack of direction.

Anything she said to Uncle Jack would make its way back to her parents. Accordingly, over lunch, Jade had picked at her sandwich and tried to sound enthusiastic about her Instagram following. It was the safest topic available, especially since Jade's Instagram efforts had started to promote the family restaurants. Beautiful shots of plated food and décor, catchy phrases, menu highlights. Jade had taken a class on social media during college, and the tricks had come easily.

Jade's mother had also been a natural at marketing. She was the one to nix her husband's original, terrible name for the first restaurant. "American Chow," she'd chided. "You do not sell dog food. You sell people food. Keep it simple."

Because Pat Coleman always listened to his wife, the first restaurant had been named Steak and Taters. Then, Steak and Taters II and Steak and Taters III. Creative variations on steak and potatoes, catering to every palate. Every Thursday there was a blue-plate special "date night," which featured live music and a free dessert.

The blue-plate special was also Jade's mother's idea. She was behind all the specials, all the ideas, all the draws. Her business savvy was twice included in the *Atlanta Weekly*. It made for an interesting story because Anita Coleman had only a high school GED, obtained after her family had immigrated from Colombia when she was fourteen. She'd taught herself English in part from watching *Mary Tyler Moore* and had won over her future husband when he was a college student and she was his waitress at a sports bar. "I came for the wings and stayed for the girl," he says anytime the story is retold.

When Jade had announced her intention to major in business marketing, her mother was thrilled. "You are like me," Anita Coleman told her, over and over. "Imagine what you can do with the right education! Anything!"

Jade squirms at the idea of telling her mother that, ultimately, she's discovered she has no interest in business—only an aptitude. Her parents were the embarrassing ones screaming with joy at every school event, particularly graduations. When they'd visited her at the PR firm—her first job after business school—they'd barely refrained from taking pictures. What would they think about her throwing away the career they'd backed in every way possible?

"If you need a job, you can always come back to us," Uncle Jack had said over lunch. The restaurants had been sold to him, a natural move considering he already handled all their accounting and had no interest in retiring. "No shame in it."

Uncle Jack had made the same offer when Jade's PR firm had downsized. But by then, Jade's Instagram following was so huge that she was being approached to promote products. Freelancing sounded better than returning to Alpharetta with her tail between her legs.

As Jade turns into her cul-de-sac, she spots Laura—the woman who'd insisted on trying a Chickpea Bite at the neighborhood watch meeting—carrying the back end of an enormous canvas out of Helen Beecham's house. A man has the front end.

Jade pulls into her driveway and hops out of the car, approaching Laura and the man as they maneuver the awkward-sized canvas down the sidewalk. It's absolutely enormous, piquing Jade's interest. She'd studied Helen's work in undergrad, and even if the canvas isn't hers, it must be interesting if she'd kept it in her home.

"Need a hand?" she asks, even though a third person might only get in the way.

"No, it's a two-person job," Laura replies, grunting. "Thanks."

"I noticed that came from Helen's house. Everything okay with her?" Helen doesn't seem the type to part with her art.

Laura shifts her end to shield her eyes from the sun. "She had a nasty fall," she tells Jade. "She's in the hospital."

"Oh, no. Which one? Maybe I could visit."

The bland smiles Jade receives tell her they don't believe her. Like when you run into an old frenemy and vaguely suggest getting coffee the next time you're both in town without also asking for a phone number.

"Wellstar North," Laura says. She pauses to rest her end of the canvas, gently, on the ground. The man does the same.

"Done. I remember she loves tiger lilies." Jade gestures at the drop cloth with her cup. "What's under there?"

Laura's eyes flicker in that direction. "A painting."

"What kind of painting?"

The man interjects, gesturing to Laura. "I'm Pete, by the way. The husband. I take it you're Jade Coleman." His eyes are amused: *What am I, chopped liver?*

"Nice to meet you," Jade says, internally chastising herself for not introducing herself earlier. She never means to be rude, but she's aware that she often comes off that way. If Jade could communicate exclusively by writing, she probably would. The ability to endlessly wordsmith to arrive at the message. Versus bumbling and fumbling for the right thing to say in the moment.

"Helen's going to live with her daughter for a while," Pete tells her. "She asked us to get this painting out of the basement. She worried about moisture on fresh paint."

"Oh, wow. It's a painting *by* her. Is it . . . any good?" Jade asks, and that was the right thing to say because Pete's face lights up.

"It's her best," he says. "Vivid, and surreal, and the imagery—it's really something. Honestly, we could have kept it at her house, but I wanted to look at it more."

"Do you think she'll show it?"

Pete's mouth twitches. "I don't know. Before the fall, I'd visited her about every night for months and she never mentioned it. Maybe it's just for her."

Or maybe Helen's too scared to show it. How terrible would it feel, not to paint for so many years, only to have your effort rejected? And Helen's from an age before social media. In her time, art reviews were written by professionals and appeared only in hard copy newspapers and magazines. Now anyone with a laptop can "comment" on any online article about anything. *That sucks, LOL.* And much worse.

"Helen has a following," Jade says, remembering her undergrad art class. No one believed Jade when she'd told them Helen was her neighbor. "People care about her art. It matters to them. She should share it."

"Maybe she should," Pete says. "But it isn't our decision. It's Helen's."

"I'll make you a proposal." Jade pulls her phone from her bag. "Let me take a picture of it. I'll write a story about it. And I'll post it only if Helen approves. I promise."

Pete tilts his head at her, considering. "I've seen your website. And your Instagram. They make what's happening here read like some slasher film."

"What's happening here *is* like some slasher film," Jade says. "But that's not all I've been writing about." Not that those stories get close to the same number of views. "I've lived here since I was a kid. Felt safe here. That's why what's happening here haunts me. I hate that it's tainting my memories. But an article about Helen, about her creating something new . . . I don't know." She shrugs. "Maybe it'll show how there are still beautiful aspects to this neighborhood. That it's not just Murder Avenue."

It's the most honest, accurate way Jade's ever described ItCanHappenAnywhere.com. Even to her parents, she's referred to it as "an experiment," downplaying it because she doesn't want them to suspect it's important to her. The articles weren't some post or tweet. They took hours. What if they weren't any good?

Pete's eyeballing Jade as if determining her level of trustworthiness. "You promise you'd delete it?"

"Absolutely. And I have accountability." She points at her house. "You know where to find me."

He sighs. "Okay, fine. Quick, Laura—before I change my mind."

The drop cloth falls and Jade bites her lip, standing back to get a better look. To absorb it. "Wow. It . . . *assaults* you, doesn't it?"

"That's a wonderful way of putting it," Laura says, but Jade barely hears her. A chill runs through her as she stares at the triptych. It makes her own posts seem amateur, clumsy. The bold bright strokes, the details. *This* is the work of a master.

"It's art," she says, realizing that actual tears have welled in her eyes. She's grateful for the reaction. Jade had almost forgotten what it felt like to be moved. "I promise to do it justice." She zooms in with her phone and captures several pictures. "Got it."

After Laura and Pete disappear down the street, Jade returns to her car and pulls out her jute shopping bag. She'd received fifty from a vendor that paid her to promote them. Their claim of reducing one's footprint on the world would be more valid if the handles didn't rip from the non-recyclable bags so easily. Jade carries hers inside, trying to ignore how the strap tears into her skin.

She unloads her Whole Foods items in the kitchen. She's required to post about all of them in the following week except for the Yogi tea, which Jade appreciates despite not getting paid to do so. Firing up the teakettle, she flips open her laptop to begin a new blog post.

To prepare, she stares at the shot of Helen's painting again. Helen has captured most of the residents, but Jade isn't there. It's not a slight, but a point of accuracy. She's not really part of the neighborhood, not anymore.

Jade snorts when she spots the detail of Tripp's image on his front porch. Helen has captured his rictus grin perfectly. "That man doesn't have a genuine bone in his body," Jade's mother liked to say.

Jade turns to her computer as a Facebook notification scrolls across the top of the screen. Three of Jade's 1,198 Friends are having birthdays tomorrow. Jade doesn't recognize any of their names, and for a fleeting moment she fantasizes about deleting her account. How much time would she save if she was never distracted by notifications or the need to get a post perfect?

The thought doesn't last long. Instead, Jade posts the picture she'd taken at lunch: a turkey-and-avocado sandwich on whole grain bread. *Awesome catching up with family.* She tags Uncle Jack and her cousin Marnie. Then, on second thought, she posts a cropped picture of the sandwich on Instagram. *With Chickpea Bites = Perfect Lunch!* She includes the link to the company website. *Healthy people like me eat this product,* her endorsement says.

Jade's an addict, she knows. And a liar, considering she went through the Taco Bell drive-through instead of finishing her sandwich.

But there are worse things to be. With a little bit of whitewashing, Jade's much prettier, more confident, and wittier online. She feels better about herself thanks to enthusiastic online fans and well-wishers, and companies like Chickpea Heaven have someone to market their products.

Online Jade is the retouched version of Actual Jade. Jade 2.0. All it takes is a few measured strokes of a keyboard. What could be the harm in that?

SOON-LI

Soon-Li has been avoiding the door ever since Tran accidentally opened it for that WAB-TV reporter, Miranda Albers. Today is the hearing on Ray's bond, and she's been circulating the neighborhood like a well-dressed vulture, attempting to gather sound bites for reactions, thoughts, and impressions. At least, that's how she'd characterized it to Tran as Soon-Li eavesdropped in the dining room.

"We have no comment," Tran had told Miranda Albers, opening and swinging the door closed in one movement.

Ten to one, the reporter had started and would end her tour of Oleander Court at Adelaide's house. Since WAB-TV had begun covering the murders in earnest after Ray's arrest, it had focused on Ray's friendship with Adelaide. It also suggested that, if guilty, Ray couldn't have acted alone. The deduction wasn't complicated to make.

"I don't get it," Laura had said to Soon-Li over coffee yesterday. "If the news thinks Adelaide and Ray are conspiring, why cover them hugging when Ray found out Adelaide was safe?" She was referring to the segment aired after Conner's murder.

"I assume they cover whatever suits them at the time," Soon-Li had replied, somewhat thrown. How was that answer not obvious?

"Do you have any idea why they might think they were working together?" Laura had continued. "It's not a crime to be friends."

Soon-Li had shrugged. It needled her, Laura asking that. Was she fishing for information? Did she think Soon-Li knew something? Soon-Li knew nothing.

After Miranda Albers leaves with a swish of her brown ponytail, Soon-Li peeks out the window. The reporter climbs into her news van, and it eases toward the Magnolia Lane cul-de-sac. Soon-Li guesses it will remain at Adelaide's house until the WAB-TV team gets what it wants. Or until they can spin the footage to make it look like they have.

It's early afternoon on a Wednesday, but Soon-Li decides it's time to call it a day. Her mind buzzes with thoughts of poor Ray, whose hearing was scheduled for the Fulton County Superior Court afternoon docket. Juliet had shared that because the docket included matters for *all* criminal defendants and Ray's last name was at the end of the alphabet, she could wait hours to be called.

Going to the kitchen, Soon-Li pops open the top of her Keurig and inserts a fresh cup. As she does, there's a pounding on the glass window of the back door. She glances at her Ring video screen and raises her eyes at the hooded figure peering into the camera. When it raises its hand to pound again, Soon-Li glimpses the green eyes and hurries to open the door.

"Thanks," Adelaide says as she slips inside. In her red hoodie and jean leggings, she could be a college student. "That reporter won't leave and I couldn't take it. I won't be a prisoner in my own house." She sashays down the hall, tracing a wood carving Tran had mounted. "Pretty. From Korea?"

"Our last visit," Soon-Li says, following her into the living room. "Those and the ducks."

"The ducks?"

Soon-Li shows Adelaide the wooden ducks on the fireplace mantel. "They symbolize the husband-and-wife relationship. If the beaks are touching, everything's great. If not"—she clucks her tongue—"no good."

"Huh." Adelaide's eyebrows knit, and Soon-Li notices the dark circles under her eyes. "If they moved on their own accord, might clue in the clueless."

It's an odd thing to say for a woman who seems to have the perfect marriage, the perfect life. After Adelaide had prematurely left the revived book club, Soon-Li had watched the entirety of *Zombie 101* out of curiosity. It was trash, most definitely, but Adelaide was believable as an undead teenager, stealing every scene from her less talented cohorts.

Soon-Li couldn't even play a tree in elementary school without being paralyzed by stage fright.

"Want a cup of coffee?" Soon-Li asks her now. "Or a glass of wine? It's five o'clock somewhere."

"Do you have herbal tea?"

"Sure." Soon-Li moves into the kitchen and Adelaide follows. She drops into a chair, resting her forehead against her hands. The double blue diamonds of her platinum wedding ring glint in the light.

Soon-Li puts the teakettle on, and Adelaide lifts her head. "I was probably caught on about half the cameras in people's back yards on the way here," she says, unzipping her hoodie and pushing up her sleeves in the warm kitchen. "I was pressed against fences like some cat burglar."

"Well, as long as you don't murder me, being caught on camera won't matter."

Adelaide laughs. "I'll try my best." Her face becomes serious again. "I wanted out of that house," she says. "But I wanted to talk to you, too."

"To me?" Soon-Li can't imagine what Adelaide would have to say to her. Hopefully it isn't about Ray, evidence of her guilt. Soon-Li only wants evidence of Ray's innocence.

"It's . . . about William," Adelaide says as she fiddles with her enormous wedding ring.

That's not a topic Soon-Li would have expected. She goes to the Keurig to finish making her coffee. "What about him?"

"That officer who's been after Ray—that Officer Moskowitz—came callin' a few days ago. And he said . . ." Adelaide's eyes fill with tears. "I'm sorry," she says as Soon-Li grabs a paper towel and hands it to her. "My hormones have been all over the place lately. I cried over a dog food commercial yesterday."

Soon-Li sits down with her coffee. "He said . . .?" She prompts Adelaide, waving off Tran as he appears in the kitchen doorway. He grabs an apple from the counter and vanishes.

"He said that William and Bambi Holiday were havin' *an affair.*" Adelaide blows her nose with a loud honking sound. "A few years ago, and maybe even more recent. And I figured, bein' able to see into their yard, maybe you'd seen somethin.'"

William and *Bambi*? Soon-Li's only encountered William a handful of times, but she likes him. He has class, kindness. He doesn't seem like the kind of man who would have an affair, let alone with someone like Bambi.

Then again, Bambi used to sunbathe in her pink string bikini in the front yard, suntan oil glistening as she propped her chin on her hands, surveying the neighborhood for admirers. William might be a good person, but he *is* a man.

"I've never seen them together," Soon-Li tells Adelaide truthfully. "Or even interacting."

Adelaide plays with the strings of her hoodie. "Have you . . . heard anything about the two of them? Gossip, I mean."

"I'm hardly the neighborhood socialite," Soon-Li says, rising as the teakettle begins to shriek. "But what about William? What does *he* say?"

"I haven't asked him."

"You haven't?" If Soon-Li had heard the same thing about Tran, she'd have confronted him immediately and resolved the situation. Though, to be fair, the idea of Tran having an affair is preposterous. He's so non-perceptive that a woman could throw herself at him and he would have no idea what was going on.

"Nope. I don't want to hear the answer," Adelaide replies. She watches as Soon-Li pours the spitting hot water into a mug.

"What if it's the right one?" Soon-Li asks her, tearing open a tea bag.

"That don't mean anything. Men're lyin' dogs."

"Not all of them. Not William."

"How do you know?"

Soon-Li takes the chair next to Adelaide's, sliding the tea over and laying out the evidence: "I've seen the way William looks at you. He couldn't look at you like that and cheat at the same time. And Marv's always home, and you're always home. Where would they have the chance to cheat?"

"Any hotel."

"William's also a doctor," Soon-Li points out. "Long hours. Less time to cheat." She wraps her hands around her coffee cup. "Did the police say when William had the affair? And how do they know for sure that it happened in the first place?"

"They skirted around the timeline. But they said a few neighbors confirmed. They saw somethin'." Adelaide dunks her tea bag, not elaborating. "I thought you might have been one of them."

"I think they're trying to play you, Adelaide. They know you're close with Ray. And Bambi's the one they can't tie her to. They're trying to make you think they have something on *you*, some motive that implicates you. Hoping to scare you into throwing Ray under the bus."

Adelaide purses her lips. "That's not all that links me to Bambi."

"What else does?"

"I slapped her, once. Don't ask me why, but she deserved it."

Soon-Li takes a sip of her coffee to hide her shock. "Okay."

"And . . . there's a note. Bambi wrote William, sayin' I was having an affair with Roberto." Adelaide rolls her eyes heavenward. "Officer Moskowitz came by with it. And it had my fingerprints on it. Yet I've never seen it before, I swear."

"What? How is that possible?" Soon-Li asks, and Adelaide shrugs.

"Your guess is as good as mine."

Soon-Li's first thought is that someone must be framing Adelaide. That's the only logical explanation, if she'd never laid eyes on the note and it tied her to Bambi's death. It provided a motive, albeit silly—to silence Bambi.

Soon-Li's second thought is that she believes Adelaide. And if Soon-Li believes Ray, *and* Adelaide—that she's right about their innocence—it means the police still don't have a clue. And as long as they don't have a clue, everyone in Oleander Court remains in danger.

Adelaide sighs, shakily. "You know," she says. "It's weird. With everything goin' on here—the murders, bein' a suspect . . . the thing I'm scared of most is losin' William."

"Which is why you should talk to him. Whatever you're assuming or thinking now—it can't be worse than that."

Adelaide tilts her head. "That's true, I suppose. But when I get my answer, I'll have to deal with that. And I won't stay with a man who sleeps around."

"Where would you go?"

"I don't know. My mama worries too much, hovers like you wouldn't believe. And I don't have much else family."

"What about friends? You must have a lot, between L.A. and Bedford."

"You don't have real friends in L.A. Besides, I go there, my failed marriage goes to page 15 of the tabloids. And my girls in Bedford . . ." She trails off, her eyes far away. "Girls don't get out of Bedford. Fact that I did don't sit well. Soon as I took that plane out of town, they figured I was too stuck-up to deal with anymore."

"You have Ray."

"Ray has a wife and a marriage to work on. I ain't gettin' in the middle of that." Adelaide turns pink. "Oh, boy. Don't tell her I said that."

"I won't."

Soon-Li's touched that Adelaide's trusted her with all this. She's always seen Adelaide as the slightest bit standoffish, but the more she sees of her, the more she understands why. What would it be like—to grow up in small town Arkansas, to have no education, and then marry a doctor and move somewhere like Oleander Court? How could you feel like you belonged?

"Do you want to stay here tonight?" Soon-Li asks Adelaide. "We have a spare room."

"Nah, but thanks." Adelaide rises to put her empty mug in the sink. As she does, she rests her hand on her stomach. Gently, unconsciously. The same way Soon-Li had touched her own stomach when she was pregnant with Lila.

When Adelaide turns, she follows Soon-Li's gaze. Her lips curve in a smile. "William gets off work early tonight. Okay for him to pick me up here?"

RAY

Ray slouches in the passenger seat as Juliet pulls into Oleander Court, half-expecting to be greeted by a horde of people wielding picket signs bearing variations on the word *murderer*.

She should have holed up elsewhere during this mess, but the complication was the dogs. Ray and Juliet had nowhere to put them, and they didn't want to be parted from them.

Ray wonders if her parents have heard about the charges, if her little sister knows. When her phone had powered back on, she'd scrolled through the relatively few texts she'd received during the thirteen days it had been out of her possession, hoping for something from Becky. Nothing.

"You okay?" Juliet asks, glancing at her.

"I've been better." Ray rubs her hand over her face, glancing down at her outfit. It feels good to be back in her normal clothes, that's for sure. "I'm just . . ."

"What?" Juliet's eyes probe hers, and Ray exhales. If she and Juliet are going to make it, she needs to say how she feels once in a while.

"I was thinking about Becky. How when people picked on me in high school, she was there."

Becky was the epitome of a normal kid. Slightly dorky, slightly awkward. Never popular, but with a handful of good friends. When she heard anyone at school trash-talking Ray—Steven, at the time—she stuck up for him.

"We used to spend all day playing with wooden train tracks in the kitchen. How can you go from spending every day with someone for *years* to not talking at all?"

Juliet, an only child, is quiet. Then she says, "Why does it have to be Becky who reaches out?"

Ray picks at her cuticles. "I don't know." What would Becky say if Ray called her? Would she want to talk? Would *any* of them want to?

Ray's family still lives in Charleston. She's seen them only a handful of times since the surgery, the announcement of which resulted in her father losing his shit so completely her mother had asked Ray to leave the house. Every time her mother calls, Ray's heart clenches because she worries it will be to relay the news that her father has died. He's always had heart trouble, always loved his sweets and red meat.

And Becky. Now a mother with little twin boys, she's a guidance counselor at their old high school. Ray knows about her life mostly through Facebook.

"Oh, shit," Ray says as they approach the house. Three news vans are parked outside, reporters bundled up against the cold winter air. Miranda Albers's red peacoat is unmistakable, and Ray slouches farther down in her seat as Juliet swings the car into the driveway, narrowly missing the perky reporter. "C'mon, c'mon, c'mon," Juliet growls as the garage door rolls upward with a grinding sound. She shoots the car inside and jabs at the opener again.

When the door closes with a final rumble, the women breathe a sigh of relief. "You don't have to talk to anyone," Juliet tells her. "Or go anywhere. I have enough groceries to last two weeks."

Inside, Ray's dogs greet her ecstatically, jumping up on her and bringing tears to her eyes. "Hi, guys," she says, dropping to wrestle with Apollo. "I missed you so much." After a long absence, Ray would usually grab their leashes and take them for a long walk. Today she'd be accosted by reporters, have microphones shoved in her face.

Ray straightens, pulling her phone out of her jacket pocket. The rest of the neighborhood already seems to know of her arrival. Adelaide, Soon-Li, and Laura have all texted.

Juliet sinks into the sofa. "Rest," she mumbles, closing her eyes and drawing her knees up. Ray joins her, straightening her wife's legs across her lap. "Thank you," she says simply.

Juliet looks terrible. Her face is drawn, new lines etched in her pale skin. Juliet hasn't complained once since Ray's arrest, but Ray knows how hard this must be on her. Safe in the jail, Ray's escaped the reporters, but what about Juliet? And what do the partners at Juliet's firm think of one of their best having a suspected murderer for a wife? They already tolerate her *having* a wife.

"I'll make dinner in a minute," Ray says. Juliet grunts, and Ray leans to kiss her cheek. "This will be over soon," she says, a bald-faced lie, before settling back against the couch. She closes her eyes, feeling the weariness in her bones.

Something *thwacks* against the window, making the dogs bark. "What was that?" Ray asks, sitting up and gently pushing Juliet's legs aside. Shadows crawl across the living room wall, and Ray realizes they've both fallen asleep. Hours have passed. It's dusk.

She goes to the window, pulling back the curtain. *Thwack!* Ray recoils as something connects with the windowpane, thinking dimly for a moment that a wayward bird had hit the house. But something yellow and glistening is sliding down the glass.

"Fag!" Ray freezes at the faint word, hoping she's misheard. Her gaze zeroes in on the group of four teenage boys gathered on the sidewalk. They're all *nice* boys, or so anyone would think—ones who ride their bikes to school and have plenty of extracurriculars to include on college applications to competitive schools. Another egg hits the window, and Ray lets the curtain drop.

"Haven't heard *that* word in a long time," she mutters, hugging her arms to her chest. A memory pushes up from the past—one where, walking home from school, Steven was surrounded by a group of boys. They'd circled on their bikes, pelting him with eggs until he'd resorted to curling up in a sitting fetal position, covering his head to ward off the blows.

And they *were* blows—with enough force and proximity, throwing an egg at someone is the same as throwing a punch. When they were finished, Steven had a black eye from where one egg had connected, bruises blooming on his arms and legs from others. Limping home to shower and hide his egg-splattered clothes, Steven had been relieved they hadn't done more.

"Were they throwing *eggs*?" Juliet asks, and Ray nods.

"That's old school."

"And they called us fags."

"Nice. Well. You know how kids are. Coming to the drama. Feeding off it." Juliet curls back into the couch, holding a throw pillow like a teddy bear. "Little shits. You need to let it roll off your back or it'll eat you up. Long time until trial."

Trial. The idea of it scares Ray to death, cuts through like a knife. It's already gotten as far as an indictment, a criminal complaint, and a bond hearing before a superior court judge.

During the hearing, the judge—a heavyset Black woman—had surveyed Ray impassively. "You have family in Charleston?" she'd asked, eyeing Ray over the kind of wire-rimmed glasses you'd expect to see on a judge.

"Yes, but we don't keep in touch much." Ray had tried not to fidget, to look the judge in the eyes. "My family is here. My community."

Goldstein, her attorney, had coached her on these words. The goal was to show she was a low flight risk.

As she spoke, though, she'd realized how little she had to tie her to *any* place, even Alpharetta. Juliet was her only real family. She didn't have a career. And her community? Ray had some friends in Oleander Court, but the rest of the residents probably thought she was a murderer.

In the end, the judge had allowed bail. Considering the severity of the crimes, the bond amount of five hundred thousand dollars was a gift. Ray was also forbidden to leave Fulton County, not that she had any plans to do so.

The release was the only positive thing about Ray's prison stay. Goldstein had finally gained access to the criminal complaint, and he'd shared the evidence the police had used to link Ray to the murders. Some of it was circumstantial, like the indication that someone left-handed had delivered Conner's fatal blow and the single footprint found in Pam's back yard matching Ray's shoe size. But then there was Ray's motive of the greenhouse dispute with Beverly, and the fingerprints found on the wine bottle that killed her.

Ray's explanation for the fingerprints was flimsy and pathetic, even to her own ears. When Laura had brought the gift bags by after Pam's party, Ray had peeked at Beverly's to see if it was better than hers. She didn't like Pam, but the idea of being handed a second-tier party bag hurt her feelings.

There was also the sheaf of papers found in Beverly's kitchen, stained red with poisoned wine. Beverly had hired a private investigator to dig up dirt on Ray, and he'd found Steven. The police presumed—probably rightly, since she was a bitch—that Beverly was planning to use the information to blackmail Ray somehow. Or that she'd already been doing that when she'd met her untimely demise. Ray couldn't prove otherwise.

The evidence that had finally triggered Ray's arrest, Ray had no clue how to explain. When scrubbing the area where Conner was whacked by his own seesaw seat, the police had noticed a strange gurgling coming from the pool filter. They'd fished out a single unused black poop bag, the same kind Ray used when walking her dogs. Officer Moskowitz had confirmed this himself during Ray's neighborhood watch meeting. She kept some right by her keys in the front entryway. Plain sight. No search warrant required.

"Oh, come on!" Ray had protested when Goldstein shared that particular clue. "A poop bag? Are you kidding me?"

Done in by a poop bag. Ray would laugh if the situation didn't make her want to cry.

"I'm starving," Juliet says now, stretching. "I can't believe we slept that long."

"I can." All her adrenaline had been expended on the bond hearing. Now that it's over, Ray could sleep for days. She glances at her closed laptop on the dining room table. "I was thinking of checking the news."

"Why? For what?"

"I don't know. To see if it's safe for me to leave the house, maybe." *To see how bad it is.*

"Absolutely not. You'd only torture yourself."

Ray exhales. Juliet's right. Once Ray opened Pandora's Box, she wouldn't be able to stop googling and clicking links between articles. Reading blogs by people who live in Albuquerque yet feel qualified to opine on her guilt. Scrolling through comments of people passing judgment on her. It would be poisonous.

"Give me your computer," her wife commands. "Now. It's for your own good."

Ray fetches her computer and hands it to Juliet. It's cool from disuse, and she vows to keep it that way. "Hide this from me," she instructs.

Juliet disappears upstairs with it. By the time she returns to the kitchen, Ray's added olive oil to a pot and is slicing open the top of their favorite Trader Joe's stir-fry. This can be a nice night in, if they pretend the outside world doesn't exist.

By bedtime, Ray's managed to somewhat relax. She has to attribute some of that to the empty bottle of malbec in the trash, but some of it is real. She'll get through this. She has to. Still, Ray swallows a melatonin pill before crawling into the covers, wanting to silence the endless chatter in her brain.

She's awakened by her Ring alarm, followed by the sound of shattering glass. The *whoop-whoop-whoop* cuts right through her as she bolts up in bed, her eyes meeting Juliet's.

Juliet reaches for the baseball bat she keeps tucked between the nightstand and the bed, springing into action.

"Wait!" Ray cries, swiping her phone and dialing 911.

There's more shattering glass, and Ray strains to place the direction. "It's coming from outside," Juliet says, and they go to the windows to draw up the curtains. When they do, Ray gasps.

The greenhouse is on fire. Flames lick from within it, the glass already coated brown. A shape hurtles through the air and connects with the glass, leaving a gaping hole. Ray's eyes go to the ground surrounding the greenhouse, where glass shards glitter in the grass.

"Little fuckers!" Juliet screams, her face contorted as she bangs the baseball bat against the window.

"Don't go out there," Ray says, grabbing at her nightgown, but Juliet ignores her, tearing free and pounding down the stairs. She wrenches open the door, waving her weapon and screaming, "Get off my property, you pieces of shit!" as she barrels down the stairs.

Bracing for bullets, Ray joins her wife as she flees to the side yard. As they turn the house corner, metal glints as two, three—no, *four* intruders mount bikes and pedal away. Was it the same kids from before?

"I bought a coupon book from that little turd on the left," Juliet snarls, and Ray remembers. A marching band fundraiser.

"Oh, shit." Ray's face crumples as she stares at the inferno. The greenhouse is a lost cause. The wooden frame sags. The glass that isn't broken is brown, black with heat. Ray's throat closes as she thinks of the delicate blooms trapped inside, their beauty destroyed by such a hateful act. She barely registers that Juliet has drawn her arm around her, is leading her away.

"I'll get the hose," Juliet says, but her tone is flat. She knows she's offering a Band-Aid for a severed limb. Ray nods, flinching as a wave of heat rolls toward her. "I'll come with you." The hose is tucked away in the garage—during the winter months, Ray uses only a watering can for her greenhouse flowers.

The street is no longer empty. Other neighbors have ventured outside, drawn by the ruckus. Ray barely registers the sound of sirens, doesn't look up to put names to figures. If she pretends no one's there, she doesn't have to say a thing.

She and Juliet cut through the front lawn to the side driveway. The floodlights are on, casting a soft glow on the concrete. When Ray glances at the closed garage door, it takes a moment for the words to register. They're jumbled all over the door, each one appearing two or three times:

Tranny

It

Dyke

Fag

Faggot

Murderer

It looks like a psychotic toddler's art project, the words scrawled in bright purple, orange, blue, and red. Paint drips down the door, pooling on the ground.

"Oh, my God." Ray's own voice sounds very, very far away.

"Oh, my God," Juliet echoes.

"Honey." Ray's sight is tunneling, and she focuses on her wife's face, her eye mask pushed comically up on her forehead in this very unfunny situation. "Why did they write . . .?" She can't say it.

Juliet pulls her in tight, her words muffled as she rubs her back. "I'm so sorry, honey."

Suddenly it makes sense. Juliet's insistence that Ray not check the news for stories of herself. She would find stories about Steven. She pulls away. "How did they find out?"

"Reporters have their ways," Juliet says. "I assume they looked into your background. And they found it weird that it began when it did."

Ray bites her lip. Any public search on "Ray Willis" shows no history before nine years ago. Even all her degrees are in Steven's name. If she was a reporter, she'd dig deeper, too.

"This isn't a bad thing, Ray," Juliet tells her, cinching her robe closed. "It's who you are. Be proud of it."

"That's easy for you to say," Ray says, swiping at her eyes as flashing fire truck lights skim across the garage, illuminating the nasty words painted there. "*You're* not the tranny."

FAITH

Faith feels horrible for Ray. It isn't fair, the police throwing her in jail and then the media going nuts, like sharks incited by a chum bucket.

The news made a huge deal out of Ray being secretly transgender. Faith didn't get that—why *that* should be the big story—but maybe that was because she knows Ray. Ray's already super different and out there. Her being a dude before wasn't that surprising.

But if Ray hadn't shared it, it was probably because she didn't want to. And now her personal business is all over the Internet.

Faith knows that Ray was released from prison yesterday, that she's probably holed up in her house. Maybe Faith can do something nice for her, like offer to walk the dogs for free or pick up groceries. It's not enough, but at least it's an effort, like giving someone flowers when they're sick.

Early morning, as she sips coffee and listens to NPR, Faith pulls into Oleander Court. She has an hour until she needs to be at the Nobles', and she'd planned on visiting Ray and Juliet first. But as Faith coasts down Magnolia Avenue, the sight of their yard makes her freeze with her coffee halfway to her lips.

Ohmygod, what happened to the greenhouse?

It's rubble and ashes, the wooden frame a charred shell. Faith remembers how Ray was reluctant to let her pull staples from the greenhouse, she was so worried about nicks in the wood. Geez, look at it now.

Faith goes to pull into the driveway, but she pumps the brake at the sight of the graffiti on the garage door:

Tranny

It

Dyke

Fag

Faggot

Murderer

Stomach twisting, Faith reverses and guns it to the end of the cul-de-sac. It's eight, which is kind of early, but Adelaide won't care. Not if Ray needs her.

Faith had meant to visit Adelaide anyway, to tell her something. She just didn't plan on doing it so early in the morning.

No one comes to the door, so Faith rings the bell again. Finally Adelaide cracks it open, her bathrobe hanging open over striped pajamas, her hair pulled back in a ponytail. A thin sheen of sweat glistens on her forehead. "Sorry," she rasps. "I was . . . indisposed. What's goin' on, Faith?"

Adelaide's clearly hungover, but Faith pretends not to notice. "Did you see Ray's house?"

"What about it?" Adelaide asks, and her face darkens as Faith tells her. "Those *motherfuckers*."

"Yeah. Um. Do you have, like, stuff I could borrow?" Adelaide's face is a blank. "To scrub off the paint."

"Oh. Sure. Follow me." Adelaide shambles to the kitchen, where she takes a canister of oven cleaner from a shelf. "This works wonders, dependin' on the type of paint. Hopefully it's the cheap stuff. And we've got a pressure washer in the garage." Adelaide drags a hand across her face. "I'll help you," she says. "Let me just . . . gather myself." She goes to the living room and curls up on the couch, a ball of misery. It makes Faith think of Judy Garland, her mother's favorite actress of all time. Judy Garland was like the most talented person ever, but she hit the bottle, too. A lot. But maybe it's not too late for Adelaide. She could still get help.

Then Faith remembers why she'd wanted to see Adelaide anyway. "I have to tell you something." She should do this now, clear the air.

"What's that?" Adelaide pulls a blanket over her head.

Soon-Li had told Laura about the note the police interrogated Adelaide about, and Laura had told Faith. And Faith remembered *she'd* tossed the envelope at Ray's neighborhood watch meeting.

"I'm the reason the police questioned you. About that note, I mean."

"What do you mean?" Adelaide pulls the blanket down, revealing her eyes.

"Bambi gave it to me to give to William. And I didn't, but then I forgot to throw it away. Until Ray's party, when I was looking for gum and found it in my pocket. I totally tossed it without thinking about what it was."

Adelaide is staring at her. She must think Faith's a moron. Who throws away evidence of a crime at a neighborhood watch meeting when there's a police officer right there? "Why didn't you give it to William?" she asks finally.

Faith toys with the tiny charms on her bracelet. The one Adelaide had said she'd liked, the one like the one she'd lost climbing a tree. "Because I met you, and I really liked you," Faith says. "I hadn't read it yet, but I figured it was about you."

"It sure was." Adelaide tucks her legs under her, moving gingerly. "Have you told anyone else about this?"

She means the police. "Yeah," Faith says. "The head investigator— Officer Moskowitz." She'd had his card from the neighborhood watch meeting. He didn't seem too impressed with the information, like he didn't believe her.

"Did you tell him how my fingerprints got on the envelope?" Adelaide says. "Because when he asked me, I sure didn't know."

Faith remembers. "I dropped it! At your house. And you picked it up, remember?"

Adelaide shakes her head. "Nope."

"Yeah, neither did I."

Faith couldn't give Officer Moskowitz that explanation *now*. He'd think she was making it up.

"Ugh. What a mess." Adelaide leans back, closing her eyes. Faith has a feeling she'll be scrubbing that garage door herself, which is fine because she totally deserves punishment.

"I'm so sorry."

"Don't feel bad. You told what you remembered. That's the most you could have done."

That's not at all true. The most Faith could have done was thrown the letter away ages ago, in her own house. Or anywhere but where she did. And then, that ship having sailed and the letter having landed with the police, she could have been clear that she was sure Adelaide had never seen it, and how she'd touched it without knowing what it was. She could have actually *remembered* something so important.

Adelaide probably would be more ticked if she wasn't so hungover. Faith watches Adelaide scrunch herself into a ball, resting her head on her knees. "Um, can I get you anything?" she offers. "Ibuprofen? Water?"

"Ibuprofen would be—oh, shoot, don't think I can have that," Adelaide says, sounding miserable. "How about Tylenol? It's on the top shelf of the cabinet to the right of the fridge."

Faith goes to the kitchen and finds the bottle as directed. As she unscrews the top, she glances at a fat paperback resting on the counter: *What to Expect When You're Expecting.* Holy crap, Adelaide's *not* hungover. "You're pregnant?" she blurts.

"Oh, yeah," Adelaide calls from the couch. "Wouldn't think somethin' no bigger than a bean could make me feel poisoned, but yes it can. I'll be like this all morning."

"Wow," Faith says as she brings the medicine and a small cup of water back to the couch. "Congratulations."

Adelaide smiles wanly, taking the water. "Thanks. I'd say it don't feel real, except my body sure is tellin' me it is." She pops the medicine, then washes it down. "Hope that stays where it should."

As Faith watches her settle into the blankets and close her eyes, it occurs to her that Adelaide isn't that much older than her. Not even ten years. She seems way older, because she's done so much with her life: moved across the country, had a career, fallen in love, gotten married. Now she's having a baby. Faith's not close to doing any of those things.

"You're being way too nice to me about this," Faith says to her.

Adelaide grunts, her eyes still closed. "No use crying over spilled milk. And you didn't do it on purpose."

"It still sucks. A lot. You might be a suspect now."

"Nah," Adelaide mutters, squeezing her eyes tighter. Pain knits her forehead. "The truth will come out. Eventually."

"I hate you going through all this because of Bambi, though. She was a crappy person. She couldn't even be bothered to remember my name even though she had me rearranging her underwear."

"Bambi had *some* redeeming qualities, I'm sure."

"I doubt that."

"I don't. Everyone's got good and bad. Put all them good and bad pebbles on a scale, see which way it tilts." Adelaide grins. "Not that Bambi had much to her. I'm not saying that."

"I'm pretty sure she was about as one-dimensional as a cardboard cutout."

"Oh, there's stuff you didn't see," Adelaide says, waving her hand. "Not everything's out in the open. And people get misunderstood. I know all about that."

Faith feels her face heat. She'd thought of Adelaide as Trophy Wife until she'd come to deliver Bambi's note and realized what Adelaide was actually like.

Still. Some people were exactly as advertised. It wasn't like *Bambi* would have ever fed a stray cat like how Adelaide does. Faith didn't have to get to know her better to know that.

Groaning, Adelaide swings her feet to the floor. "Okay. Let's go scrub us some graffiti."

It takes an entire hour of scrubbing and spraying before Faith and Adelaide admit defeat. The color of the nasty words is gone, but the outline is there, like the second page of a notebook where someone used a sharp pencil on the first. "They're gonna need a new door," Adelaide finally concludes. There's color back in her cheeks, and she hasn't paused to dry heave in a while. Faith wonders if she made her own mother that sick when she was pregnant.

When Faith dips her scrub brush back into her bucket, the garage door starts to rumble. As it raises, Adelaide puts her hands in the air. "Don't shoot!"

The garage isn't small, but it's cluttered with junk. A lot of it gardening materials meant for the greenhouse. Just looking at it makes Faith feel bad all over again. Ray and Juliet are both coming toward them, weaving their way around the cars wedged between the junk.

"You guys didn't have to do this," Juliet says, glancing at Faith's hands. Her fingers are rubbed raw from scrubbing for so long.

"Like, obviously we did," Faith tells her. "You guys didn't deserve this."

Adelaide sits down on the driveway. "Who did it, anyway?" she asks, and Juliet tells her about some high school kids vandalizing their property. Faith knew the type—over-achieving, popular kids who got away with crazy parties because adults never believed they'd do anything wrong. "We called the cops," Juliet finishes. "See how *that* looks on a college application."

"It probably won't even show up," Faith says. "Their parents will throw money at the problem and make it go away." Kids like that never have consequences. They're above that.

Ray shrugs. "I can't even think about that right now. I'm numb."

Juliet rubs her back. "Don't worry, honey. Once the numbness fades, the rage will settle in."

Faith checks her phone. She's really late to get to Laura's, even though she'd texted her why. "I should take off," she tells everyone.

"Okay," Ray says, her eyes meeting Faith's. Her smile is so sad, it makes Faith want to cry. "See you later, kid."

Laura's waiting at the open door, hugging herself against the cold. "Saw you through the window. Get in before you freeze to death."

Faith hops up the stairs and into the inviting warm air. She drops to untie her shoes. "We didn't get the words off the door," she tells Laura. "They'll have to replace it."

"That's awful. And when they replace it, maybe it'll happen again." Laura shakes her head, looking troubled.

"They're having a really rough time," Faith says as she puts her hat on the hook by the door. "Have you talked to Ray at all about it?"

"Only by text. I asked her if she needed anything."

"She needs company, probably. You should invite them both over for a game night tomorrow."

"I doubt they're up for games."

"I bet they are. It'll take their minds off stuff."

Faith only stays at Laura's for a few hours. Enough time to help with a few things—cleaning up the basement and in the kitchen. Before she leaves, as she goes to grab a Coke from the fridge, she notices that Laura has added something to her calendar whiteboard for the following day: *Ray and Juliet, Game Night at 7.*

Faith grins. Laura's gotten Ray to agree to a double date. Ray deserves that.

TRIPP

The plates have been moved when Tripp goes to retrieve one for dinner. He opens six cabinet doors before he finds them on the shelf below the glasses, which had previously housed Sandy's casserole dishes. With a stab of irritation at the change—he'll discuss this with his wife later—Tripp grabs a blue-rimmed china plate and dishes out a generous heaping of lasagna. Gone to Dacula to visit her aging parents in their assisted living center, Sandy had left him the meal he'd requested.

But where are the rolls? Ah, there they are. A quick zap and they'll taste like they're straight out of the oven. Or so Sandy says.

Tripp covers the lasagna and places it in the microwave, jabbing the buttons. As he waits for the cheese to heat and bubble, he wanders to the front window. Raising the curtain, he finds an empty, dark street. The streetlight in front of Tripp's house has been burned out for a week. He'll have to talk to Stacey Denton about it again. That damn woman's too flighty to be trusted with the HOA.

That was one good thing about Pam—maybe she was a tad obnoxious about being president, but she always got things done.

Next door, Helen's front porch is lit. Tripp hasn't seen the old woman since her fall, but he understands she'll recover. He also understands she's going to live with relatives in Kentucky or thereabouts and her house will soon be up for sale. With any luck, the new neighbors will take better care of the yard. Tripp's grown tired of writing letters complaining about Helen's upkeep to the HOA and asking for appropriate action.

And will there be any takers? It boils Tripp's blood to think of the handful of FOR SALE signs dotting Oleander Court. The lower list prices are killing his home value.

The microwave beeps, and Tripp drops the curtain. He notices the pink roses on the accent table across from the front door. When did Sandy have time to go to the store? Her seven-layer lasagna takes hours, and today was also her day for the washing and ironing. Every Tuesday.

Tripp adjusts the roses before fetching his dinner. They're slightly off-kilter. If Sandy's going to buy flowers, she should make sure they look right. They're the first thing one sees when opening the door, and a first impression is key.

Swapping the lasagna for the rolls, Tripp pours himself a glass of pinot grigio from the open bottle in the fridge. He inhales as he takes the first sip, savoring the bite of the wine. It's been a stressful week. According to both Zillow and Redfin, his house value has dropped another fifteen grand.

Tripp now regrets contacting Officer Moskowitz. It was a misfire to shift attention onto another resident, especially considering the media attention. Now it seems that housing values will never recover. Who cares about square footage and architectural detail when your neighbor might murder you?

Tripp's food is ready, but he's no longer hungry. How did he get here? All this work, such *effort*, and the end result is living in a neighborhood dubbed "Murder Avenue." The unfairness of it fills him with rage.

Headlights wash through the curtains, and Tripp wanders to the front foyer again. The headlights cut as the car turns right, into the Colemans' driveway, and Tripp's grip on his glass tightens. It's that Jade, the Instagrammer. She has nothing better to do in her life of leisure—of *slothfulness*—than idly post updates about murders that make it sound like Oleander Court is some crime-ridden *barrio* like the one once occupied by her mother.

Jade Coleman shouldn't be on Instagram. If immigration laws were the way they should be, Jade Coleman wouldn't be living next door. She wouldn't have even been born, as her mother would have remained in Colombia where she belonged.

No one will ever know that Tripp has these kinds of opinions. Both at his firm and in his capacity as city councilman, Tripp is very active with the Latino community. Publicly, he is fully in favor of diversity, equal rights and opportunities, and in pumping resources into impoverished areas with an enhanced Latino demographic.

Obviously. A vote is a vote.

Tripp watches as Jade slams her car door and glides to the house. So arrogant, her living alone and unafraid. Does she think she's invincible, so special the killer will spare her?

After Jade disappears into her home, Tripp retrieves his dinner, utensils, and a clean linen napkin. He takes them into the dining room, arranging them at his spot at the table. His fork is slightly too far away from the knife, so he nudges it closer. There. Now he can begin.

Tripp eats methodically, pausing between conservative bites of lasagna to drink his wine. When he's done, having timed the completion of the meal with the finishing of his glass, he loads the plate into the dishwasher and pours himself another glass of wine.

He checks the time. Sandy won't be home for at least two hours. She always stays until the center closes, and it takes her an hour to drive back. More, if Sandy stops for gas or to pick up some last-minute groceries.

Tripp carries his glass to the basement, careful not to spill on the cream carpeting. Flicking on his impressive array of equipment—to fully turn on the television and PlayStation, seven switches must be engaged—Tripp thumbs through his DVDs until he finds *The Matrix*. It's a movie he watches over and over again. Anytime he can't decide what to watch, he lands on *The Matrix*.

Popping it into the PlayStation, Tripp takes a sip of wine and settles into one of the overstuffed movie chairs. He presses the button to raise the footrest.

For the next few hours, Tripp allows himself to be swept away into the dystopian world of the future, one where Keanu Reeves is young and chiseled. Tripp prefers him that way, compared with his grittier *John Wick* roles, but he'll take him either way. (He has the *John Wick* trilogy on Blu-ray, too, along with every other Keanu film.)

When the credits roll, Tripp takes his empty wine glass and bottle upstairs, his ears pricking for signs of Sandy. She's still not home. Now he remembers—tonight was the night she'd planned to stay over in Dacula, in order to help her parents with an estate sale at their old home. Tonight, Tripp has the house to himself.

Not that it makes much of a difference. At exactly ten o'clock every night, after softly saying goodnight to her husband, Sandy retires to the bedroom to begin her nighttime routine of brushing her teeth, washing her face, and applying various creams and lotions. Tripp stays up later, remembering her existence only when settling into his bed in the same room and taking care not to wake her. That might prompt conversation.

Still, it is somewhat nice to have the house to himself for a change, the license to roam without Sandy's eyes following him, a half-question always formed on her lips. Tripp fixes himself a plate of cheese and grapes and takes it down to the basement. *Matrix: Reloaded* isn't nearly as good as the first movie in the series, but Keanu has other films. *Point Break*, for example. Tripp has always found that movie highly underrated.

As Tripp pads down the stairs, he hears a muffled sound. A rustling from the guest room. Then it stops.

"Hello?" he calls out sharply. "Anyone there?" Grabbing a pool cue from the unused pool table in the open space of the basement, he opens the guest room door with a jerk, flipping on the light. "Hello?" A quick sweep of the room tells him it's empty—of a living soul, that is. Tripp had known that Sandy was using this room as a staging area to collect items for donation, but he'd had no idea of its state of clutter. The green floral bedspread is covered with old clothes stacked neatly and arranged by type. Taped-closed boxes are pressed up against the wall, in between the bed and an old nightstand. Others on the floor are assembled but empty. Tripp tosses them on the bed as he circles it, dropping to look underneath. Nothing but plastic storage containers.

Air *whooshes* through the vent near the ceiling, blowing at the curtain nearby. It rustles.

Tripp smiles, resting his hand on his chest. He should have known there was nothing to worry about—since the murders, Tripp has spent nearly ten thousand dollars on additional security equipment, to include a motion detection camera installed at every point of entry. Upon triggering of the sensor, Tripp is texted a video of the activity on his porch, back patio, or at any other door. The videos are also dated, time-stamped, and downloaded to a database maintained by the security company. The pricey measure ensures that no one comes into Tripp's house without his knowing about it.

Despite the reassurance, Tripp exercises his due diligence by searching the rest of the room and the connected bathroom. The only thing he finds amiss is the blankets hastily piled in the closet. They almost reach his waist. Making a mental note to chastise Sandy the next day, Tripp closes the door on the mess and leaves the room.

Popping the next Blu-ray into the PlayStation, Tripp goes to inspect the selection in the wine cellar. Sandy finally has taken the time to sort the wine. The bottles have been arranged by type, the boxes from the cases delivered last week discarded. It's time for a nice riesling, or maybe a chardonnay. Tripp selects one from his miniature refrigerator and removes a new glass from his hanging rack. Then he runs his fingers over the top ledge of the door, his fingers closing around the metal key. Inserting it into the lock to the room housing his treasures, he takes a sip of the full-flavored wine. This one would make an excellent pairing with goat cheese.

Leaving the key in the doorknob, Tripp moves into the room, rolling his sleeves down against the cold. Going to the war uniform serving as the centerpiece of the small area, he raises a hand to caress the rough material. Remembering himself at the last moment—he'd never risk compromising the integrity of the fabric—he lets his hand drop.

Is that a speck on a frame? Tripp squints at the wartime poster, moving closer to inspect it. Tripp rarely cleans the room—only a light dusting every now and then is warranted—but this looks like an actual smear.

As Tripp moves around the table housing the war uniform, the door slams closed. It happens so suddenly that he jumps, wine sloshing over the rim of his glass. "Shit," he mutters, on reflex glancing to make sure no liquid has spilled on or near his heirlooms.

Then he realizes he may have a larger problem. The door to the room is firmly shut, and it locks from the outside. Is he *trapped*?

"Hello!" Maybe Sandy's home. That doesn't make sense on a number of levels—nor does any explanation for her having closed the door—but Tripp clings to the possibility.

Tripp tugs on the door. It's locked, and Tripp sets his glass down to push with both hands, bracing his feet. The door is as unyielding as a wall. "Hello! Sandy!" he screams, even though he knows by now it can't be his wife on the other side of the door. He pounds on the wood, but his fists barely make a sound as they land. "*Hey!*" He's greeted by silence.

His phone! Tripp pats himself down, looking for his iPhone, then elicits a loud curse. He knows exactly where the device is—sitting neatly lined up with the PlayStation controller and TV remote in the other room. So close by, yet so far out of reach.

Maybe whoever's out there is there to burgle the home. Let them. Tripp's safe in this room. They'll leave once they're through ravaging the house, and tomorrow Sandy will come home and find him. Not the best situation, but it's much better than the one experienced by four of his neighbors in recent times.

Tripp moves the table with the war uniform closer to the wall. If his visitor swings open the door, he needs to be in a good position to confront them.

If only the Walther P38 was operable. Tripp will have to rely on his fists, and he was never one for fighting. He's never even thrown a punch before.

Tripp faces the door, flexing his hands. *Come and get me, you son of a bitch.*

His nose pricks with the scent of something acrid. What is that? Tripp sniffs the air, his eyes widening. Is that—smoke? No. No, it can't be.

Why not?

Tripp goes to the door, placing his hands against it. Is it warm? He can't tell. Maybe he's imagining things.

In a moment, however, the unmistakable smell of smoke permeates the air. *The fire alarms will go off,* he thinks, but there's nothing special about his fire alarm system. He'd sunk all his money into security. The Schulman house is equipped only with battery-run smoke detectors that shriek their alarm.

Tripp presses his hands against the door. It's certainly warm now, and his eyes are beginning to water. What can he do? The room is windowless and airless, save for the crack under the door. Tripp imagines a fire raging in the basement, flames licking at his movie room chairs and engulfing his speakers.

Smoke is pouring into the small room now, and Tripp pulls his shirt over the bottom half of his face, coughing and wheezing. It feels like his lungs are being scrubbed with sandpaper, and his eyes water against the toxic air.

"Help!" he screams, his lungs burning. The effort hurts, and the word erupts into a fit of coughing. "Help!" He bangs on the door again even though he knows the effort is useless. His head swims, the room tilting crazily, dangerously, and he slides to the floor, wheezing. "Sandy," he calls, just once.

Sandy usually comes when she's called, but not today. As Tripp's vision narrows to a black pinprick, he manages one last look around his room of treasure. And he realizes he won't be remembered as the city councilman who lived on Murder Avenue.

He'll be remembered as the Neo-Nazi who died in his tomb of Hitler artifacts.

Transcript of WAB-TV Atlanta

Aired January 21

[7:08:137] MIRANDA ALBERS, WAB-TV CORRESPONDENT: I'm standing outside the home of city councilman and prominent lawyer Tripp Schulman, whose residency on Murder Avenue—a subdivision otherwise known as Oleander Court in Alpharetta—has come to a grisly end. Late last night, as his wife was away visiting family, someone set fire to his home after having trapped him in the basement. Authorities were summoned when his next-door neighbor spotted the smoke and called 911. With me is Jade Coleman, the neighbor who made that call. Jade, what was going through your head as you did that?

JADE COLEMAN: Panic. Fear. I don't know. With everything else going on in Oleander Court—the other murders—I didn't have any hope in making that call.

MIRANDA ALBERS: It must be terrifying to have something like this happen so close to home. As I understand it, many other residents of Oleander Court are fleeing the area until the killer is caught. Do you have similar plans?

JADE COLEMAN: I-I'm not sure. Honestly, only a few weeks ago I'd come back here after being gone for years.

MIRANDA ALBERS: Oh? Why is that?

JADE COLEMAN: I have a website. ItCanHappenAnywhere.com. I started it when the murders began, and I felt the only way I could make it authentic was if I was actually here.

MIRANDA ALBERS: I see. Well, I hope you stay safe. Oh! *[Moves away]* This is Officer Moskowitz, who has acted as the lead investigator since the homicides began. Officer Moskowitz, any idea how the killer managed to escape the Schulman home without being detected?

OFFICER JOHN MOSKOWITZ: It appears the killer escaped through a storm window in the basement. The house next to the Schulmans' was empty, so they once again evaded being captured on camera.

MIRANDA ALBERS: Very interesting. That sounds like a bit of luck, but that also sounds like someone who knows the neighborhood.

OFFICER JOHN MOSKOWITZ: Yes, that's a fair assessment.

MIRANDA ALBERS: And Ray Willis, who was arrested for three of the murders, is now out on bail. Tell me—you don't think she's the culprit here, do you? To pull off something like this mere days after her return home? And if that appears unlikely, doesn't it call into question her arrest in the first place?

OFFICER JOHN MOSKOWITZ: I'm not going to comment on Mrs. Willis's charges.

MIRANDA ALBERS: Well, thank you for the information you did share. Hopefully, the next time I interview you there will be a break in the case.

And there you have it. Tragedy on Oleander Court continues with the loss of another upstanding member of our community. On behalf of the WAB-TV staff, our sympathies go out to his friends and family, with the continued hope that the person or persons behind this senseless horror are soon brought to justice.

[UNAIRED FOOTAGE]

MIRANDA ALBERS: Okay . . . what? She came back to Murder Avenue *voluntarily*? What kind of moron does that?

PAUL HANSCOMB: The same kind of moron who dies by taking a selfie on a cliff.

MIRANDA ALBERS: Nice she got to plug her website on the air.

PAUL HANSCOMB: I'm calling it now. She gets it next.

MIRANDA ALBERS: This isn't a horror movie.

PAUL HANSCOMB: I'll give you ten-to-one odds.

MIRANDA ALBERS: *[Pauses]* Make it twenty.

LAURA

When Laura wakes up on Tuesday, it feels like she's moving underwater. She doesn't usually take sleeping medications—despite the assurances on the bottle, she can't believe they aren't habit-forming—but she'd given in the night before, dry-swallowing a Tylenol PM when she'd woken, wide awake, at one in the morning. She'd imagined she'd heard police sirens, so she'd downed the pill, crawled back into bed, and pulled Pete close.

Today the family is visiting Helen at the hospital, where she's recovering nicely. Luckily—and amazingly, considering Helen's age—the breaks to her wrists and leg were stable fractures. And while she's been treated for hypothermia caused by the coldness of the basement, there have been no complications. Against doctor's orders but with his grudging consent, soon Helen will be transported to her daughter Erica's home in Tennessee, where she'll receive outpatient rehabilitative care paired with regular visits from a physical therapist.

Yawning, Laura wrinkles her nose at her dry mouth. She grabs her phone as she goes to fetch water, then does a double-take at the missed voicemails and texts from Soon-Li. Heart sinking, she unlocks the phone and stabs at the first text, which was sent right before she'd woken up last night:

Let me know you're safe. Standing outside the Schulman house. Thought you'd be here.

Laura rushes outside and leans over the balcony railing to peer at the house next to Helen's. There's nothing amiss, at least not from this vantage point. The police and the media must have come and gone.

Shivering in the cold, Laura calls Soon-Li, who picks up immediately: "Laura? I figured you were okay—the killer usually only hits up one house at a time—but still. Did you hear? Tripp's . . . dead."

"How?"

"Smoke inhalation. Someone trapped him in the house."

Laura puts her hand over her mouth. Pete hadn't liked Tripp, and Laura can't say he'd endeared himself to her, either, but he was still a human being. "Was Sandy home?"

"Nope. Away visiting her parents."

Stepping into the foyer, Laura closes the door behind her. Nicole's coming down the stairs and holding up her phone. Her eyes are wide as saucers. "Maddy saw it on the news. Another one." Her voice cracks. "Mom—I can't. I can't live here anymore." Her voice breaks, tears glistening in her eyes.

"I have to go," Laura tells Soon-Li. "I'll call later. Baby," she says to Nicole as she disconnects, "I don't know what to say." It's early, she has a dull headache, and her mouth still feels dry and fuzzy despite the glass of water. She's not equipped for this conversation. "Maybe we could go live with Grandma and Grandpa for a while."

"Fine." Nicole's arms are crossed as she sits down with a thud on the bottom stair. "Wherever isn't here."

Laura comes to sit next to her, playing with the dark hair so much like her own. "Your father and I will discuss logistics in the afternoon." She's still reeling from the news about Tripp, at the same time wondering why she's even surprised. She remembers his portrayal in Helen's painting, the grimace-smile. *Rot.*

Laura nestles against her daughter, grateful when she doesn't pull away. It's hard to predict when Nicole will reject affection. Laura still yearns for the days she could pull Nicole into her lap for a story, drawing her arms around her tiny frame, breathing in the scent of her baby shampoo. "We'll figure this out," she tells her. "I promise."

What is there to figure out? It can't be whether to leave. Only how long to stay away, or whether to come back at all.

An hour later, the family is walking through the glass doors of the hospital, which slide open to greet them with a whoosh of warm air and the scent of antiseptic. Through the labyrinth of halls and levels, they find Helen's room, a steady beep emitting from a machine. A vase of bright orange tiger lilies on the nightstand brightens the room. She's sitting up in bed, flipping through television channels with one cast-covered hand. Her eyes light up when she spots the family hovering at the door.

"The Nobles! Come in. Will be good to have some company besides this idiot box." She tries to gesture, but she only manages to drop the remote. "Oh, my. That's about the sixth time today."

Laura goes to retrieve it, placing it on the plastic tray pulled down over Helen's bed. Her water cup is empty. "Would you like some more?" Laura asks her.

"No, thank you. The trips to the bathroom are quite a process." She shifts in the bed, wincing as she hits a pain point.

"Can I adjust you?" Pete asks, and Helen directs him as he works the buttons on the side of the bed. "Ah, that's better," she says when he's finished. Laura knows it must drive her mad that she can't do it herself.

The kids are happy to visit Helen, but there's not much for them to do in a hospital room. When they begin to show signs of restlessness, Laura pulls out a ten-dollar bill. "Why don't you kids get something to eat?" she suggests. "Hospital cafeterias actually have pretty good food." She doesn't need to tell them twice.

"What's new?" Helen asks once the children are gone. Laura opens her mouth to share the news about Tripp before closing it again. Helen doesn't need to know that *both* houses flanking hers are now crime scenes.

"I have something for you," Pete says after the awkward pause, digging in his pocket for his phone. "Jade Coleman—remember how she has an . . . online story?" he asks since blogs are still a foreign concept to Helen. "She finished the one on your painting. Can I read it to you?"

Pete had shown Laura the draft earlier, and it surprised her. It was *honest*—a stunted artist's reaction to the greatness of another.

And interestingly, Laura found a parallel between the article and the painting. Jade had verbally captured the contrast between the Oleander Court of Before versus Now. Helen did so visually.

Laura watches Helen as Pete reads the ending paragraphs:

I've spent these last few weeks studying Helen's painting, sometimes finding myself drawn to her house at the center of our cul-de-sac. The neighbors say she sat on her porch for hours, staring at the neighborhood through the latticework of her trellis. Observing—assessing, I know now. Her brilliant mind putting together the pieces and imagery that would become the basis of this latest work. Her greatest work.

Helen must know it isn't only about the neighborhood. Every artist's work draws from themself—a yearning, a struggle, a desire. I see that in this painting of years lost. Of a past Helen couldn't and didn't want to shake. I see the narrative of Helen, who has been out of the public eye for so many years.

She's no longer hidden behind the latticework. We see her.

When Pete finishes, Helen is still, her hands still gripping her blankets. Only her throat moves, her Adam's apple twitching. "Wow," she says finally. "That's some story."

"I was surprised by how well it turned out," Pete says, sinking into a chair by the window and pulling it closer to Helen. "I expected sensationalist fare. And when I really started digging through her articles— she's talented. It's a shame she wastes it by promoting products on Instagram."

"It's reverent," Laura contributes quietly, watching a single tear slide through the crevices of Helen's cheeks. It finally stops, glistening, at the edge of her chin.

"Yes." Helen coughs. "And quite right. Everyone wants to be seen."

Laura thinks of Helen situated on her porch swing, watching the neighborhood residents passing by on the sidewalk. Some acknowledged her—a quick wave, a word. But so many others didn't. It was easy to pretend not to see the woman behind the trellis.

"She can share it," Helen tells Pete. "Why not?"

"She'll be thrilled," Pete says, already tapping away at his phone to send Jade a text. As he does, his phone buzzes. "Ha! Wouldn't you know it? The kids are lost. Be right back." He leaves the room, the phone pressed to his ear. "Nicole?"

Alone with Helen, Laura doesn't know what to say. During these last few weeks, Laura's often sneaked away to contemplate her own image in the triptych. She feels vain for doing so—like poring over old yearbook pictures to lament younger skin, thicker hair.

"Something's troubling you," Helen says. "Spit it out."

"Oh, it's nothing."

Helen appraises her with those clever, shrewd eyes that Laura has come to learn see everything. "Clearly not."

"Is that how you see me?" Laura asks finally. "In the painting. I seem . . . desperate."

"Oh, dear." Helen struggles to adjust her position, but she's pinned in place. "Is that how you read it?"

"How else would I?" Laura mimes hands pressed against glass, the grin Helen had slashed across her face.

"Darling, it's surrealism. The nature of surrealism is exaggeration."

"Ah. That explains it, then." *Great, I'm snapping at a hospitalized old woman.*

Helen tilts her head. "Was I wrong?"

"No." That's why Laura's so upset. In coming to Oleander Court, she'd wanted so badly to become part of the neighborhood's fabric, to seamlessly fit into the social scene of parties, barbeques, and book clubs. To be a part of a society she'd never been before. She'd seen the opportunity of moving there as a fresh start—like beginning a new school where no one knew what a dork you were, where a new haircut and a growth spurt could make you someone different, better. The InfoHealth sale had made that possible, or so she had thought.

"Wanting to fit in isn't the worst thing," Helen says, playing with the cup she wouldn't let Laura refill. "But it could be worth thinking about why it's so important."

Pete comes in, the children trailing behind. "Found them! Only a hall corner away, turns out. What'd we miss?"

"Not much," Laura says, her cheeks reddening. Pete doesn't know that she's embarrassed about her portrayal in Helen's painting. He himself has nothing to be sensitive about. Helen has him raking the leaves, for goodness' sake. *Pete is industrious and helpful,* the image says. It couldn't be less objectionable.

"We're going to miss you," Pete says as they leave. "The neighborhood won't be the same without you."

"The neighborhood isn't the same *with* me," Helen points out. "That's why I'm leaving." She gives a sad smile.

Faith's car is in the driveway when the family arrives home. Laura had needed help with tidying and preparing a dinner with actual nutritional value. When they walk through the garage door, the air is fragrant with carrots and broth. Faith's famous minestrone is simmering on the stove.

"You're too good to be true, Faith," Pete says as he slips off his shoes.

"Yeah, I'm basically the best." Faith finishes stirring the soup and rests the ladle on a paper towel. "How's Helen? And how was game night yesterday?"

Laura unbuttons her coat, unwrapping her scarf from around her neck. "Game night?" she repeats.

"Yeah. Last night. With Ray and Juliet."

"Oh, they cancelled. I went to bed early instead." Should she mention what happened to Tripp? Even after the events of recent months, Laura's unsure of how to bring up the subject: *And by the way, there was another murder.*

"What? I thought it was set." Faith starts slicing the celery with vigor.

"Ray changed her mind. Said she wasn't up for it."

"Well, that sucks," Faith mutters to herself, and Laura notices the dark circles under her eyes, like purple bruises. Faith adores Ray, Laura knows—she's mentioned over and over how funny Ray is, what a good person.

Faith hasn't shown an emotional reaction to Ray's arrest, but that doesn't mean she doesn't care. She just doesn't wear her feelings on her sleeve, like Laura does.

"Ray will be okay," Laura tells her, even though she has no basis for saying so. "Helen, too. She's healing really well for such an old gal."

Pete laughs, opening the fridge to remove a beer. "What? It's almost five," he says at Laura's glance.

"I still can't believe she fell down the stairs," Faith says as she adds a pinch of basil to the soup. "And that she had to lie there until you found her. That's so awful."

"Especially because of how she was spooked first," Pete says as he opens the utensil drawer. "I'm glad she didn't wake up. The poor thing might have had a heart attack, lying there and worrying that the killer was coming for her." Expertly, he flips off the bottle top.

"What do you mean, spooked?" Faith pauses, jar of minced garlic in one hand and tiny spoon in the other. "Like, she thought someone was in the house?"

"Yeah," Pete says. "She thought she heard something. And tripped when she turned around." He takes a drink of his beer. "But there was no one after her, thank God."

Faith's face is pinched. "Geez," she says, picking up the garlic again and untwisting the top. "I didn't know that. I hate thinking of that. She's so nice. And funny, too. Like, half the time she'll make some comment and you won't realize it's funny until half a second later. She's crazy clever."

Laura puts her hand on Faith's back as she reaches in the cabinet above her for the soup bowls. "Don't worry about Helen. Her daughter will take good care of her now."

"Yeah, but she didn't have to fall," Faith says. "She never would have, if she hadn't been worried about being next on the list."

"Well, I guess we'll have to blame it on the murderer," Pete says.

Faith adds the garlic and shakes the rest of the spices into the soup. "This'll be ready in about twenty minutes," she tells Laura. "I have to go. I totally forgot I was supposed to pick up my friend at the airport. She'll be ticked if I make her wait."

"Oh . . . sure," Laura says, surprised at the sudden departure. Faith's not the type to forget things. Then again, everyone's been jumpy lately, forgetful—including herself. "Drive carefully, okay?"

After Faith leaves, Laura finds herself wandering into the dining room to, once more, look at Helen's painting. As always, her eye is drawn to her own image, the expression on her face.

This time, Laura steps back to see the triptych as a whole. The ugliness of the middle panel, the waste, and the garish caricatures of her neighbors. That's when she sees it—the same way the image in an ambiguous drawing will flip from a duck to a bunny, an old crone to a young lady, with a refocusing of the eyes.

At the hospital, Helen had told her to think about why fitting in in Oleander Court was so important to her. Why was it? From the time she'd arrived in the neighborhood, she'd seen the rot herself, smelled it. Pam, gossiping about everyone and judging with a quick swipe of her eyes. The general obsession with appearance and opulence, with a few notable outliers.

The tragedy of Laura's figure isn't that she's looking out on something she can't have. It's that she wants it in the first place.

As Laura stares at the picture, she realizes how foolish she's been. She'd wanted to belong, but in what sense? She'd never throw a party just to show off, or judge a neighbor for their landscaping.

And she and Pete didn't choose Oleander Court because it was the place to be. They chose it for their family. The safety, the schools. The house that had felt like a home the moment they'd stepped inside.

Laura leans forward, stopping just short of touching one of the apples in the middle panel of the triptych. The rot, the waste. She's not part of it.

And because she's not part of it, Laura suddenly understands that she will be spared.

ADELAIDE

William had burst out laughing when he'd picked up Adelaide outside Soon-Li's house. "Are you going incognito?" he'd asked, taking in the white-framed glasses Soon-Li had let her borrow.

"Sure am."

It had felt like a lifetime had gone by since Officer Moskowitz had come calling the day before. William and Bambi Holiday. It couldn't be true. Every time Adelaide thought about it—especially when her imagination added any kind of detail—her stomach heaved.

"I need to talk to you," Adelaide had said during the short drive home, and he'd turned to look at her.

"Everything okay?"

"I guess we'll see."

Tension crackled as William followed Adelaide into the kitchen from the garage. She'd folded her arms, pacing the length of the marble island. A crystal bowl held pears, oranges, and apples artfully arranged during the cleaner's last visit. Perfect, perfect, perfect.

"I'll just get it out," Adelaide said, her heart tapping painfully as she looked into William's concerned eyes. *Hopefully* she'd get it out. She'd been Ms. Waterworks lately. "I need you to tell me the truth."

"Okay . . ." William said slowly. "The truth about what?"

"Were you havin' an affair with Bambi Holiday?"

William's eyes widened. "Who told you that?"

Not, *Of course not,* or *What?* Instead, *Who told you that?*

"Oh, God. It's true!" Adelaide's voice, high and tinny, frightened her. She'd spun on her heel and headed for the stairs, her trembling hand gripping the banister.

William followed, grabbing for her, but she'd wrenched away. "Don't *touch* me." Bounding up the stairs like a rabbit, she'd raced for their bedroom, fully intending to slam the door behind her.

"Adelaide. Adelaide. *Adelaide!*" As she'd reached the room, something in his tone made her look back.

"What?"

"It was years ago," he'd said, raking his hand through his hair. "Years. Before I knew you."

"Was she married then?" Adelaide snapped.

"Yes. And I'm so ashamed. They took vows. And I—" his voice cracked.

"—helped her break 'em."

"I'm not going to make excuses," William said.

"I'd like to hear some excuses," Adelaide responded, hands on her hips. "What would make you fool around with a married woman? You're better than that. Least, I thought you were."

William spread his hands. "She came over once. Getting signatures for some zoning thing for her pool house. She ended up staying for a drink. It turned into two. She didn't have anywhere to be, and I wasn't on call for once. That was the first time it happened. It was an accident."

"Oh, I just hate accidents like that," Adelaide said sarcastically. "When a woman falls and is impaled on a man's penis. Such a terrible tragedy."

"You asked!" William was quiet for a moment. "I was so terribly lonely," he'd said finally. "Every day. And then she showed up on my doorstep, smiling at me. Making it easy. Letting me forget for a while that I didn't have anyone."

Adelaide didn't say anything. She went to the bed to sit down.

"It was casual. Fun. That was all. She didn't ask anything of me, and I didn't want anything from her."

"Except sex," Adelaide was quick to clarify.

"It wasn't even that. It was the companionship. The intimacy."

Adelaide was trying to wipe the image of her husband having "intimacy" with Bambi Holiday when he'd continued: "And then one day," he said, coming to sit next to her, "I stopped at Starbucks. And I tried to claim a pumpkin spice latte that was not rightfully mine." Adelaide smiled back at him, at the memory. She couldn't help it, damn him. "And I saw you. And, Adelaide—" He'd paused, his jaw working. Adelaide let him push her hair behind her ear. "Adelaide, it was like coming home, looking into your eyes. I don't care if that sounds like a line. I looked into those green eyes, and I was done for."

"Well, my great beauty has felled many a strong man," Adelaide said, laughing nervously. He was staring at her so intently.

"No." He shook his head. "It was you. And then I got to know you— this scrappy, smart girl who'd pullled herself up by her bootstraps. So strong, so hardworking. Funny. Adelaide, I've never met anyone like you. I get to *be* with you." He'd paused, as if choosing his words, how to explain.

"It's not that I'd never do anything to jeopardize that. It's that it would never even cross my mind."

Tears blurred Adelaide's vision. She'd spent so much energy worrying that she'd never be good enough for William. That she didn't deserve him, because he was a doctor who came with a ready-made home in a place like Oleander Court. And she was, what? Nobody. Nothing.

William had never seen her that way. God, what a fool she'd been.

"Being with Bambi was a mistake," William said, his hand over hers. "But it's not one I made after I met you. I promise you that."

"Why did you lie to me, then? And keep lyin' to me? You coulda fessed up at any time."

"I was ashamed. At first, I didn't want to say anything that would make you run. And after, I worried how you'd react to my not having been truthful." His eyes held hers. "I'm sorry. For all of it."

A great relief had filled Adelaide. It was as if she'd been holding her breath for years, and she'd finally realized she didn't need to anymore. He was telling the truth, but he'd also screwed up royal. Not even William was perfect, and knowing that made her want to flat-out cry with joy. She didn't want a perfect man, because she'd never be the perfect woman.

She'd decided not to tell him about the baby right then. It was too much. Instead, she'd decided to think of another way to tell him, one that was even better than spelling it out on a tray. One they'd both remember forever.

Now, though, she needs to do it soon. Every morning, she hauls herself downstairs to throw up in the privacy of the bathroom off the living room. And it takes everything in her to act like she doesn't feel like she's been beaten by a stick when she kisses William goodbye each morning. As soon as he's out the door, she goes back to dying on the couch, but even the actress in her has trouble putting on a show until then.

It was an accident that Faith had found out before William. Before anyone else, actually. Adelaide hadn't meant to leave the baby book out on the counter—she'd been thumbing through it as she waited for her tea—but she's not worried. Faith's the kind of girl who can keep a secret. After all, she'd kept Adelaide's even though it turned out there was nothing to hide. *Roberto.* Ridiculous. She'd picked flowers for his wife, for God's sake. Invited him in for breakfast with her husband sitting right there at the kitchen counter.

Even after much googling, nothing seems right. There are hundreds of cute baby announcement ideas, but none of them are Adelaide and William. One night, though, as Adelaide listens to William snore softly as she drifts into sleep, the idea simply appears. She falls asleep quickly, a smile on her face.

The next day is a rare morning off for William. "Let's go to Starbucks," Adelaide says, pulling him out of bed. The morning sickness is slightly better today—she doesn't feel like she's crawled out of a trash can—and she beams at him as they get ready.

At the café, Adelaide whispers to the barista when William's out of earshot, studying the merchandise for sale. When his drink comes up—a grande extra-hot latte this time, as pumpkin spice lattes are seasonal—William's name is called. He thanks the barista as he grabs it from the counter, not sparing it a glance as he takes it to the sugar station.

As he reaches for the canister of sugar, he takes a second look at the black wording on the side of the cup:

Dad

September 20

For a moment, he stares at it. Then he turns to Adelaide. "Is it—? Are you—?"

She nods. "I am. We're going—" she begins, but he's crushing her in a hug, raising her off the floor. He kisses her as the small crowd gathered in the café stares.

"I can't believe it," he says, pulling his forehead to hers. "Are you sure?"

"Two tests and a doctor visit," she tells him. "Better be sure."

"I'm going to be a dad." He raises his arms. "I'm going to be a dad!"

"You're embarrassin' me," Adelaide tells him, but it's fine. More than fine. She'll always remember the moment her typically reserved husband shouted in Starbucks about becoming a father.

On the way home, they stop at a gas station. "I'm gettin' a bottled water," Adelaide tells her husband as he fills the tank, closing the car door with her hip. She walks inside, running her hand over her flat stomach. How long until she shows?

Choosing a liter from the selection, Adelaide breezes past the newspaper display. As she does, her own face catches her eye—a publicity shot from *Zombie 101* juxtaposed with a candid shot of Ray unlocking her front door. A picture of Juliet is below the two. It looks like a professional photo lifted from her law firm's website.

"The Lesbian Love Triangle of Murder Avenue." It's the *Star Gazette*, the lowest of the low when it comes to tabloids. Still, people read it—lots of people. Adelaide snatches it and marches to the counter with it facedown. "Just these," she says, hoping the teenaged cashier will scan the paper's barcode without flipping it over.

He flips it over. His eyebrows practically shoot into his shaggy hair as he compares the front cover of the tabloid to the woman in front of him. "I've never been on the cover of a magazine," Adelaide says as she picks up her purchase with as much dignity as she can muster. "No such thing as bad publicity, right?"

She pages through the magazine after she slides into the car. It's all garbage—rampant speculation on all fronts—and it's not easy to read. According to the tabloid, she and Ray are murdering, secret lovers, with Juliet caught in the middle of their pure evil.

The worst is her old mug shot. Where'd they even get that? Adelaide winces at the picture, glad the purple eyeshadow had at least rubbed off before they'd taken the shot. "Couldn't turn down a dare, could you?" she berates her younger, dumber self.

She'd expected the news to get nasty. The media's been having a field day with Ray-as-Steven ever since it was announced. It was only a matter of time before Ray's relationship with a younger woman down the street got blown up into something it wasn't. Sex sells. Always has, and always will.

Adelaide hates to think of Juliet's reaction to all this. Seeing her own face splashed across a tabloid, but as an afterthought. The real story is with Adelaide and Ray, secret lovers.

Juliet's opinion of Adelaide isn't getting better anytime soon.

JADE

As soon as Jade had seen the smoke curling up from the base of the Schulman house, she'd known it was too late. Still, she'd raced to dial 911 and hoped that maybe, this time, the emergency would amount to nothing more than a pan left on a stove.

It didn't. As Jade had watched a white-shrouded body wheeled out on a stretcher, a sob racked through her. She hadn't really known Tripp, and her impression of him hadn't exactly been positive. But he was a person, and he was dead, and he used to live right next to her.

Rather than go inside and lock the door, she'd stayed on her porch. She was rooted there, unable to stop staring at the activity at the Schulman house. And she didn't want to go inside and be alone with her thoughts. Jade wanted her mother to comfort her.

As Jade stood there, frozen, a reporter had hustled up her porch steps, extending her microphone and a wide smile. Jade doesn't remember exactly what she said. She was in shock.

Since Tripp's murder a week ago, Jade hasn't spent a single night in her house. She hates that—that she can't feel safe there. The wraparound porch, which hugs the entire house, was where she'd learned to ride a bike, going around and around until it drove her parents crazy. The wall by the refrigerator is where they measured her height. (The chart is still on the wall.) They still have the same couch she'd cried on when Tommy Slater broke her heart in high school.

Jade has packed up and moved in with Uncle Jack's family, staying in a guest room with exercise equipment pushed against the wall. It makes her feel like a kid again, and not in a good way. Like Jade's there because she doesn't have her shit together in her personal life or career, which is exactly the case. She's twenty-eight and drifting. *Floating.*

Every night, Jade stares at the ceiling, waiting for sleep. She doesn't want to get out of bed, because any unusual night movements will be reported back to her mother, who will in turn tell Jade she's not sleeping because she's haunted by Oleander Court. That she needs to come to Tampa to see her father's new restaurant.

Pat Coleman's retirement is now over, just as everyone knew it soon would be. He'd fallen in love with a dumpy little seafood place and offered to invest in its renovation and menu upgrade. He'll be the head chef, of course. The owners are thrilled.

Her parents have already asked Jade to provide her marketing perspective. They say they could use her Instagram skills.

Jade loves the idea of helping her parents, and she will, but the drifting is driving her mad. She doesn't want to continue Instagramming about products she doesn't believe in. Over the last six days, she's posted about "organic" toothpaste, earth-friendly sanitary pads, a fruit juice so bad she thought it was spoiled when she took a sip, and a granola cookie so hard it required a long dip in milk before Jade could take a bite without breaking off a tooth.

On Instagram, however, all those products are good finds. Amazing! Jade loves them all. And of course, here is the link for purchase.

Every day, Jade gets up early and drives to Oleander Court. None of the murders have ever happened during the day. Jade comes home, locks the door, and checks every possible place a killer could be hiding. Then she works on her website in the kitchen, back facing the wall and her father's largest knife next to her laptop.

Jade's last article has gotten a tremendous amount of attention. It has over three hundred comments, some of them praising Jade's writing. A literary agent even emailed her, asking if she'd thought about writing a book about "Murder Avenue."

That reach-out had jolted Jade. When Jade was in undergrad, she'd written a book—a long, unwieldy romantic comedy not unlike those she enjoyed at the time. She didn't tell anyone about it. She didn't ask anyone to read it. Instead, she'd sent out emails to literary agencies all over the country, fantasizing about the moment she could tell her parents about her resulting book deal. The achievement would not just be a sign, but *proof* that Jade was meant to get an MFA instead of an MBA. Her parents would be confused about the switch, but they'd understand.

Nothing happened from the effort. No agent, and no book deal. And then the deadlines came for applying to schools. Jade applied to MBA programs, not MFA programs. Just like her parents wanted, especially her mother. Anita Coleman hadn't had the chance to go to business school, so Jade would go for her. Jade put the book away in her computer files and never looked at it again. But she's thought about it a lot, especially during her year of Instagramming after her PR firm downsized.

What was she doing, wasting herself like this? What would it take to get her to stop? To have the courage to go for what she really wants? To have a chance to one day make a contribution like Helen's magnificent painting? She has promise. She knows that now.

The agent who reached out was from an agency Jade recognized. Before she can second-guess herself, Jade writes back, letting her know she's not interested in writing a book about "Murder Avenue," but that she'd be interested in another angle. The juxtaposition of the old neighborhood with the new.

She wonders what the agent will think of the article about Helen's painting. She's holding on to it, teasing her followers with a countdown to "Oleander Court making history." The first public release of a Helen Beecham original in forty years.

Jade sends the email and rises from the table, draining her coffee and heading out the front door. The contact doesn't mean anything, but it brings Jade back to six years ago, the hope that filled her chest every time she saw a new email from an agent in her inbox. She takes her phone and walks outside, bracing against the cold air.

In the front yard, Jade snaps a picture of her home. She takes another of the tree out front, the one that used to have a tire swing until the branch snapped. Then she moves down the sidewalk, taking picture after picture of houses, elements of Oleander Court. She's outside for nearly an hour, her hands chapped and pink by the time she's come full circle.

Jade barely notices the cold. In the hall closet, her mother has dozens of scrapbooks. Each one has a theme—holidays, birthdays, favorite places. The latter including the neighborhood, of course. When Jade returns inside, she'll leaf through them, looking for the same images she's just taken. She'll use the contrast as the basis for stories—before and after. Jade's not exactly sure how she'll execute it, or the exact theme, but the prospect of figuring it out exhilarates her.

For the first time in a long time, Jade suspects she'll sleep fine that night.

RAY

oberto and his crew are almost finished with removing the remains of Ray's beloved greenhouse from the lawn. After its destruction, Ray had come out to her side yard to find what remained—a single lavender orchid somehow completely unharmed by the flames. When a piece of glass had shattered, it had created a makeshift shelter for the plant. Using her gardening gloves, Ray had carefully unearthed the flower from the rubble and planted it in a ceramic pot she'd recovered from a shelf in the garage.

Now it sits on her kitchen counter. Is it a reminder of how hated she is? Or that, no matter what, survival is possible?

As Ray peers out her curtain, a white van pulls up alongside the sidewalk. A man wielding a large camera jumps out and snaps pictures as Roberto's men carefully rake up what's left of the glass shards. It's taken them the entire morning to remove the thousands of pieces from the brittle grass, to comb the yard for slivers. After this, they'll plant topsoil where the greenhouse used to be. Soon it will be like it was never there.

The cameraman steps on Ray's lawn as he moves closer to Roberto's crew. Normally, Ray would fly out the door. Inform him to either get lost or get ready to taste his own camera, since Ray was about to shove it up his ass.

Today, a shot of her is exactly what he wants. So, instead of defending herself and her property, Ray stays hidden.

She can't even go out for another scrub at the garage door. Talk about a photo op. Instead, Ray's called a company to come out and replace it.

When Roberto's done, he knocks on Ray's door. She opens it reluctantly, almost expecting a cameraman to pop out of her bushes like a jack-in-the-box. "All finished, Mrs. Willis," he says, his handsome face creasing in a smile. "The patch will be gone in no time."

"I'll get my checkbook," Ray says, but Roberto holds up his hand.

"No fee," he says. "We are happy to do it. But sad this happened to you."

God, he has kind eyes. No wonder Adelaide's so crazy about him and his little girl. "You don't have to do that."

He shrugs. "No. But we all want to." From the truck, Miguel—the young guy Ray always talks shit to about football—raises his hand. Ray waves in return, tears filling her eyes. The kindness moves her, as had finding Adelaide and Faith in her driveway. It showed her she wasn't alone in this.

"Thank you," she says.

After the truck leaves, carting away the pieces of Ray's place of solace, she sinks into her couch, pulling her computer into her lap. She won't read the news stories. Every nasty word hurts. Instead, Ray finds herself accessing Facebook, drawing up Becky's profile. Ray's Friends with her little sister, and Becky posts frequently. It's not hard for Ray to keep track of the major (and minor) events in Becky's life: lunch at an Italian restaurant with friends, birthday celebrations, complaints about the weather.

Ray goes to Becky's photos and is surprised at the option to access "photos of you and Becky." When she clicks on it, she finds several extremely unflattering photos of herself from the one Christmas she and Juliet had spent with Ray's family. It had been horribly awkward, with no one knowing how to act. Juliet had tried too hard and come across as abrasive, grating. Ray had taken offense at everything her parents said. Everything had a double meaning, every comment an insult. She'd been depressed for weeks after the visit.

Still, Becky's kept the pictures. She's "tagged" Ray in them, too, meaning that Ray could have found them anytime.

As Ray is clicking through Becky's photos, the garage door rumbles. A minute later, Juliet comes through the door. Her face is drawn, and she sinks into the love seat across from Ray. "God," she says, draping her arm over her face. "What next?"

"Can I get you anything?" Ray asks, snapping the laptop closed. She's surprised Juliet didn't say anything about it.

"Water," Juliet says, removing her arm from her face. "Ray."

"What?" Ray asks, taking in her wife's anguished look. "What happened?"

"I was . . ." Juliet swallows. "I was let go today."

"They *fired* you?"

Juliet nods.

"Those *fuckers*!" Ray is outraged on behalf of her wife. Juliet's given Ponce, Prince & Cushman the best years of her working life. She's spent twelve hours a day holed up in her office, taken her work home with her. She's landed her own clients, found brilliant solutions, earned her way up. And they were *firing* her?

"Are they, though?" Juliet says miserably. She reaches into her handbag, pulling out the *Star Gazette*. The couple's own faces gaze back at them from the cover. "Honestly, they've been extremely supportive since . . . everything." *Your arrest for murder.* "But when this hit, suddenly they were getting calls from clients, asking me to be pulled off their accounts. Some threatened to walk if I worked there at all."

Ray swallows. Like most jobs, Juliet's is at-will. Until she made partner, she had no "right" to keep her job, no recourse if she got fired. Not unless she was discriminated against, and could she really argue that was the case? Juliet's firm would lose money if it kept her. Letting her go was a business decision that made complete sense.

"Some of the clients hadn't even known I was a lesbian," Juliet says. "Despite—well." She gestures to herself. With her short hair and pantsuits, Juliet did fit the stereotype. "Now they do." Juliet never offered her orientation to clients. Less was best when dealing with the conservative older men who ran the companies that hired Juliet's firm.

"So now what?" Ray asks.

"They gave me four months of severance," Juliet says. "That was actually generous, considering they didn't have to offer me anything."

"Generous, my ass. That's half the partner bonus you would have gotten in two years." Remembering the water Juliet had asked for, Ray fetches it from the kitchen and brings it to her wife. Juliet swallows it all in a few gulps.

"Ray," she says, wiping her mouth. "What are we going to do?"

"We have plenty of savings. We'll be okay."

They don't, though. Since Ray's settlement, her savings have gradually dwindled away. And they're not big spenders, but they have expenses. The mortgage, house repairs. Just last year, replacing all the front windows had run them fifteen thousand dollars.

Juliet sets the glass on the coffee table, cradling her head in her hands. "What are we going to do?" she whispers. "I can't get another job. Who would hire me with all this going on?"

Ray doesn't have an answer for her. "All this" is all about her. The trial might not be over for eight months. In the meantime, any prospective employer would google "Juliet Willis" and find the cover of the *Star Gazette*.

They've also been informed that an excellent criminal defense might cost an entire year of Juliet's salary. Now there's no salary.

"I feel physically ill," Juliet says, rising.

"I'm running you a bath," Ray announces. "Bath bomb, bubbles—the works. And while you're in there, I'll order a pizza. A cheap one," she adds. "Come, come." She grabs Juliet's arm, guiding her upstairs. Juliet's been taking care of her for weeks. It's time Ray returned the favor.

Upstairs, Ray plugs the bathtub and turns the knobs, watching water gush from the faucet. Growing up in Charleston, Ray never had a bathtub like this—it was the same standard, rectangular bathtub you'd find in a hotel. The bathroom floor was yellow tile, which her mother grumbled about cleaning—those cracks were a bitch—with sea accents like the pastel shell-shaped decorative soaps, which Ray had tried to eat as a kid. Twice.

Memories—or, rather, details—keep assaulting Ray like this lately. She assumes it's some pathological need for her parents, the nurturers, during her time of need. That's what her therapist would say.

"It's all yours," Ray says once there are enough bubbles for Juliet to float away on. As her wife strips off her clothes, kicking them to the side,

Ray feels a pang of guilt. When did Juliet get so thin? She looks like a scrawny cat. She lowers herself into the bubbles, shooting Ray a smile through closed lips.

"Thanks, babe."

"Take your time." Closing the door behind her, Ray pads down the stairs. Pulling her iPhone from her pocket, she unlocks the screen. Already her heart is pounding.

Ray remembers the day she told her parents about her gender-affirming surgery, how her mother had asked her to leave the house because of her father's reaction. After, Ray remembered it as being *thrown* out of the house. But was that what had happened? Becky had followed her to her car—feet bare, arms wrapped around herself. It was October. "Drive around for a while," she'd told her older sister. "He just needs some time. It's . . . huge, you know?" Ray had practically snarled as she'd peeled out of the driveway, shutting off her phone. She hadn't stopped driving until she was back in Georgia. What if she hadn't shut off her phone? Or if she'd driven back?

And her parents hadn't completely disowned her. They still tried, a little—cards, and the occasional call or text. She never reached out, not even when she wanted them. Needed them. She figured the contact was unwanted, but had she ever tested that theory?

Exhaling shakily, Ray scrolls down her contacts list and hits a button. Maybe it will go straight to voicemail. Or the ringing will cut off with the unmistakable indication of a declined call.

"Hello? Ray, how are you holding up? We've been waiting for you to call."

Ray doesn't hide the sob that rises from her throat. "I've missed you, Mom."

SOON-LI

Soon-Li misses the quiet activity of Oleander Court. It was like a perpetual loop of a dull but comforting soundtrack. She'd never realized that she found peace in it.

The neighborhood isn't quiet anymore. It's silent, still, and not only because of the horror that's befallen Oleander Court. It's because it's emptying. Of the twenty-three houses in the neighborhood, nearly half are vacant—either because a resident was killed or because the inhabitants have packed up and left. Oleander Court is a shell of what it used to be, and the absolute, utter silence crackles in Soon-Li's ears like static.

Cradling her mug in her hands, Soon-Li glances at her elliptical. It's once again draped in wet clothes. Maybe she should invest in a treadmill instead. Something where she could feel her feet beating against the belt, her earbuds blaring music and keeping out dark thoughts.

Oh, sure. The Jungs could use two clothes racks.

Tran comes down the stairs, dressed in a suit he'd had tailored but still doesn't seem to fit him. His hair is combed over his thin spot. "Wish me luck," he tells her as he places his leather attaché case on the kitchen table. He only uses it when meeting prospective clients.

"Good luck," Soon-Li says, going to kiss him. He doesn't need it. Their firm's reputation speaks for itself. In fact, right now they're hunting for new employees—ones with Top Secret security clearances—who can support its newest Department of Defense contract. While Soon-Li typically has no role with the HR functions of the firm, she wouldn't trust anyone else to hand-pick the candidates. That's what she's supposed to be doing today—poring over the résumés to determine who the firm wants to engage.

In a moment Tran's out the door, and Soon-Li taps her fingers against her mug. She wanders to the front windows. Across the street, Laura's climbing into her car, and Soon-Li raises her mug to her lips even though she knows it's empty.

Soon-Li can't shake the uneasy feeling she has about Laura. On Halloween night, it was Laura who ran off to investigate Beverly's house. And Laura had gone to Pam's party. She would have known about the floating staircase, the alcove with its wide windows.

Ray's fingerprints had been found on the wine bottle that poisoned Beverly. Meanwhile, it was Laura who had shown up on Ray's doorstep after Pam's party, carrying the gift bags for both women. Leaving Ray alone while she used the restroom.

And the dog poop bag found in Conner's pool drain? Laura has a dog, too.

Soon-Li puts her mug in the dishwasher and goes to her home office. Closing the door behind her, she locks it via the padlock and goes to her swivel chair. She has several screens hooked up to her computer monitor, and she switches them all on. Already, her palms are sweaty. She enters the double passwords needed to access her computer and watches the screen load. Her hands are shaking as she types in a series of numbers.

Soon she's drawn up the IP addresses of all computers and laptops located in a quarter-mile radius. On another screen, she pinpoints their exact locations, designated in red dots on a map. There are forty active computers on Jasmine Lane and Magnolia Lane. Soon-Li starts in order, beginning with the first house on the left when entering the subdivision. The Womacks.

This is called "ghosting," a delicate craft impossible for most engaged in the art form of computer hacking. Soon-Li's practice doesn't focus on computer hacking, but cybersecurity is its close sister and she is one of the few who can do what she's about to do.

Swiftly typing a series of codes, the screen of Soon-Li's computer melts away to reveal a different desktop, one with far more folders than Soon-Li's own neat arrangement and a screensaver of a smiling family.

Chewing on her lower lip, Soon-Li goes to work sweeping the contents: browsing the folders, accessing the applications, logging into email and bank accounts with workaround passcodes, reviewing browser and search history. After an hour of careful perusing, she's found nothing. It's time to move on to the next computer.

If anyone were to find out what Soon-Li was doing, she wouldn't just lose her security clearance and destroy her company's reputation. Federal statutes criminalize her current activities, assessing weighty monetary penalties and jail sentences for each act of access.

They won't, however. "Ghosting" is named as such for a reason. Like an apparition, Soon-Li will slip in and out of each computer without leaving a trace. But when she's done, she might have the answers she needs, ones that have eluded the police so far.

If they point to her new friend, Soon-Li will deal with that when the time comes.

FAITH

After the Greyhound bus drops her at the town center of Johnsonville, North Carolina, Faith walks the two miles to her aunt's house. It feels good to stretch her legs, to feel her muscles straining as her breath escapes in puffs of air. Johnsonville looks just as she remembered it from when she visited last February, which isn't surprising since it's looked the same since Faith was born. The fountain at the traffic circle changes color in the summer, but it's turned off now. Nothing to distract anyone from the gold paint chipping off its sides, like an aging tree.

Faith smiles as she passes the pie place. It smells like apple today. Her aunt Connie always said she'd never leave Johnsonville because she'd never leave a town that always smelled like pie. Connie was simple like that—a sweet woman who laughed a lot and still believed in God (also a lot) after her husband died from lung cancer even though he didn't even smoke. The other guys in the factory where he worked did, which was beyond a bummer. How much did it suck not to smoke when you probably wanted to—for years and years and years—only to die because other dudes couldn't help themselves?

Faith shifts her backpack, adjusting the straps that keep slipping down her puffer coat. Her boots pinch, and she's practically limping by the time she makes it to the gravel road that leads to her aunt's old house. It's hidden behind scraggly trees, and Faith breathes out shakily when she turns the corner, tears stinging her eyes. This is where she and Nick drew on the garage floor in chalk, where they built hideouts in the two acres of woods behind the house, where Faith and her aunt and mother spent hours making cookies, soups, cakes—whatever—as Nick clutched his stomach and whined that he was starving.

The house looks abandoned, but that's probably because Faith knows it is. Under Connie's will, everything went to Faith's mother, Connie's only sister, and Faith's mother won't come here. A NO TRESPASSING sign is fixed under the oak in the front yard, but it looks like an afterthought.

Like Johnsonville has robbers, anyway. It might feel way different from Alpharetta, but it's just as safe. Probably safer now, given the murder spree in Oleander Court and a killer still on the loose, ha ha. Funny how money can't prevent tragedy.

Faith reaches in the cavity of the oak, her fingers scraping until they close around the key to the front door. She'd have been way annoyed to get all the way here and be locked out. She'd forgotten her own key back home. She unlocks the door, her nose prickling in the stale air that hasn't moved in months. Connie's house smells like an old lady house now.

Only now it isn't Connie's house. It feels so weird, like any second Faith will hear the floorboards creak and her aunt call out "Oh, no! Hired goons!" like she always did when Faith's mother let herself in with the oak tree key. The house is so silent it gives her the creeps, and Faith turns on the TV just for the company. A soap opera's on, the kind Connie and Faith's mother always made fun of but were secretly way into.

Dropping her backpack on the kitchen table, Faith traces a line of dust in the shadow box that holds Connie's Precious Moments collection. Connie had loved her Precious Moments figurines, and it makes Faith sad to think of them sitting alone on the shelf, gathering more dust each day that Connie's not there to care for them.

Faith wanders down the narrow hallway that leads to the rest of the house, hooking a right into Connie's bedroom. Geez, was shag carpeting ever cool? Faith sneezes as she sits at Connie's desk, opening her aunt's laptop. Faith knows all her passwords, which are all the same—variations of Connie's birthday combined with the name of her favorite cat. It's a good thing no one's tried identity theft on her aunt, because it would take them two seconds. She even kept her social security card and *all* her passports in an unlocked drawer in her desk. Faith had found them once when she was looking for a pen.

Even though it's sad to be here, Faith's glad she came. She's been spending loads of time in Oleander Court, and it's getting to her, especially seeing what Ray's going through.

And Juliet, now. Faith can't believe she got *fired* over Ray's arrest.

Plus, Faith has a mission. She's going to look through Connie's stuff and see if there's anything worth selling. There's lots that Faith would never get rid of—like the Precious Moments figurines—but there's bound to be something valuable. Connie used to go to auctions, and she'd lucked out a few times by accidentally buying something worth way more than she'd paid for it. Then she'd re-sell it using this online auction house she told Faith all about. Faith will use that same auction house. She already has two items to sell, and they're worth way more than anything she'll find in Connie's house.

Faith logs in to her aunt's computer, navigating to her Wells Fargo bank account. The one not mentioned on any of the estate documents, maybe because Connie had forgotten to include it. It's the student account Connie got after she went back to college online, the "goofing off" one she only used for her Netflix charge. The ID and password are unchanged, and Faith rubs her forehead as she logs on. Yup. Still active. Netflix is even still taking its money every month.

The door to Connie's walk-in closet is open, and Faith drifts over, wrinkling her nose at the clothes crammed tight together on metal hangers. Connie liked thick "cozy" sweaters that took up a lot of room. Faith lifts a sleeve to take a sniff, to see if it still smells like her aunt's vanilla perfume, but it's the same musty scent as the rest of the house. Yuck.

As Faith rifles through a rack of Connie's clothes—where did she even get sweaters that ugly?—she remembers Bambi Holiday's ridiculous walk-in closet. It seriously looked like something you'd see in a movie about a spoiled rich girl, only in the movie the spoiled rich girl would learn valuable lessons about herself and what's really important in life instead of dying in a gross bathtub electrocution.

Faith had enjoyed sorting and categorizing Bambi's stuff, since that kind of thing's right up her alley, but it had pissed her off how much that woman had. Like, did she really need ten versions of the same black dress? Or those thirty-seven pairs of strappy sandals? She could have donated like two-thirds of her closet to charity and not even noticed.

Faith had also enjoyed pretending she didn't know what Dolce & Gabbana was. Like, hello. *Obviously*, she did. But she couldn't resist screwing with Bambi.

Now Faith navigates to Netflix, browsing the selections. She's not going to think about Oleander Court for a whole weekend. She's not even going to answer text messages—although now there aren't nearly as many annoying ones, considering the worst people in the neighborhood are gone. Faith puts a few movies on her Watch List and gets up. It'll be dark in a few hours, and she needs to get to the grocery store. All that's in Connie's pantry are expired cans of vegetables, paper plates, and Trader Joe's wine, probably put there by Faith's mother. There's no Trader Joe's in Johnsonville.

An hour later, Faith returns from the store. She'd also stopped by the pie place, where they sold her a half-priced one because they were about to close for the day and because Rebecca, the owner, knew her and made a big deal about seeing her again. "You're so grown up!" she'd shrieked. Faith had a hard time carrying everything back without squishing or dropping anything.

Back at Connie's house, Faith plugs in Connie's laptop at the kitchen table. She preheats the oven for pizza and opens a bottle of wine. Faith doesn't really like wine—it burns her throat—but getting hammered while eating pizza and watching movies instead of thinking about what's happened in Oleander Court sounds way awesome. By the time the pizza's done, Faith's done with one glass and feeling great.

Faith pours herself another glass of wine, biting the rim as she watches Jennifer Aniston in some movie about a hefty girl with beauty queen aspirations. Faith's mother would watch anything with Jennifer Aniston. She'd love this movie.

If she was here, Faith would tell her about Adelaide and how she'd used beauty pageants to get to a better place. Her mother would respect Adelaide. They'd get along. Faith could see her hanging out on the couch with Adelaide and Ray as they joke and stuff their faces.

Faith jumps up and gulps a glass of water, grabbing another slice of pizza from the top of the stove. She blows her nose with a paper towel as she sits back down, clicking into a new tab on the computer so she can hear Jennifer but not see her. She browses Billboard and Rotten Tomatoes, and she even visits Jade's website, ItCanHappenAnywhere .com. Jade has some countdown to "Oleander Court making history." Some gimmick about the murders, no doubt. Seriously, Jade has no shame. Laura had even mentioned that the other day, Jade was wandering around the neighborhood and taking pictures. There has to be some privacy law against that.

Then Faith goes to Fox News.

"State May Seek Death Penalty in 'Murder Avenue' Killings."

A rock forms in Faith's stomach. *Ohmygod.* Is this for real? The death penalty? Against Ray? What evidence do the police have against her? Faith's been trying to get details out of Laura since Ray's arrest, but Laura's been annoyingly vague. Maybe she doesn't want Faith to know, out of some weird desire to protect her or something. Or maybe Laura really doesn't know anything.

If the police are after Ray because of the greenhouse drama, that's just stupid. Who kills someone else over four walls of glass? And besides, Beverly was so awful, she'd probably pissed off plenty of other people just as much as she did Ray. Why aren't the police looking at *them*, too? Why the focus on Ray?

Faith doesn't know what the police are thinking. She only knows they're on the wrong track with Ray.

They have to be, because Faith knows who the killer really is.

LAURA

"I should have done this a while ago," Laura mutters Wednesday morning as she clicks through images in her home office. She'd googled "vacation packages," and the results were impressive in both quantity and quality. Laura could rent the family a villa at Nassau Paradise Island in the Bahamas, where she and Pete could enjoy cocktails on white sandy beaches while Nicole and Ben played in the aquamarine water. Or she could reserve a hotel room overlooking the Seine, the Eiffel Tower and Paris's many other charms within walking distance. There were cruise packages to Europe, dirt cheap options in Mexico, and a guided tour to climb Mount Fuji in Japan during cherry blossom season. Especially on a cold winter day, the options are infinitely appealing.

"Whatcha doin'?" Pete asks, startling her so much, she jostles her coffee.

"That!" she says, gesturing to the liquid sloshing in the mug. "*That* is why I need a vacation. I'm on edge. We're all on edge."

"You're not supposed to be looking for a vacation," Pete tells her. "You're supposed to be looking for somewhere for us to live." Then, a second later as Pete breathes over her shoulder, staring at the screen, he yelps, "Ooh! Japan!"

"You have the attention span of a hummingbird," Laura tells her husband. "But, look—I was thinking. Maybe once the kids are out of school, we treat ourselves. Don't you think we deserve it?"

"Absolutely. Let's do it." Pete's phone buzzes, and he pulls it out of his pocket. "Duty calls," he says as he wanders away.

Laura rests her chin in her hands, studying the options. She hadn't planned on going abroad with the kids until Nicole graduated from high school. Now, though, they have the money, and they've been through a lot in these recent months. A trip would be a nice diversion.

An ad for a Greece cruise pops up, and Laura remembers Faith telling her about her plans with her mother. Four years is a long way off, and Faith works so hard. Could *Laura* maybe buy the trip for them?

Laura clicks on the link and winces. It's way too expensive. It's not that Laura wouldn't pay for it—she would in a heartbeat—but she imagines Faith and her mother squirreling away all their money, saving for a trip they'd earned. For Laura to swoop in and "take care of it" would probably insult them.

Still. Maybe Laura could put out some feelers when Faith returns tomorrow. She's still out of town, visiting her friend Casey at Yale.

The doorbell rings, making Laura jump again. "You gotta chill out," she tells herself, swiping at her forehead as she pops up from her chair. When she comes back, she'll do as she was supposed to do and start looking into extended stay options in St. Louis. Given the circumstances, the kids' schools have given them permission to finish out the year remotely if Laura and Pete wanted to take the option.

Laura hurries down the stairs and finds Erica on her porch, tapping on her phone. "Hey!" Erica finishes tapping and shoves the phone into her purse. "I came for the painting. It's the last thing for the U-Haul."

"I'll get Pete," Laura says, glancing into the house. "*He'll want to say goodbye,*" she stage-whispers.

"Thanks."

"What do you think you're going to do with it?" Laura asks as she leads Erica inside. "No, keep them on," she adds as Erica starts taking off her shoes.

"I really don't know," Erica says, about the painting. "I've never been in the art world."

Pete comes out of the living room, hoisting the painting. "*Noooooo!* Don't take it!" he protests even as he sets it at Erica's feet.

Erica jangles her keys. "Sorry, Pete. But you can visit her whenever you want. Mom, too." She rubs her eyes, yawning. "Ugh. I've been up since five. I wanted to do a load of Mom's things—everything for my place to feel like her place. Considering it took broken bones to get her out of this house, I understand she likes familiarity."

"Ya think?" Pete asks, shifting so Erica can grab one end of the canvas. "You steer," he tells Erica as Laura holds the door open for them. Gently, they maneuver the painting down the stairs and into the waiting U-Haul.

Pete and Laura wave as Erica pulls away from the curb. "That's one good daughter," Pete comments. "Think Nicole will take care of us like that when we're old?"

"Absolutely." Laura tugs on his sleeve as they walk inside. "Hey. A trip. Let's do it."

Pete raises his eyebrows. "Really?"

"We should. Life is short, you know?" She sobers as she looks out into the neighborhood, the empty sidewalks. The half-hearted FOR SALE signs. Six months ago, a house in Oleander Court wouldn't even need to be listed to be sold.

"We'd have to get the kids passports," Pete says, and Laura nods. "I know. We can do it."

Pete rubs his nose. "I admit, I'm stoked at the idea. Ben would love to see Stonehenge. And Nicole would love London. All those Jane Austen novels she's been reading. God! I can't believe she's reading Jane Austen already."

Laura had been thrilled when Nicole picked up *Emma* from her office bookshelf. "If you read that," she told Nicole, "I'll take you to Fancy Tea."

Nicole had grinned. "I outgrew tea when I was about five, Mom." But she'd acquiesced, letting Laura take her to a local teahouse which specialized in finger sandwiches and dipping cookies. After, they'd gone shopping, because Laura "needed a clothes makeover." Nicole is now in the age of makeovers.

Laura retreats back to her office and plays with the mouse to enliven the screen. How long would it take to get the kids passports?

SOON-LI

S oon-Li's fingers fly over the keyboard, furiously typing. With a glance to the computer screen, she sees it's almost six thirty. Tran won't be up for an hour, so she has time to finish up the task of ghosting the last two houses in Oleander Court. She's been faithful to her pattern, keeping Laura's house next-to-last based on its location in the neighborhood.

The sick feeling in her stomach is still there. Soon-Li's profession involves a deep respect for following the rules, for using her talents only for lawful purposes. She's never bent the rules, let alone broken them so completely. She tells herself it's for good, that the laws are there to prevent acts in a completely different ballpark from what she's doing now, but it doesn't help. Soon-Li has always been a black-and-white kind of person. Either it's wrong, or it isn't, and ten different criminal statutes and the certifications she makes when renewing her Top Secret clearance tell her this is certainly wrong.

Regardless, she plugs away. Over the last week and a half, Soon-Li's found time to infiltrate the computers of all of her neighbors except these last two. One took her nearly all day: who knew the Dentons would have five different computers between them? Stacey and Scott didn't seem like likely suspects, that was for sure, but Soon-Li went through the motions anyway, accessing accounts and emails and browsing search terms until she was satisfied that both Dentons had nothing to do with the recent murders.

Criminal nature aside, the act of snooping gnaws at her. She'd felt awful when her eyes landed on a series of bills reflecting that Stacey has breast cancer. And almost as much so when she found unsent drafts of emails Ray had written to her family. Ever since the news had begun reporting on Ray's transgender status, different aspects of Ray's person- ality had suddenly made more sense, slotting into place like pieces to a jigsaw puzzle Soon-Li hadn't realized were missing. No wonder Ray was so boisterous, so loud. It was a defense mechanism.

Only Ray hadn't shared this with Soon-Li. Soon-Li had learned it only by breaking into Ray's computer. Soon-Li hates herself for the se- crets she's learned about her neighbors—secrets she's stolen, basically— but it's too late. She can't undo the knowledge or how she obtained it.

Soon-Li straightens her back, wriggling in her chair. She's been at the task since five, silently stealing from bed as Tran snored, oblivious. If he awoke early, she'd tell him she was catching up on emails, and he'd believe her.

Jade is next. Jade only uses a laptop, so there's just one device to peruse. As Soon-Li does, she reflects on how different the outward Jade is from the one reflected in the files here. Jade appears so shallow—nothing more than a whitewashed Instagrammer obsessed only with her social media presence and related concerns. Her computer content paints a completely different picture. Jade is close with her parents, emailing and Facebook messaging with them constantly. Jade donates monthly to the Humane Society, and she gets daily alerts from a half dozen literary magazines and blogs. Every post to her new website has multiple drafts, and Soon-Li pauses on one that recounts a child- hood summer revolving around ice cream truck visits: "When A Push-Up Pop Was Enough." It's lovely, sincere.

After finishing with Jade's computer, Soon-Li takes a shaky breath. It's time.

The Noble family has a number of electronics: two desktops, three laptops, and an iPad. Soon-Li accesses the iPad first, browsing quickly once she realizes it belongs to Ben. Pete's work computer reflects he's much more tech-savvy than Soon-Li was aware. He and Tran should be better friends. Laura's work computer is clearly only for professional purposes, a family photo serving as the desktop wallpaper.

Soon-Li's heart pounds as she skims through Pete's personal laptop, already anticipating what she might find on Laura's. There's nothing of note on Pete's, other than that Laura is a very lucky woman. Weeks in advance, Pete started visiting sites to find her the perfect Valentine's Day gift.

Hands shaking, Soon-Li types in the series of numbers and letters needed to access Laura's laptop. Pete's computer desktop melts away, revealing a desktop photo of Laura and Pete. *This could be it*, Soon-Li thinks as she digs into Laura's search history. Maybe she'll find search terms inquiring how to dismantle or avoid a security system. Or researching odorless, tasteless poisons. Or how to electrocute someone in water, as most appliances have safety features to prevent it.

Soon-Li's eyebrows knit as she scrolls through the many searches Laura's conducted over the last few months. Nothing, nothing, nothing. The only conceivably suspicious search is a series of inquiries into international destinations and passports, and even that one proves innocuous. All hotel searches list four guests. Laura's planning a trip for the family.

Next, Soon-Li accesses Laura's email, using electronic alerts to direct her to Laura's credit card accounts. Nothing looks strange.

Something bumps overhead. Someone's awake—Tran, most likely. Soon-Li bites her lip as she clicks and scrolls faster, searching for something, anything that could be an answer. There's nothing.

Footsteps thud on the staircase, and Soon-Li swiftly turns off her equipment, jumping up to leave her workspace. By the time Tran turns the corner into the kitchen, Soon-Li's placed her mug under her Keurig dispenser and is waiting for her second stream of hot brew. "Morning, honey," she tells him as he grins sleepily at her.

"Morning." He yawns as he leans to retrieve a coffee cup. "I must have slept like the dead. Didn't hear you get up."

"I was quiet."

How does she feel about this discovery? Or, rather, non-discovery? Soon-Li should be relieved—she didn't *want* Laura to be the killer. She likes her, and she likes what Nicole has done for Lila. And Soon-Li didn't want to find that another neighbor was behind all this.

But there is still no answer, no clue to end the killings. After her invasive and time-consuming exercise of ghosting, Soon-Li feels like she's earned the key to a treasure chest and opened it to find cobwebs.

That's not the worst thing, though. Soon-Li's search was supposed to be a means to an end. To find *something* that would justify a rule-breaking she otherwise finds unfathomable, unforgivable. Instead, she's empty-handed.

Meanwhile, next September when Soon-Li applies for renewal of her Top Secret clearance, she'll be required to attest to her integrity. The full functioning of her moral compass. For the first time, she might not be able to do that.

Her hands wrapped around her mug, Soon-Li wanders to her front windows, looking out at the street. When her vision blurs, she realizes she's crying, for the first time in years. She's compromised herself. Her values, her adherence to right and wrong.

If her ghosting had led her anywhere, would she feel differently?

She'll never know.

Through the glass, an Amazon van turns onto Jasmine Lane, braking when it arrives at Jade's house. A white AT&T car is parked in front of the Noble home.

Soon-Li lifts her coffee to her lips, carefully sipping the hot liquid as she studies the slender woman who crosses through Jade's yard to reach the porch steps. Was this the same woman who brought all the neighbors' Amazon packages? And for how long? Weeks? Months?

Soon-Li couldn't describe a frequent delivery person if her life depended on it. They were just there, like hedges. The Amazon truck came through the neighborhood at least a dozen times a day. Ditto with FedEx. And the entire neighborhood was serviced by Comcast and AT&T. Added up, there were dozens of inconspicuous individuals with access to Oleander Court. And they were all viable suspects.

But Soon-Li is done trying to figure it out.

"Tran!" Soon-Li shouts, and her husband peeks around the kitchen doorway, newspaper in hand. (Tran always loved an actual newspaper.)

"You okay?" he asks. The Jungs are not shouters.

No, she thinks, but she musters a smile. "I was thinking," she says. "It's not healthy for us to stay here. Not for Lila. Who knows what she hears in school?"

Tran grimaces, taking a sip of his coffee. "I have been thinking the same."

"There's no reason for us to stay here," Soon-Li says. "After we select for the DOD project, let's get out of here. Go to Pennsylvania. Stay until this is over. And if it's never over, we sell."

The words hang in the air. They'd promised each other they'd never move again. The process was too costly, too inconvenient.

"Okay," Tran says, and it's decided. Soon-Li will be packing up what's left of her and leaving the neighborhood.

ADELAIDE

"I wish there was somethin' I could do," Adelaide says, tapping her fingers on the counter as she waits for her teakettle to boil. "I feel so useless."

"It's not your problem to solve," William tells her.

"All right then. Can you give them all your money?" Adelaide asks, half-serious. Ever since the news about Juliet's job, Adelaide's been nauseous, and it's not all morning sickness. How are Juliet and Ray going to survive?

"They could live with us," William jokes, taking a second mug from the cabinet and removing the tin of tea options. "I'm sorry, but I'm going to be glad when this part of solidarity is over." Tea isn't William's favorite, but he's been drinking it since Adelaide has to forgo coffee. The teakettle shrieks. "Oh. Boy. The water's ready," he says in a monotone.

"Ray says Juliet can't sue her firm for firin' her," Adelaide says. "That they were just protectin' their interest."

"That may be the case." The teakettle hisses as William pours the water. "And it doesn't look good, suing your employer. Makes a prospective one look at you with pause."

Adelaide chews her lip, mulling this over. She's read between the lines of Ray's story about her departure from her former law firm.

"When this all blows over, maybe they'll hire Juliet back," Adelaide says as she squeezes honey into her tea.

"How long does a trial take?"

Adelaide sighs. "You're not makin' me feel better."

"I'm sorry. But really, unless you can catch the killer and exonerate Ray, there's not much you can do."

Adelaide rubs her stomach, thinking. A smile lights her face as an idea occurs to her. "You're wrong. Put on a nicer sweater. We've got a house call to make."

After finishing their tea and scouting outside—no news vans this time—Adelaide and William walk to Ray and Juliet's house and ring the bell. It's Juliet who opens the door, looking wan.

"Come on in." There isn't a trace of irritation in her voice, just weariness. Maybe getting Juliet to like her isn't hopeless. "How are you feeling?" Juliet asks as Adelaide and William slip off their shoes. Adelaide had shared her big news with Ray the same day she'd spilled the beans to William.

"Better," Adelaide says. "I barfed just once today!"

Ray's on the couch, flipping through TV options. She cranes her head to see her guests. "Hey," she says listlessly.

Adelaide's mama used to get like this every once in a while, too. When the world had busted her up, when people at the diner where she worked left cigarette butts in their coffee instead of tips on the table. She'd curl up on the couch until she mustered the strength to move again, and then she'd be right as rain.

It always took something to get her moving, though. The Little Miss Harvest Moon Pageant. Adelaide's debut on the high school theater stage. Don's fortieth birthday party.

Ray needed something to get her moving, too.

"Come on, now," Adelaide says, sinking into the seat diagonal from Ray. "It can't be all bad."

Ray groans, putting her pillow over her head. "Don't Pollyanna out on me, Adelaide. Let me wallow."

"You talked to your mama," Adelaide tells her. "That's a good thing."

Ray removes the pillow, a glimmer of a smile around her lips. "They're coming to visit the week after next," she says. "Becky, too, and her family."

"That's great!"

"Yeah, they should take advantage of our space before we lose the house."

Juliet rubs her forehead as she takes a seat next to Ray. "She's a beam of sunshine, isn't she?"

"The sky is falling," Ray moans, pulling the pillow over her head again. "The glass is half-empty."

"Snap out of it," Adelaide says, sitting up straighter.

"Eh. Why bother?"

"Well, for one thing, you're gonna have to scrape yourself off that couch for when your family visits. You want them to see how pretty your house is, right?" Ray grunts, but Adelaide knows she's listening. "And also, my kid's godmommy ain't no downer." She looks at Juliet. "God-mommies. I assume it's okay she has two, considerin'."

Ray sits up, her hand over her mouth. "You want *us* as the godparents? You're sure?"

Adelaide and William had talked it over. Not like he had a say, anyway—she's the one incubating the little critter as it tries to kill her. Now, he nods. "We can't imagine anyone better," he says.

"Obviously, you're who we want," Adelaide adds. "You're both strong, amazin' women. And what's going on is awful, and testin' that, but you'll get through it, especially since you have each other to lean on. Even if every once in a while one of you acts like a big baby." Juliet smirks at Ray, taking her wife's hand.

"You have to say yes," Adelaide says. "No one else will do."

Juliet kisses Ray's hand, her eyes meeting Adelaide's. "Yes. Of course. We'll be the best godmommies anyone's ever seen."

RAY

"Here's the guest room," Ray says, leading her parents down the hallway. "Bathroom's right off it. It should have everything you need. Towels, soap, shampoo."

"Thanks, Ray," Mr. Pritchett says, rolling his suitcase into the room, the wheels clicking against the hardwood. "This is nice."

"Thanks." Ray and Juliet had decorated the space ages ago—in warm shades of green, blue, and gold that complement the white dressers. There were other little touches, too, like mottled vases with peacock feathers and shelving with plants you'd swear were real. Ray would have asked her parents to appreciate the amenities ages ago if she wasn't such a chickenshit.

But now, what better motivation than the ticking clock before your trial for triple murder and possible resultant incarceration? Or even death?

"Do you need anything else?" Ray asks, hovering in the door and picking at her cuticles. They've been a mess lately. "We could run to the store." It's an empty offer. Ray and Juliet wouldn't show their faces anywhere.

"This is perfect," Ray's mother assures her, putting a hand on her arm. It's warm, and soft, and Ray tries to ignore the tears prickling her eyes. She'd almost forgotten how her mother *felt*.

Ray leaves them to settle in. Juliet's in the kitchen, and Ray reaches across her to gulp from her glass of wine.

"Excuse you," Juliet says mildly, removing a second glass from the hanging rack. "Here's your own."

"Sorry. I'm just—"

"I know. It'll be okay. They're here, aren't they?"

Ray had been so nervous to call them. What if they said no? Ray would know it was an excuse—both of her parents are retired, and they have no problem with traveling. But as soon as the offer had left her lips, her mother had accepted.

"Don't you need to ask Dad?" Ray had asked, and her mother had *pssshed*. "He'll be thrilled," she said, so honestly and easily that tears had stung Ray's eyes. "When do you want us there?" They'd settled on two Fridays from then. Becky and the rest would follow the next day. The kids had soccer practice on Fridays. For this first night, Ray's plan was to engage her parents with a dominoes game while plying them with alcohol.

Ray's parents emerge from the guest bedroom a few minutes later. "Nice crown molding," Ray's father says, his eyes flicking toward the ceiling of the dining room.

"Thanks. I did that," Juliet says.

"You don't say. You know, I did ours myself, and . . ." They launch into an extremely boring conversation about house repairs. But it's a conversation. Ray removes the dominoes from the cabinet over the microwave and puts them on the dining room table. "Help yourself to wine," she tells her mother as she clears the table. "White's in the fridge."

"I love your cookie jar." It's a white-and-black cat holding an orange fish. Ray had thought of her mother when she'd found it at Hobby Lobby. She loved ceramics, had even taken a class when Ray was little. The result was a lopsided glazed bowl fit only to hold bathroom potpourri.

"We never use it, but me, too." Ray grabs a stack of plates and puts them next to the snacks: Juliet's seven-layer dip, a veggie tray, walnut brownies. She glances at her wife, who is now enthusiastically chatting about storm windows. "Babe? A little help?"

"Do you want a beer or some wine?" Juliet asks Ray's father.

"I'm more of a beer man," Ray's father says, and Juliet removes two from the refrigerator. "I'll follow your lead," she tells him, removing the bottle opener from the utensil drawer.

Ray's heart twinges. Juliet hates beer.

Everyone sits at the table and Ray explains Mexican Train, the game.

The rounds go slowly at first, then faster and faster. Ray's father emerges as a natural. They shit talk over the game, and they laugh about random topics. Ray's father accuses her mother of cheating.

"What does it matter?" she shoots back. "You're kicking everyone's ass."

Since when does Ray's mother swear? Ray had been holding her own potty mouth in check ever since she'd walked through the door. What else about her parents would surprise her?

"Excuse me," Ray says between rounds and as Juliet tallies the scores. Ray goes to the bathroom, closing the door.

In the mirror, Ray's face is flushed, her hair frizzing. She pushes it behind her ears, studying the new pimple above her left eyebrow. Who knew you could get pimples after forty?

Raucous laughter filters into the room. Juliet hasn't laughed like that in a while.

Ray smiles softly, thinking of what Juliet had been like when Ray first met her. Loud, forward. She'd had enough pride to make up for Steven's lack thereof.

Juliet's always been after her to stop being so down, so negative, but Ray had always accepted that she was a negative kind of person. Why? It's being negative that's gotten her to the bottom, triggered her Dark Days instead of helping her find sunshine. Made her keep away from the people now sitting in her kitchen—people who had unhesitatingly accepted her invitation as if they'd been waiting for it for years. Maybe they had, and there she'd been, terrified to give it. Terrified of a rejection that wasn't going to come. Making her lose *years* she could have had with them, countless moments and memories. Her throat tightens to think of it.

As Ray stares at her image, she *sees* herself. She's Ray Willis, and what the fuck is wrong with that? Nothing. It's who she was born to be, and she'd had the courage to become Ray while a lesser person might have remained Steven in his misery. Ray Willis is funny, and good to those she loves, and once upon a time she was also a kick-ass lawyer. If she puts her mind to use, to a good cause, she could be one again.

Ray hasn't been to a support group in a while. She used to go as an effort to feel better about herself, to gain hope. To hear stories from others who have been through what she's been through and found peace with themselves. Who managed to have pride in who they are.

When Ray goes again, it won't be for her. She'll be the one with a story to tell. The one where she looked in the mirror, and finally found her pride.

JADE

Jade wrestles with the door on Tuesday, her last day in Alpharetta. Her mother has purchased her a plane ticket to Tampa, a not-so-subtle nudge to get her daughter away from the danger in Oleander Court. She leaves tomorrow.

When Jade had received her ticketing information via email, she'd had to smile. Trust Anita Coleman to be bossy from hundreds of miles away.

Jade gives up on the door, putting down her coffee to work her key in the lock. It finally turns. Even though it's only mid-afternoon, she goes through every room, inspecting for anything out of order and turning on every light. As she does, she pauses at each room, thinking of the stories her mother read to her in her bedroom, imagining her father shaving in front of the master bathroom's mirror, seeing her mother rifling through the walk-in closet for the perfect date outfit. Every square inch of the home has memories, and as Jade wanders from room to room, she realizes she's saying goodbye.

She comes to the lower level. Her mother's scrapbooks are laid out on the dining room table, now marked with sticky notes and tabs. After Jade had walked through the neighborhood the other day, catching it through the camera lens of her iPhone, she'd pored through the books to find matching images. An idea for a collection of essays has taken root in Jade's mind, and she's been outlining her intentions.

The literary agent who had reached out to her likes the idea. She wants to see an outline and Jade's first fifty pages, and they'll go from there. It's not a promise of representation—far from it—but it could be, eventually. And more than that, it's motivation for Jade to keep at the project. Validation that her efforts are worth making.

Even without this nudge, Jade knows she'd finish this. Reading the articles she's written over the last few months, she's proud. These aren't Instagram posts that will fade like vapor into cyberspace. They're a con-tribution. Nowhere near the level of what someone like Helen has to offer, but a contribution just the same. And the more Jade works at it, the more she tries, the better she'll get.

Now Jade realizes the error of her twenty-two-year-old self. She shouldn't have expected anything from that one draft of a book. She didn't even let anyone else read it, hadn't thought seriously about changes or structure. The fact that nothing came of it shouldn't have taught her to give up. It should have taught her to try harder, to calibrate. Everyone starts somewhere, but Jade didn't have the courage to continue.

Jade's phone vibrates with a text. Her mother is at the grocery store and wants to know what Jade wants to eat. Jade is about to text her back when the doorbell chimes.

Squinting through the peephole, Jade sees the back of a UPS man, and on her welcome mat she finds a square white box. Another Instagram product delivery. Jade wonders what it is this time. A fruit roll-up with the consistency of leather? "Earth-friendly," itch-inducing shampoo?

Jade doesn't want to think about Instagramming. #leavemealone, #postityourself. She leaves the door closed and returns to the kitchen, where she sits down and calls her mother. When Anita answers the phone, Jade hears the background sounds of the store—piped-in music, the murmur of other shoppers.

"Something's wrong," her mother says almost right away. "You sound different. Is everything all right? Where are you?"

"I'm in the house, but don't worry. I'm being careful. Every light is on. And I'm leaving soon." Jade only needs to gather up the last of the photographs she'll use from the scrapbooks, and she's off. "But, Mom. I need to tell you something."

God, this is hard. It reminds Jade of the time she'd shoplifted a tube of mascara when she was in junior high. Three of her friends had done it, too, but Jade's mother was the only one who marched her daughter back to Target to apologize.

Jade opens her laptop, watching it flicker to life to show the dashboard to her website. The website Jade pretended was just some hobby. That it didn't really matter.

"Mom, I want to go back to school," she says in a rush. "To be a writer. Maybe fiction, maybe journalism."

"What? Where is this coming from? What about Instagram?"

Jade clicks on the draft article about Helen's painting. She expands the image. The triptych is so magnificent. She thinks of how she felt the instant she first saw it. And that gives her the courage to begin to talk. To tell her mother, the person who has always supported Jade, why she wants to be a writer. Jade talks and talks, the words flowing out of her once the dam is open.

When she's done, her mother is silent. Ominously silent. "Say something," Jade pleads. She clicks on her post. The countdown is over. Helen's painting is now live on the Internet.

Jade feels awful, like a spoiled brat. Anita Coleman grew up with nothing, and Pat Coleman hadn't exactly been born with a silver spoon in his mouth. Meanwhile, Jade didn't even have to pay for the education she's decided she doesn't want.

"I never knew you felt this way," Jade's mother says finally. "It is a surprise." Her accent is always heavier when she's thinking. Or upset.

"I didn't know how to tell you. You were thrilled to have me in business school. The marketing—all that. I didn't want to disappoint you."

"But, Jade—you're so good at that kind of thing. I am very confused."

"I'm sorry, Mom." Jade's voice catches.

"Do not apologize to me," her mother says, and Jade's heart twists. But then Anita continues: "Never apologize for what you want. If this—writing—is what you want, then of course we support you."

"But you were so proud of me getting my MBA." Jade is restless. She rises from the table and opens the patio door. The back porch is drenched in sun—an early February day that hints of spring. She closes the door behind her, going to lean against the railing.

"No, my love. I was proud of *you*, for getting what you wanted. My dreams are irrelevant. If we had the same dream, well, that would be wonderful, but are we the same person? No, we are not. And am I the kind of woman who wants to live through her daughter? Accomplish what I could not? You think that?"

"No, of course not, Mom."

"I have done just fine without an *MBA*." Anita says it like it's a dirty word. "Don't you think?"

"Yes, but you *invested* in my MBA. And I'm telling you I was wrong to make you do that. Doesn't that bother you?"

"Why would that bother me? What is the point of what we have done—all this money we have—if we cannot use it to help our daughter follow her dreams? If it has taken you this time to understand what yours are . . . well, you have gotten there. Some people never get there. At least you are being honest with yourself. And I am proud of you for that. Every day, I am proud of you."

"Really?"

"Do not ask stupid questions," Anita Coleman says brusquely, and the moment is over. "Look into schools, get a plan. We will figure it out."

Jade feels like she's seventeen again, looking into colleges with her parents. And she doesn't mind.

"What about Instagram, though?" she asks.

"What about it?"

"I hate it, but I don't think I could stop," Jade admits. "The money's too good."

She's also addicted to her account, can't stop checking the number of likes and followers. She'd love to cut herself off, but she can't. That's what addiction is.

"You could stop gradually," her mother suggests, but that won't work. Jade can't "kind of" be on Instagram.

"Maybe I—" Jade's ears perk up, and she stops mid-sentence.

"What? What is going on there?" Her mother's voice is sharp.

"Calm down." Jade turns to the house, but all she sees is her own reflection in the patio doors. "I could have sworn I heard the refrigerator door open." It's a heavy one that sticks from suction, often requiring a nice tug. "Maybe the killer's a milk drinker."

"Do not joke. You can't be too careful."

"True, but I'm also jumpy." Jade would never tell her mother about the kitchen knife she keeps out when she's home.

"I'm glad you will be gone tomorrow. Wait until you see this new restaurant. So much work. Your father is in heaven."

They chat for a few more minutes, and Jade can't stop smiling. She isn't a disappointment. Her mother had scoffed at the very idea while making a rather obvious, sad point: how many people *never* figure out what they really want? Jade's only twenty-eight, and she's on her way.

When they're done, Jade goes inside to retrieve her laptop. As she does, she frowns. *Could* she have heard the refrigerator opening? She hadn't closed the door to the back patio all the way, and sound travels over the hardwood. And she can't shake the feeling that someone has been in the house. She senses their presence, their energy.

Jade goes to the front door to retrieve the package left by the UPS man. As she reaches the door, she pinches her nose. She'd forgotten to lock it. How could she be so careless?

It's one thing to expose herself to danger by being in Oleander Court. By leaving a door unlocked, by not being vigilant, she's practically inviting it in. She's glad she'll be nowhere near Oleander Court as of tomorrow.

Opening the door, Jade bends to scoop up the box, then stops short.

It's gone.

LAURA

A s Laura waits for her friends to arrive, she can't help but think how sparsely attended this book club meeting is, compared with her last—and also her first—one. Back then, she'd frantically arranged food on trays, procured an entire crate of wine, and tried on ten different outfits in an attempt to fit in with the other well-dressed ladies. It feels like a lifetime ago.

Today it's only Adelaide and Ray. There's almost no one else to invite, and Laura hadn't bothered. Even Soon-Li is absent, packed up and gone to Pennsylvania to stay with family.

"When are you coming back?" Laura had asked her, and Soon-Li had shrugged. "We'll see," she'd said, which wasn't an answer.

Now, Laura sips her water on the front porch, eyeing the three water goblets she'd set out. Today is Wednesday, and it's every bit as nice as it was yesterday. She's taking advantage of the warm sunlight that will melt away into a chilly evening. On his dog bed, Costco dozes beneath the glass table, releasing an audible snore with each breath.

Ray slouches into her chair when she arrives first, wrapping her hands around her glass. "We going to talk about this book, or what?" she asks, and Laura has such a sense of déjà vu she shivers.

"What?" Ray asks.

"Those were the first words you ever spoke to me, you know," Laura says, and Ray cocks her head, considering. "Hey, I think you're right.

"I'm less interested in this book than in what happened next door," Ray continues, nodding subtly in the direction of the Coleman house. "Do you really think the killer was inside?"

"Killer was inside where?" Adelaide asks as she comes up the porch stairs, looking wan. She's pregnant. Laura knows because Ray's practically taken out an advertisement to announce her future godmommy status.

"You don't know?" Ray pulls out her phone and taps on it. "Don't you read Jade's blog?"

Adelaide shakes her head as she slides into her chair. "Should I?"

"Geez, girl. What's wrong with you? This shit's interesting even if you aren't worried about murder," Ray says, shoving the phone at her. "It's there, at the bottom. The comment with a picture."

Just that morning, someone called *guesswho* had posted to Jade's article about Helen's painting:

How does it feel to know you were supposed to be next?

The scales may have tipped in your favor, but it's time your Instagram lemmings know what's really in your kitchen. XOXO.

Beneath it, they'd included a shot of a pantry overflowing with junk food.

"There goes her branding," Ray says as she reaches for the wine bottle. "I knew she was full of shit. Stacey Denton says she used to pay her for babysitting with chocolate chip cookies."

"Apparently, the killer came for her but changed their mind," Laura says, her stomach twisting just thinking about it. They could now be discussing the sixth murder in Oleander Court.

Adelaide's been quiet, studying the phone. "*The scales may have tipped in your favor.* Why does that sound so familiar?" she murmurs, her pretty face furrowing.

"Kind of cryptic," Ray says. "Scales of justice?"

Adelaide takes a sip of water. "Maybe. Or maybe it's some weirdo sittin' in their basement in Portland, spoutin' nonsense for attention."

"But the picture was really Jade's pantry," Laura tells her. "And Jade says they stole a package, too. Someone was actually there."

"That could still be kids." Adelaide helps herself to the dip Laura had set out. "Gettin' in on the action on Murder Avenue, takin' a souvenir."

She shrugs, crunching into a chip. "I don't know. Just seems weird there'd be one the killer couldn't pull off."

Laura considers. *Could* the post have been a prank? She draws up the blog on her own phone, scrolling to the post. Expanding the image with her fingers, she zeroes in on the items in the pantry. There's something off. What is it?

"The olives!" she exclaims.

"The olives?" Ray repeats, throwing back a mouthful of wine.

"Look at the jars. Second shelf from the top. There's a reflection. At least, part of one. A hand."

Adelaide and Ray grab their phones, clicking as Laura waits impatiently. "I don't see what you mean," Ray says after a moment.

"Zoom in on the second jar from the left. The big one. You can see the edge of the hand holding the phone."

"Oh." Ray squints as she peers at the image. "You're right. And look—there's a string. Around the wrist. See?"

Laura zooms in too close, and the image becomes fuzzy. She expands again, and she sees what Ray means. There *is* something looped around a slender wrist.

Blood roars in her ears. She shakes so violently that she has to put down the phone. It clatters onto the table.

Adelaide is eyeing her with concern, a hand on her belly. "Laura? Are you okay?"

She can't breathe. Laura puts her hands on her knees, trying to catch her breath. Ray hops from her chair. "Laura." She rubs her back. "It's okay. In. Out."

Laura shakes her head. "It's not a string," she chokes out. "It's a bracelet. Faith's bracelet. The charms are so tiny, the bracelet looks like barbed wire from far away."

Ray draws up the image again. "It could be a hair tie wrapped around their wrist," she says, but Laura shakes her head. "It's too bumpy to be a hair tie. Don't you think?"

Adelaide's face has turned white. "I remember where I heard that expression. *I* said that. To Faith. We were talkin' about Bambi. I was tellin' her she couldn't have been all bad, and Faith said"—she pauses, considering—"she said something about how you could always fit people in one slot or another. And I said somethin' about scales. About putting people's good and bad pebbles each on there to see which way it tilts."

Ray breathes out. "This is all circumstantial. A lot of people wear bracelets. We can't even *see* the image well. We have, what? Half a wrist to go on. And the talk about scales, good and bad—that's not a new topic."

"Have you heard from Faith today?" Adelaide asks Laura.

"No," she admits, gulping down her water. She needs to keep a clear head. "But she doesn't usually work on Wednesdays."

Should she text her? Call her? Or wait until she shows up at the house tomorrow and confront her? Question her? There could be an explanation.

But now that Laura thinks about it, it fits. Faith is the one person who had access to the houses of every victim in Oleander Court. She'd never been on Laura's radar, because of her age and also because it was *Faith*, but kids younger than her have done worse.

And what about how Faith reacted to hearing that Helen had fallen down the stairs because she was spooked? She'd acted more than upset. She'd acted *guilty*. Like the news bothered her. Which it would have, if she was the reason Helen had been on edge.

You're being ridiculous, Laura tells herself. Faith could have been grumpy for any number of reasons. Or non-reasons. She was a teenager, after all.

Besides, so what if Faith had posted the comment? She hadn't hurt Jade. Instead, she'd outed her for being a phony. Laura had witnessed Faith's conversation with Jade at Ray's neighborhood watch party, seen her roll her eyes. It wasn't exactly *moral* to enter someone's home without permission, or to swipe a package from the front porch, but both were a far cry from murder.

But the person who had posted the comment used the handle *guess-who*. And referred to Jade as almost being "next."

"Do you know where she lives?" Ray asks. "Maybe we could go there. Surprise her. If it's nothing, then we know."

"I'm sure it's nothing," Laura says with a confidence she doesn't feel.

"What are we going to say when we show up?" Adelaide asks, and Ray shrugs.

"We'll figure it out."

"I made cupcakes," Adelaide offers, and Laura frowns at the change of subject.

"It's our reason to show up," Adelaide explains.

"That's a pretty crappy reason," Ray says.

"You got a better one?" Adelaide shoots back.

"Nope."

Soon Laura is navigating her way to Faith's house with the help of Google Maps. She only knows the address because it's on the employment contract she'd asked Faith to sign. All Faith's wages were under the table—Laura didn't want Faith to have to bother with taxes—but Pete had insisted on an agreement to spell out Faith's rate and basic expectations. At the time, Laura had thought Pete was being ridiculous.

The ladies arrive at a modest, one-story white house straddling the line between Alpharetta and Roswell. Faith's car isn't there, unless it's in the garage. Laura hurries up the sidewalk and rings the bell, glancing anxiously through the windows. The curtains are pulled closed and the house is dark, silent.

The moments tick by. "She's not home," Laura says finally, turning the doorknob. It moves easily. Faith hadn't locked it. Laura exchanges a glance with Ray before stepping inside, flicking on the light.

The house is as neat as a pin. As Laura walks through the living room, which is made warm by the floating shelves containing personal touches—wooden figurines, piggy banks, fake African violets—already she gets the sense of emptiness.

The kitchen gleams, the counter bare except for a fat envelope with a woman's name: IRENE. The only clutter is the boxes stacked in the corner, clearly marked by room or contents: kitchen, living room, linens, women's clothing.

The women peek into the bathroom as they walk down the hallway that leads to three rooms. It, too, is sparkling clean, the counter completely empty. There isn't so much as a toothbrush.

The doors along the hallway are closed. When the women explore, one room looks like it belongs to a teenage boy, with *Avengers* posters on the wall and a bulletin board of pictures. The room is much too clean for a teenager. The next is the master bedroom. As Laura opens each, a mustiness fills her nostrils. Neither of these rooms have been occupied for some time.

Realization dawns on Laura as she pulls the door to the master bedroom closed. How many times had she invited Faith's brother and mother over? Numerous times, but not enough. She should have tried harder. She might have known.

Laura's heart hammers against her ribcage as the trio head silently for the room at the end of the hall. The door is ajar, and when Laura pushes it open she finds a bedroom with a lovely dark-finished dresser and matching four-poster bed with a hunter green bedspread neatly tucked underneath the mattress. Another fat envelope rests on the bed, this one with Laura's name on it.

The three women look at one another. "Go on," Ray says. "Open it."

Laura opens it, her eyes boggling at the money fastened with a black clip. "Holy—" She counts it. All hundred-dollar bills. "There's a hundred thousand dollars here." She opens the letter, her eyes tearing through the words. When she's done, she clears her throat. "It's to all of us, really." She reads it aloud:

> Laura,
>
> By now Ben's gotten to the bottom of his Froot Loops so you found my note telling you to come here. I'm sorry it's such a lame way of telling you goodbye, and that I didn't do it in person, but I know you understand why. The nature of an escape is doing it in secret, right?
>
> Anyway, I wanted you to know how much I appreciate what you've done for me. And that you're one of the best moms I've ever seen. Nicole and Ben are so lucky. I know you came to Oleander Court to give them this crazy, amazing life, but I hope you know all they really need is you.
>
> The money is for Ray to re-build her greenhouse. I'm not sorry for what I've done, but I'm sorry for how it affected other people and that I didn't think about that. If I'd have known what Ray and Juliet, and

Adelaide (Though not as much; did you hear they're offering her TV roles again? People are gross) had to go through, I wouldn't have done it. Ray is basically the coolest person I've ever met, and Adelaide is the most interesting. I'm going to miss them.

In case it's not totally obvious, this is my confession. It was me! If the police go to my aunt Connie's house in Johnsonville, North Carolina, they'll find everything they need to prove that, and that I did it alone.

Please tell everyone goodbye, and thank you for making me feel like part of your family.

—Faith Martin

"Where did she get the money?" Ray asks as Laura hands her the clip of bills. "She couldn't have saved up this much from working in the neighborhood."

"And where do you think she went?" Adelaide asks, face drawn, hands on her belly. Alpharetta is close to Hartsfield International Airport, the world's largest airport, so Faith has plenty of options.

"I don't know," Laura says, even as she's tapping away at her phone. There's only one place Faith had ever mentioned going, and the only one that makes sense now.

When she finds the one flight available that day, her stomach twists. It was scheduled for a departure of three hours ago, but it's delayed. It won't leave for several hours.

"You know something," Ray demands. "Spill it."

"She's going to Greece." They deserve to know.

"Then she'll be at the airport," Ray says. "Should we call Moskowitz?"

Laura puts her phone away. "Pam. Beverly. Bambi. Conner. Tripp." As she says their names, Ray's and Adelaide's faces involuntarily twist in disgust. "Faith wasn't right—"

"She committed murder," Ray interjects.

"—but was it *purely* wrong?"

"According to the criminal charges I've been defending, yes, murder is flat-out wrong," Ray says, and Laura thinks of Helen's painting.

The rot. Faith had been cutting it out.

"How about we . . . give her a head start?" Laura offers, tentatively. "If we call the police now, she's a sitting duck at the airport."

Adelaide spits out a laugh. "Have you lost your marbles? Why would we let a murderer leave the country? Greece," she mutters. "I've always wanted to go there."

Laura feels crazy, suggesting they let Faith go. She's read news stories where families have protected a son or daughter guilty of terrible crimes, wondering at the time why they didn't march the child up to the police department themselves. Judging them for not doing so.

Now, though, in the situation—and having looked at those empty rooms, so carefully and lovingly maintained—she can't bring herself to turn Faith in. Not yet. Not without giving her something of a chance. "I don't know," she answers Adelaide, quietly. "Why would we?"

For a long moment, the women stare at each other, each lost in her own thoughts. Their own reasoning.

Laura, who has her own daughter she loves so fiercely.

Ray, who finally has her family back.

Adelaide, who has fought for everything she has.

Finally, Ray clears her throat.

"So," she says. "When do you think we found this note?"

FAITH

As the customs official stared at her passport, Faith had tried to keep her cool even though she was totally freaking out inside. The guy who'd forged it boasted he'd never had anyone get busted, but considering his line of business he could have been full of crap. Images of being led away in handcuffs swirled in front of Faith's eyes until the official handed it back to her, smiling blandly.

"Have a nice flight, Ms. Reynolds."

Faith Martin no longer exists. Now there's only Annabelle Reynolds.

Now, Faith—Annabelle, but really always Faith—rests her forehead against the cool window of the plane and closes her eyes. In only eleven hours, her plane will touch down in Athens. Already she's brokered a deal with a nice couple who rents their upstairs loft to visiting students, wired them the rent for the first three months. She's nervous about carrying so much cash on her—one hundred and thirty-seven thousand dollars, netted mostly from using the online auction house recommended by her aunt Connie—but soon it will be safely divided among three banks common all over Europe.

Maybe Faith should have chosen somewhere in Latin America as her escape route. The exchange rate would have been better, that's for sure. But Faith's mother wanted to go to Greece, and she hadn't gotten to because two Christmases ago in Johnsonville some shitty driver had barreled his SUV into the side of her Chevy Cobalt, killing Beth Martin and her son, Nick, and leaving her sister Connie to die five days later.

That same shitty driver, a fine upstanding member of the Raleigh elite, had somehow only been sentenced to three years of jail time thanks to the efforts of an extremely skilled, extremely expensive team of lawyers. Some judge had decided the lives of the people Faith loved most were worth *three years* of freedom.

Since Faith had been eighteen at the time, legally an adult, she could be on her own. That worked out considering she didn't have family other than the three people who had decided to go to a movie while Faith stayed in because of a cold. She'd inherited Connie's house—which Faith couldn't sell because that would totally break her heart—and she worked odd jobs to pay the rent on the one she'd once lived in with her mother and brother.

Then Faith had come to Oleander Court. She didn't have a problem at first. Laura was nice, and Faith was happy to help out the family. She'd put up her ad for childcare services in part because she was lonely, and the Nobles had been kind to her. They treated her like part of the family instead of an employee, and Faith never thought much about how rich they were.

But then Laura had introduced Faith to the other people who lived in the neighborhood, and Faith thought about how rich they were all the time. She couldn't help it. They loved showing it off. Paying other people to do everything for them. They couldn't even be bothered to blow their own leaves off their yard.

The people in Oleander Court—a lot of them, at least—were just like the dude who'd run a stoplight and paid his way out of the life sentence he'd deserved. Why did they get to live in a place as nice as Oleander Court, ordering other people around and not even appreciating what they had? Something in Faith had snapped.

That was why Faith had stolen from both Pam and Beverly. She also knew no one would notice, or care. It wouldn't hurt anyone. Everyone in Oleander Court had so much, they couldn't keep track of what they had.

Faith didn't expect to take it further than Pam and Beverly. It had been so easy. Pam's show-offy gift bags meant *anyone* at the party could have poisoned Beverly. And Pam didn't have a security system. All Faith had to do was go up the floating staircase when no one was looking, and—once Pam was alone—open the shutters so they'd bang against the wall and make her come look. Then—bam! No more Pam.

Then Faith had run to Walmart and grabbed items as fast as she could to make it look like she'd been shopping for a while. Her time-stamped receipt was her alibi. She'd wished that Officer Kramer would have paid more attention to it, because she was pretty proud of being so clever. Or maybe she should have just been grateful the police weren't smarter.

Bambi was more of a gamble. Faith knew that Marv and Bambi hadn't installed their Ring security system, because she'd heard them talking about it through the heat register in Bambi's walk-in closet. Still, someone could have spotted her—either when she cut around the back of the house or when she was climbing the trellis. She'd been lucky that Helen lived between the Holidays and the Schulmans—her only security system was posting herself on the front porch.

The old curling iron was a lucky find. Faith had been looking for a humidifier at Goodwill and found the ancient piece of garbage, cord wrapped around it, at the bottom of the bin. It had probably been there for years.

She'd been on the fence about Conner. He was a dad. But Faith knew that sometimes having no dad at all is better than having a shitty one. The only thing Conner would ever give any of his kids was a complex. Gabby, especially. Faith caught her measuring her stomach with Tracey's sewing measuring tape once and wanted to cry for her.

Faith had been sorting the Boyles' mail when she saw a package with "Important Benefits Election Forms Inside" marked on the front. When she'd opened it, Faith realized it was for Conner's life insurance policy through his work. She'd tabbed all the places for him to checkmark and sign, then left it in his office with everything he needed to drop it in the mailbox. If Faith went through with taking care of Conner, Tracey and the kids would be set for a long while.

Faith had been there when Tracey was dealing with having to leave for Scottsdale early. She'd watched the kids while Tracey ran around packing and Conner hid in his office playing *Call of Duty* even though he wouldn't see his kids for a week. He'd kept texting, too. Conner was always texting. And he always kept his phone in his pocket, where no one else could see it.

Faith pretended to leave after Tracey and the kids did. But then she'd skirted around the house and waited for it to get dark. She had a feeling Conner was waiting for someone, and he was the kind of sleazeball who would make use of his heated pool and hot tub in an affair.

Faith had decided: If she was wrong, she'd go home and avoid the Boyle house from then on. If she was right, well . . . Conner would have brought it on himself.

He'd brought it on himself. As Faith had swung the wooden seat to the seesaw at his dumb, fat head, she'd been grateful for all those years of rugby practice. Goodbye, Conner.

Then there was Tripp. He wasn't as annoying as some of the others, but he was probably the evilest. A Nazi collection? Really? Also, he totally abused his wife. You could spend twenty minutes with Tripp and Sandy and know something was up. She acted like some kicked dog. Once Faith had grabbed the top of her arm and she'd practically howled in pain. *Where are you getting bruises, Sandy?*

Faith had found Tripp's little artifacts room when she was rearranging the wine cellar. A silver key was on the ground, and Faith was curious. It had to go to the room that was catty-corner to the wine cellar, the one that was always locked.

Faith expected maybe a weapons room. She wasn't prepared for the door to swing open to *that*. It was like a war museum, meaning whoever kept it had lots of pride in it.

Sandy used Faith's services more and more during Tripp's last days. Faith thinks she was lonely. Faith liked Sandy okay, even though she was a little boring. Maybe she'd be less boring without her asshole Nazi of an abusive husband ordering her around all the time.

Tripp's death was also supposed to serve a larger purpose. Faith thought Ray would have an airtight alibi for Tripp's death by being with Laura for a game night. And if she had nothing to do with Tripp, the police might think they were on the wrong track with the other murders. Instead, Ray had canceled because she wasn't up to it.

Come on, Ray. Help a girl out.

Faith hadn't come to Tripp's house the day he died. That's why the police didn't find her on his security cameras. Instead, she'd been at his house late the night before, bringing groceries for Sandy so she'd have time to cook Tripp his eight-course meal of choice while she was gone the next evening.

Faith had told Sandy she'd see herself out once she was done organizing clothes intended for Goodwill in the downstairs guest room. Instead, she'd curled up in the closet and gone to sleep. That was also where she was hiding when Tripp investigated the guest room—had he moved the top blanket aside, she would have had some explaining to do. Once she'd started the fire, Faith had stacked Goodwill boxes so she could escape out the storm window. It was a tight fit, but she'd managed.

Jade was supposed to be next. Faith had her pegged from the beginning—as a spoiled, entitled rich kid who wasted her talent on brainwashing the ignorant masses. As complex as a doorstop.

Jade had never hired Faith, though, so Faith didn't have access to her house. The only way she could think to get to her was by sending something that looked like it came from an Instagram sponsor. Coconut water with a splash of poison—the same Faith had used on Beverly—seemed a fitting way for Jade to go considering how many minds she'd poisoned through Instagram, ha ha.

Faith made sure it was a brand that actually looked good. Jade was such a poser, Faith's main worry was that Jade wouldn't actually take a sip.

Since Faith had sent the package with tracking sent to a burner phone, she got a text alert for all major events during transit. The alert signaling that the package had been delivered pinged like two seconds before another alert notified her that Jade had published another blog. Faith had read it, and it was beautiful—all about Helen's painting of Oleander Court and what the neighborhood had meant to Jade. A confession that she was floundering. Faith had been impressed that Jade had the ability to be so real.

And reverent of something with such power. As Faith had studied Helen's triptych, she'd understood how her actions had been interpreted by the old woman. An attempt to remove the nastiness of beautiful Oleander Court, to eliminate those who tainted it.

Only, what she'd done hadn't restored the neighborhood to its former self. That wasn't possible. Sometimes, once something spoils, there's no going back. People like Conner and Pam might be gone, but it was only a matter of time before someone just like them moved in.

Faith had been at Laura's house when she got the alerts. Laura was upstairs folding laundry, and Pete was probably trying to do squats in the garage. The kids were at school. She'd jetted from the house and found the package she'd sent Jade. Should she save Jade by taking it away? She'd thought about what Adelaide had said that day—how people aren't always what they seem.

Maybe it went both ways. Like, Tripp seemed like such a great citizen on the surface but he was really a steaming piece of crap. Jade seemed like a vapid waste of space, but she had something to offer the world. It was hidden by her own dumbass self—what with the Instagram posts promoting dried toenails and all—but it existed all the same.

As Faith had stood on the porch, trying to decide what to do about the package, she'd heard a voice. Jade was on her back balcony. Glancing to make sure the coast was clear, Faith tiptoed to the side of the porch. The whole thing was wraparound, marble, and she could have walked right up to Jade if she'd wanted. She could see her through the long windows at the back of the house, facing away, her feet up on a cushioned lounge chair. Deep in conversation as she took advantage of the weirdly warm February weather.

On impulse, Faith tried the door. It was unlocked. Seriously, were the people in Oleander Court *trying* to get murdered?

Jade's house had the exact same floor plan as Laura's, and Faith wanted to see one thing. Jade was all tree-hugging and granola on Instagram, but what did she keep in her kitchen?

Keeping an eye on Jade through the window, Faith opened her refrigerator. Tons of Diet Coke. Instagram Jade wouldn't drink Diet Coke.

Faith headed for the pantry and had to stifle a laugh. Holy crap. It was like a kid with a credit card had been let loose in a supermarket. There were Doritos, Fritos, chocolates, and Cheez-Its galore. The only grown-up items were a row of olives in glass jars on a middle shelf.

Faith turned around and was confronted with a bulletin board. Pictures were tacked up on it, so many they overlapped one another. It was Jade at all different ages. She was alone in some—eating an ice cream, on the zipline at Roswell Area Park, graduating from high school. In most others she was with her parents. Her mom was a short Hispanic lady who looked a lot like Jade, and her dad was a tall white guy who looked nothing like Jade.

There was one with Jade and her mom that really got to Faith, because it was the kind she and *her* mom would have taken. One where their cheeks are squashed together and they're both laughing so much, you can see all the way to their back teeth.

Faith had backed away, her eyes trained on Jade's mother. She didn't want to be the one to take away that laugh. And besides. What had Adelaide said to her?

Everyone's got good and bad. Put all them good and bad pebbles on a scale, see which way it tilts.

Maybe Jade had some bad pebbles, with her stupid obsession with social media and Instagram fraud, but she wasn't all bad. Not if she could write the way she could. And she had parents who loved her, who would miss her.

Faith knew she was finished. She'd turned, snapped a picture, and jetted from Jade's house, grabbing the package off the doorstep as she went. No more.

Faith spent the rest of the day making arrangements and cleaning the house so her landlady, Irene, wouldn't feel totally screwed. It was actually perfect timing. The money from the auction proceeds had hit her aunt's bank account, with Pam's necklace and Beverly's Fabergé egg netting over two hundred thousand dollars combined. It would have been more, if Faith could have authenticated the pieces, but she didn't want any scrutiny. Faith cashed the cashier's check ordered in her actual name and used a credit card she'd applied for in her aunt's name to purchase "Annabelle's" plane ticket.

The money for Ray had been way trickier. She'd had to withdraw it in cash, because she doubted Ray would get to keep a check. Faith had shown up at the bank in a wig and with Connie's driver's license and social security card in hand. It was a good thing everyone said Connie and Faith looked alike, and that the driver's license was almost ten years old—on the verge of expiring. If she'd been caught there, Faith probably would have been toast on everything else. Maybe the public didn't know about the missing Fabergé egg and necklace, but the police sure did. And where else would Faith get so much money?

The next morning, Faith was about to leave the house for her flight when she remembered something. When she'd signed up to follow Jade's blog, she was required to create a username and password. *Guesswho*, she'd selected as her user name, authenticating her account with a dummy email address.

That day, *Guesswho* made her first comment on Jade's blog. On the latest article, Faith uploaded a picture of Jade's pantry—in all its filthy glory—and captioned it:

How does it feel to know you were supposed to be next?

The scales may have tipped in your favor, but it's time your Instagram lemmings know what's really in your kitchen. XOXO.

Then Faith's plane had been delayed for nine hours. As she'd sat in the airport, she'd sweated bullets as she kept refreshing the replies to her comment:

Is this for real?

Is that really your pantry? You. Are. FAKE!
OMG did the killer post that?

By the time Faith boarded the plane, she was a nervous wreck. If anyone found out she'd posted, all they had to do was go to her house and find the note she'd left for Laura. There was no trace of Annabelle Reynolds or where she was going, but duh—it would begin at Atlanta's *international* airport. Faith had considered scrapping her plans and hopping a flight to Mexico, but she didn't know if the airlines or customs would be able to see two separate international flights booked for Annabelle Reynolds on the same day. In the end, she'd decided to sit tight.

And now, here she is.

"Miss?" A stewardess with a cart smiles politely at her. "Would you like anything?"

"A Sprite, please."

It had been her mother's favorite.

Transcript of WAB-TV Atlanta

Aired March 15

[7:05:11] MIRANDA ALBERS, WAB-TV CORRESPONDENT: Hello, I'm Miranda Albers, coming at you with an exclusive interview with some of the surviving residents of Oleander Court, a neighborhood in Alpharetta which until roughly a month ago was terrorized by a murder spree with seemingly no end in sight. But now—thanks to the heroic efforts of these women—it has.

With me are Ray Willis, Adelaide McKenzie, and Laura Noble. Ray, we understand all charges have been dropped against you, is that right?

RAY WILLIS: That's right.

MIRANDA ALBERS: Is there anything you want to share about that?

RAY WILLIS: *[Pauses]* Well, it's nice this living nightmare has ended. I'm going to appreciate looking out my window and not seeing your news van, Miranda.

MIRANDA ALBERS: *[Laughs awkwardly]*

RAY WILLIS: But at this point, it's about picking up the pieces. And some of those pieces were broken before all this sh—*stuff* hit the fan. Like reconnecting with my family.

MIRANDA ALBERS: That's lovely.

RAY WILLIS: And realizing I shouldn't care about people who scrawl slurs on my garage. Those kinds of people are the reason I couldn't accept who I was, even as a kid. And those kinds of people can go fuck themselves.

MIRANDA ALBERS: Mrs. Willis, I have to remind you *we're live.* Now! Adelaide McKenzie—known as Adelaide Holt to her fans—how does it feel to have your name cleared as well?

ADELAIDE MCKENZIE: Feels great, especially since vultures like WAB-TV and the *Star Gazette* are leavin' me alone.

MIRANDA ALBERS: Well, I hardly think WAB-TV and the *Star Gazette* are in the same category.

ADELAIDE MCKENZIE: Really? I'm pretty sure both y'all camped outside my door.

MIRANDA ALBERS: And I hear you're volunteering now?

ADELAIDE MCKENZIE: Nice transition. Real smooth. But yeah, I'm working with the drama clubs of some local high schools. Encouragement's the best thing to give kids with talent.

MIRANDA ALBERS: Mrs. Noble, you were the one who made that call to the police. The one who finally exposed Ms. Martin. How did it feel to make that call? After you'd spent so many months getting to know the young woman, having her play with your children, trusting her with your home?

LAURA NOBLE: It was hard, that was for sure. But in my heart, I know I made the right decision.

MIRANDA ALBERS: Five murders, and another one planned. It's terrible to imagine. Do you think Ms. Martin is evil?

LAURA NOBLE: *[Pauses]* That's hard to answer. Faith targeted those she thought had more bad than good. That's why she let Jade go—because the balance tipped in her favor.

MIRANDA ALBERS: You passed the test too. After all, Ms. Martin was in your house more than anyone else's, and here you are.

LAURA NOBLE: Did I, though? Maybe everyone has a bit of that rot Helen depicted in her painting. At what point are you rotten, not good? What makes the scale tilt?

MIRANDA ALBERS: That's a very deep question, one to which we'll likely never have the answer. Now, as I understand it, there's been no trace of Ms. Martin since she vanished. While I'm sure the police have asked you this, Mrs. Noble, do you have any idea where she might have gone?

LAURA NOBLE: *[Looks to camera, smiles]* None at all.

ONE YEAR LATER

ADELAIDE

As Adelaide reaches the beach, she pauses to unstrap her shoes. She kicks them aside as she stretches her swollen toes. Red welts are forming where the stilettos pinched her feet, and she sighs as her toes sink into the powdery white sand. During the day, Ornos Beach on Mykonos is warm—baking in the sunlight—but not at night. Adelaide runs to the water, wincing when the tide slithers through cool foam to cover her feet. The saltwater stings.

She shouldn't have come here. She's tried to belong for how long? Four years now? But trash is trash, and as cute as her accomplished husband insisted it was when she pronounced quinoa "quin-yew-wah" or squealed when her Sephora box came in the mail, she was aware her novelty was slowly wearing thin. As her mama always said, *cheap gold looks pretty, but in the end it runs a ring around your neck.* That's when it gets chucked.

It's heartbreaking, really. She'd thought she'd loved him. She'd thought he loved *her.* And with so much that had happened between them, she can't believe this is where they've ended. On this beautiful island off of Greece, sharing a house with strangers—his *colleagues,* he calls them—and pretending everything is just peachy. This was supposed to be a second honeymoon, but really it's his way of softening the blow. She'd found the papers in his office.

She hasn't called her own lawyers. She couldn't stand to. It would make it real.

And besides. Where would she go? Her mama's trailer ain't big enough for another body.

She hears it. Soft footsteps? A sigh, swallowed by the constant beating of the waves? Whirling, Adelaide trembles at the figure before her. They advance, a stone—broken from the walkway, perhaps?—held high over their head.

"No," Adelaide gasps, hating the whimper in her voice. Lord, when did she become so weak? She glances up the beach, but there's no sign of life. Their host had boasted about owning a mile of beachfront, the complete privacy of his property. *La di da*, she'd thought at the time.

Adelaide backs away, the water lapping higher at her ankles, making her dress stick to her. It hinders her, the mass of the water weighing her down.

It happens so quickly. A slice of movement, and then—

"Cut!"

Goose pimples prickle Adelaide's arms from what must be her fourteenth fall into the Aegean Sea, her fourteenth death. Roger, her murderer, leans to help her from where she's sitting in the shallows, the water licking at her.

"I think we've got it," Paul, the director, says as a set crew member comes to wrap a robe around her. "Adelaide, that was amazing."

"Thanks," Adelaide says, both to him and to the bottle of water offered to her. "It's been a rough night. Leave a girl to a night walk, will ya?" She tips the bottle at Roger, who shrugs apologetically. "Don't look at me. I'm the body double," he says.

He's there for staging purposes only. A neo-noir director, Paul's style is snatches of imagery, the allusion to danger and violence. Let the audience fill in the gaps.

"That's a wrap," Paul announces, and a quiet cheer goes up from the crew. It's been a long day—a long week, actually—though Paul's demands are worth it, considering they're all hooking themselves to his rising star. Adelaide had seen him on-screen at the last two Golden Globe ceremonies—and not in the peanut gallery, either. The follow shot they'd just filmed comprised less than a minute of film, yet it had taken hours to shoot. Hopefully it would repay them in award hardware.

As if on cue with their dismissal, Adelaide feels the prickle of her milk coming in. Daniella will be six months old next week, and the only hard thing about accepting this part was leaving her. She's staying with Ray and Juliet, and FaceTiming is a poor substitute for being with her. Holding her, smelling her. Adelaide still can't believe she's hers.

Adelaide wanders toward the hotel with the rest of the crew. This night was physically demanding. She'd walked up and down the cliff so many times, it strained muscles she hadn't known existed. She reasons it will help her lose the baby weight faster. It's almost gone, and William insists that most of it is in her boobs. It's sweet of him to lie to her.

Being here—not just on the island of Mykonos, which is gorgeous, but shooting this part—still feels surreal. Adelaide had snorted when Lance, her agent, had told her she should audition for Louisa. "Yeah, and then after that, I'm gonna go win me the big teddy bear at the county fair."

Each achievement seemed equally unlikely. Paul Cooney, the director, was big league, and a summer job at the Milk Bottle Knockdown had taught Adelaide that those poor teddy bears were never liberated. But Lance had insisted that she appear for the screen test, which was only available because the original actress had a scheduling conflict, and Adelaide had been feeling soft towards Lance because he'd stuck by her in the *Zombie 101* aftermath. Also, Lance told her the interior shots would all be local—at some mansion in Dunwoody. Adelaide had only a few scenes on Mykonos, the location Paul insisted was necessary to capture the tone of the film.

Somehow, after a total of four screen tests and readings, Adelaide had landed the role. And the more she's gotten into the head of Louisa, really lost herself in the character, the more she's realized she's worthy of it. Maybe she'll be the one stealing the centerpiece off the table at the Golden Globes this year. She's unlikely to get the cute little statue, but she'll press a rose and be damned proud of it.

For now, her hotel suite is paid for by Blurred Lines Productions, and her husband—her real one, not poor Louisa's scoundrel—is already fast asleep in its king-size bed. The work trip is doubling as a vacation for the couple, because Lord knows they could use it after so many sleepless nights with Daniella. Adelaide slips the key card in the door and makes a beeline for the bathroom, grabbing her breast pump off the counter.

William's up when she emerges. "How'd it go?" he asks sleepily, reaching for her over the covers.

She curls into him, still feeling the cold sand beneath her feet. There will be grit in the bed tomorrow, but she's too tired to shower. "Good, I think. Paul said I was amazing."

"Then it was more than good," William mumbles into the covers. "We'll celebrate tomorrow."

Adelaide's already asleep.

"What do you think of this for Ray?" Adelaide asks the next morning, fingering a bright orange dress hanging from a rack featuring other vibrant patterns. "Too much?"

"Is any outfit 'too much' for Ray?"

"Good point." Adelaide removes it, folding the silk over her arm. "Now I need to find something for Juliet." Ever since Juliet's firm quietly took her back, she's scaled back her hours. She'd spoken up about need-ing a work/life balance, and they listened. Maybe Adelaide could find her a decoration for her office. Or something for their playroom. The couple had finally submitted their adoption paperwork, and prospects looked decent considering they weren't limiting themselves to infants.

"POH-soh KAH-ne?" Adelaide asks the vendor perched on a wooden stool, using one of two phrases she's learned in Greek: *How much?*

"Sixty Euro," he replies.

Adelaide extends three bills. "Ef-caree-STO." *Thank you.* Now she's out of phrases.

"God, this place is gorgeous," William mutters as they continue walking past the stalls of bright red tomatoes, of pungent fish, of bread. The street is unique, resembling more a private outdoor patio than a thoroughfare, with misshapen gray stones sanded down to be smooth underfoot as one navigates the narrow passageway. Cement steps lead to the second-floor entrance of nearly all buildings, small balconies over-looking the walkway below.

Adelaide twines her hand through William's as the passageway opens to the seafront curving into the city. Across the way, dazzling white buildings are cut into the hillside, spilling down to the bright blue ocean, the docks. It's an assault of color Adelaide's never witnessed—the brightness, the openness. Far out on the ocean, sailboats look like paper boats.

A restaurant occupies this side of the seafront, and William raises his eyebrows at Adelaide. "Yes, please," she says, and moments later a trim woman is ushering the couple to a patio table shielded from the sun by a wide canvas umbrella.

As a waitress appears to pour tap water, Adelaide's mind wanders to a person never far from her mind. Faith. Once, during a shopping trip to the outlets near Alpharetta, Adelaide had seen a girl with a similar gait, her hair pulled back in a messy ponytail. Even though she'd known it was crazy, Adelaide had pushed through the crowd until she'd caught up with her, only to find that the girl looked nothing like Faith.

Below, hundreds of people wander the docks, the beach. Thousands of tourists pass through Mykonos each year. They all escape *real* notice—during this lovely day of wandering, Adelaide can't recall the details of a single face they've passed.

Faith had been in Greece. Athens, according to Laura, but Mykonos is a hop, skip, and a jump away. Could Faith have ended up here? Maybe fleecing rich tourists as an overpriced "island guide" for her own amusement, or penning a novel in a flat overlooking the very market Adelaide had just visited. Blending in, going unnoticed.

"Penny for your thoughts?" William asks her, and Adelaide shakes her head.

"Just thinkin' of how blessed I am," she says, scanning the crowd. An Asian couple breaks free from the throng, and Adelaide thinks of Soon-Li. The Jung house is still on the market, and no one in Oleander Court has heard from the former lady of the house. Gone without a trace.

A group of four girls pass in front of the restaurant. They look like locals, with their easy smiles and lack of iPhones snapping pictures of the waterfront. As Adelaide's eyes settle on them, she's grateful for the large white sunglasses that hide her gaze. She's staring at the girl on the fringes of the group—the one with a bracelet threaded around her thin wrist. Adelaide can't make out its detail from so far away.

Adelaide knows it's basically impossible. Faith most likely moved on to somewhere else months ago. She's one smart cookie, and smart cookies don't stay in one place—or near it—waiting to get caught.

Still, Adelaide can't fight the feeling of unease she has as she continues to stare at the girl. The near-impossible *is* possible. Adelaide is Louisa, after all.

The girl feels her gaze. As the rest of her group moves on without her, she pivots slowly, shading her eyes. Backlit by the sun, her features are shadowed. Then she turns and keeps walking.

She could be any girl. Or she could be one girl in particular.

Adelaide will never know.

ACKNOWLEDGMENTS

Every writer stands on the shoulders of others. No book would exist—at least, not in the form it reaches readers—without inspiration from other works, without input from writing partners and beta readers, or without support. *Neighborhood Watch* is no exception.

Thank you, first, to my husband, Scott Reida, who believed in me and kept me writing despite nearly a decade of rejection.

Thank you to my mother-in-law, Marianne Reida, for her enthusiasm and little pink highlights over early drafts.

Thank you to my parents, Bill and Joyce Schauerte, for buying me every book in the *Sweet Valley High* series and making going to the library an Event.

Thank you to my wonderful editor, Ryan Smernoff, for the insights you brought to this book and for breathing life into Oleander Court.

Thank you to my writing partners, Claire Fayers and Veronica Canfield, who have been with me through multiple projects, submissions, and agents over the years. I cannot begin to express how grateful I am to have the both of you during this process. All of it!

Thank you to Frans Vischer, for your editorial insight and notes. And on behalf of my babies, thank you for the drawing of Fuddles, the obese cat in your delightful series.

Last, but not least, thank you to Landry Parkey, the one who discovered *Neighborhood Watch* and found it advisable to publish a book about "terrible people getting murdered."

ABOUT THE AUTHOR

S arah Reida is an attorney whose work focuses on assisting veteran businesses performing federal government contracts. As an author, Sarah has published two middle grade books: *Monsterville: A Lissa Black Production* (2016) and *All Sales Final* (a *Kirkus Reviews* Best Indie Book of 2020). She lives with her husband and two young children near Atlanta, Georgia.